BLACK FLAG

Surviving the Scourge

Dave Klapwyk

Klyk Publishing

For the best editor ever!

DAVE

Copyright © 2020 Dave Klapwyk

All rights reserved

The characters and events portrayed in this book are fictitious. Any similarity to real persons, living or dead, is coincidental and not intended by the author.

No part of this book may be reproduced, or stored in a retrieval system, or transmitted in any form or by any means, electronic, mechanical, photocopying, recording, or otherwise, without express written permission of the publisher.

ISBN: 978-1-7773444-1-2
Cover design by: Erica Rogers Design

If you write it, I'll buy it.

                                                     MOM

CONTENTS

Title Page
Copyright
Epigraph
Chapter 1 — 1
Chapter 2 — 7
Chapter 3 — 12
Chapter 4 — 15
Chapter 5 — 21
Chapter 6 — 31
Chapter 7 — 40
Chapter 8 — 53
Chapter 9 — 58
Chapter 10 — 62
Chapter 11 — 66
Chapter 12 — 70
Chapter 13 — 73
Chapter 14 — 80
Chapter 15 — 87
Chapter 16 — 96
Chapter 17 — 101
Chapter 18 — 108

Chapter 19	114
Chapter 20	119
Chapter 21	123
Chapter 22	132
Chapter 23	140
Chapter 24	151
Chapter 25	163
Chapter 26	172
Chapter 27	179
Chapter 28	189
Chapter 29	197
Chapter 30	208
Chapter 31	216
Chapter 32	231
Chapter 33	239
Chapter 34	248
Chapter 35	252
Chapter 36	263
Chapter 37	272
Chapter 38	276
Chapter 39	283
Chapter 40	284
Chapter 41	286
Chapter 42	290
Chapter 43	291
Chapter 44	294
Chapter 45	295
Chapter 46	298

Chapter 47	301
Chapter 48	304
Chapter 49	306
Chapter 50	308
Chapter 51	316
Books In This Series	321
Acknowledgement	323
About The Author	325

CHAPTER 1

The elevator opened. Before any of them had made a step out of the elevator, there was a crazed scream. The origin of the crazed scream became apparent when an equally crazy shirtless man with a hatchet ran past the elevator. Streaks of blood could be seen across his torso. His long scraggly hair flowed in the air behind him as he disappeared from view.

Joe shook his head in disbelief. It was just ten minutes ago when he was peacefully eating a sandwich in his office.

Things can change rapidly.

The office where Joe Lortier had sat eating his ham and cheese sandwich would more aptly be described as a maintenance room or a shop. It was also his lunchroom, his workroom, his storage room and his sanctuary. The room was in the basement of his apartment building. Although it was midsummer, and there was no air-conditioning, the room was comfortable.

The pair of fluorescent lights on the ceiling were not enough for a room this size and added to the claustrophobic feel. Joe didn't mind. In fact, he loved his little sanctuary. Being the maintenance engineer, (as he liked to call it), for three buildings had its perks. He was able to tap into one of the cable lines to connect his television which he had found in one of the big dumpsters out back. Other than a single black horizontal line near the top, it was a decent 40-inch plasma smart television.

The room contained an old recovered and repaired fridge, a sink with running water, some cupboards, a small electric grill and a old but comfortable couch. There was a second room connected by a small door to his shop where he kept his tools.

On the television a news anchor talked about the virus commonly known as the Scourge. She explained that the high mortality rate of the virus was compounded by the fact that it had an unusually long incubation period.

Joe had his lean, six-foot frame stretched out on the couch. He was watching television, eating his lunch when his cell rang. Not many people had his number. He didn't have many friends or family, and the only people that called him were his boss Hank, Blender, or one of the tenants asking to get something fixed. He swallowed his last bite and answered the phone.

"Hello."

"Yeah, Joe, you need to get over to Building Two."

It was his boss, Hank. Hank Masterson was an annoying overweight man who owned several properties in the City of Ingerwood. He was rich, overbearing, and perpetually sweating, but he signed his pay cheque, so Joe had to be nice to him.

"Oh, hi, Hank. I'm just having lunch right now. What's going on?"

"Room 65 has a problem, and you have to hurry."

"Can't it wait like 10 minutes?"

"No!" Hank was yelling now. "I just got a call from the cops. They need you to let them into Building Two. Something about a man with a small axe."

"Wouldn't you call that a hatchet? And why are the cops there?"

"It's some druggy threatening to hurt someone. You need to get your lazy butt over there NOW!"

"Okay, okay, I'm on my way." He hung up the phone.

I'm not lazy, and I'm entitled to a lunch break.

He stuffed the rest of the sandwich in his mouth, turned off the television and grabbed the ring of keys hanging by the door. Joe walked down the hall past the laundry room and climbed the stairs to the rear emergency exit. When he opened the door, he had to squint as he was hit with the bright summer sunshine.

There were three buildings on Pochatok Street he had to look after. Building One was the 100-year-old building where he had his office. Building Two was adjacent to it and had a wide assortment of tenants, including recent immigrants, poor families and students. He was sure there was a drug dealer on the sixth floor. Across the road was Building Three, which was filled with rich, young families. It didn't come as a surprise that the cops had shown up to Building Two. It got most of the problems.

He walked between the buildings to the front where he saw a police K-9 Unit SUV pulled up to the curb and a small group of onlookers.

"Are you the super?" one of the two policemen standing by the front doors asked. Both men appeared young. One was lean and tall, and his police issue pants were almost five centimetres too short. The other policeman was short, stocky and muscular. The tall policeman was addressing Joe.

"I'm Officer Reginald, and this is Officer Mike." He pointed at muscles, who nodded. "We need you to open the door."

The front doors to Building Two were glass double doors that were always locked. Tenants had keys, and all visitors had to buzz in. Joe walked up to the doors and found the large brass key and unlocked the door. He opened it and stood back to let the two men in.

"I heard that someone has a hatchet up on six," Joe said, following them to the elevator. The hallway was too small for all three of them to walk side by side, so Joe was walking behind them. Even then, Reginald and Mike were barely able to walk beside each other.

"A small axe, actually," said Mike, as he almost knocked

over the fake palm tree beside the elevator "Do you know who lives in apartment 65?"

Joe didn't bother arguing about the axe as they boarded the elevator. "Nope, I'm in charge of the maintenance for multiple buildings, and I don't know most of the people that live in them. I have heard about drug dealing on the sixth floor."

Mike looked at Joe as he mashed the button for the sixth floor. "Why didn't you report it."

"I only heard things. I never saw any drug dealing," said Joe.

"I bet Roxie could sniff it out," said Reginald.

Mike shook his head. "She's not a detection dog."

"Oh yeah, right," said Reginald. "Where is your dog today?"

"She's got the day off," Mike answered.

The elevator opened. That's when the crazy, bloody shirtless man ran by.

"Wait here," Mike held his hand up to Joe, stopping him from taking a step forward.

Joe looked at Mike's hand. "I have no intention of going out there."

Reginald unbuttoned his holster, pulled his revolver and stepped out. Mike quickly followed. The elevator doors closed, and Joe pushed the button for the ground floor. He could feel his heart beating faster, and he tapped his foot nervously. He just wanted to get back to his sanctuary and hide till this was over. Finally, the doors opened. He waited a moment, half expecting to see a bloodied man run by, but all was quiet. He cautiously stepped out of the elevator, looking both ways. To his right was the doorway to the stairwell and to the left was the short hallway to the entrance. He began walking fast to the left towards the glass doors. Suddenly, he heard the doorway to the stairway open behind him. He turned around to see the door fly open, with the crazy Hatchet-man exploding out the door. His hatchet was in his hand above his head, and he was running right at Joe. He didn't have time to turn and run or get out of the way. The hatchet came down towards Joe's head. He dodged to the left, diving into the fake palm tree. Crazy Hatchet-man tripped and fell hard on the linoleum, his hatchet flying out of his hand and sliding across the floor. He scrambled to his feet and ran to the front doors, leaving the hatchet behind him. The man struggled with the door, finally opening it and running outside. As Joe untangled himself from the ridiculous looking palm tree, Reginald burst out of the stairwell door. His long legs carrying him swiftly across the floor and out the front doors after the crazy man, who was now without a hatchet. A few seconds later, Officer Mike emerged from the stairwell door, panting.

Apparently, he spends a lot of time with the weights in the gym but doesn't do much cardio.

The officer looked down at Joe. "Don't touch the axe."

"It's a hatchet."

"What?"

"Never mind, I promise not to touch the weapon." He pushed the tree back into place.

The officer seemed to get his second wind and continued his pursuit. Both policemen and the bloodied crazy man were nowhere to be seen by the time Joe exited the building. A small group had gathered to see the commotion.

Laurel and Harvey stood holding hands beside a group of kids with a basketball. Laurel and Harvey were a middle-aged gay couple that lived on the first floor of Building Two. They were congenial and even had Joe over for a chicken masala a couple of weeks ago. He couldn't help thinking of them as Laurel and Hardy.

"Are you okay, Joe?" asked Laurel, "Did that guy have a gun or something?"

"No, he had a hatchet, but he dropped it," Joe replied.

"Isn't a hatchet a small axe?" asked Laurel.

Joe rolled his eyes.

One of the kids with the basketball yelled at Joe. "Is he a Scourge zombie?"

Laurel turned towards the kids. "It's not that kind of virus."

Joe started walking away. "Let the cops know that I'll be in my office in the basement," he yelled back to Laurel and Harvey.

When he finally made it back to his sanctuary, Joe's adrenaline was starting to wear off. The sweat was dripping off his short black hair. He hadn't been this scared since his late wife told him she was dying many years ago. He started thinking about her, but promptly shook the depressing thoughts out of his head. He walked to the fridge and rummaged around till he found the small bottle of Crown Royal he hid for special occasions. He had a cheap bottle of Canadian Club too, but this was definitely a special occasion.

As he grabbed a small plastic cup from the cupboard, he heard a noise from the tool room.

He wasn't alone.

CHAPTER 2

Monique Broderick sat at her desk with her head in her hands.

Is it lunch yet?

She was the project manager of graphic design at the ER Advertising Agency in downtown Ingerwood. She had her own small office. It had a veneered particleboard desk with two monitors, a dusty shelving unit and an old grey filing cabinet. The only redeeming feature was the large bay window that overlooked the main street. The office was simple and efficient, but that was not how she felt right now.

She was eight months pregnant, and she had a storm of emotions swirling around in her head. It was almost 11 o'clock, and she hadn't done much work yet. She rubbed her neck and tried to straighten her back. There was a knock at the door.

"Come in," she called out.

The door opened, and one of the designers walked in. Clarissa was young and energetic. "Monique, I was wondering if you had a chance to look at the sample layout for Jean's Animal Food ad mock-up?"

Monique stood up, and walked around the desk. "Is that it there?"

Suddenly she saw movement out of the corner of her eye and instinctively looked out the window. The dark shape of a body silhouetted by the afternoon sun dropped past the window.

She looked over at Clarissa. "Was that a man that just fell past my window?"

Clarissa stared, wide-eyed at the window. "I think he had a blue tie."

They both ran to the window to look, but couldn't see where the man had come from or where he had gone. "Let's go find out," said Clarissa.

They both left the office. "Someone jumped off the roof!" announced Clarissa. The entire office floor went from a hushed din of office chatter to a raucous flurry in a few seconds. Many of them clamoured to get a better view out the window. Some checked their phones. Others ran to the elevators to get to the main floor.

Monique went to the stairs. The elevators would be full, and the stairs were hard on her swollen feet, but they were only one floor down from the roof. She managed to climb the stairs to the roof but was out of breath when she reached the top.

I need to get into better shape when this baby comes. Maybe I can join a baby walking group.

The door to the roof was usually unlocked. Although it was technically not allowed, many of the workers came up here to eat their lunch or sneak a cigarette. She opened the door and stepped out into the heat. The blazing sun and humid air were a stark reminder that she was working in an air-conditioned office.

She didn't see anyone else on the roof. When she reached the edge, she awkwardly bent over to get a better look. This hurt her back as well as her protruding belly. Instead, she decided to go on her knees and crawl. Once she made it to her knees, she looked over the edge. A small crowd had gathered around the body. The man was on his back, his legs sprawled unnaturally. He had a blue tie, and there was a large pool of blood by his head. Monique gasped at the sight. With great effort she made it back to her feet and went back inside.

After the police, ambulance and fire trucks had come and gone, Monique's boss called a meeting, and all the employees gathered together in the cafeteria. It was standing room only, and she was grateful for the young man who offered his seat.

I bet he used to think I was hot nine months ago. Now he's just nice to me because I'm pregnant.

Clarissa glared at the man next to Monique till he gave her his seat.

Drake Thomas, the general manager, stood at the front shuffling paper, before silencing the noisy crowd.

"Thank you all for being here."

"I'm pretty sure we didn't have a choice," whispered Clarissa.

"I have two items to discuss. First, we are all distraught about Andrew Davis, who has succumbed to his injuries, and our thoughts and prayers are with his family at this difficult time."

Clarissa leaned in and whispered in Monique's ear. "His family is dead, so that would be useless."

"What?" she whispered back.

"His wife died last week, and he found out that his kid died this morning. That's why he jumped."

Drake continued. "Second, we have also heard of many recent tragic deaths from the ongoing Scourge pandemic. Our business model has undergone many adaptations, and we continue to follow all government protocols. We were initially going to transition to a work-at-home model next week. However, due to the recent upsurge in cases in our community, we are going to expedite this transition. Please pack up your laptops, and current files, backup all work in progress, and be prepared to begin working from home starting immediately."

The crowd began to murmur amongst themselves, and Drake attempted to regain control.

"People, people, please. We need to remain calm." The murmurs turned to louder chatter, and he finished his announcement. "Please talk to your supervisors if you have any other questions." He scurried out a side door.

Everyone pushed, shoved, talked and yelled as Monique sat silently. Clarissa looked over to her. "Are we going? Do you need some help?"

"I'm not in a rush. I'll just wait for the mad rush to subside."

"I'll wait with you."

The two of them waited until everyone had left. "Okay, can we go now?" asked Clarissa.

"Now, I'm hungry. Is it lunch yet?" asked Monique.

They walked over to the cafeteria counter, but the cashier and cooks had all left."

"Where is everyone?" asked Monique, "what are we supposed to do now?"

"A pregnant woman has to eat," said Clarissa as she walked behind the counter.

"What are you doing?"

"You and your baby need food, so I am feeding the needy." She grabbed a large set of tongs. "What'll it be, ma'am?"

That afternoon she packed her laptop and some of her files. As she hugged Clarissa goodbye, Monique noticed that her skin was warm to the touch.

"Clarissa, are you okay? You feel like your burning up."

"I am feeling a little sick all of the sudden, but I'm sure it's nothing."

"Your nose is bleeding," said Monique, becoming increasingly worried.

Clarissa felt her nose. "It's the dry air-conditioned air in here."

"Should I take you to the hospital?" asked Monique.

"No, you go home. I'll be fine. I just need to rest, and so do you."

"Are you sure?"

"Yes, I'm sure," said Clarissa, "but you call me when you have your baby. I want to be the first friend who holds her."

"You will. I'll see you later, okay?"

Monique left ER Advertising Agency and walked to the bus stop. She waited outside of the bus shelter in the uncomfortable heat with her laptop case weighing heavily on her shoulder. Eventually, the bus creaked to a stop and a small line formed at the doors. She was the last to get on and was about to step on to the bus when she was suddenly pulled backwards. She was released just as fast and discovered her laptop case was no longer on her shoulder. A man dashed away with it. Monique was in no state to run, so she reached into her purse to find something to throw. She pulled out the first thing she felt and flung it at the thief. Her make-up mirror clattered to the ground as the man disappeared around the back of the bus. She rolled her eyes and boarded the bus without her laptop or her mirror.

"Are you okay, Ma'am?" the concerned bus driver asked.

"No," she answered, "I'm pregnant."

On the bus ride home, she fell asleep and had to get off at the next stop, take the bus going the opposite direction and finally made it home before the government-imposed curfew.

As she walked home from the bus stop, she called Clarissa on her cell. Her boyfriend answered. Donny told her that Clarissa had collapsed in a taxi on her way home from work. She was currently in intensive care at St. Jude's Hospital, but was unresponsive. Monique cried the rest of the way home.

Her husband, Kevin, greeted her at the door and asked her the worst possible question: "How was your day, honey?"

CHAPTER 3

Joe knew he wasn't alone in Building One because the noise he heard was not normal.

Building One was built in 1912. The tenants were mostly elderly and didn't make much noise. However, it had an old boiler heating system which created a wide assortment of strange banging, clanging, and creaky sounds as it pushed hot water up five floors through its ancient pipes. It was currently the middle of summer, and the boiler was off. There was no central air conditioning system like in the newer Building Three, so the strange creaky noises were usually minimal until at least late September.

The noise he heard in his tool room sounded more like shuffling than creaking. It was as if a small animal was rummaging through his tools.

Maybe it's a racoon.

Last week he was called over to Building Two and found a family of racoons nesting at the bottom of the garbage chute. However, it would be difficult for a racoon to get into his little room as he usually kept the door shut and locked.

He heard the noise again, this time a little louder.

I think I left the door open when I went left. What if the Man Without a Hatchet is hiding in my shop?

With the knowledge and experience of a man who has watched hundreds of horror movies, he knew better than to go towards the noise. He set his cup of whiskey on the counter and took a step towards the door to the hallway.

"Mr. Lortier?" A small voice from behind him whispered.

Unless Hatchet-less man had been kicked in the family jewels, that voice had to belong to a little girl. He turned around to find a young dark-skinned girl with tight braids in her hair peeking around the corner.

He breathed a sigh of relief. The girl was Ayesha. She could have been 11 or 12 years old. It was hard for him to tell. Her mother was raising her by herself on the third floor of Building One. They were one of the few people in Building One who were not over the age of 70. He had met her mother a couple of times but didn't see her much because she worked nights at an all-night diner downtown. Ayesha's mother made her play outside, so she could sleep during the day. Ayesha was a bright, friendly girl, and Joe couldn't help but look out for her.

"Ayesha, what are you doing here?"

"I'm hiding." She looked nervously around Joe.

"Is someone chasing you?" he asked.

"No, we're playing hide-and-seek, and Zach is looking for me. He'll never find me in here."

"You're not supposed to be in here."

"Sorry, but the door was open."

"A bad man's running around, it's not safe. You should go inside with your mother."

"Mom's sleeping. Besides, the cops took him away already."

"What? How do you know that?"

She pulled out her phone, which barely fit in her jean pocket. "Zach just texted me. He said the guy had a little axe."

"It's a hatchet."

"Found you!" A young, pudgy boy a little older than Ayesha with thick-rimmed glasses appeared at the door.

"You must be Zach."

"Who are you?"

"I'm Joe. You kids shouldn't be out playing. You know there's a very dangerous virus out there."

Zach pushed his glasses up his nose. "My uncle says we already either have it or we're immune."

"Fine, but you should not be playing here. Get out and stay away from Building Two, I don't think it's very safe over there for you kids."

"It's okay, Mr. Joe," Zach said, looking at his phone. "That guy with the hatchet is gone now."

Finally, someone who knows what a hatchet is.

Joe looked at Ayesha and pointed to Zach. "You trust this guy?"

"He's fine. He's smart. His family just moved into Building Three, and he's 12."

"I'm 12 and a half."

The two kids took off, running down the hall.

He worried about them. He worried about the virus. He worried that he may one day die of the Scourge.

He grabbed the remote and turned the television on.

According to the news many people had the virus but didn't know it till just before they died. It had a six-month incubation period where the carrier didn't have any symptoms. It was extremely contagious, and was already widespread in many countries around the world before scientists knew it existed. The virus grew inside the body slowly and covertly until suddenly it attacked the major organs. The infected person would die within days from lung or coronary failure. For many people, the incubation period was ending.

Joe grabbed his cup of whiskey and changed the channel. He sat back down on the dusty couch and watched.

The channel was reporting on the mass protests. In response to the increasing deaths due to the virus, shutdowns and curfews were imposed. Many people were upset that their rights were being suppressed and were angry that more wasn't being done to find a cure. They went out into the streets to demonstrate and protest. This caused more shutdowns and curfews, which caused more people to be upset and scared. Like a dirty rolling snowball, the cycle continued.

CHAPTER 4

Later that same night, a few blocks north on Pochatok street, Monique and Kevin were finishing dinner.

"What are we going to name the baby?" Monique asked.

"I don't know, maybe Alexandria?" suggested Kevin.

"Nah, too long. How about Lee?"

"Is that even a girl's name?"

"Yes, it can be."

"Oh, I know…Autumn."

"Like the season?"

As Monique looked across the table at her husband, she saw a dark shape pass by the back window over the sink. Her heart skipped a beat. "What was that?"

"What?"

"Behind you…I saw someone go by the window."

He turned around to look. "I don't see anything."

The baby kicked inside her, and she held a hand up to her belly.

Kevin looked at her. "Are you okay? Are you having the baby?"

"No, she just kicked."

"I'll do the dishes. Maybe you should take it easy."

"What about the guy?"

"What guy?"

"The guy in the back yard. You need to go check it out."

"Oh yeah, right."

He left the kitchen and went out the back door into their little backyard. They had a late dinner that night, as Kevin had to work an extra hour at the factory, so it was dark outside. As soon as he stepped onto the back porch, the automatic exterior light came on.

"I don't see anyone," he called back.

"Can you please walk around the house once to make sure? I *know* I saw someone walk by the window."

While he was gone, she washed the dishes and left them to dry on the rack. She went to the bedroom to change for bed. Kevin walked into the bedroom. "You going to bed already?"

"Yes, I'm tired after doing the dishes."

"Oh yeah, sorry about that, I would have done them."

"Sure you would," she said.

"Hey, I was just got talking to the neighbour, Janice. Her husband, Mike says a lot of the other cops have died and some of the ones that are left are not showing up for work. She says they're thinking of leaving too."

"Glad you could have a nice little chat with our pretty neighbour while I did your dishes." She shook her head, and with great effort, climbed into bed.

"Don't be like that. I said I would do them, and I would have done them eventually. You're the one that sent me outside."

"So, it's my fault that there's someone lurking outside or that you take a half-hour to walk around the house just to get out of doing the dishes?"

"Hey, I worked all day at the factory. What did you do? You were home all day."

"I was working at home all day, and I have been carrying around our baby for the past eight months."

"That baby is a gift. A gift from God!"

"Well, I don't think there's room in this bed for anyone other than me and this gift of God. So why don't you go sleep on the couch which was a gift from my parents."

He stormed out of the room, and she turned out the light

and tried to sleep. She was angry, upset, sore and tired.

How could he treat me like this? There was a time when he told me I was a gift from God. Now that I'm huge, he treats me like a...I don't know what. And now what, he's out there watching television like he doesn't care? Why does this have to be so hard? Why does God think it's a good idea to have a baby in a pandemic, anyway?

Eventually, her tired body won out, and she fell asleep.

She woke abruptly when she heard a thump. She turned to wake up Kevin, and realized he wasn't there. Monique pulled the covers back and got out of bed. The night was warm, and she decided to forgo the slippers. She walked quietly to the bedroom door and opened it. There was the sound of muffled voices in the living room, and she stopped. The voices were two men, but she couldn't make out what they were saying.

Do I call out or go and hide? Is Kevin talking to someone?

She padded down to the end of the hallway and peeked around the corner. The living room was dark, but lights flashed on the walls and ceiling. Then she realized Kevin had fallen asleep with the television on. Kevin was sleeping soundly on the couch.

Why do you get to sleep peacefully?

Monique walked silently into the living room. She found the remote and turned the television off. The room was dark and silent. That's when she thought she heard rustling outside.

Do I wake him, or will that just make him mad again?

She went to the front window and peered outside. The bright street light in front of their house allowed her to see most of their yard, but all she saw was an empty front yard and an empty Pochatok street.

I'll have to get heavy curtains for the baby's room so that light doesn't keep her awake.

She heard a noise from the back of the house.

Monique walked through the living room into the kitchen, which was lit only by the clocks on the stove and microwave. She went to the window over the sink that overlooked the backyard, but it was dark outside, and she couldn't see anything. Leaning across the sink, she cupped her hands around her eyes to see better. At that moment, the sensor light on the porch turned on. A dark hooded figure paused mid-stride on the porch and looked right at her. She screamed.

Her scream was short-lived when a gloved hand covered her mouth and an arm wrapped around her neck from behind.

She froze in fear.

From behind her, she heard Kevin say something as he awoke. Monique reached for the knife block, but her attacker pulled her away from the counter. The back door opened, and the hooded figure entered.

Kevin flew out of the living room straight at the attacker's head. The man bent over with an *oof* as Kevin's head collided with his stomach. The intruder fell backwards and hit the back of his head on the side of the table. A short black and green knife clanged to the floor. The man lay on the ground unconscious. Kevin stood up with a mixture of surprise, pride and anger. He took a step towards Monique and her attacker, but the cold steel of a knife materialized on Monique's throat, and he stopped.

"Don't step any closer," the man said.

Kevin put his hands out in front of him. "Okay, okay, take it easy. Let her go."

"Just back up and keep your hands in the air," the man with the knife said.

The hooded figure on the floor was still not moving, and the black and green knife lay beside him.

"Please don't hurt her," Kevin begged. "She's pregnant. Just take what you want."

A plan formed in Monique's mind. Before she had time to decide if it was a good idea, she screamed. "Aaaah! I'm having contractions!"

The man's grip loosened, and the knife was no longer pressed to her neck. She keeled over and groaned again. "Aaaaah! I think stress has induced labour. Aaaah!"

She fell to her knees. Kevin went to take a step, and the man held the knife out towards him. "Back up!"

"But she's having the baby, I have to help her," he implored.

As the man's focus shifted to her husband, Monique put her hands out on the floor to steady herself. Her hand sliding to the black and green knife. She snatched it up and held it at her side.

Her attacker looked down at her, and she pretended to point at something and mumbled.

"What?" he said leaning down, "What are you saying?"

She mumbled again, and the man leaned in closer to her, his knife still pointed at Kevin. As soon as he was within reach, she swung the knife up with all her strength, and it plunged it deep into his throat. There was a crunching, slurping sound, and blood began to pour out. He dropped his knife and brought his hands up to his throat. Both knives clinked to the floor. Monique stood up as the man slumped against the cupboards. Blood seeped out between his fingers, and he made gurgling noises as he gasped for air and then was silent.

Kevin grabbed her in his arms, and they both wept.

They managed to duct tape the unconscious man before he woke up. Kevin called 9-1-1, and an hour later, the police showed up. They arrested the hooded man and removed the other body. The police took their statements and told them that there had been several robberies and home invasions in the neighbourhood.

When the police and paramedics had left, Kevin and Monique sat on their couch. Monique had stopped crying, and Kevin had stopped shaking.

"I'm sorry about earlier this evening," said Kevin, "I was a jackass."

"I'm sorry too. I have a lot of emotions, and I'm pregnant and..."

"You don't have to apologize. Besides, you saved our lives."

"You helped too," she added.

"I can't believe you stabbed a man in the throat. You're like a pregnant Wonder Woman."

"Olivia," she said.

"What?"

"I think we should name the baby Olivia."

"Oh." He paused for a moment. "I like it. Olivia, daughter of Monique, the Wonder Woman!"

They laughed, talked and cried into the early morning hours. She eventually fell asleep in his arms.

CHAPTER 5

Two weeks later, Joe shaved his dark stubble and left his apartment to get some groceries. It was convenient living in the same building where he worked, especially since he didn't need a car to get to work. It was a way to keep himself insulated from much of the world with so many reminders of his late wife. It was nice to get out and do some grocery shopping.

He patted his small paunch.

I need to start walking more.

It was early Saturday morning. The clouds were darkening, and the wind was starting to pick up. He considered going back inside to get his umbrella but changed his mind. He only had one and a half blocks to walk to get to the closest bus stop. The traffic seemed to be busier than normal for a Saturday morning in mid-August, but he didn't think much of it as he boarded the bus. He walked to the third from the back seat and slumped down next to the window. A young couple sat in the back, looking nervous and talking in hushed tones.

Joe pulled out his phone and texted one of his few friends, Blender.

<You up for darts tonight?>

Sherman Waters was his real name, but everyone called him Blender. He wasn't even sure why anymore. That had been his name since he had known him in high school. It might have had something to do with how he liked to blend his foods.

Blender was the best man at his wedding and a good friend ever since. He was twenty pounds overweight, had a long beak-like nose and wavy brown hair. Blender loved to eat, and Joe liked to drink and play darts. Almost every Saturday night, they would head down to McFaddy's Irish Pub for a game of darts and a few drinks. Blender went for the chicken wings and poutine while Joe went for the dart games and Canadian whiskey. They both went for each other's company.

He looked down at his phone and read Blender's response.
<I dunno. Maybe we should order in>
<What? Why?>
<Watch the news. Things are getting out of control>
<Fine, my place at 8. I've got the booze and Netflix>
<K, I'll bring the pizza, wings and garlic bread>

Joe put away his phone. The hushed tones from the couple in the back were getting louder.

Suddenly the bus screeched to a stop. Joe lurched forward, hitting his head on the seat in front of him. His phone slipped out of his hands and slid under the seat in front of him. He looked up, rubbing his head. A pickup truck had blown through the lights, and the bus driver had stopped just in time. The truck, however, had swerved to avoid the bus. It had suddenly stopped due to an immovable concrete hydro pole, and its hood was now puffing out black smoke. Thunder crashed somewhere in the distance, and the sky was getting ominously darker. People were running frantically to get wherever they were going. He wasn't sure if they were trying to beat the storm or for some other reason.

"End of days..." The hipster-looking guy in the back had now graduated from hushed tones to a louder voice that made Joe turn towards him. The hipster had a neatly trimmed beard and a flat tweed cap.

Joe looked at him quizzically. "Saturday is the end of days?"

The bus suddenly moved forward, sending his phone sliding to the back of the bus.

The hipster's young wife seemed a little overweight. Her

short-cropped blond hair was messy, and her cheeks were flushed. She appeared out of breath as she chewed ravenously on a granola bar. It took great effort for her to bend over and retrieve the phone. Her husband looked right at Joe.

"This is exactly what the Book of Revelations talks about, the seven angels with the seven plagues."

His wife reappeared with Joe's phone in his hand. "Got it!"

She then waddled down the aisle using the seats for support and handed Joe his phone. It was then that he noticed that she was pregnant.

"Thanks," he said, taking the phone from her, "When are you due?"

"Still got another two weeks." She slowly returned to her seat.

An ambulance siren sounded in the distance. The bus slowed down again as a firetruck passed the bus on the right, its horn and siren wailing.

Joe watched as it turned right at the next intersection. "They're going the wrong way. That truck is behind us."

Hipster ignored the comment. "This is it, your final chance to put your hope in God."

"I think I'll go to the grocery store first." Joe reached up and rang the bell for the next stop.

"Yea, that's where we're going too. Got to get the necessities – flour, coffee beans, and pickles." He reached his hand out to Joe. "The name's Kevin, and this is my lovely wife, Monique." She was using both arms to help support herself as she made her way to the door. She nodded to him.

"Nice to meet you both. My name's Joe."

They all got off the bus and stepped back into the windy dark day. The rain had just started as they waited to cross the street to the grocery store. Ray's Grocery was not a very big store, nor was it the cheapest. But it was the only one in the neighbourhood, and Joe didn't want to endure the 45-minute bus ride to the chaos known as downtown.

Ray's was an old grocery store that was the anchor store for a small strip mall. It was usually a little busy, but today was different. The parking lot was almost full, and many people had their carts loaded up and were running to their cars. They appeared to be running from more than just the storm.

"Wow, this is looking intense," Kevin said, his eyes wide.

"Guess we better get going before Armageddon," Joe replied. The three of them crossed the street as fast as Monique could manage.

When they reached the other side of the street, Kevin looked over to Joe. "Armageddon is a place, not an event. It's the location of the final battle."

"Well, the final battle for pickles and coffee may be upon us," Joe laughed.

At the same time, all of their phones went off. It was the emergency alert system alert.

Joe clicked his phone off without looking at it. "What's going on?"

When Kevin pulled his phone out, a baseball rolled out of his pocket. He stared at his phone, clicking frantically, reading and scrolling.

Joe ran to grab the rolling baseball. "Well, what is it? A big storm coming? Because I could have told you that." He handed the ball back to Kevin. The rain and winds were beginning to pick up.

"A state of emergency was declared," he mumbled, still scrolling and reading. "There have been major incidents of social unrest around the country."

Monique stretched her back. "So, it wasn't a state of emergency when millions of people die of the Scourge, but it is when people start protesting and looting?"

"Millions?" Joe asked.

Kevin looked up from his phone. "Don't you watch the news, man? This Scourge, killed a million people, just last week. This is the plague from Revelations 6."

"I think I missed that Sunday School class. What's with the baseball?"

"I've had it since I was a kid. I went to a Blue Jay's game and got it signed by..."

He didn't get a chance to finish his sentence. He was interrupted by the crack of gunfire coming from the direction of Ray's grocery store. That's when everything got worse. People began streaming out the front doors. Shoppers were being trampled. Carts were overturned, punches were thrown, vehicles crashed into each other, and there was a lot of screaming. As if on cue, the rain and winds turned into a full-blown storm.

"Okay, so no groceries today," Joe said. "We need to get out of here."

Monique began to breathe rapidly. Kevin put his hand on her shoulder. "What's going on? Are you okay?"

She was breathing so heavy she could hardly speak. "I'm...fine...just need...a second."

"How far to your place? Can you guys walk?"

"We live about ten blocks south on Pochatok Street."

"I'm just another two blocks south of that. I'll walk with you—strength in numbers, right?"

"We normally walk it, but she's a little too pregnant to be walking. That's why we took the bus."

The rain was beating down, the thunder was getting louder, and the winds were making it all worse. Smoke was beginning to billow from a broken window in the side of Ray's Groceries, and the parking lot became clogged with soaked panicked shoppers trying to escape.

Joe ran down the sidewalk, grabbed an empty shopping cart and ran back to the couple. "What if she rode in this?"

"Okay, but not too fast. The sidewalk is bumpy. I don't want to knock the bun out of her oven." Kevin took the cart from Joe and pushed it over to his wife.

Monique was finally catching her breath. "Do I get any say in the matter?"

"Do you have any better ideas?"

"Fine, but not too fast." Kevin put his baseball in his coat pocket, and he and Joe both awkwardly helped her into the cart.

"Everything is going to be fine, and we are only borrowing this cart. I will return it tomorrow." Kevin insisted.

Joe started to walk down the sidewalk. "I think that's the least of Ray's problems."

Indeed, the world around them appeared to be falling apart. It looked like there might have been a power interruption due to the storm, and the traffic lights were out. The intersections were an apocalyptic parking lot, and much of the traffic was clogged up.

They started their trek south. Kevin pushed Monique at a decent pace against the rain and winds while Joe made sure the way was clear. The rain began pounding down harder, and lightning struck close to their location. The cart clacked over the sidewalk cracks sounding like a train going over a road crossing. There was a lot of honking and yelling and sirens. The rain splashed down, and the wind whipped large raindrops at their faces. Behind them, more shots rang out, followed by shouting and cursing.

Joe turned around to look and then stopped walking. He stood with his mouth and eyes wide with disbelief. Kevin saw his astonished expression and stopped as well. The three of them looked back down the road.

There were five or six guys with baseball bats, golf clubs and one had a rake. They were walking up to cars, yelling at the occupants and then putting stuff into bags.

"Are they robbing people?" Monique asked.

Joe couldn't believe his eyes. How could things go downhill so fast?

"Isn't it a little early in the apocalypse to be pillaging?" asked Kevin, stopping the clacking cart.

A large heavily bearded man with a white bandana and a black skull on his head was yelling at the occupants of the car closest to them and then suddenly swung the rake at the car smashing the window. A baby crying could be heard in the back.

Out of the corner of his eye, Joe could see Monique reaching into Kevin's pocket and pull out the baseball.

The three of them were about 15 metres from the rake guy. It was about the distance from the pitcher's mound to home plate. It might have been luck, skill, or the strong will of a soon-to-be mother. Whatever it was, it was a very accurate pitch. Monique grunted as she lobbed the ball towards Rake Man. They all watched as the ball soared through the air. Rake Man turned as the ball smacked him right in the nose with a large crunching sound that could still be heard over the loud rain crashing to the pavement.

They all watched, frozen in place with disbelief. Monique was the first to break out of her spell. "Remember how I said to go slow...I changed my mind."

They both sprang into action. Kevin resumed pushing the cart, but this time faster.

"Go, go, go!" Joe yelled. The rake guy was holding his nose, and blood was now pouring on to the pavement.

The three of them ran as fast the cart would go without tipping through the torrents of rain.

The cart sounded like a speeding locomotive as it clacked noisily over the cracks in the sidewalk.

Kevin was running with a look of fierce determination on his face. "That was my lucky baseball!"

"Who cares about your stupid baseball. If it was so lucky, why are we running for our lives?"

"Because you threw it, and the lucky ball hit its mark!"

"I thought you didn't believe in luck. Just God's will."

Joe turned back to see if they were being chased. He could see Rake man wipe his bloody nose, and start running towards them. He had an angry look on his face.

Kevin and Monique were still arguing as they ran past a large transport truck stopped sideways on the road.

"I don't think it was God's will that you throw my ball away." He was running and panting heavier now.

"Maybe, but you have to admit, that was a good shot." She pushed her wet blond hair out of her eyes.

"Only if you want to make that gardener from hell mad."

"Hey, he was tormenting that family, and I had to do something."

Joe glanced behind them and saw their pursuer was gaining on them.

"Hey Kevin, you wouldn't happen to have a lucky bat, would you? We need to slow this guy down."

They passed the truck that had merged with the hydro pole, that they had seen from the bus. There were a couple of officers at the scene. Joe yelled at them as they got closer. "Help, a big guy with a rake is trying to kill us!"

The officer was bent down, looking inside the pickup. He looked up just as the three of them ran by, the grocery cart clacking down the sidewalk.

"Whoa, whoa, whoa. What's going on here?" It was Officer Mike, the policeman that had chased the hatchet guy out of Building Two.

The three of them didn't stop, but Joe pointed behind him at the rake guy. By the time Joe looked back again, Mike had his gun pointing at Rake man. Behind him, the other five pillagers were now gathering.

Kevin was breathing heavily and had slowed down. "I think that cop is my neighbour."

Joe beckoned him forward. "Don't slow down now. That cop might not be able to stop all of Rake man's friends."

"No, it's fine. We live here." Kevin was bent over, trying to catch his breath. He pointed at the small red brick semi-detached house across the street.

"Okay, I'm just down the street a bit. I'll see you," said Joe.

Kevin reached out his hand. "Thanks a lot. Keep safe, and I'll pray for you."

Joe shook his hand. "Okay, thanks. If you ever need anything, I'm in the Masterson Apartment complex, Building One, Room 501."

The two of them helped Monique out of the cart. "You stay safe, and I hope things get back to normal before your bun is done."

"Thanks."

Joe ran down the street towards his apartment.

He could hear the sound of sirens and more thunder. The rain was finally starting to slow down. He thought he heard a shot being fired from the direction of Rake man and his gang of unruly pillagers.

He ran faster.

Panting, he finally arrived at his apartment. He struggled to catch his breath.

I probably should try to get into better shape.

In front of Building Two, he saw a crowd had gathered. Some with umbrellas, while others stood beneath a large sycamore tree. The rain and wind had somewhat subsided, but Joe was now thoroughly drenched.

An ambulance was parked in front of the building with its back doors open. A stretcher came out of the building with someone on it. He walked closer to try to see who it was, but the body was covered in a white sheet. Two paramedics wheeled it towards the back of the waiting ambulance. Laurel followed behind, his hand over his mouth and his whole body shaking as he cried.

"Laurel, what happened?" Joe yelled as he jogged over.

Laurel paused and looked up at Joe, who was now standing beside the ambulance.

"It's Harvey. He's...just...gone." He managed to say between sobs.

The paramedics expertly folded the legs of the stretcher in and pushed the stretcher with Harvey on it into the back of the ambulance.

"How?"

"It was...the Scourge...it...he just...his heart...it happened so fast...and..."

"I'm so sorry, Laurel." He wasn't sure if he should hug him or put his hand on his shoulder or say something else. He felt too awkward to do anything.

The paramedics jumped out of the back of the ambulance, shut the doors and climbed into the cab.

Laurel and Joe stood on the wet road watching the ambulance drive away. Water from the leaves of the large sycamore dripped down around them, making big blooping noises as they collided with the large puddles below. Joe could barely hear the sounds of the commotion across the street or the small river of water and garbage flowing down the side of the road into the sewer. He barely noticed the sounds of various sirens going off in what sounded like many areas of the city, and he ignored his phone notification dinging in his pocket. All he heard was Laurel crying as the two of them stood there on the edge of the sidewalk. He knew the pain Laurel was feeling. He still felt the pain from when Jenny died. It wasn't as sharp and visceral as when it happened ten years ago. It was more of a dull ache now. It still hurt. For a moment, the painful memories pushed their way back to the surface.

They stood in the rain for a long time.

CHAPTER 6

The notification he had ignored while standing with Laurel was from Blender. Both of Blender's parents were sick, and he wasn't going to be able to come over that night, but promised to come over the following Saturday. That was fine with Joe as he needed some time alone with depressing music and a bottle of cheap rye.

The following week was long. The virus seemed to be hitting full force, and over 50 people from his three buildings had died. There were protests and unrest all over Canada, the United States and around the world. Joe wasn't sure or cared what exactly they were protesting. There was talk of possible terrorist attacks and wars brewing in the Middle East and Indonesia. The president of the United States hadn't been heard from in three days, and rumours were that he was dead. The food supply chain was breaking down, and many stores and businesses were overrun or looted. There were reports on social media that a vaccine was being developed in China, but the mainstream media had so far been unable to confirm the stories. He hadn't seen Laurel since the day Harvey died.

He sat in his apartment on a cloudy Saturday afternoon, debating if he should venture out to find a grocery store that hadn't descended into chaos. His apartment was a double apartment. When he first got his job working for Hank Masterson, Hank agreed to pay him minimum wage but got free rent in an apartment of his choice. A month later, an elderly

WWII vet named Roger Waxworth in the apartment next to him died. When Joe went in to clean it out for new tenants, he discovered that the kitchen pipes had been slowly leaking for a long time. Roger had been cleaning up the leaky water but had never got the leak fixed. When Joe tried to replace the kitchen plumbing, he discovered rot and mildew had crept up the walls. He had to rip out most of the kitchen cabinetry and part of the wall. On the other side of that wall was Joe's apartment. This happened just as Hank was having Building Three built. He didn't have any money to fix the wall and kitchen, so he told Joe that if he fixed it, he could have the apartment. Joe ripped out the wall, put up a beam for support and expanded his apartment to now include Roger's. His old apartment remained much the same, but he tore apart Roger's apartment so that it was a spacious open rec room. It had two large long old windows, a big leather couch, large screen television with surround sound, a pool table, a wet bar and a dartboard. Unlike his tiny sanctuary in the basement, his open-concept apartment was expansive and roomy.

On television, a music video showed scantily clad young women with too much make-up dancing and singing. The pop music from the video rang out on his surround sound speakers.

His phone rang, and he muted the television.

"Joe, this is Hank," said the voice on the phone, "You need to clean out Room 222 in Building Three." He sniffled and coughed.

"Are you okay? You sound sick," said Joe.

"I'm fine. Can you please just do your job and clean it out?

"I thought they just moved in?"

"Well, they died, and the Westons on the top floor want the apartment for their kid."

"Okay, I'll clean it up next week."

"No, you need to get it ready by Tuesday. I need you to go in there today and start getting it ready."

"Fine, I'll check it out right now."

He was bored anyway, so he thought he should at least see what kind of shape it was in. Building Three was new, and most of its tenants were rich, and half of them hired housekeepers.

Knock, knock, knock.

He hadn't buzzed anyone in, so he thought it had to be one of the other tenants in his building.

When he opened the door, he was surprised to find Blender standing there.

"How'd you get in the building?"

"I have my ways." Blender smiled as he walked around Joe and headed straight to the kitchen. "You got any food?"

Joe closed the door.

"Not really. And what are you doing here? I have things to do, you know."

"No, you don't." He opened the fridge and started moving stuff around. "No beer, no milk, no nuttin'."

"I thought your parents just died. Shouldn't you be in mourning."

Blender tasted a piece of cheese. "Nah. He was only my stepdad, and he was a total idiot, and my mom didn't think much of me since they got married."

"You know you would have got along with them better if you weren't still living in their basement at 30 years old."

"First of all, I'm only 28, and second of all, this cheese tastes funny."

"Look, I have to go to Building Three to check on an apartment of a couple that died. Maybe you should come back later.

"No way. I'm coming with you. Building Three has all the *richie rich* people in it. Maybe we'll find some cool stuff, like a safe with millions or leftover pizza."

"I'm sure the family has already taken away most of the good stuff, but if you want to, let's go."

When they got to Building Three, the first thing they noticed was a tall police officer getting into his car.

Joe waved to get his attention. "What's going on?"

"Are you in charge of *this* building too?" It was Officer Reginald. Today his pants reached his shoes.

"Oh, hi Officer Reginald. Yes, I look after this building too. What's going on?"

Reginald had his cruiser door still open. "Someone broke your window."

"Who?"

Reginald looked like he had been working non-stop for the past two weeks. He had dark circles under his eyes, his shirt and correct length pants were full of wrinkles and dirt stains. "I don't have time for this. I've got real problems out there," he said, then ducked his lanky frame into the cruiser.

Joe leaned in closer. "Where's your partner today?"

He was sitting in his car, but the door was still open. He looked up at Joe with sad, tired eyes. "Mike's dead."

"What? How?"

"Some whack job killed him with a rake. Do you believe that? An effin' rake! Mike was all excited about finally having trained his dog and then this. Look, I got to go."

He shut the door and drove away.

Blender ran up to him, chewing on a small piece of something orange and blue.

"What was that about?"

"Remember how I told you about my escape from Ray's Grocery?"

"Was that the time some guy with an axe tried to kill you?"

"It was a hatchet, but no, this was the pregnant lady in the grocery cart. Anyway, that crazy guy with the rake must have killed Officer Mike."

"Who's Officer Mike?"

"He's the guy that saved me from the hatchet guy in Building Two. Never mind - what are you eating?"

Blender took another bite. "Oh, this is cheese."

"It's blue."

"It doesn't taste like Blue Cheese."

"That's because it's cheddar cheese with mould!"

Blender rubbed the blue off. "If you're trying to avoid brushes with death, you should try not poisoning me?"

Joe knocked the cheese out of his hand before he could take another bite. "Don't eat that. That guy with the rake that was chasing me and my grocery cart brigade killed Officer Mike."

"How do you get to have so many harrowing adventures? Nothing ever happens to me."

"I could live without my terrifying brushes with death."

They walked up to the front doors to Building Three. The big bay window beside the front door was smashed.

Joe reached to unlock the door as Blender walked through the broken window. "Are you going to fix this?"

"Not now." Joe unlocked and opened the door, and then met Blender already standing on the other side.

"I'm hungry," said Blender.

They walked across the shiny new linoleum floor now covered in tiny pieces of safety glass towards the elevator. Joe pressed the up button.

"How are you not sick from eating bad cheese?"

He patted his overweight belly. "I've got a stomach lined with titanium."

"That doesn't even make sense."

The elevator door opened. A small brown bundle of a child with black braided hair sat hunched in the corner, crying.

"Ayesha, what are you doing here?"

She continued sobbing.

"This isn't even your building. Where's Zach?"

Her face pressed against the wall. She refused to respond.

They stepped inside the elevator, and Blender looked at the buttons. "What floor?"

"Two." He turned to the girl on the floor. "Hey, Ayesha, where's your mother? Do you need me to take you home?"

Without turning away from the corner, she shook her head.

The door opened on the 2nd floor.

"We'll be back in a minute. Don't go anywhere."

They exited the elevator leaving the girl behind.

"You're just going to leave her there?" asked Blender.

"Doesn't look like she's going anywhere. This building is pretty safe. We'll get her on our way out."

They walked a short way down the plush carpeted floor to Room 222. Joe found the master key and opened the door. "I'm hoping they don't have much stuff-"

They walked into the room, but then stopped when they heard Reggae music. The apartment wasn't empty. The living room in front of them still had furniture, and the walls had baseball and landscape pictures. The shelves contained books and knick-knacks. Shoes and sandals sat messily in front of the closet, and spring coats and a baseball hat hung on the black hooks by the door. Beneath the coats was a small silver dish filled with an assortment of keys and a large Blue Jays key ring. A glove and aluminum baseball bat sat in the corner.

"I thought you said they died." Blender moved Joe aside, so he could walk around him into the room.

"Wait!" Joe whispered loudly.

Blender paused. "Did you just whisper loudly?"

"I hear someone."

"That would be Bob Marley," he whispered loudly back. "And why are we whispering loudly? Doesn't that defeat the purpose of whispering?"

"Someone's in the kitchen."

They both stopped and listened. There was a clinking sound coming from the kitchen.

"This sounds like the start of another of your harrowing adventures where you encounter brushes with death," said Blender

"Hello?" Joe said a little louder and walked into the living room where he could see into the small eat-in kitchen.

"Hey, Zach," he called out. Zach was sitting at the dining room table, eating a mini-wheat type cereal without the frosting.

Joe looked back to see Blender flat against the wall with a bat in his hands.

"Are you coming?" asked Joe.

"I just wanted to make sure you didn't die first."

"Don't worry, its safe, George Bell."

Blender walked out into the living room, still clutching onto the bat.

"Who's George Bell?"

Joe ignored the ignorant comment.

"Blender, this is Zach. Zach, this is Blender." He pointed back to his friend.

Blender finally put the bat down at his side. "Hey Zach-man, whatcha' eatin'?"

"Blender?" said Zach, his mouth still full of cereal and milk. "That's a funny name, and what's with the bat? This isn't the zombie apocalypse."

Joe sat down at the table across from Zach. Blender opened the fridge and pulled out the milk.

"Zach, what are you doing here?" asked Joe. "This isn't your apartment."

Blender grabbed a bowl from the cupboard, found a spoon and sat down beside Zach. "Zachariah is a weird name too, big guy?"

"First of all, don't fat shame me, baseball boy, to cover up your insecurities and obvious cowardice and two, that milk is bad."

Blender poured the cereal into his bowl. "Where is the frosting on this cereal."

Joe attempted to interrupt. "Hello? Why are we sitting in a dead person's apartment eating mini-wheats?"

Zach looked at him with a serious look on his face. "These aren't mini-wheats."

Blender poured his milk and went to take a bite. "He's right, they don't have frosting, so they're not mini-wheats."

"Yeah, more like small hay bales."

Suddenly Blender spewed his milk across the table towards Joe, who moved to the side just in time.

Zach continued eating. "Told you it was bad."

"But what are you eating, then?" Blender dumped his bowl in the sink.

"This is almond milk. It lasts longer."

Blender rifled through the cupboards. "Yeah, well, that's gross. It's not milk unless it comes from a farm."

Joe waved his hand in front of Zach to get his attention. "Again, what are you doing here? How did you even get in?"

"I got hungry, okay? They hide their key above the door, in that little crack."

"But why are you even here?"

"The Florento's family died, and my family is gone. I ran out of food, so I came here, looking for chocolate. I didn't find any chocolate, but I did find some almond milk and this weird cereal."

"What? Your family died?"

"My dad left on a business trip when I was three. He never came back, and I hope he's dead. My mom ran off with some landscape gardener guy, and I haven't seen her since."

Joe discovered a can of something and sat back down beside Zach. "Did he carry a rake?"

Zach looked at him with a quizzical look. "What? I don't know. She told me to find my Uncle Ted and stay with him, and she would come back for me when they got settled. Whatever that means."

"Oh, Zach, I'm so sorry, I'm sure she'll come back."

Zach tilted his bowl up and drank the last of his milk. "My mom hardly even paid any attention to me. I was raised mostly by Uncle Ted, anyways."

"Blender, what are you eating? That stinks!"

"It's sardines. It's good for the brain."

Zach barely paused, eating his cereal. "You need all the help you can get."

"And where is Uncle Ted?" Blender asked, still scooping up his sardines.

Zach put his bowl down and plugged his nose. "I don't know. He left a couple of days ago. Said he was going to find some food, but never came back."

The three of them suddenly stopped talking when they heard the front door close.

Blender picked up his bat. "Did you leave the front door open, Joe?"

"Uh, you came in last, so technically you left it open, and put that bat down before you hurt someone."

Ayesha peeked her little brown head around the corner. "What stinks?"

"That would be Blender here." Zach pointed a thumb to his left.

Ayesha wiped the remnants of her tears off her face with the back of her arm. "That's a silly name. Is there more cereal?"

Over a meal of sugar-less hay bales with almond milk, Ayesha told them that her mother had died. Her aunt was supposed to look after her but never showed up. She too had run out of food, was all alone and didn't know what to do.

"Well, both of you are coming back to my place. I've got lots of space, and we're going to figure out where you kids can go," Joe announced.

"Joe, I was hoping for a harrowing adventure, not starting a daycare. Can we at least find some food first?" asked Blender.

Joe attempted to call Hank back to let him know that he had checked the Florento's apartment, but Hank wasn't answering. Blender and the kids convinced him to look for food in the apartment before they left.

The Florento's had prepared for the apocalypse. They had boxes of canned and dried food stored away in a spare room. Strangely they also had several cases of toilet paper, which seemed like an odd supply to be storing. Zach found a newer model laptop and a box of electronic paraphernalia. Ayesha grabbed a box of Disney Blu-rays. The three of them made several trips carrying the boxes of food and supplies back to Joe's apartment.

CHAPTER 7

The world around Joe appeared to calm down over the next few weeks. People were still dying of the virus, but there seemed to be less chaos in the streets. He wasn't sure if it was because society was calming down or there was so few people left.

He called Child Services to find out if someone could take the children. After waiting over an hour to talk to someone, they told him that because he was taking care of the children, they would be on the bottom of their priority list. They promised to send someone as soon as they could.

He still wasn't able to reach Hank, his boss.

The power stayed on, and grocery stores, hardware stores and other essential services had limited hours. Half the grocery store shelves were empty, and most of the protests had died down. The government was bailing out many businesses and sending cheques to keep the remaining population from extreme poverty. The hospitals and morgues became overrun. There was more talk of China developing a vaccine. The government enacted curfews and martial law to help curb looting and vandalism.

Joe, Blender, Ayesha and Zach lived together in Joe's apartment for the rest of the summer. They played video games, watched television, went for walks and even had a dart tournament. Zach hated darts and had thrown a wild shot in frustration, which had stuck briefly in the side of Blender's right thigh. Joe fixed leaky pipes, replaced the window in Building Three, and kept most of the remaining tenants relatively happy. He still hadn't heard back from his boss, and Hank's voicemail was full. They had some food left, which they were rationing. Joe and Blender made a couple of trips to the grocery store, but the shelves were almost empty.

August rolled on, and Mother Nature had decided to present another heatwave for its final summer performance.

Blender was cooking grilled cheese in the kitchen. Ayesha was watching the first Frozen movie again while Joe napped, and Zach browsed the internet. Joe's window air conditioner struggled to keep up with the hot summer sun.

Zach was commenting on the latest news that no one but him ever seemed to pay attention to. "Did you know that the virus isn't as bad in China? There is talk that they already have a vaccine or may have had one the whole time."

Nobody responded. Joe mumbled some half-asleep retort while Blender flipped the bread over in the pan. Ayesha was still engrossed in Elsa's song.

"Hello...morons." Zach was frustrated by their lack of attention. "You know the world could end and you idiots wouldn't even know it."

Blender flipped his grilled cheese over again in the cast iron skillet. "That would suck, especially if grilled cheese was going to be my last meal. If I had known, I would have cooked steak or lobster. Or both – surf and turf, baby."

"Okay. Seriously guys, this is major news."

Blender heard the sound of breaking glass from outside. "What was that?"

"The voice of reason." Zach didn't look up from the computer screen.

"No, outside." Blender walked over to the window and pushed it up as far as it would go.

Joe woke up. "What are you doing? You're letting the cold air out."

Blender stuck his head out the window and looked down. "I

heard breaking glass."

Zach now looked up from his computer. "If he falls out, I'm claiming that grilled cheese."

"Guys, I'm trying to watch something here," Ayesha said. "This is the best part."

"Let it go, Ayesha," laughed Joe as he stood up and stretched. "Is it the Building Three window again, because I just fixed that." He squeezed beside Blender, and they both looked out the window.

The sun was performing its last act of the day, still giving off some of its remaining light on the outside world. The shadows were lengthening, but they could still see a lot from the fifth floor. They saw a group of about 20 rough-looking biker types. They gathered around the front entrance to Building Three. The front window was smashed again. Two pick-up trucks, an SUV, three vans, a yellow school bus, and about a dozen Harley-Davidsons were in a line on the road. The biker at the front was directing his followers, and he wore a white bandana with a black skull on it. He held a sawed-off shotgun in his hands.

"That's the rake guy!" Joe exclaimed.

Blender was still beside him, looking out the window. "That doesn't look like a rake."

As they spoke, the man in the bandana looked up at them. Blender pulled back inside, and Joe bumped his head awkwardly on the window when he tried to do the same. He backed away from the window.

He looked over at Blender. "Did he see us?"

"I don't know."

Ayesha paused her movie and ran to the window. "What is it?" She started to move the blinds aside to lookout.

Joe stopped her and pushed the blinds back. "Get away from the windows."

"What are they doing?" asked Blender.

Zach was still looking at his laptop. "Looks like they're robbing Building Three."

"How would you know?" Blender walked back to the kitchen to grab his sandwich.

"I have a camera set up outside that's linked to my laptop. I'm watching it right now."

Joe walked over to Zach to look over his shoulder. "Where did you get a camera?"

"I grabbed it from the Florento's place, hooked it up last week. I have a couple of them set up." He pointed to the screen. "This one is mounted on the top of Building One, looking across the street to Building Three. If I zoom in..."

They were all gathered around Zach's laptop. On the screen, they could see the entrance to Building Three. Some of them stood guard outside the entrance while others carried boxes, electronics, food and other items out to the waiting vehicles. Most of them were armed. They had bats, knives, machetes, a cricket bat, and one had a short shovel. Nobody carried a rake.

"What's that?" Joe pointed at a second-floor balcony near the top right of the screen.

Zach fiddled with some buttons, and the view zoomed out.

"No, over there."

"I'm working on it, hang on."

As Zach adjusted the controls, the picture shuddered briefly, then moved right, up, and then zoomed in on a balcony on the fourth floor.

A large overweight man stood at the balcony doorway with one hand on his hip, and the other held a cricket bat that rested on his shoulder. A mother and her two young children sat cowering in the corner of the balcony. In front of them, the father stood between the mother and kids and the man with the cricket bat. He was holding his head, which appeared to be bleeding.

"Is that a cricket bat?" Blender was eating his grilled cheese as he hovered with the others looking over Zach's shoulder. "Who even plays cricket on this side of the pond?"

Ayesha had to push her way through to see the screen. "That man looks like he's hurt."

Joe stepped aside a little to give her a better view. "What

are they doing? Zach, can we see the street?"

"Can do." He adjusted the controls again, so they could see the entrance to Building One and part of the street.

"Can you zoom in further?"

"No, that's as good as it gets. This camera is mounted on the roof of the building, so that's pretty far away."

"How many cameras do you have?"

"Just two, and both are on your building. One on the roof and the other in the lobby."

They watched as men and some women carried their looted items to the waiting vehicles on the street.

"It looks like they are robbing the whole building!" Joe pulled out his cell phone. "We better call the cops."

After an agonizing five minutes, he finally got through. The operator said the police are currently backlogged, but help was on the way.

They watched for the next 20 minutes as Building Three was emptied of all food and valuables, and still, no police showed up. The sun had completed its final act of the day and retreated behind the dark curtain of the horizon.

"What are they doing now?" Blender asked.

The man with the white bandana was pointing across the street as others started marching towards Building One.

"This is not good," said Zach as he moved the mouse and clicked a different camera icon.

The screen went black for a moment, then came back up. The screen showed the inside of the lobby. They were able to make out faces peering through from the outside.

"What are we looking at, Zach?"

"That would be the other camera in the lobby downstairs. I think we're next."

Ayesha stepped back. "Are they coming to kill us?"

"No, no, Ayesha, it will be fine. The police are on their way." Joe said, but he wasn't sure he believed it. He put a hand awkwardly on her shoulder. It seemed like the right thing to do.

Blender was back in the kitchen. He was stuffing cans of

food into a backpack. "We need to get out of here."

Joe looked up at him. "What are you doing?"

"I'm packing up the food."

"Uh-oh." Zach was still watching the screen. "They're in."

Joe looked back at the screen as Ayesha moved closer to him and grabbed his arm. The armed gang had broken through the door and were now streaming into the lobby.

"We've got to go," said Joe.

Blender paused his food stashing. "Where are we going to go if they are already in the building?"

Ayesha was still clinging to his arm. "What if we just let them have our stuff, maybe they won't hurt us."

Joe watched as Blender threw his backpack on, walked across the room and grabbed his bat. "What are you doing?" asked Joe.

"I'm going to protect our food." He stood at the door in a batter's stance.

"I don't think so, Braveheart. We need to get to the roof."

Blender put his bat back down at his side. "Oh, good because I really don't like fighting."

Joe walked towards the door. "Ayesha, Zach, let's go. Now!"

"Are we sure we don't want to let Babe Ruth here take them on?" Zach closed the laptop and joined them at the door.

Joe opened the door to the hallway and looked both ways. He couldn't hear or see anybody.

"Okay, let's go."

As they left, Blender pointed back to the apartment door. "Aren't you going to lock your door?"

"No. They're going to get in anyways, no sense having a broken door too."

He led them to the closest stairwell. Following closely behind him was Ayesha. Behind her, still carrying his bat as menacing as he could, was Blender. At the back of the group was Zach. "Isn't a cricket bat bigger than a baseball bat?"

Blender looked back at Zach. "It's not the size of the bat that counts, it's how you-." He stopped mid-sentence as Joe opened the stairwell door, and they heard yelling and footsteps coming from the stairs below. They froze as the footsteps got louder.

"The other way!" Joe whispered loudly. They turned as one and ran down the hall in the opposite direction.

Blender was now leading the pack as they passed the elevator doors. "What did I say last time about whispering loudly?"

The elevator dinged behind them as they reached the stairwell at the other end of the hallway. Blender opened the door and let the rest of them go past. Just as Joe entered the stairwell, the elevator doors opened. Blender took off up the stairs. Joe stopped to look back through the small window in the stairwell door. One of the other tenants had opened their door at the same time as two burly men exited the elevator. The old man was Mr. Isper. He was over 75 but was always happy and full of energy. He was saying something to the men when one them pushed him to the ground. Another skinny man with long red hair came through the opposite stairwell doors. They all entered the old man's apartment as the red-haired guy, who looked to be out of breath, walked towards Mr. Isper.

"Are we going?" Ayesha appeared beside Joe, tugging at his arm as he watched through the window. Blender and Zach were already at the top of the stairs trying to open the door to the roof.

"Joe, Ayesha," Blender called down, "are you coming? The door's locked."

Mr. Isper was yelling at the red-haired guy, his arms flailing.

Joe reached into his pocket and pulled out his key ring. He removed the key for the roof and handed it to Ayesha. "Here, bring this to Blender and get on the roof. I'll be there in a second."

She grabbed the keys and ran up the stairs. When Joe looked back through the window, Red was kicking Mr. Isper as he crouched in the fetal position on the floor.

Joe ran through the open door and dove headfirst into Red, knocking him to the ground. Joe was not a fighter and had rarely even been in a fight, except for joining the wrestling club for two years in high school. Red squirmed out from under Joe and stood up. Joe rolled over and came up in what he was sure was a fighting stance. His fists came up like Rocky Balboa. He had a few centimetres and about 10 kilograms on Red. He was feeling confident now that he had successfully knocked the guy over on his first charge. That confidence turned to fear when Red pulled a Crocodile Dundee sized knife out of his pants.

Where was he keeping that knife?

Joe glanced down at Mr. Isper. He wasn't moving or making any noise.

Rather than using his fists in a knife fight, he made a dash for his apartment door and almost fell inside. Red was right behind him. Joe looked around for anything he could use a weapon. He made a move to the knife block in the kitchen just as Red threw his knife. The large knife flew end over end and smacked Joe in the back of the head, handle first. The knife clanged across the floor. Both men dove across the kitchen floor towards the knife. Joe's head was stinging, and his vision was a little blurry. Red easily beat him to the knife. Joe backed up on his butt, sliding backwards towards the rec room. Red stood above him with the knife in his hand.

"End of the line, hero."

Joe reached behind him and felt around for something, anything he could use to fight. His right hand came across one of his favourite championship darts, which he immediately grabbed and threw with all his might towards Red. The dart shot through the air and lodged itself into the centre of Red's forehead.

That's a triple 20.

Red pulled the dart out and threw it to the ground. This gave Joe enough time to get to his feet and run through the rec room. He felt a sharp, hot pain in his left thigh and looked down to see Dundee's knife sticking out the side of his calf. The knife then fell out of his leg and onto the ground. He yelled in pain and grabbed his leg, as he stumbled to the ground. Red was walking over but was having trouble seeing as blood now streamed down his forehead and into his eyes. He stumbled towards Joe, who was now up against the wall below the window. Red wiped the blood out of his eyes and charged. Joe grabbed the knife on the ground and staggered to his feet, just as Red plowed into him. Red's hands were on Joe's throat. He gasped for air but couldn't breathe. It felt like his larynx was being crushed. Joe let go of the knife and tried to pull the hands away from his throat, but he was rapidly losing consciousness. The room seemed to spin, and his vision went blurry, and he closed his eyes.

Suddenly he was able to breathe again. The hands around his neck loosened. He opened his eyes and looked back into his attacker's face. He had a look of confusion on his face as he stared back at Joe. There was something wet on Joe's stomach and below on his family jewels.

Oh no! I've been stabbed in the balls. I'll never have sex again!

Red staggered back a step. The knife was protruding from *his* stomach. It was hilt deep, and blood was hemorrhaging from the wound. Joe stepped aside as Red began falling forward towards him. Red clasped at the window knocking the blinds down and revealing the open window behind it. He placed both hands down on the sill looking through the window into the black night.

Joe wasn't sure if he should run, punch him or help him. He took a step forward. "Are you okay? I should call someone or…"

As he got closer, the man pulled the knife out of his stomach and stabbed clumsily towards Joe. He ducked, then slipped in the blood now pooled on the ground. Joe landed face-first in the blood. When he looked up, he could see Red had the knife in both hands above his head and was preparing to bring the knife down onto the back of Joe's head. Joe grabbed both of the man's ankles and pulled. Red fell backwards out the window and disappeared into the darkness, taking the knife with him.

Joe sat for a moment, stunned. Then he heard talking and yelling outside the apartment door, and he broke out of his stupor. He scrambled to his feet. It sounded like someone was about to come through the open door, so he ran to the second door that was once Mr. Waxworth's apartment door on the other side. Just as he reached it, a man with a white bandana with a black skull on it came through the first door. It was the cop-killing, rake wielding psycho who now carried a shotgun. Joe noticed that his nose looked a little crooked.

For a moment, they both stopped and looked at each other. Then the man looked at the blood all over the floor below the open window and then back to Joe.

Joe flung open the door and flew out into the hall. He tripped over Mr. Isper, who now appeared dead. Joe scrambled back to his feet and limped over to the far stairwell door. When he opened the door, he found Ayesha lying in the stairwell landing. Dead.

He took a quick intake of breath and bent down. "Oh no, Ayesha."

"Joe!" she came back to life and wrapped her little black arms around his neck.

"What..." the sound of Black Skull following in his footsteps and tripping over Mr. Isper brought Joe back to the other terrifying reality. The one where he was being chased by a man with a shotgun.

He was about to race up the stairs to the roof, when he heard men banging on the doorway to the roof. He changed his mind and ran down the stairs, Ayesha still clinging to his neck. Her legs were wrapped around his waist. He ran down the stairs as fast as he could limp with the extra 35 kilograms strapped to his front. Black skull ran up the stairs thinking they had gone up, giving him a few precious seconds to descend two more floors.

Joe could hear that more men had joined Black Skull in his pursuit. He opened the door to the 2nd floor, hoping they might think he had gone that way. However, it was the fire door and automatically closed. He took off one of his shoes, threw it into the 2nd floor hallway and stuck the other shoe into the doorway to keep it open. He limped down to the first floor and stopped, listening. It sounded like they were following his misdirection.

The first floor was filled with other members of the raiding party, so he ran down the last flight into the basement level. He wasn't sure if they were following him or not, but he didn't want to find out. Joe began to run down the hallway when he heard people running down the opposite stairway. He put Ayesha down and reached for his keys, opened the door to his shop, and the two of them ducked inside. He turned on the light and locked the door.

They could hear voices and footsteps in the hallway for a few minutes. At one point, someone banged on the door and tried to open it, but eventually, most of the voices and noises faded.

The two of them sat quietly on the couch. Ayesha hugged her knees and started to shake.

"What's the matter, are you okay?" Joe asked. He wasn't sure what to do. He tried to comfort her but was coming down off his own adrenaline high and had to force himself to not break down crying. The two of them sat there for almost ten minutes and were finally starting to calm down when Ayesha's phone chirped.

It was Zach. He and Blender were on the roof and were safe. Joe realized that he had lost his phone at some point. He told Ayesha to text Zach back and that they should all stay where they were until the cops showed up.

"Hey, you're bleeding." She pointed to the blood covering his shirt and pants.

"Oh no, that's not mine." He looked down at his shirt but then noticed the pain in his calf. He slowly unrolled his pants to reveal the still bleeding wound. "This blood, however, is mine."

"Are you shot?" Ayesha had an empathetic grimace on her face.

"No, it's only a flesh wound," he said with a British accent.

She looked back at him, confused. "And that's a good thing?"

"Never mind. I got a large knife thrown at me. Grab that cup, fill it with water and pour it over my wound."

She ran to the sink, filled a mug with water and emptied it slowly on his cut. Once the water washed away the blood, he could see that the slice wasn't very deep.

Ayesha pulled the first aid kit off the shelf and opened it. She dabbed at his leg with a piece of gauze. "Hold still."

"Do you know what you're doing?"

"My mom's a nurse. She did teach me *something* useful." She pulled out a roll of gauze and proceeded to wrap his leg. "Where's your wife?"

"Gone. Ouch, be careful that hurts."

"Gone where?"

He adjusted his position on the couch, which was suddenly uncomfortable. "She died 10 years ago."

"How?" She finished wrapping his leg and expertly tucked the end of the gauze under, so it was secure.

"Cancer." He pulled his pant leg back down over his wrapped leg, then got up to pour himself a cup of whiskey. "Do you want any water or anything?"

She nodded, and he rinsed out a mug and filled it with water for her. He sat back down beside her.

"That must have made you very sad," she sipped from her mug as if she were savouring hot chocolate.

"It was a long time ago."

"Your still sad."

"Yeah." He took another sip of his whiskey.

"What was her name?" She took another sip of her water.

"Jenny."

"What was she like?" She put her mug down on the side of the couch.

"She was perfect."

"How come you never found another wife?" Ayesha yawned and rubbed her eyes.

"Never met the right person, I guess."

"Do you think you will ever find someone perfect?" She shifted closer to him and leaned her head on his arm.

He looked down at her. "What are you, my therapist? You're only 10 years old. What do you know about love?"

"I'm 11, and I don't know much about love. I don't even think my mother loved me." Her eyes closed as she talked.

"Of course, she did. All mothers love their kids."

"What do you know about kids; you don't even have any," she said quietly. Her face was nuzzled up against him.

They sat in silence for a moment.

"I have you," he finally replied.

She said nothing. He leaned his head forward and moved a black braid from her face. She was sleeping.

CHAPTER 8

Monique sat on the couch, breathing heavily and deliberately.

In through the nose, out through the mouth.

"Do you need…" Kevin started to ask but was interrupted when Monique held up her finger, indicating that she needed a minute.

She continued concentrating on her breathing.

It would have been nice to take a few prenatal classes other than just the ones online.

Like many other non-essential services, in-person prenatal classes were shut down due to the pandemic. There were online classes only.

As her breathing slowed and the pain subsided, she looked up to see a dark pair of canine eyes looking at her. They only had Roxie for a week, but she was already very protective of her.

Roxie had been with Officer Mike for four years as part of the canine unit. He had responded to a call about a man with a rake and was ambushed and killed by a gang on Pochatok Street. Roxie hadn't been reassigned to another officer yet.

Mike's wife Janice was left to look after their three children. Shortly after Mike was killed, two of their sons died of the virus. This left Janice with their remaining daughter and Roxie. Janice decided to leave with the daughter to live with her mother and asked Kevin and Monique if they wanted the dog.

After their traumatizing home invasion, Kevin and Monique had tried to get an alarm system installed. However, alarm companies were not considered an essential service many were no longer open. Kevin bought some heavy-duty locks that he had to install himself. The locks didn't offer much security, so they gladly accepted the offer to look after the big German Shepherd.

Roxie immediately clung to Monique, following her around the house. When she sat down on the couch and started breathing heavily, the dog sat and watched with a concerned stare.

Monique recovered and sat up straight. "How long since the last contraction?" she asked.

"45 minutes," replied Kevin, looking at his watch.

"Okay, so I'm not having the baby yet."

Kevin rubbed her back gently. "Shouldn't we go to the hospital?"

"I suppose we should be going soon."

"I'll grab the duffle bag."

Twenty minutes later, they were standing at the bus stop waiting. The sun had retired for the day, and the night was beginning its shift. A teenage boy stood leaning against the bus shelter, scrolling through his phone. The boy looked up from his phone. "Looks like no more buses today."

"What? Why not?" Kevin asked.

The boy let his skateboard drop and shrugged his shoulders. "Reduced service, I guess." He hopped on his skateboard and rolled down the sidewalk.

"I'll call a cab," said Kevin as he pulled out his phone.

Monique's back hurt, but she hadn't had a contraction for a half hour.

"I can't get through," he said, "they must be *really* busy."

"What about an Uber?"

"I ran out of data yesterday. Where's your phone?"

"I left it at home. It's a work phone, remember, and I hate

answering work calls after hours."

"Maybe we should have bought a car."

"It's so expensive. Besides that's what public transit is supposed to be for." Suddenly Monique keeled over in pain. When she recovered, Kevin looked at his watch.

"It's been 35 minutes," he said. "They're getting closer together." Monique thought for a moment. "Do you think the neighbours took their bicycles?"

"You are not in any condition to be riding a bicycle."

"No, but they have one of those kid trailers that hooks on the back of a bicycle."

They walked back home and, using the key under the rock in the petunias, opened the neighbour's front door. Kevin walked through the house and into the garage. When he opened the garage door, Monique saw a shiny blue jeep. "Why don't we take the jeep?"

"It's one thing to borrow their bicycle without asking, but I'm *not* stealing their jeep."

They found a red bicycle and a small bicycle trailer that they managed to connect to the back. The trailer was meant for two kids, but Monique was able to squeeze inside with the duffel bag behind her. She had to have her knees slightly bent to fit, but it was tolerable. They put a blanket underneath her for added comfort. There was only one pink bicycle helmet, and Monique insisted Kevin needed to wear it, since he was the one on the bicycle.

They closed the garage door and rolled down the driveway. The sidewalk was far too bumpy for Monique, so they opted to take the road. Fortunately, there were lights on the bicycle and trailer, so this reduced the chances of getting run over.

Monique had done a fair bit of cycling before she was pregnant and figured it should take them about an hour. Although with Kevin's driving, an hour and a half.

There was little traffic, and the air was still warm. Six months ago, this would have been the perfect night for a late-night cycle. Tonight, however, was a little different. There was the constant sound of a siren from somewhere in the city. Some stores were closed, some were boarded up, and there were few people out on the street.

Up ahead, they heard shouting, and as they got closer, they could see a large group of protesters coming their way. They were chanting, shaking their fists in the air in unison and taking up the entire street and both sidewalks.

"Detour!" yelled Kevin as he turned down a side street at the next intersection. The side street was notably quieter, and the sounds of the protesters behind them faded.

Kevin slowed as they came upon a large white transport truck. The truck looked out of place on the narrow side street. As they passed, Monique could see the back of the truck was over half full of bodies. People in blue and white hazmat suits were loading full body bags onto the growing pile. The truck was parked outside of a large senior's residence with a black ribbon tied to the front sign.

Kevin slowed to a crawl as they watched.

"Keep going, Kevin!" Monique suggested loudly.

They turned up the next street to get back to the main road to the hospital. The road was all residential houses. Most were older homes, many with uncut grass and untouched flower beds. Some houses were boarded up and there were few people out on the sidewalks. There were few other vehicles on the streets.

"Ahhh!" yelled Monique, "Stop!"

Kevin pulled to the side of the road.

One of the exceptions to the empty city was a group of about ten teens and twenty-somethings on the road ahead of them. The group straddled the curb with some of them on the sidewalk while the rest stood on the side of the road. Many had beers in their hands while others were smoking various substances.

Kevin steered to the far side of the street, hoping to get around them. One member of the group said something to the others, and they moved to block the entire road.

Kevin rolled to a stop in front of them. "Look, guys, we need to get through."

"There is currently a special toll for this street," said the leader of the group. He wore a large black hoodie, dark wide pants and a branded baseball cap. He looked at Kevin's helmet and laughed. "Especially for dorks with pink helmets."

Others in the group laughed.

Monique was getting impatient but remained in her seat.

"Look," said Kevin, "We don't have any money and…"

"Oh really," the leader of the group interrupted as he stepped closer.

Monique had had enough. She almost tripped on her face as she gracelessly extracted herself from the tiny trailer. She walked up to the leader of the pack with her distended belly pressing up against the man.

"Do you want to rob us at the same time I'm giving birth?!" she yelled.

He stood motionless with a stunned look on his face.

"Unless you want my water to break over your designer shoes, I suggest you step aside!"

The man took two steps back. "Um…maybe we'll just charge you double next time."

Monique struggled to get back into the trailer but then felt strong hands under her arms as she was gently lowered down. She looked up at the gang leader who was now helping her.

"Thank you," she said.

He looked down at her with a smirk. "We may not always be good people, but we're not savages."

"Not yet," she called back as they cycled down the street to St. Jude's Hospital.

CHAPTER 9

Early the next morning, Joe and Ayesha were both rudely awoken by the sound of someone banging on the maintenance room door and the notification chirp on Ayesha's phone. The police were at the door, and Zach was texting to say the police had finally arrived. Joe and Ayesha opened the door and came face to face with four policemen all decked out in full riot gear. The police led them out of the room and outside. There were lights and sirens and a lot of yelling. Blender and Zach had come down from their night on the roof and reunited with Joe and Ayesha.

Blender looked at Joe. "What's with all the blood? Are you hurt, and where are your shoes?" he asked

"It's a long story," said Joe. "Let's go check out the apartment."

As they walked back inside the building, Laurel came running up behind them. "Joe, are you alright? What happened?"

"I'm fine, thanks Laurel. Are you okay?"

"Yeah, my apartment's been cleaned out but I'm not hurt."

"That's good. We were just about to check out mine." He led the procession to the elevator, up to the top floor and down the hall to his apartment.

Laurel stood beside Joe with his hand on Joe's shoulder. Zach and Blender stood on the other side, and Ayesha clung to his hand. The five of them stood silently inside the doorway.

His apartment was trashed. The kitchen cupboards were

open and now mostly empty. One of the cupboard doors hung awkwardly from one hinge. The fridge was open and emptied except for some condiments and a rotten apple. Most of the furniture was upturned. A side lamp lay broken on the floor. One of the windows was broken. The blinds on the other window that Joe had flung Red out of were barely hanging on. They swung in and out of the open window in the early morning breeze. There was blood everywhere. The television, sound system, and Zach's laptop were gone, as was the last of their food stash. There were clothes and books strewn across the room. It looked like someone had taken a machete to the pool table, and his dartboard was gone.

Why would they take my dartboard?

The five of them stood looking at the disaster previously known as their home. Joe looked around at his friends and realized they were waiting for him to say or do something.

I'm the leader of this little group of survivors at the end of the world. I should say something inspiring.

"We will rebuild!" he exclaimed.

Blender looked at him with a quirky smile. "Right, you build a new television, and I'll go build some food."

A voice from behind him interrupted their reconstruction plans. "Is there an Ayesha Norsburg and Zachary Wiles here?"

A woman and three men with business cards that said 'Child Services' swooped in to take the kids. Joe briefly tried to protest, but they insisted they would be taken care of. Zach was mumbling about his laptop, and Ayesha just looked stunned. Blender said something to him about checking in with his parents. Laurel left to go check up on his neighbour. Then one of the officers told him that his apartment was a crime scene, and he would have to stay in a hotel for a few nights while they investigated. For a few brief dizzy moments, he stood there alone.

It all happened so fast. He felt detached from what was going on around him. The crazy events of the night before, and so many things happening at once overwhelmed him.

I killed a man. My apartment is trashed. The police are everywhere. Blender and Zach are gone. I'm homeless. The world's gone mad. Ayesha's gone. I'm alone, again.

He walked down to his shop in the basement, grabbed the bottle of Canadian Club and walked out of Building One. While drinking straight from the bottle, he walked past the policemen and paramedics. He walked past the tenants trying to ask him questions. He walked down the streets aimless and in a daze. He kept drinking. He walked past the ambulances, police cars and Harley's outside the building. He drank some more. He walked past the sycamore tree he had stood under with Laurel as they watched the ambulance take Harvey away.

Now it was him being taken away. Except it *wasn't* him being taken away. It was everyone else that was leaving. He felt more alone now, than when he walked out of Patmos park where he had poured out Jenny's ashes. His mind swirled with cheap rye as he took another swig.

For hours he wandered aimlessly, and drank until the bottle was empty.

Eventually, he stumbled into Patmos park. The park was filled with large maple and pine trees. A small paved pathway wound its way through the centre. He sat with his empty bottle of Canadian Club on one of the many park benches that lined the pathway.

I miss you, Jenny. Why can't you be here with me now? You left me. Everyone left me. I'm alone in this dying world, and no one cares.

He got up from the bench and walked drunkenly down the path until he came upon a gang of four hoodlums skulking towards him. One of them had a white bandana with a black skull.

That's him.

The sadness and anger bubbled inside him like magma.

This was the man who tried to kill pregnant Monique. He killed Officer Mike, and his friends killed Mr. Isper, and they trashed his apartment. It's his fault that Zach and Ayesha are gone. It's his fault that I'm alone.

His anger erupted. He charged at the man with the white bandana with a black skull, knocking him over. On the ground, he pounded the man with his empty bottle. His rage and grief unleashed as he reigned blow after blow down on the man's head and face.

Somewhere he heard a woman's voice. "Stop, please stop!"

Jenny? Is that you?

He paused from his frenzied violence for a moment. It wasn't Jenny. It was a woman's voice he didn't recognize. His blurred vision cleared somewhat, and he looked down at his victim. The man did *not* have a white bandana with a black skull. He had a Chicago White Sox baseball hat. The hat was now covered in the man's blood. Beside him, the man's wife was pleading with him, and two kids were crying under a small maple tree.

Out of the corner of his eye, he saw a man in black – a police officer - running towards him. The last thing he saw before he blacked out was a big black police baton swinging towards the side of his head.

CHAPTER 10

When Joe woke up, he heard screaming. It was a woman in the distance, and it was getting louder. He opened his eyes. He was facing the ceiling, and fluorescent lights were moving slowly past. But the lights weren't moving, he was. He was lying on a stretcher being pushed down the hallway of a hospital. His leg hurt, his head hurt, he had a pounding headache, his throat was dry, and his tongue felt like sandpaper. His right hand was handcuffed to the stretcher. A nurse with short black hair, dark skin and tired deep brown eyes peering out from behind a mask pushed him down the hall. Both sides of the hall were lined with patients on stretchers. The nurse parallel parked his stretcher in a gap between an older woman who wasn't moving and a blond teenage boy who kept coughing.

The sound of the screaming woman in the distance stopped.

"Guess she had her baby." The nurse said as she examined his head. She gently touched the bandage on his head. "Now, you're not going to give me any trouble, are you?"

"No, I...what's going on?" He rattled his handcuff.

"You did some bad stuff. You are at St. Jude's Hospital. You've been arrested, and I need to make sure you don't die before you go to jail."

The memories of his volcanic eruption of violence at Patmos park came flooding back to him. He felt ashamed of his actions and a deep aching remorse.

How could I do something like that? I beat an innocent man in front of his wife and kids? What kind of person have I become? And now I'm going to jail, and no one knows or cares. I deserve it. I deserve to die.

His eyes began to well up.

"Okay, you big baby, hold still." The nurse cut away his pant leg near his knife wound and unrolled the gauze that Ayesha had applied. He thought about Ayesha. A tear rolled down his cheek.

"Looks like it might be a little infected." She wiped away the dried blood and yellowish pus from around the wound and poured some alcohol on it. It hurt, but he was too numb to care.

"Might as well just let me die, Miss ..." He read the name tag on her shirt. "...Norsburg."

I've heard that name before.

"Nope, you're not allowed to die until the police have taken you away, then you are their responsibility. Now don't go anywhere. I have to get a stapler."

He lay back, closed his eyes, which were still wet from his crying, and tried to go to sleep.

"Joe? Is that you?" someone was shaking him. He looked up to see a familiar face.

"Kevin...what are you doing here?" He managed to sit up but had to steady himself as the room spun around him.

"I'm having a baby. Well, actually Monique already did, but...what are you doing here? Are you okay? What's with the shackles?"

"Let's see - a gang of looters broke into my building, and one of them attacked me with a knife – I killed him and threw him out a window. Then I hid in the basement with a little girl. The next morning, I found my apartment had been ransacked, and the little girl and boy that were living with me were taken away, and my best friend left me. Then I got very drunk, walked into a park and beat some innocent person to a pulp with a bottle. I *thought* it was the guy that ransacked my apartment." He took a much-needed breath. "The same guy, I might add, that chased you and I down the street from the grocery store!"

"Sound like you've had a rough time of it," said Kevin.

"Excuse me, you can't be here." The nurse returned with her stapler. "I've got work to do, and this man is *not* allowed visitors."

Kevin backed away. "I'll come back later and show you my baby girl, Olivia."

The nurse proceeded to staple his wound.

"Norsburg, Norsburg," he mumbled, and then louder: "I know that name!"

"Oh yeah, how's that."

"Are you related to Ayesha Norsburg?"

"She's my niece." She dabbed at the stapled wound and re-wrapped it with gauze just as her niece had done the day before. "Do you know her?" she asked.

"I was looking after her when her Mom died."

"Why aren't you look after her now?"

"I have enough problems of my own. I don't need to be looking after that brat too."

She stormed off, leaving him sitting alone, shackled to his stretcher.

Joe lay back and closed his eyes. Visions of violence, sadness and guilt kept him from sleep. About a half-hour later, someone unshackled him from his stretcher and handcuffed him to the handrail on the wall.

"Sorry, buddy, we need the stretcher. The cops will be here shortly to bring you to your new home," said the nurse.

He sat on the hallway floor with his handcuffed hand over his head attached to the guard rail. It was uncomfortable and even painful.

I deserve this. I deserve worse. I deserve whatever jail holds for me too.

He had nodded off when Kevin's voice woke him. "Isn't she

beautiful?" Kevin was standing next to him with a newborn baby in his arms.

"Yeah, congrats, Kevin, that's great." There wasn't much feeling in his voice.

"Amidst all this chaos," Kevin looked around him at the hospital hallway full of sick and dying people and then to the newborn baby in his arms, "there is still hope for the future."

"Not for me, there's not."

Kevin gently rocked his baby in his arms. "There is always hope. God gives us little miracles sometimes, like Olivia here, to remind us that he still cares."

"I don't think he cares for me. Not after what I've done."

"God will always forgive, no matter what you've done."

"The world around us is dying, I've lost everyone I've ever cared about, and I'm on my way to jail, and you talk about a God of hope?"

Little Olivia fussed a little. "Do you know what St. Jude is?"

"I believe it's the hospital where I am currently being incarcerated."

"Yes, but St. Jude, do you know what he's the patron saint of?"

"No, I'm not Catholic."

The baby started crying. "He's the patron saint of lost causes." Kevin stood up as Olivia appeared to get more agitated and was starting to cry. "I've got to get this little gal back to her mother."

"Okay." Kevin was staring down at the floor.

"Don't lose hope, Joe. You're a decent guy, and there's still hope for you. There's always hope."

He walked down the hall and disappeared around the corner. The blond teenage boy on the stretcher next to Joe had stopped coughing and was now dead silent.

Did he just die? I'm not a decent guy, and there is not much hope for this world and definitely not much hope for me.

CHAPTER 11

Monique woke up in the hospital bed, sore and still tired. She shared the room with three other people, and not all of them were new mothers. St. Jude's Hospital was overloaded and understaffed, so they were unable to have dedicated maternity rooms. Most of the other patients in the room had privacy curtains that hid them from her view. The patient beside her was no exception. It looked like his family was coming in to visit him. Monique assumed the woman was his wife, and the toddler was his son. They were talking and crying loudly, and the wife peeked around the curtain. "I am so sorry; we did not mean to wake you."

"Oh, that's quite alright, I've slept enough already," she answered.

The toddler walked through the curtain and fell towards Monique's bed. He grabbed at the sheets to steady himself, causing them to pull off the bed.

"Oh, I'm *so* sorry again to disturb you," the mother apologized again.

"Really, it's fine. I'm going to have to get used to it soon."

"Are you pregnant…or…"

"I gave birth just a few hours ago."

"Wow, you recovered quickly. Where is the little one now?"

Monique pointed at Kevin, carrying Olivia into the room. "There she is."

Kevin handed the baby to Monique.

"There's my precious," she said.

The wife looked at Olivia with a look of melancholy in her eyes.

"Would you like to hold her?" Monique asked.

"Are you sure, I mean..."

"Absolutely," said Monique. "My name's Monique, and this is my husband Kevin, and this tiny miracle is Olivia."

The mother handed off her son to her husband, who was now looking on. "My name is Lily, and that's my husband Garret and my son Mason." She pointed to the man in the bed and the little boy sitting at his feet.

Lily carefully held Olivia in her arms, and her lips appeared to be quivering slightly.

Mason watched his mother. "My brother Tommy is gone to Heaven."

"Yes, that right," said Lily, "but Mommy and Daddy are still here with you."

Olivia could see the tears welling up in Lily's eyes as she gently rocked Olivia.

Monique leaned forward in the bed and hugged Lily, who was still holding the baby. "I'm so sorry. I can't imagine what you're going through."

When they had finished hugging and crying, Monique asked, "Is that why you're here?"

"No, it's been two weeks since he passed," Lily answered, "Garret here hurt his nose."

Garret was holding a gauze pad up to his nose. "I did *not* hurt my nose. Some crazy man with a bottle attacked me."

"Don't exaggerate, honey. He was too drunk to hit you very hard."

"I might have a concussion."

"Don't be such a baby," Lily scolded him.

Kevin interrupted their spat. "Did this man have dark hair, mid-30's, bit of gut, and did he hit you with a bottle in a park?"

"Yes," said Garret, "how did you know?"

"Look, I'm very sorry," said Kevin, "He's my friend, and he's going through a *really* difficult time right now."

Garret looked angry.

Kevin continued. "It's not an excuse. He was wrong to hurt you. I think he mistook you for the guy that ransacked his apartment."

"What?" said Monique, "What are you talking about, Kevin?"

Kevin looked back at Monique. "Remember the guy that you hit with a baseball?"

"You hit someone with a baseball?" asked Lily.

"He was breaking into people's cars," explained Monique.

"Anyway," continued Kevin, "That same man that chased us that day, broke into Joe's building and trashed the place. Joe was angry and drunk. He thought Garret here was that same man. That's why he attacked him."

A police officer entered the room. "Mr. Garret Kavanagh, I need to ask you some more questions."

"Sure," said Garrett, "what do you need to know?"

"We're not pressing charges," stated Lily.

"We aren't?" asked Garret.

"No, dear, we are not. Your nose isn't even broken. Besides, do you want to go to court to testify and all that other stuff for a bloody nose?"

Garret's shoulders dropped in resignation. "Fine."

"Are you sure, sir?" asked the officer.

Garret nodded.

"Okay, I'm going to keep him overnight at the local jail to make sure he's sobered up. He may still be charged with drunk and disorderly," said the officer and then left the room.

Monique reached out to touch Lily's hand. "That was very kind of you."

"Oh, don't worry about. Now, we should let you and your baby rest." She turned to leave.

"Can I ask a favour of you?" asked Monique.

"Sure, anything, what do you need?"

"You wouldn't happen to have an extra baby seat, would

you?"

CHAPTER 12

Joe was taken to the Ingerwood Police Station. In the morning they put him on a bus that drove for over five hours to the Abitido Jail outside of the capital city of Commerce. When Joe arrived, he was placed in a cell with two other men who had already claimed both bunks. He had to sleep on the cold hard floor with nothing more than a dirty blanket and hard pillow.

His cellmates were a skinny, scraggly looking guy named Jimmy and a nervous middle-aged man with thick glasses named Benaiah.

Jimmy mostly kept to his top bunk and slept. He rarely spoke. Joe never spoke much either. Jimmy would sometimes stay in the cell when everyone else went to the cafeteria to eat or for the daily free time in the yard outside. Joe was pretty sure he was sick.

Benaiah talked enough to make up for Jimmy's silence. He even talked in his sleep. He talked about the virus and how he heard the Chinese were immune, but most people in North America were not, and they were all going to die. He also talked about the insurrection in the States and that it was going to start a civil war in that country, and many were going to die. He talked about wars on the other side of the world. Bombs were dropping, and troops were being mobilized. He talked about how so many people had already died. The government was falling apart, and civil society was crumbling.

Gangs were taking to the streets and killing for food and supplies. He talked about how the food supply chain was broken, and people were starving to death. Pretty much all his stories and theories ended with people dying. Joe didn't mind all the gloomy talk. He didn't care about anything.

One morning Jimmy was dead. Two guards with masks showed up. They opened the cell door, checked Jimmy's pulse, loaded him on their stretcher and left. Joe was sure he should have been sadder about it, but he was just relieved to finally have a bed. The top bunk wasn't very soft, and he could feel the springs through the thin mattress, but it was still better than the cold, hard concrete floor.

They were given a few hours every afternoon to go outside to get some fresh air. The early September air was still warm, but the heatwaves had abated. A small group played basketball on the concrete court while some prisoners exercised in the outdoor gym. Most of them talked amongst themselves in various groups around the yard and under a small wooden pavilion.

The only people Joe knew at the jail were his cellmates, Jimmy and Benaiah. Jimmy was dead, and that afternoon Benaiah was working with a group of prisoners doing janitorial work in the administration wing. So, Joe was alone. He wandered around the yard contemplating his transgressions. As he passed by the pavilion, a short heavily tattooed Latino with a thin moustache and too many earrings stepped in front of him. Joe was looking down as he walked, and deep in his misery. He almost walked right into the man, but stopped just in time.

"Where you going, Pendejo?" The Latino stood with his hands on his hips. "You think you can just walk wherever you want?" A group of six other prisoners stood behind, trying to look as menacing as possible. "This area here," he pointed at the pavilion, "this is Rafael Javier's house. Do you know who Rafael Javier is?"

Joe just stood there, staring off into the distance. "I don't know, and I don't care." He scratched at the dark stubble on his chin.

The man pushed him. "That would be me, fresa? And you didn't ask my permission to enter mi casa, did you?"

Joe was barely paying attention. He knew that if he antagonized this man, he would get a beating. Just like the beating, he gave that poor man in the park.

Joe slapped Rafael across the face as hard as he could.

Rafael returned the slap with a backhand across his left cheek, causing Joe to stumble and fall on his back. Like a wake of vultures, Rafael's group crowded around him and began kicking him. Joe didn't fight back or try to block the blows. They kicked his legs, kicked him in the stomach, and kicked him in the back. He felt the searing pain and continued taking the kicks. This was his punishment. This was his penance. Maybe, they would kill him and then it would be over. In the distance, he thought he could hear yelling from the guards. After a couple of vicious strikes to the head, Joe passed out.

Joe woke the next day in the prison medical station. His body hurt everywhere. His legs and arms were bruised, he had a couple of broken ribs, two black eyes and a mild concussion. The nurse told him his wounds would heal. He wasn't sure if that was true.

They bandaged him up, gave him some aspirin and sent him back to his cell.

CHAPTER 13

The government had been sending emergency money to all Canadians still alive, since the shutdowns. Neither Monique nor Kevin had gone to work for weeks, but they still had food and most essentials. It was still possible to get items from some stores if you could find one that was open. There was an initial run on many essential items, but the devastating death toll reduced the demand. Online ordering was not always reliable, as many warehouse workers and delivery drivers had either died or stopped going to work.

The garbage truck was coming once every two weeks instead of weekly, but it was still reliable. For that, Monique was grateful, since this meant she could still use disposable diapers.

Olivia was four weeks old and growing fast. Monique was changing her diaper on the floor while Roxie sat watching, when Kevin walked in.

"Where did you go?" asked Monique.

The dog got up to greet him.

"I went to Joe's apartment," he replied, rubbing Roxie behind the ears.

"Is he back yet?"

"No, but I did meet his friend Blender."

"That's a weird name."

"That's what I thought. It looks like Joe is still in jail, and this Blender guy is taking care of his apartment."

"When will Joe be getting out?"

"I don't know. Blender hadn't heard anything."

"We should go to the police station and find out where they're keeping him. We should at least visit him. Other than when he drinks too much, he seems like a nice guy."

"Okay, I guess I could go to the station and ask."

Monique pressed the final tape securing the diaper and lifted the baby. "We're coming too."

"I don't know if that's a good idea."

"We need to get out and give this little one some fresh air and some visual stimulation."

"I don't want you guys to get sick or…"

"The virus is airborne, and we are either going to die of it or we're immune. Staying in the house is not healthy for either of us, is it?" She directed the last part to Olivia.

"Fine, but what about the dog? Are we going to leave her here?"

"Nope, we are taking her with us for protection."

"They won't let her on the bus, will they?"

"I can be very persuasive."

They packed the diaper bag, put the baby in the stroller, put Roxie on a leash and walked to the bus stop.

The bus was running at reduced service but still ran twice per day. There was no one else at the stop as they waited, and the bus appeared to be empty when it arrived.

Kevin stepped onto the bus carrying the stroller and swiped their bus passes. The dog walked up the steps in front of Monique and Olivia.

"Whoa," the bus driver said in a muffled voice from behind his shield, "no dogs, unless their service dogs."

"There's nobody on the bus, and have you been out there lately? We need protection. There are some bad people out there." She held up the baby. "You wouldn't want this tiny innocent baby to be orphaned, would you?"

The driver rolled his eyes. "I've told you the rules, and now I'm going to check my rear-view mirror. I hope I don't miss any dogs getting on my bus while I'm not paying attention." He made an exaggerated gesture of looking out the window at his mirror.

With the baby, the dog and the stroller, it took them some time to get settled in their seats in the middle of the bus.

"I can't believe that worked," said Kevin.

"I told you, I can be persuasive. Besides, no one cares much about the rules anymore. There are more important issues, like staying alive, that makes these trivial rules unimportant."

The bus wasn't quite empty. At the back of the bus was a young boy and girl, who were whispering to each other.

Monique peered over her seat, "Are you kids okay?"

The girl had dark skin and neat braids in her hair. Her eyes were red and puffy. "We're fine, thank you." She reached up and pulled the bus stop cord. The bell sounded, and the bus began to slow. The girl nudged the boy, and they both stood up and made their way to the rear door. The boy had thick glasses and messy hair, and they both carried full backpacks.

The bus stopped, the doors opened, and they both got off. The doors closed, and the bus slowly regained speed.

Monique pointed to an apartment building that was hollowed out and blackened from a recent fire. "Isn't that where Joe lives?"

"No, he's across the road at the older building, there." He pointed across the road.

A half-hour later, they got off downtown, two blocks from the station. The morning air was warm, but the cool wind reminded them that summer was over. They passed by a group of older teens on the sidewalk, but once they saw the big German Shepherd, they ignored them. Downtown was calm. Half the businesses were closed, and many people were now staying indoors. Others, however, had taken the opportunity to loot and vandalize. There seemed to be a steady stream of various sirens wailing across the city. Traffic was steady, but there were not the usual traffic jams.

They moved from the relative calm of the downtown to the chaos inside the Ingerwood Police Station. The lobby was the size of a basketball court. There were two rows of seating on the left and a large reception counter to the right. At the back of the room were double doors that led into the rest of the station. The lobby was filled with people. One officer was sitting beside a prostitute arguing. Beside him, two officers were struggling to control a large angry woman. Near the back, a large group of elderly men and women were arguing. A long line started at the reception desk, snaked around the seating and ended near the entrance. Men and women of various ages, sexes and ethnicity talked, argued, yelled and whispered in the line. Policemen and women constantly streamed in and out of the double doors at the back of the station. It was loud and chaotic, and it didn't feel like the air conditioning was working.

They made their way to the end of the line, which only took them a couple of steps. An officer walking by noticed the dog. "Sorry guys, no animals allowed in here."

"Really," said Monique, "have you looked around?"

The officer took a second look at the dog. "Wait a second, is that Mike's dog?" He knelt to pet the dog. "Hello, Roxie." The dog's tail wagged as the officer gave the dog a thorough rub down.

"Janice left the dog for us to look after," said Monique. "She left with her daughter to live with her parents."

"I'm Hal. I worked with Mike. He was a good guy, and he loved this dog. I'm glad someone's looking after Roxie."

He finished petting the dog and walked away.

It was over an hour before they finally made it to the front of the line. They stepped up to the counter. A sweaty overweight policeman with red-rimmed glasses was behind the plexiglass. "How can I help you?"

"We're looking for my friend, Joe," said Kevin. "He was arrested two weeks ago."

"What's his name?"

"Joe."

"Last name?"

"Um... I don't know. He was arrested for hitting a man in the park and was taken to St. Jude's."

"I'm going to need a little more information than that, sir."

"Garret," said Monique, "the man he hit was Garret Kavanagh, his wife was Lily, and they had a child named Mason."

"And those are the names of the victims?"

"Yes."

"I'm going to need more information..."

"Can't you just look up Garret Kavanagh on your computer?"

"Let's see." The officer made a few mouse clicks and pecked on the computer. "Looks like I have a Garret Kavanagh who was a complainant."

"What about the guy that hit him?"

"That would be Joe Lortier."

"That's the guy." Monique was a little excited now. "Where is he?"

"Looks like he's been sent up to the Abitido Jail just outside of Commerce City."

"I was told the charges were to be dropped!" said Kevin, his voice rising in frustration.

"That could be."

"We talked to the Kavanagh's," said Monique, "We were there when they told the policeman that they weren't going to press charges."

"Sorry, but that's not what it says here." The policeman pointed at his monitor.

"Where is the officer that arrested him?" asked Monique, "Can we talk to him?"

The heat in the room was making the policeman sweat, which caused his red-rimmed glasses to slide down his nose. He pushed them back up. "The arresting officer...was...oh! I'm sorry it looks like Officer Bryson is no longer with us. He died a couple of days ago."

Monique was getting impatient, as was little Olivia. "Well, who is the officer in charge of this case now?"

"I don't know. You're going to have to wait for his arraignment hearing."

"Well, that's…" Monique was not able to finish her sentence.

A single gunshot rang out and echoed across the lobby. Instantly, everyone dropped to the floor except for one large angry woman. She stood at almost two metres tall and wore a flowered one-piece dress. Somehow, she had managed to steal one of the officer's guns and was swinging it around like she was going to spray paint the room with it.

One policewoman was laying on the ground behind her, she started to get up, but the woman swung around and pointed the gun at her. "Don't you dare, you scum. You're all scum. This stupid Scourge is going to kill us all, and you all act like nothing's going on!"

Monique lay on the ground, her body covering the baby. Kevin lay down close by, his hand holding Monique's. Roxie sat next to them like a sentinel, watching the woman with the gun as she kept shouting at her captive audience.

"You know we are all going to die anyway…" she stopped suddenly when she thought she heard a noise in Monique's direction. She whirled around, and when she saw the dog watching her, she shot in their direction.

Monique heard the thump of a body falling behind her. Roxie sprang forward towards the woman. Monique watched with trepidation as the dog leapt over the people lying down. Roxie used the prostrate prostitute as a springboard and leapt into the air. Her jaws clamped down on the woman's arm, and she fell backwards. The gun fell from her hands, and blood sprayed out of her wrist. Roxie had a lock-tight grip and was not letting go.

Monique handed the baby off to Kevin and ran to the dog.

"Roxie!" she yelled, "Let go!"

Roxie was still attached to the woman's arm as the woman

flailed and cried out.

Officer Hal ran over. "Off!" he yelled with an authoritarian voice.

Roxie immediately released her grip and sat down by Officer Hal.

Four other policemen cuffed the large bleeding woman and dragged her through the rear double doors.

Hal handed Monique his card. "Here's my card. Call me, and I can go through some very useful commands for this dog."

Monique thanked him and ran over to hug her husband and daughter. As she hugged them, she noticed a stream of blood flowing out from behind the reception counter. She released Kevin and Olivia from the hug and peered around the counter. The large man behind the counter was lying on his back, not moving. He had a red hole in his chest, and his red-rimmed glasses were lying on the floor in a pool of blood.

"Help! We're going to need some help here!"

CHAPTER 14

The previous night Ayesha lay on her back on the top bunk, sweating. She was staring at the ceiling when she heard a voice from below. "You awake?" It was Zach. He was having the same problem she was. Neither of them were able to sleep with the stifling heat. The top floor was hot and humid, and the Flagenmeyers insisted on keeping the windows closed 'in case someone tries to steal you'.

Their foster parents weren't bad people, but this was not how Ayesha pictured her perfect family. When she lived with her mother, she was often ignored or yelled at. Most of the time, her mother was either sleeping or at work. No one ever told her about her father, except that he left when she was born. At least when she lived at Joe's apartment, everyone liked her.

She longed for a family like they had in the movies - one with a father, mother, brother and sister. Joe felt like a father, although she wasn't sure what having a father felt like. The Flagenmeyers seemed to dislike both of them. Zach said it was because they had twin girls that had both died of the virus. When they tried to replace them with Ayesha and Zach, they ended up resenting them because they were not as good as their own children. She was glad Zach was here with her. Zach was her best friend, and they made a good team. Right now, all they had was each other.

Ayesha rolled over and hung her head over the side of the

bed. "Yes, I'm awake. It's way too hot up here to sleep. Why don't they have an air conditioner?"

"They say it's too expensive to feed us and pay for an air conditioner," answered Zach.

"I hate it here," she said.

"Me too."

"I miss Joe and Blender."

"I miss chocolate."

"Why don't we go back to Joe's apartment?"

"I wish, but I don't think that's going to happen. Besides, that place was trashed."

Ayesha thought for a moment. "Joe said he wanted to rebuild."

"I think he was joking."

"Maybe, but I still want to go back."

"I don't think the Flagenmeyers are going to bring us back, and neither will Child Services."

"But what if we just left?"

"What?" he said, his voice rising, "you want to just leave?"

There was a loud banging on the door. "Shut up in there and go to sleep!"

She reduced her volume to a whisper. "You want to stay?"

"No, I do not," he whispered back.

"Why don't we pack our bags, sneak out and take the bus back to Joe's? I bet he'd be happy to have us back."

"Are you serious?" His voice started to rise again.

"Shhhh," she replied, "I hate it here. They won't even let us watch television."

"They won't give me access to a computer."

"We should leave at night, so they don't see us leave."

"Okay, let's do it. What night do you want to leave?"

"Tonight."

"Really?"

"Yes, why not?"

"Okay."

They got changed out of their pajamas and packed their

backpacks with some of their clothes. The television downstairs wasn't on, so they assumed the Flagenmeyers had gone to bed. Once they snuck past their room, Ayesha and Zach ran down the stairs. Ayesha tip-toed towards the front door, but Zach veered into the kitchen.

"Where are you going?" she asked.

"I'm packing some food and looking for chocolate," he answered.

They both heard a door open upstairs.

"No time!" said Ayesha.

Zach stuffed a box of Cheerios in his backpack and followed her out the front door. Behind them, they could hear a voice calling. They ran across the driveway and down the sidewalk without looking back. It was dark out, but the street lights lit up their path.

"Can we slow down, please?" Zach was panting and had to slow to a walk.

Ayesha looked behind, no one was following them. "Okay, we can slow down now. What time does the bus run around here?"

Zach was still catching his breath. "It only runs twice a day now. Once in the morning and once in the afternoon."

"So, we have to wait till morning? What are we supposed to do all night?"

"I don't know, this was your idea. Maybe we could..."

Several dark figures seemed to materialize in front of them. They all wore dark hoodies and black baseball caps.

"Oh crap, we have to run again, don't we?"

Ayesha pointed down a side alley. "This way."

They both ran down the alley. The streetlights weren't able to light their way, and they almost tripped over some garbage bags. They could hear footsteps behind them, and they ran faster. Ayesha was quicker on her feet, and she led the way taking random turns down streets and alleys. She noticed a basement window, in a red brick building and ran to it. Zach helped her push it open so that they could squeeze through.

It was pitch black inside, and Ayesha hung from the window sill, but her feet still didn't reach the floor.

"I can't reach the floor," she called up to Zach.

"Just let go and bend your knees. It can't be that far."

She squeezed her eyes shut and let go. The drop was not as far as she was afraid it might be, and she landed gently on a concrete floor. Zach dropped down from the sill but tripped when he landed and fell on his butt.

"Ouch, that hurt," he said.

"Did you bend your knees?" she asked.

"I think I bent my butt. Where are we?"

"I don't know. Do you have a flashlight?"

He fished a flashlight out of his pack and flicked it on. The basement was full of kegs and bottles. A large wine rack ran along the sidewall.

"Now what?" asked Ayesha, "Should we go upstairs?"

"I guess. If we have to wait here all night, I don't want to sleep on this concrete floor."

They climbed the stairs and opened the door at the top. The room was lit only by the lights under the glass shelving behind the bar. There was a pool table, dartboard and three large-screen televisions.

"Is this a bar?" asked Ayesha.

"Yes, I think so."

"It looks like Joe's apartment."

A leather couch and some plush chairs sat in the corner by the pool table. Ayesha lay on the couch, and Zach took one of the chairs.

"At least this is not as hot as upstairs at the Flagenmeyers," said Ayesha.

"And no one's going to bang on the door yelling, 'shut up?'"

"Do you think Joe misses us?" asked Ayesha.

"I think he does."

"Are you glad that we left the Flagenmeyers?"

"Yeah, that place sucked, but you know what would have really made me happy?"

"What?"

"I would have been really happy if we had broken into the basement of a chocolate factory."

"No, a candy-floss factory."

"A sausage factory."

"A cake factory."

"A laptop factory."

They laughed and talked till they were both too tired to keep their eyes open.

Just as they had both fallen asleep, the sound of keys rattling in the front door lock woke Ayesha. She sat up and listened. There were voices outside.

"Wake up, Zach." She shook him by the shoulders. "There's someone here."

He opened his eyes and was about to say something when Ayesha covered his mouth and put her finger to her lips. She pointed to the front door.

He realized what was going on and followed her lead when she ducked behind the pool table.

The door opened, and a little bell hanging above the door dinged. They could hear two people entering and talking to each other.

"I don't know Bill," said one of them, "all I know is that the silent alarm went off. You check the basement, and I'll check the washrooms and office."

As they both left the room, Ayesha motioned Zach to follow, and they ran to the front door. As silently as she could, she turned the handle and opened the door. The tiny bell above the door dinged, and they ran.

The street had a few brightly lit stores, streetlights and a couple of cars were driving by. They were close to downtown, and there were a few people out. Once she checked that they weren't being followed, Ayesha slowed down to a walk.

Zach was out of breath again. "Why do we have to keep... on...running?"

"Maybe if you didn't eat so much sausage and chocolate,

you would be in better shape," she said with a smile.

"Where are we now?" he asked.

"I think I know where we are," she said, looking up and down the street, "and stop looking so scared."

"I am scared."

"People are looking at us, and someone is going to call the cops, so just pretend like we know where we're going."

They kept walking.

"Do we know where we're going?"

"Yes, it's just down here."

They walked down the sidewalk, towards the brightly lit corner restaurant called, "Nevil's All-Night Diner."

"Wait!" yelled Zach when they were a few metres from the entrance. He pointed down the sidewalk where two police officers were walking straight towards them.

Ayesha and Zach stopped and looked in fear. Just before the officers were about to walk into them, they turned into the diner.

"We need to wait till they're gone," said Ayesha.

"Can't we just go somewhere else?"

"No, this is where my mother works – or used to work. Penny works here, and she'll help us."

"I don't know..."

"She might give us free chocolate shakes."

"Let's wait."

A few minutes later, the policemen led a large angry woman in a flowered dress, who was yelling, out the front door.

Once they had left, Ayesha and Zach went into the diner. There were a few diner patrons including a grey-haired man at the far end of the diner bar who was slumped over and appeared to be sleeping. There was also a group of noisy teenagers at one of the booths.

A waitress in a striped dress walked over to them. "Ayesha? What are you doing here?"

"Hi, Penny," said Ayesha.

"Come, sit down over here," she motioned them to an

empty booth. "Who's your friend?"

"I'm Zach."

Penny looked at the other customers to make sure she wasn't needed and then sat down opposite them in the booth. "I'm really sorry about your Mom, Ayesha."

"Thanks."

"So, what are you doing here in the middle of the night?"

Ayesha decided to tell her part of the truth. "It was really hot in the house, so we left for a bit."

"Where are you staying?" she asked.

"We're at a foster home," Ayesha answered.

Penny pointed at them. "You're going back, right? Otherwise, I will have to call them."

"Of course," chimed in Zach, "We'll be back in the morning. Do you think maybe we could get a chocolate shake?"

"Absolutely, big guy. Did you guys need some food too? The cook back there is bored anyway. What do you want?"

Zach rubbed his hands and licked his lips in anticipation. "Do you have a menu?"

After they ate too much food and drank too much chocolate, Penny came to take their dishes and garbage. "Are you kids going back now?"

"It's kind of scary out there," said Ayesha, "would it be okay if we stayed here till the morning so we can take the bus?"

"Won't your parents – foster parents be worried?"

"I can text them," said Zach.

"Okay, come with me." Penny led them to the break room in the back. They managed to get a few hours of sleep before the sun rose the next morning, and Penny's shift was over. They washed the sleep out of their eyes in the bathroom and walked to the nearest bus stop. They used the tip change that Penny gave them to pay for the bus that took them to Pochatok Street.

CHAPTER 15

The next day Kevin and Monique made numerous phone calls to the police station, the courthouse and a lawyer. The phone lines were becoming unreliable, and often nobody would answer the phone. When they did get through, they got little information on the status of Joe's case. All they knew was that he was being held in the Abitido Jail.

Monique decided that they should check up on Joe's apartment. They took the baby and the dog for the short hike up Pochatok street. As they approached the apartment, three jets screamed overhead.

"Are those military jets?" asked Monique.

"It looks like it. What do you think they're doing?"

"I have no idea. It's not like they can bomb the virus."

Kevin pointed at the old brick apartment building. "Is this it?"

"I think so."

"How are we going to get in?"

"Maybe the superintendent will let us in," said Monique.

"Isn't Joe the super?"

"Oh yeah. Somebody here must be able to let us in. Let's try his apartment just in case."

Kevin pressed the buzzer for 501.

A voice crackled through the speaker, surprising both of them, "Hello?"

"Um...hello," Monique stammered, "We're friends of Joe's,

and we wanted to check up on his place. Who are we speaking to?"

"I'm Ayesha. I'm not supposed to let in strangers."

"Is that a little girl's voice?" Kevin whispered.

"It sounds like it," she whispered back.

"Is your Dad or Mom there?" she asked.

An adult's voice came through the speaker, "How do you know Joe?"

Kevin answered, "Blender? It's Kevin, we met last week."

The door buzzed open. Kevin held the door for the stroller and the dog. They took the elevator up to the fifth floor and knocked on Room 501.

A man with a long thin nose and greasy brown hair opened the door. "Kevin, come in. This must be the infamous baseball throwing Monique I heard about."

Blender, Ayesha and Zach introduced themselves to Kevin, Monique, Olivia and Roxie.

Kevin and Monique sat on the couch and relayed the story of Joe going to jail, the charges being dropped and how they had been unable to find out when he might be coming back.

Blender told them that both of his parents had succumbed to the virus. He didn't want to be alone, so he came to be with his friend, Joe. He had begun cleaning the apartment while he waited for Joe.

"Then yesterday, Ayesha and Zach showed up," he said. "They were living here for a bit with Joe before he went to jail. They say they escaped their foster home and took the bus here. Personally, I think they missed me."

"Not likely," Zach chimed in. He was tapping at his phone.

"I can't believe he's in jail all the way in Commerce City," said Blender.

Ayesha was petting the dog. "How do we get Joe back?"

"I think I should drive up to Commerce and at least visit him."

"I want to come too," said Ayesha.

"It's too dangerous, dear," said Monique, gently rocking the baby.

"It's too dangerous for you too, Monique," said Kevin, "Things are happening fast out there, I think it would be safer for the baby if you stayed here. Besides, it's a five-hour trip."

"The thought of driving for five hours with the baby doesn't sound like much fun, but you want me to stay at home alone?"

"You'll have the dog."

"Why don't you stay here?" asked Ayesha.

Monique looked at Blender, "I don't want to impose…"

"Hey, it's not even my place, but there's lots of room. You're welcome to stay and you can help me look after these brats."

Zach was still looking at his phone. "We can take care of ourselves."

"One little problem in this plan," said Kevin, "I'm going to need a car."

Monique stopped rocking the baby. "What about the neighbour's blue Jeep?"

The next morning, Kevin went back home and borrowed the blue jeep. He drove it out of Ingerwood towards Commerce City. Although it was late September, it felt like summer was still hanging on. The highway was not busy, and he had trouble finding a gas station that was open. He made it to the Abitido Jail before nightfall. Abitido was a medium security facility that featured double seven-metre high fences. The parking lot outside the administration building was almost empty.

He walked up to the front doors and pressed the red button beside the door. Nothing happened so he pressed it again. Above him a video camera with a green blinking light stared at him. He waved at the camera and pressed the button again.

"How can I help you?" said a voice from the speaker above the door.

"I'm here to visit one of your prisoners."

"You need to call ahead to make an appointment."

"I tried; you're not answering my calls."

There was a brief pause, then, "Visiting hours are over."

"Please," he pleaded, "I've driven a long way to see my friend."

"Sorry, visiting hours are over."

"When are your visiting hours?"

"Try again tomorrow."

"When I come back tomorrow, then can I visit him?"

"Not likely."

Exasperated, Kevin started to walk back to his car. He noticed a man standing outside one of the side doors lighting a cigarette. Kevin walked over him. "Excuse me, can you please tell me what's going on here? Why can't I visit my friend?"

The man took a long drag from his cigarette. "I don't know what to tell you, pal. We are short-staffed. Some guards have died from the virus and others just stopped coming to work. We don't have the manpower to facilitate visits."

"But my friend hasn't even had his arraignment, and the charges were supposed to be dropped. Can they just keep him without his day in court? Is that even legal?"

"It's a state of emergency, buddy. They can do what they want." He pinched off the ember and put the last half of his cigarette in his chest pocket. "Sorry, man."

"Wait, give me two minutes," said Kevin. He ran back to his jeep and grabbed a piece of paper. He wrote a quick note and handed it the man.

The man took it, opened the door and disappeared into the building.

It was getting dark, and Kevin was too tired to drive all the way home, so he decided to find a hotel. He drove into Commerce City until he found a small motel that was still open. The Manor Motel was a long one-story building with 25 rooms and a reception area at the end. The grumpy, old motel owner would only accept cash. The rooms were cheap, so he didn't mind the lack lustre service.

There were only four other vehicles in the parking lot including the silver sedan that was parked in front of the room next to his. As he unlocked his door, his neighbour's door opened and a man with messy red hair walked out. He stared at the ground as walked slowly to his car.

"You, okay mister?" asked Kevin.

"Yeah, I'm fine," he mumbled. He got into his car and drove away.

When he entered his room, Kevin realized the low price he paid for the room was barely worth it. The once red carpet was blackened with stains and almost worn down to the floor beneath. The wood panelling covering the walls was warped away from the wall in places. Cracks snaked across the ceiling and white paint was bubbled up in the corner. There was a chain securing the television and no clock radio on the bedside table. The bathroom wasn't any better. There was black mould on the walls of the shower and he could see some of the grey backing through the mirror. Fortunately, there was cool running water which he splashed generously on his face.

He decided to not take his chances under the bed sheets and lay on top with his clothes on. He stared at the ceiling and prayed. He prayed for Monique and Olivia that they would be safe. He prayed for Joe, that he would find peace. He prayed for himself that he would be a light in a darkening world.

Is this it, God? Is this how it ends? Have you gotten fed up with this sinful world and decided to end it? Or is this part of the Tribulation – the beginning of the end days? Why was I not taken up in the Rapture? What do you want from me, God?

He fell asleep thinking, and praying and asking God unanswered questions.

Kevin woke from the sound of his neighbour's door opening and closing. He turned the television on, but the few stations that were still running had reruns of old sitcoms. He fell asleep again.

When he awoke a second time, he wasn't sure what had woken him. He went to the window and opened the curtain. The silver sedan was parked beside his again and the other three vehicles were parked in the same spot. There was a large rusty red pickup truck parked at an angle by the reception.

That's when he heard something from the room beside him. He held his ear up to the panelled wall, and confirmed that what he was hearing was crying. It was muffled crying, but the man next door was definitely crying.

Is this what God wants me to do – help my neighbour?

He left his room, walked over to the door beside his and knocked. The crying stopped, and he heard the man click in the chain lock and the door opened as much as the chain would allow. The man's face appeared in the opening. "What do you want?"

"I just wanted to make sure you were okay."

The man's eyes were red and wet. "Well, I'm not okay, if you must know, what do you want?"

"I just thought if you need someone to talk to…"

"I don't need to talk to anyone."

Kevin could smell his sweet liquored breath. "Do you have any more whiskey?"

"No, just cinnamon schnapps."

"Care to share?"

The door closed, the chain lock was disengaged and the door reopened again.

"You might need to bring your own chair," the man said, "These finely furnished suites only come with one chair in each." His attempt to have a snooty accent was hampered by his drunken slur.

Kevin ran back to his room and returned with his chair. The room was a mirror image of his room. The only difference was that there was someone sleeping under a blanket on the bed. The man, who introduced himself as Lorne offered him the bottle of schnapps. "Sorry, no glasses."

Kevin put the bottle up to his lips and took a sip. The sweet liquor burned as it went down.

"That's it?" The man said loudly, "if you want to drink with me, you need to take a swig, not a sip."

Kevin obliged and the schnapps felt like molten lava. He coughed and sputtered.

Lorne let out a bellowed laugh. "That's the spirit! Burn, baby burn!"

Kevin took a few breaths to try to expel the hot fumes. "Aren't we going to wake…". He pointed to the bed.

"She won't be waking up for a very long time."

"Oh."

Lorne took the bottle back and took another swig. Then he reached over to the desk and grabbed a box of After Eight chocolates. He took the lid off and handed it to Kevin. The cool chocolate mint was soothing.

"Are you married, Kevin?" asked Lorne.

"Yes I am, and I have a baby girl, Olivia."

"Well I don't have kids. My Agnes couldn't have any. It was sad at first, but you learn to live with these things. You adapt. We loved each other, and we travelled lots of places together, played cards and went to parties. We had lots of friends and went to church. I had a good job as a horticulturist. We lived in six different houses in five different cities. We fought, we laughed and we loved. But we always had one thing that remained the same." He took another swig of schnapps.

"What's that?" Kevin asked.

"Every Friday night we would sit and talk. She would have her cinnamon schnapps and I would have my After Eight mint chocolates."

Kevin looked at the almost full box of chocolates. "Is that Agnes in the bed?"

"Yes, that's my Agnes," he said.

"She's not going to have schnapps anymore is she?"

"Agnes got sick a couple of days ago. She had a major headache and couldn't get out of bed. I took her to Commerce City Hospital, where they said she had the Scourge and would be dead in a day or two. She didn't want to die in a hospital, so I started to drive her home. It was a two-and-a-half-hour drive, and she was just getting worse. I was afraid we wouldn't make it home before she died. We stopped at this crummy motel and when she laid down in the bed she seemed to be doing better. Tonight is only Thursday, but she wanted to have her schnapps one last time with me. I left to go get the schnapps and mints, but when I returned, she had already died. So, I pulled the blanket over her head and opened this bottle of schnapps.

There were sounds of yelling and breaking glass outside, so Kevin went to the window to look out. When he pulled the curtain back, he saw a bottle with a flaming rag sailing through the air towards him. He scrambled back and yelled at Lorne, "Get back!"

As he yelled, the window shattered as the bottle crashed through. It hit the end of the side table and exploded sending liquid flame across the table and onto the bed. Lorne and Kevin rolled to the back of the room. The blankets on the bed and the curtains were engulfed in flames.

"Are you okay?" yelled Kevin.

Lorne stared at his wife on the flaming bed, and said nothing.

Kevin grabbed him by the arm. "We have to go, now!"

Just as they were about to run across the flames to the door, another Molotov cocktail crashed into the room. The fire spread across the carpet making it impossible to cross to the door. Kevin took Lorne by the arm, lead him into the washroom and closed the door. Lorne calmly sat on the edge of the tub. Kevin took the lone towel and wet it down in the sink before shoving it in the gap at the bottom of the door.

He looked at Lorne sitting with a lost look on the edge of the tub. "Get in the tub, Lorne."

He obliged and crawled into the tub and Kevin followed. He closed the curtain and started praying, "God, please help us now in our hour of need. Let us not fall by the hands of wicked men…"

"Wait!" Lorne interrupted. "Are you a praying man?"

"Yes, I believe in God and…"

"Can you do me a favour? That guy that hung beside Jesus on the cross – he asks at the last minute for God to remember him in paradise." Lorne held one hand to his stomach and the other still clutched the schnapps. "I'm not a bad guy that deserves to die, but I'm kind of like that guy, asking at the last minute to go to Heaven."

"What do you mean the last minute? We're not dead yet!" said Kevin.

Lorne moved his hand away from his stomach to reveal a large piece of glass protruding from his abdomen. Blood seeped out and dripped into the tub. "I am."

"We need to get something to stop the bleeding..." Kevin went to get up out of the tub.

"No!" yelled Lorne. Then in a calm quiet voice – "Don't bother. I'm not going to make it. It's okay, I'm going to be with Agnes..."

His breath was becoming more difficult, and Kevin could hear blood starting to fill his lungs as he spoke in a raspy timbre. "I have no one, Kevin. I have no kids and my friends are either dead or old." He reached into his pocket and pulled out a set of keys and handed it to Kevin. "I live in a big house on the outskirts of Commerce City. There's lots of food, its fully furnished and it has a big fenced-in property. I'd like you and your wife and daughter to have it." His breaths were short and laboured. "The address is on that orange key fob. The alarm code is the year of our wedding nearly 50 years ago – 1973."

"I don't know what to say, Lorne I..."

They could hear sirens wailing outside and smoke was creeping through the gaps in the door.

Outside the door the firemen were yelling and spraying water on the fire.

Lorne looked Kevin in the eye as he took his final breaths. Kevin repeated the words of Jesus to the man hanging beside him, "Verily I say unto thee, today thou shalt be with me in paradise."

Lorne stopped breathing and sagged into the tub.

CHAPTER 16

The next couple of months at the Abitido Jail went by like a blur. Joe didn't antagonize anyone else since Rafael. And, since he sucked all the fun out of a good beating by not fighting back, no one else bothered him.

The dark stubble on his face grew into a full beard and he started to lose his little paunch.

His friendship with Benaiah grew, and his wounds began to heal. Joe's anguish dulled and his depression diminished a little, not unlike their food rations, which diminished a little every week. Many of the prisoners got sick and died from what he assumed was the Scourge. Every time one of them died, two guards would come and put the body on a stretcher and take it away.

One morning Joe and Benaiah sat across from each other eating their breakfast of oatmeal and crusty bread. Benaiah was doing most of the talking, as usual. A large man with a curly moustache stood guard by the door. The cafeteria was half full.

"How long have you been here, Joe? Two months?"

Joe nodded. "Something like that."

"Why haven't you been arraigned? Do you even know what you are being charged with? There is something called justice, and what about the right to a fair and speedy trial?"

"Whatever, I don't care. I'm guilty anyway."

"That's for the courts to decide. Your innocent until proven guilty."

Joe changed the subject. "What kind of name is Benaiah?"

"It's the kind of name my mother gave me. Its Jewish. I miss my mother. I miss my wife and two children. Did I tell you I have two children? Well, they're not children anymore, they're adults now. One of them is married. Nice girl. I'm not sure if they're even still alive. You know I haven't even heard from…Oh yeah! I almost forgot. You got a letter."

"What? No one even knows I'm here. And how do you have a letter for me?"

Benaiah pulled a crumpled piece of paper from his back pocket. "I know a guy who knows a guy. Just kidding, I do know the guy who mops floors in the administration wing. Theodore was my cellmate during my first stint. Anyways, he says that they are getting rid of old letters and correspondence. They weren't delivering any of the letters to the prisoners, so we don't know what's going on outside. He managed to rescue a couple of letters before they got shredded. I think things are getting pretty bad out there. I heard that at least half the guards have died, and I think more than half of the prisoners have died too. I heard that in China the Scourge isn't…"

"Just give me the stupid letter." He grabbed the paper from Ben.

"Hey no need to be rude. My wife was rude. That was one of the reasons we divorced. She couldn't even…" Benaiah continued to prattle on as Joe read the letter. It was from Kevin.

Dear Joe: I hope this letter makes it to you. It was the only way I knew to get in touch with you. I talked with the police and managed to speak to the guy you hurt. He said you were too drunk to hurt him that bad, and we convinced him to drop the charges. I'm working on getting you released soon, but things have gotten very disorganized, and no one will tell me anything. I keep trying to visit you, but they won't let me. Monique and the baby are doing well, and I trust that God will help us and you through these troubling times. I went to check on your apartment and met up with Ayesha, Zach and Blender. I brought them up to date on your situation, and they are very much looking forward...

The letter was stained and ripped. The rest of the letter was missing.

He interrupted Benaiah, who was still rambling on. "Where's the rest?"

Benaiah shrugged, "I don't know, my dog ate it."

Joe reached across the table and grabbed him by his collar and yelled. "I NEED the rest of this letter!"

Benaiah put his hands in the air in surrender. "Hey, don't shoot the messenger. That's all I got. Theo said he just grabbed some ripped-up letters and stuffed them in his pocket. They were supposed to be shredded, and he was lucky to get that. He asked me if I knew a 'Joe' and gave me that letter."

Joe let go of his collar and put his head in his hands.

"You know, when I took accounting in college, a dog literally ate my homework. It was an essay assignment on the benefits of accrual accounting, and the dog was one of those Pitbull types..."

Joe closed his eyes and put his head in his hands. He had a lot of questions.

When was this letter sent? I hardly hurt the man in the park? Why haven't they released me yet if the charges were dropped? Why are Ayesha and Zach back at my apartment? Where are their foster families or orphanage or wherever they got sent to? Where are child services? Is Blender at my apartment? What am I supposed to do now?

Joe rubbed his beard and looked up at Benaiah, who was still talking. "I need to get out of here," Joe said, interrupting him.

"Oh, now you want to leave?"

Joe slammed the paper down onto the table, making a loud bang that echoed off the cafeteria walls. The guard gave him a warning glance then resumed massaging his curly handlebar moustache.

"Look," he said, gritting his teeth, trying not to yell or

strangle Benaiah. "Is there any way I can get my arraignment thing and get in front of a judge?"

"Why, what happened?" Benaiah picked up the letter and read it. He sat back in his seat and crossed his arms. "So, does this mean you're not as evil of a guy as you thought?"

"Maybe, but Ayesha might need my help."

"Who's Ayesha? Is she your wife? I thought you told me she was dead. Is this a new girlfriend? You know I should get me a girlfriend. That might be easier if I lost some weight. Although with this food, that shouldn't be hard. I think I've already lost…"

"Benaiah. Stop talking. Answer my question."

"What was your question again?"

"How do I get my arraignment?"

"Oh yeah, I don't know. One of the guards might know. The only one that even speaks to me has that funny moustache. I had a moustache in college…"

"Benaiah, he's right there!" He pointed at the curly mustached guard. "Ask him."

"Okay, fine, I'll see what I can do."

They both sat there for a moment.

"Well?" Joe asked.

"Well, what?"

"Are you going to ask him?"

"Now?"

"Yes, RIGHT NOW!" he yelled.

Curly moustache man walked towards them. "Is there a problem here?"

"No, no problem, Alfonso. My friend here would like to know when he might get his day in court. He's been here for months now, and he hasn't even been officially charged yet."

Alfonso leaned in towards them, talking quietly. "Not anytime soon. Things out there are not good, Ben. We are not supposed to tell you guys anything, because the boss says he doesn't want the prisoners to panic. All I can tell you is, don't hold your breath on anything happening in the near future."

He stood back up.

"Why, what's going on out there?" Joe asked, but Alfonso was already walking away. "What do you think he means that 'things out there are not good'?"

"I don't know. It could be the virus is getting worse. Maybe there's been a war. Or maybe the Russians have nuked us. No, it would more likely be the Chinese or North Korea…"

"Ben?"

"What?"

"He called you Ben."

"Oh yeah, only my mother calls me Benaiah, but I thought I'd try out my full name for a bit to see what it felt like."

"So, you lied to me about your name?"

"No, technically, that *is* my name. But you know it did sound awkward when you said it."

"Well, we need to get out of here, *Ben*."

CHAPTER 17

Later, Joe and Ben sat outside on a bench overlooking the basketball court.

It was a cool November afternoon. They had frost a couple of nights, but the small amount of snow that had fallen had melted away.

The basketball court concrete was cracked in places, and the nets no longer had any netting. A small group of prisoners were playing a friendly game of basketball. Puffs of steam blowing out their mouths as they ran back and forth on the court, chasing the bouncing ball.

"What do you think about trying to escape?" Joe asked.

"I think you're not the first person to try. This place is designed to *not* let anyone escape." Ben rubbed his head. He was balding, and the bare patch on his head felt cold in the light November wind.

The players bumped each other as they ran down the court.

Joe rubbed his leg where he had been cut. It was almost healed now, and it no longer hurt when he touched it. "But now there are fewer guards, and if the world is as bad as they say it is, maybe the guards that are left don't care."

"Maybe, but then why don't they just let us go? What if we just wait until the guards stop coming to work and then we can just walk out of here?"

"And what if we get locked in our cells and abandoned? Do you want to die in here?"

"No, I don't want to die at all. That is why *death by prison guard* isn't appealing to me."

One of the players stopped in front of them. He had his hands on his knees and was trying to catch his breath. He was well over six feet, was well-muscled and had a tattoo of a hammer and sickle. His blond hair was short on top and shaved close on both sides. He looked menacing except that he was always smiling. He looked over at the two of them on the bench.

"You guys planning an escape?"

The sudden interruption startled Ben, and he almost fell off the bench. He pushed his glasses nervously. "We were just talking."

"Oh yeah? Well, talk to me." The other players continued their game as the man sat down beside them.

"We were thinking it might be better to get out of this place before we're abandoned," Joe said.

"And we were thinking that staying alive in here might be better than getting shot on the way out." Ben shook his head at Joe.

"The name's Sargent Kolikov. Adrik Kolikov, but they call me Ubi." He extended his hand and shook both of theirs. "I tend to agree with your friend here. I don't want to starve to death in here."

"I'm Ben, and this is Joe. They call us Ben and Joe. I suppose you would like to join our little team of desperadoes."

"Look," he said to them while watching his friends run to the opposite side of the court, "I can help. My buddy's and I were thinking that since the number of enemy combatants has dropped significantly, we may have a tactical advantage."

Ben rubbed his hands together, trying to keep them warm. "They also have the advantage of being armed. What do you plan to do, Captain Gung-ho, overpower them with your bare hands?"

"Exactly. But not just any bare hands, trained bare hands that have been in worse situations than this." He nodded to the players, now arguing over who was going to get the ball which had bounced off the court and down the hill. "Tank, Stretch, and I are former Canadian Forces, and we can fight."

"Well, I'm an accountant," and I can evade things like taxes and hopefully death. And what kind of name is 'Stretch' and 'Tank'?"

"They're our call signs or nicknames, like Ubi."

"What kind of name is Ubi anyway?"

"It's short for Ubiysta."

"Is that Russian?"

"Yes, it's the Russian word for killer."

"Oh." Ben paused before continuing. "I knew a guy named Obee. He was a computer programmer. He was definitely not an Ubi. If he had a call sign, it would have been *Big Nerd*. He was a smart guy, though. He had the entire periodic table memorized. I'm not sure what that had to do with computers. I used to help him with his taxes..."

"Does he always talk this much." Ubi looked at Joe.

"Yes, even in his sleep."

Ubi got up from the bench. "Well, I think we should plan for our great escape before we're all too starved to think."

Ben looked up at him. "You know, nobody in *The Great Escape*, survived, right?"

"Well, then this better be the *Greater Escape*. We'll reconvene at 1400 tomorrow." Ubi re-joined his friends in their game.

Over the next couple of days, Joe, Ubi, Tank, Stretch and reluctantly, Ben, made plans for their greater escape. During the afternoon free-time in the yard, they would gather by the basketball court and go over the plan.

It was early on a cool crisp morning when they initiated their plan. As usual, there were two guards on duty in the cell block. They both had radios and batons and one of them had keys. The only time they would open a cell was if someone was in danger or if someone had died.

Joe and Ben waited anxiously in their cell for Ubi to make the first move. They didn't have to wait long.

"Guard, guard!" Ubi yelled from across the cell block. "Stretch isn't breathing. I think he's dead." The two guards walked over and said something Joe couldn't quite make out. One of them was talking on his radio. About 15 minutes later, two more guards with masks and a stretcher came to Ubi and Stretch's cell. The guard with the keys opened the cell for them. The two masked guards wheeled the stretcher into the cell.

"Okay, that's our cue," said Ben from his cell on the opposite side of the cell block, "hit me."

Joe grabbed Ben and threw him up against the bars making as much noise as he could. "Guard! Help me! He's trying to kill me!" yelled Ben.

One of the guards came over. Joe made sure the guard was looking then threw a decent right cross at Ben's face, hitting him a little harder than he intended. Ben slumped to the ground as the guard banged on the bars. "Hey, settle down in there."

Ben stood up as Joe stood in what he thought might be a boxer's stance. "Come on, pudgy, let's see what you got."

Ben stood up and kicked Joe square in the balls. Joe keeled over, wailing. Then Ben grabbed Joe in a choke hold and squeezed. Joe's arms flailed wildly. "Help, he's killing me."

The guard banged his club on the bars. "Johnny, get over here, I need to go in." Johnny was the guard with the keys. As Joe was pretending to fight Ben, he stole a glance over to Ubi's cell. He could see them quietly overpowering the masked guards.

Johnny came over and turned his key in the cell door and opened it. He pulled back his club and was about to hit Ben, but paused when he heard what sounded like a bat hitting a watermelon behind him. When he turned, he watched his fellow guard slumped to the ground. Ubi stood behind him with a guard's uniform that was a couple of sizes too small.

The guard nimbly pulled his Taser from its holster and aimed it at Ubi. "Don't move!"

Ubi put his hands in the air, smiling. The guard stepped out of the cell and grabbed his radio with his free hand. Before he could depress the button on his radio, he was hit hard on the side of the head and crumpled to the ground. Stretch, who was also dressed in a guard's uniform, stepped over him and wiped his baton on the side of the downed guard's pants. Stretch was about an inch taller than Ubi, and his uniform was even more ill-fitting then his cell-mates. "Okay, we have to hurry up before someone sees something on the cameras."

Ubi grabbed his guard by the ankles and started to drag him into the cell. "I thought you said there were no cameras out here."

"I said there were no cameras in the cells," Stretch responded. "If they're paying attention, they might see us out here." The two of them dragged the unconscious guard into the cell.

Ben released his hold on Joe. He took off his glasses and rubbed his cheek. "I think you broke my jaw!"

Joe slowly stood up, rubbing his throat. "Well, if I can't have kids now, I'm blaming you. Did you have to kick me right in the nuts?"

"I wanted to make it real - like your punch."

"Okay, you fools, time to initiate Phase Two." Stretch said as he and Ubi dragged the second guard into the cell.

Joe put on a guard's uniform while Ubi grabbed the ring of keys off the guard's belt and went to open Tank's cell. Stretch ran to grab the stretcher. When he got back, Ben lay down on the stretcher with a blanket over him. Tank, who had been alone in his cell, put on the other guard's uniform. Like his nickname suggested, Tank was built like a tank. He was just shy of six feet and was mostly muscle. Those muscles now bulged under the tight-fitting guard's uniform.

Joe looked at the three others dressed as guards. "Okay, you all look stupid." None of their uniforms fit at all. The cuffs of Ubi's sleeves were almost at his elbows, Stretch's pants reminded Joe of Officer Reginald. Tank's shirt made it look like he would explode into the Incredible Hulk.

"I'm going to have to do the talking. You guys stay behind me," said Joe.

He led the way to the doorway out of the cellblock. Ubi walked behind him, and Stretch and Tank pushed the stretcher with Ben on it. Some prisoners were awake now and were yelling to be let out.

"We better hurry," said Joe, "Before the control room gets suspicious."

The only way out of the cellblock was a caged room with locked doors on either end. There were cameras, an intercom speaker, and a microphone outside both doors as well as inside the cage. The intercom and cameras were connected to the control room. The guards got buzzed into the holding area inside the cage. Once the door closed behind them, the next door would be unlocked. Both doors were controlled by the guards inside the control room.

The five of them walked up to the first camera. Joe pressed the intercom. "Coming out!"

The intercom crackled. A voice said, "Who are you?"

Joe looked down at the key card around his neck. "It's Ramirez. We got another dead one to take to the morgue."

"You look different, Ramirez."

"New haircut." Joe had black hair like the guard whose uniform he had taken, but his was a little longer. He hoped it was enough.

"What's with the whole caravan? You can't all come out."

Joe looked back at the small procession behind him and made a quick decision. "No, it's just the two of us and the body." He looked at Ubi, who nodded and whispered something to the others. Ubi covertly handed off the ring of keys. Stretch and Tank started walking back into the cellblock slowly, the keys dangling from Tank's hands.

The door buzzed, and Joe walked into the cage. He was followed by Ubi, who pushed Ben in the stretcher. From under the sheets, Ben whispered, "Now what? What about your two guys?"

Ubi responded, barely moving his lips. "Plan B, they'll come in behind us."

They stood inside for a moment. Joe wondered if they had been found out, and if they were now trapped inside the cage. His heart hammered against his chest. Finally, the intercom came back on. "Close the door fully behind you."

Ubi swore under his breath and closed the door behind him. He then nodded through the cage at his friends on the other side. They returned his nod and disappeared.

"Plan C," he whispered through his teeth.

Ben stirred under the blanket. "What's Plan C?"

Ubi put his hand on Ben to stop him from moving. "Shhh, no more talking. Things are about to get hairy."

CHAPTER 18

Over 500 kilometres west, in the city of Ingerwood, in Building One on Pochatok Street, Monique was feeding her baby. Ayesha and Zach rolled pool balls back and forth, and Blender was baking cookies in the kitchen. Kevin was still not back from his latest trip to try and visit Joe at the Abitido Jail.

"Miss Monique," said Ayesha, "I really want a television and a Blu-ray player, so I can watch my movies."

"I told you before, you can just call me Monique."

"I want a laptop," said Zach as he rolled the eight ball with a backspin towards Ayesha.

In the kitchen, Blender mixed the dough with a wooden spoon. "Yeah, well, I need some chocolate chips. Cookies without chocolate chips are just boring."

Over the last couple months, they had gotten settled into Joe's apartment. Blender had cleaned up the mess left by the looters and threw out some items that had been broken during the break-in. This included the television and Blu-ray player. The pool table was still in the apartment, but the green felt was ripped and the pool cues were broken. The dartboard and laptop were both stolen and most of their food stash. It was more dangerous than ever outside so they had to entertain themselves inside the apartment.

They were still able to get most essential items and food if they could find stores that were open.

"I think you should all go shopping!" Monique announced one morning. They all stopped what they were doing and looked at her with anticipation. "I will stay here with the dog and the baby, and you should go take a trip downtown to see if you can find some stores to buy essentials. I would like some vitamins and some healthy foods."

"Like chocolate chips," said Blender

"I mean more like fruits and vegetables."

"I want a television and a Blu-ray," said Ayesha.

"I still want a laptop," said Zach.

"I have a credit card," said Monique, "but I'm not sure how much is on it."

"Most places are just taking cash," said Blender, "but I know where Joe keeps his secret emergency stash." He ran to Joe's bedroom and disappeared.

"I have some cash too." she pulled her wallet out of her purse.

The dog barked and there was a knock on the door. "I'll get it," said Ayesha and Zack at the same time. They raced each other to the door. When they opened it, they saw a tall man with thick blond hair and a big smile on his face.

"Well, hello there, kids - and dog," said Laurel.

"Aren't you that gay guy from Building Two?" asked Zach.

Ayesha elbowed him, "That's rude, Zach."

"What?"

"That's okay. I'm Laurel. I *am* gay, but I hope to be known as more than just the gay guy from Building Two." He rubbed the top of Roxie's head.

Monique walked over. "Hello, is there something we can help you with, Laurel?"

"I'm looking for Joe. Is he here?"

"No, I'm sorry, he ran into a bit of trouble. My husband has gone to see him in jail right now. Are you a friend of his?"

"Yes, I…"

"Laurel, is that you?" Blender came out of Joe's bedroom.

"Oh, hi, Blender. I hear Joe is in trouble."

"Why don't you come in Laurel. This is Monique. Have you met Ayesha and Zack before?"

"Yes, I've seen them around. The last time I saw them was right here." He looked at the baby in Monique's arms. "And who's this?"

"This little miracle is Olivia."

They sat, and ate cookies (without chocolate chips). They talked about the Scourge, the looters and how society seemed to be falling apart.

"It gets lonely in my apartment all by myself and..." said Laurel.

"Why don't you come to live here with us?" said Ayesha.

"I don't want to impose, but..."

"Do you have a television?" asked Ayesha.

"I do..." he said.

"When you move in here, can you bring your television?" asked Ayesha.

"Do you have a laptop?" Asked Zach.

"What about chocolate chips?" asked Blender.

Laurel looked at Monique.

Ayesha said, "Can he live here with us?"

"This isn't even my apartment, why are you asking me?" said Monique and then looked at Blender.

"Hey, don't look at me, it's not my place either."

The apartment door opened, and Kevin walked in.

"Kevin!" shouted Monique.

Laurel held his arms out to take the baby. "Here, I'll take her."

She handed Olivia off, ran to her husband and gave him a loving embrace. "How's Joe? Did you get to see him? What happened, and why does your hair look singed?"

"It's a long story," he answered, "Do I smell chocolate chip cookies?"

"I wish," said Blender.

"Laurel's coming to live with us," said Ayesha, "he's Joe's friend."

"He's gay," said Zach.

Kevin looked confused. "Do you guys like living here in this little apartment?"

"No," said Zach, "it's boring. There are no laptops and no game systems."

"We don't have a television either," said Ayesha, "But Laurel's going to bring his."

"The dartboard's gone," said Blender.

"It *is* getting a little crowded in here," admitted Monique.

"I don't have to move in," said Laurel sincerely.

"I found a place," said Kevin. "It's a big place with a big yard."

"Is it a mansion?" asked Ayesha.

"Yes, it's a mansion, and it's just outside of Commerce city, and I'm sure it's big enough for all of you to have your own room, even Laurel."

"We can't afford a mansion," said a wary Monique.

"It was given to me. It's free!"

They all started talking excitedly to each other. Even Roxie could sense something happy was happening and ran from person to person, her tail wagging.

"How are we all going to fit into your little stolen Jeep?" asked Monique

"I have a PT Cruiser," suggested Laurel.

"Pack your things, we're moving out!" announced Kevin.

"How did you manage to get a mansion?" asked Monique.

"I'll explain on the way."

The five-hour trip to Commerce City was long but after being cooped up in an apartment it was bearable. They had to stop multiple times on the way to change the baby, stop to eat and allow everyone to go to the washroom.

Monique was excited and apprehensive. She was excited to move into a big house, and she hoped it was safe and had food. However, she was also anxious, and she had a million questions.

What will it be like with this growing group of people all living

in the same house? Was she expected to be a den mother? Was this going to be a cross between a commune and an orphanage? Is this part of what Kevin would call God's plan? Were they all going to survive this pandemic? Would she come back to Ingerwood when this was over and go back to work at the advertising agency? Would the government keep sending emergency money? How long was this pandemic going to last?

A million questions, but no answers.

They left the highway and drove for another 20 minutes down a few country roads before they found the front gate to the mansion.

"I just want to warn you guys," said Kevin, "I haven't actually seen this place, so don't get your hopes up. Lorne said it was a big house, but he didn't say how big."

The entry gate was bordered on either side by two brick columns. A 3-metre-high fence stretched out in both directions. One of the brick columns had the address and a sign with *Veilig Estates*. The other had a metal bracket holding a security keypad. Ayesha and Zach were restless with anticipation as Kevin typed 1-9-7-3 into the keypad. The black iron gate rolled to the side with a loud creak. Both vehicles drove through, and the gate creaked closed behind them. The laneway was bounded on both sides by immense maple trees. The laneway turned to the left, and the view opened up. The large three-story stone manor was surrounded by immaculately kept gardens and shrubbery. There was a separate three car garage to one side and rolling green grass all around.

"No way..." said Zach, "This is awesome!"

Ayesha smiled and clapped her hands in glee while Monique stared silently with her mouth open.

Blender did a clenched-fist pull-down. "Yes!"

They drove up to the front steps. When the vehicle doors opened it was like they had pulled in to Canada's Wonderland. Zach and Ayesha exploded out of the car and ran up the steps, yelling, laughing and talking. Roxie took off running out into the yard to pee and sniff.

The group huddled around the front door as Kevin fiddled with the keys. He opened the ornate oak doors, and they filtered in. Ayesha and Zach climbed the grand winding staircase to claim their rooms. Blender went to the kitchen to inspect the restaurant-sized amenities. Laurel went out the back door and discovered a pool with a large deck. Kevin found the study with a large hardwood desk and a vast collection of books. Monique used one of the many bathrooms to change Olivia's diaper. They found a white pickup truck in the garage.

Over the next few weeks, they got settled into their new home. Since they were close, Kevin drove the blue jeep to the Abitido Jail once per week but was refused each time. Ayesha found a movie theatre room and a library of Blu-ray movies, which included many kid's movies. Zach helped her hook it up and would sometimes watch movies with her. Zach found a laptop which he connected to the internet. The connection was not reliable. Many sites were either not updated or not working at all, but he tried anyway. Blender was happy in the kitchen. He found a full freezer and racks of canned food in the basement. After dinner, he would often go to the rec room, where he found a dartboard. He would throw darts by himself, and when anyone asked to play with him, he said none of them were as good as Joe and he would rather play alone. Kevin tried to keep up the house and grounds. He cut the lawn, trimmed the hedges, and cleaned the floors. Kevin also managed to keep his beard neatly trimmed.

Monique spent a lot of time looking after Olivia, but was able to hand her off to Laurel, so she could have a break. Laurel was in a perpetual sombre mood. He spent much of his time sitting by the pool or wandering the grounds with Roxie and didn't talk much.

CHAPTER 19

Not far away at the Abitido Jail, Joe was in the midst of his escape attempt. He and Ubi stood over the stretcher with Ben, waiting for an agonizing couple of seconds in the cage. Joe's heart felt like it was going to beat out of his chest.

What is Plan C? What does he mean things are about to get hairy? Why don't they open the door already?

Eventually, there was a buzzing sound, and the 2nd door opened. Joe resumed the breath he didn't know he was holding and walked out of the cage. The three of them exited the cage and stood at the beginning of the hallway. The door clanged closed behind them.

Suddenly a deafening klaxon siren sounded, a spinning red light flashed overhead, and a voice boomed over the loudspeakers.

"Attention, all personnel, we have a Code Orange. All Class I guards remain at your station. All Class II's report to Cell Block F2. We have a Level One security breach."

Joe looked back at Ubi. "What's going on?"

"It's all part of Plan C. Keep moving."

Joe continued walking down the hallway. "What did you do?"

From around the corner, a group of four guards charged down the hallway towards them. They wore helmets with face shields, knee pads, elbow pads, shin pads and body armour. The guards were dressed in black, carried batons in one hand a large plexiglass shield in the other. They were running towards them. Joe froze.

This is it. This is where I die. If I don't die, I'm about to get severely beaten. Again.

"Step aside," one of them said as they marched past.

"What's going on?" Joe asked Ubi.

"Stretch and Tank just opened up all the doors in our cell block."

"What? Why?"

"It's all part of the backup plan in case we didn't all make it out of our cell block. They might be able to get out in the ensuing riot and confusion."

The two of them pushed Ben down the hallway and through a second set of double doors. Down the next hallway was another security station, just before the exit. Ben got off the stretcher and walked in front of Joe with his hands behind his back, pretending to be their prisoner. They all walked as casually as they could up to the security station. This station consisted of a booth with two guards and a locked door with a swipe card reader.

As they approached the booth, one of the guards yelled out from the booth, "Where are you going?"

Joe spoke for the group. "Prisoner transfer."

"Not now. We're on lockdown. They've got something happening in F2. Nobody in or out till we get the all-clear."

Joe looked at Ubi. "Now what? You have a Plan D?"

Ben spoke up. "The basement. We might find a way out there. The guard's locker rooms are down there. There might be another way out."

Ubi looked at Joe. "Let's go."

They walked back down the hallway till they found a stairwell. The three of them shuffled through the stairwell door and down the stairs. They walked down another hallway past the guard's lunchroom and into the changeroom. The basement was quiet, and there didn't appear to be anybody around. The only sound was the prison alarms and their footsteps echoing across the changeroom.

"Now what?" Joe asked, looking at Ben.

"I don't know. I said there *might* be a way out down here. At least there are no other guards down here."

Ubi ran further into the changeroom. Ben opened some lockers until he found a uniform that might fit him. The locker also had a set of keys, including one for a Mercedes that he put in his pocket.

"Over here, guys!" Ubi called out from the other side of the changeroom. "I found a window."

Ben scrambled to put on the guard's uniform as fast as he could and joined Ubi and Joe by the window. The window was barely big enough to fit through and was at the top of the wall. There was steel mesh that was affixed to the window, and a large lock held it in place.

"Now what?" asked Ben. "Do you happen to have a key for that? You know I used to know a guy who could pick locks. He tried to pick the lock to his cell door once. He didn't do it, mind you and got himself thrown in solitary. I hear they don't even give you a toilet in solitary. You have to go…"

Ubi ran out of the changeroom. They heard some clanging, and running water in the other room. He returned carrying a large steel pipe, that was still dripping water.

"Found the key," he said and then slipped the pipe between the lock and the door, using the pipe as a lever.

They heard voices from the stairway. "You better hurry," Ben said.

Ubi pushed as hard as he could till the pipe began to bend, but the lock remained intact. The voices were getting louder, and they could hear loud footsteps coming down the stairs.

"Come on, let's go. They're almost here."

Ubi hit the lock with the pipe, swinging at it hard. On the 3rd swing, the lock finally gave out and clanged to the floor.

"Who's down here?" someone yelled from out in the hallway. They could hear the guards entering the lunchroom, and it would be only moments until they found them.

Ubi bent open the metal cage and started to pull himself up. The guards could be heard on the other side of the change-room. Once he climbed out the window, Ubi helped Ben and then Joe out the window just as the guards ran into the room.

Outside, the air was cool, and a light snow was falling on the frosted ground. They ran away from the window towards the employee parking lot. Ben pulled out his key and pressed the unlock button repeatedly. "This car has to be around here somewhere."

Finally, a black Mercedes honked, and they all ran towards it. Behind them, the guards were yelling.

As they approached the car, Ubi held out his hand towards Ben. "Give me the keys. I'm driving." Ben handed him the keys and got in the back of the car. Ubi got in the driver's seat, and Joe climbed into the other side. The guards were getting closer as Ubi started the car and sped towards the main gate.

The gate was over 20 feet high. It was reinforced with steel tubing and topped with razor wire. It was also closed. Orange lights flashed on top of the guard tower beside the gate, and two guards stood on top of the tower. One of them had a long rifle with a scope.

"We're all gonna die!" Ben yelled from the back.

"Go, go, go!" yelled Joe.

Ubi put his foot down hard on the gas pedal, and they sped towards the gate. A shot rang out just as they were about to collide with the gate. Ubi's head exploded just as the car impacted the gate. Joe was saved by the airbag that deployed. He felt Ben's head hit the seat behind him. The car wasn't able to get through the gate which was now folded around the car. Joe slapped at the airbag to push it down. He looked over at Ubi, whose head was a mess of flesh, bone and blood. Joe vomited on the deflating airbag. From behind him, Ben was passed out. Through the smashed window beside him, Joe saw the muzzle of a large gun pointed at his head.

Ben was taken away to the infirmary and treated for a mild

concussion, and Joe was placed in solitary confinement. He remained there for one week - and it *did* have a toilet. It gave him time to think and contemplate his life and current situation. He thought about Ubi and tried to block out the image of his head exploding. The only way he found he could escape the horrible images was to look ahead.

He needed a plan and a purpose. Joe missed Ayesha, Zach, Blender, Kevin and Monique. H wanted to get back to them. At the next opportunity he *would* get out of this prison and back to his apartment.

When he emerged from solitary, he was put in a cell alone. He met up with Ben during the next free time in the yard. Ben had suffered a concussion and a sprained wrist; it was still wrapped up. Ben told him that Stretch and Tank had been moved to a different cell block and that none of their crew had made it out. He also heard that due to the attempted escape, ensuing mini-riot, and the fact that there were now fewer guards and prisoners, they were being transported to a different facility. They were conglomerating many of the prisons into one large facility somewhere out east. Further away from his friends.

CHAPTER 20

It was a cool November evening when Laurel walked into the study.

"You are a good person, Kevin." He stood at the side of the desk, looking at the photos hanging on the wall.

Kevin put the book he was reading down. "Thank you, Laurel."

"You're also very polite to me."

"Of course."

"You are more polite to me than to anyone else."

"Well, I-."

"You are polite to me because you believe that homosexuality is a sin."

"I never said that."

"I know, but it's how you feel. I can't help who I am. I loved Harvey in the same way you love Monique."

"I know, I never meant to –"

"It's okay, that's not why I want to talk to you. You are not a perceptive person, Kevin. You spend a lot of time in this study surrounded by all these books, but have you ever looked at the photos on the wall?"

"No, I didn't think it was important."

"Sometimes, Kevin, you are blissfully unaware. What did Lorne look like?"

"I don't remember – I think he had red hair. Why?"

"These photos show a nice couple. He is bald, she is beautiful, and their son is going to a prestigious university in the States."

"What?"

"He was a lawyer, and she was a doctor." He pointed to the plaques on the wall.

"How do you know that? That's not possible."

Kevin was agitated, but Laurel remained stoic.

"As I said, you are not very perceptive. If you were, you would know that there's a safe behind that painting? You would know that Lorne did not own this house, but was only the groundskeeper. You would also know that there are enemies at your gates and more on their way."

"What are you talking about?"

"There is a toolbox with gardening implements that has Lorne's name on it. He lived with his wife in the guest house out back. You didn't even know there was a guest house, did you? Also, I've seen a woman and man looking through the gates. How many hours do you spend cleaning this place? It's a full-time job, isn't it? It was for the couple that used to do it. Every day they cleaned this big house, and all they got was minimum wage. When the bald man and his beautiful wife died from the Scourge, the housekeeper went home. She sat with her husband in their tiny apartment and realized that no one would know if they moved into this house. By the time they worked up the nerve, you guys had already moved in. They know that this is not your house. She may have worked here for many years, and she thinks she deserves this house."

"How do you know all that?" asked a flabbergasted Kevin.

"Consider it an educated guess. Unlike you, I pay attention to my surroundings, and I know people. I know that the son of the couple that lived here may have got bored living in his little frat house. You see how he is smiling in all these pictures with his parents. He loves them, and he will come back here to find them and claim his inheritance."

"How do you know he's still alive?"

"In the top drawer of that desk is a sticky note with a password. That password allows access to the computer in front of you. The email server doesn't appear to be working anymore, but the last correspondence from him was not that long ago. It's not a sure thing, but he could be alive, and on his way here."

"Why didn't you tell me any of this before?"

"You never asked. You treat me with politeness, but I'm not really a part of your little clan. If you want to be the leader of this group – although I think Monique would make a better leader – then you need to treat everyone with respect and utilize their abilities and talents. That's how you make a successful team, and you are going to need a successful team to defend this house you are squatting in."

"Why are you telling me this now?" asked an exasperated Kevin.

"You really are *not* very perceptive. I'm dying, Kevin." Blood trickled from his nose, his eyes rolled back, and he collapsed onto the carpet.

"Monique! Someone! Help!" He cradled Laurel in his arms.

Monique came running into the room with Olivia in her arms. "What happened? Is he okay?"

"I think he's sick."

Blender helped Kevin carry Laurel to the couch in the living room. Zach and Ayesha came running when they heard the commotion. Roxie followed them in, sniffed Laurel, and sat by his side.

"Is he dead?" asked Zach.

Ayesha gave him a little push. "Don't say that."

Laurel was still breathing.

Monique knelt beside the couch and held his hand. When Laurel opened his eyes, she pushed the hair covering his eyes aside. "It's okay, Laurel, we're all here for you."

"We should take him to the hospital," said Kevin.

"I'll bring the car to the front," said Blender.

Laurel lifted his other hand to stop them. "No, you don't need to do that."

"The hospital can't help him," said Monique. "He has the

Scourge."

"You knew?" asked Laurel.

"Of course, I knew," she said.

He started coughing, and blood leaked out the side of his mouth. He squeezed her hand and started whispering. Monique leaned closer to hear.

"Take care of them, Monique."

"You go be with your Harvey," she whispered back.

"You should-." He never finished his sentence.

Kevin took Blender to the shed to find shovels. He noticed the toolbox with Lorne written in black marker on it. Kevin put the toolbox under the bench out of sight. They buried Laurel in the back yard. Each of them said something they liked about Laurel, and Kevin said a little prayer.

The next day, Monique walked into the study as Kevin was putting picture frames into a box.

"What are you doing?" asked Monique.

"I'm putting some of these photos away. I don't like looking at people I don't even know all day. I was thinking we could get Zach to print our photos and hang them in here."

"That might be nice," she said.

"Laurel said that he saw someone lurking outside the gate. Have you seen anybody?" asked Kevin.

"No, but I don't walk that way often. Is this something we should be worried about?"

"No, it's nothing to worry about. I'll check it out, but I'm sure it's nothing."

Over the next week, Kevin walked out to the gate twice a day, but saw no one. Kevin looked in the drawers of the desk and found another sticky note that had the combination to the wall safe. He found stacks of money. He and Blender made trips into Commerce City to buy food and supplies every two weeks. There were fewer stores open, and the shelves were emptying. They paid cash to have the large propane tanks filled, and the government provided electricity for free. The government also set up stations for handing out food rations.

CHAPTER 21

It was early December when Joe and the other prisoners were loaded into buses. The day was cold and grey as Joe and Ben climbed aboard a modified school bus. It was painted dark blue and had metal guarding on the windows. A second blue bus drove behind them. Their hands and feet were shackled together on short chains. A guard with a shotgun sat behind the driver. Joe sat against the window beside Ben, who talked non-stop. He pretended to listen and nodded once and a while as he stared out the window.

Snow was falling lightly, adding to the dirty slush already covering the city. A few vehicles were driving through the wet snow on the roads, and many abandoned cars lined each side of the street. Several businesses were boarded up or had their front windows smashed in. A few buildings were burnt to the ground, and others were still smoking. There were signs indicating where C3's were located and small black flags hung outside some homes. He watched two light-armoured military vehicles go by. A few people were out walking, but the streets were mostly abandoned. Before the blue buses left the city limits, they stopped briefly at a well-armed military blockade. The buses drove east on the highway away from Commerce City. The highway was almost empty. Several vehicles were abandoned in the ditch or on the side of the road. The bus drove on through the thin layer of slush covering the highway for a few hours before Joe nodded off to sleep.

They stopped once, for everyone to do their business on the side of the road and eat stale pitas. He watched as the guards on the other bus dragged a dead prisoner off the bus and laid him on the side of the road, then covered his body with a blanket. They stuck a short pole with a black flag on it in the ground beside him.

They got back on the bus and resumed their trip. The bus crossed the border into Quebec, past Montreaux without stopping. Just over four hours later, they pulled off the highway at the Chateaugay exit. They stopped briefly at a military checkpoint before the pair of buses drove into an industrial park and stopped outside a large warehouse with the sign: Jean's la Nourriture Pour Animaux.

The guard at the front of Joe's bus with the shotgun stood up. "Okay, people time to get off."

"This is the jail?" someone asked.

"No, this is the halfway point. We will sleep here for the night and finish our trip to the Big House tomorrow." Joe still didn't know where their final destination was.

The group exited the bus and walked towards the large warehouse, dragging their chains through the slushy gravel. The prisoners from the second bus were doing the same. As they approached the building, Joe looked back and watched a guard carry a dead prisoner off the bus.

Joe and Ben joined the line as it wound its way into the building's glass front doors. They went through a small lobby and into a large open area in the building. It smelled like dog kibble.

There were stacks of dog food against the walls. The building didn't appear to have been abandoned for very long. As they herded everyone inside, Joe noticed Tank was in the line from the other bus and nodded to him.

It was still cold inside, but at least it was dry. The guards handed out blankets and bottles of water, and the prisoners settled down for the night. As Joe and Ben laid out their blankets in their little corner, Tank walked up carrying his blanket roll.

"Hey guys, do you mind if I bunk up with you?"

"No problem," said Ben, "We haven't seen you since..."

The big guy looked up with a melancholy look on his face. As he unrolled his blanket, he simply said, "yeah."

Joe was lying on his side on a blanket with his head propped up. "Look, I'm sorry about Ubi. I know he was your friend."

Tank sat on his blanket. "Where ever he is right now, I bet he's bragging about how he died by a gunshot to the head."

Ben lay back on his blanket with hands behind his head. "Where's Stretch?"

"The Scourge got him. More than half of my cell block died last month."

"Sorry to hear that, Tank."

"Thanks, I have no one left..."

"You have us."

The three of them lay silent. Listening to the hum of other conversations going on around them, until Ben spoke up. "I think a lot more people have been dying lately. It's like a second wave of the virus or something. I know a doctor in Elora. I did his taxes. He said that the second wave was going to be worse than the first. He told me that this could be the virus that wipes out all humanity. I think he might have been exaggerating, kind of like he tried to do with his tax write-offs."

They continued talking in hushed tones further into the night. A couple hours later they heard a commotion outside the front doors. The three of them joined the other prisoners as they huddled around the doors leading into the lobby to find out what was going on. Joe had a hard time seeing much. He had to look over the other prisoner's heads, through the open doors to the front lobby and out the glass entrance doors. The guards were yelling at someone, but Joe could only see a silhouette. The man stood in front of a vehicle whose lights were pointed at the front doors. He was gesticulating wildly. The guards had their guns pointed at the man and were yelling at him.

Joe thought he recognized the man's voice. "I think I know that guy!" Joe said to Ben and Tank. They were in the middle of the group of about 50 others trying to see. Tank looked at Joe, "Do you want to get closer?"

"That would be nice, but..."

Before he could finish, Tank lived up to his namesake and began plowing through the crowd. Joe followed close behind him. Many of the prisoners got mad about being pushed aside and would turn angrily to confront the interloper. However, once they saw the large beast of a man with menacing scowl, they stepped aside.

Joe and Tank eventually made it to the front of the crowd. The man was now on his knees, and two guards were next to him. One had a shotgun pointed at his head, and the other was yelling. A flashlight shone briefly on the man's face.

Joe couldn't believe it.

What is Kevin doing here?

Joe yelled as loud as he could, "Kevin, over here! Kevin! It's me! Over here!" He waved his arms frantically.

Kevin seemed to pause briefly and tried to look around the guard in front of him. Joe yelled again, "Kevin, I'm here!" One of the guards grabbed Kevin and led him back to his jeep. Kevin reluctantly got inside the jeep.

The guard inside the factory building cocked his gun. "Okay, the show's over, back inside." The lights of the jeep swept around to face away from the factory, and Kevin drove away.

With frustrated groans, the group of prisoners walked back to their bedrolls. The guards sat back down on chairs under the glow of the red exit lights at the exits. The other fluorescent lights were turned off, and other than the red glow over the guards, the factory was plunged into darkness.

Back in their little sleeping area, Joe, Ben and Tank lay down on the chilly floor.

"Did you know that guy?" asked Ben.

"That was Kevin." Joe rubbed his wrists, which were getting

red and sore from the shackles.

"The guy from the letter?" Ben rolled over uncomfortably. "What was he doing here?"

"I have no idea what he's doing here."

"Maybe he's come to bust you out," Tank interjected.

"You know," said Ben, "This might be a good time to make another escape attempt. I heard that another guard died today. How many do you think are left?"

"Not many," answered Tank. "I bet if we could convince a few others to join us, we could overpower the few guards that are left and make a run for it."

"You know I can hear you morons." One of the guards shone his flashlight in their direction.

"We were kidding?" said Ben. The conversation ended, and they tried to get comfortable. Joe heard Ben snoring as he slowly fell into a cold restless sleep.

Despite the non-stop sounds of ankle and wrist cuffs jangling every time someone moved, Joe fell asleep. He woke briefly sometime during the night when he heard whispering and doors creaking open and closed. Moments later it went quiet again and Joe went back to sleep.

Joe woke with a start to talking and shuffling from many of the prisoners across the factory floor.

He rubbed his eyes and sat up. His back ached, and he felt cold and clammy. "What time is it?"

Tank was sitting up. "Something is happening."

"Is it breakfast?" Joe asked, stretching.

A few of the prisoners were looking out the small windows into the lobby. Others were talking in hushed conversations that were getting louder.

"Wake Ben up, it's time to go," said Joe. "What do you think is going on?" he asked Tank as he knelt down and gently nudged Ben.

"I think they're gone," said Tank.

Ben was still sleeping, and Joe pushed him harder. "Who's gone?"

"The guards."

"Where to?" Joe asked as he shook Ben harder.

"I don't know, maybe they left."

Joe grabbed Ben by the shoulders and shook him hard.

"Is he dead?" Tank asked, looking down at Ben.

Joe reached down and plugged Ben's nose.

Suddenly Ben's eyes opened, his body tensed. He swung his arms wildly at Joe who stood up. "You're a deep sleeper."

Ben stood up beside the two of them. "What's going on?"

"The guards are gone," said Tank.

A door opened, letting in bright morning sunshine. There was shouting, and the prisoners started leaving. They used the two side exits, walking past the empty chairs that the guards had sat on the night before.

The factory where they slept emptied. Joe, Tank, and Ben followed the group going into the lobby. There were no guards anywhere. Some of the prisoners were leaving out the front door. Others in the lobby were taking turns using a key on a large ring to unshackle themselves. When it was his turn, Joe used the key to liberate himself and then Ben and Tank. The three of them spilled out the front door with the rest of the former prisoners.

Both buses were gone and everyone was running in all directions away from the factory trampling the fresh layer of snow in the empty parking lot.

"I don't think we have to run," Joe spoke first. "The guards abandoned us last night. I think they drove away in the buses." They were not dressed for the weather and Joe rubbed his hands to try to keep them warm.

"Where to now, boss?" Tank asked Joe, as he rubbed his freshly freed wrists.

"Why am I the boss?" asked Joe.

"You're the brains," Tank replied, "I'm the brawn, and he's not going to last two days out here." He pointed at Ben.

"Hey, you should be nice to me. You may need me to do your taxes someday."

"I doubt that."

"Okay, that's enough kids," said Joe, "We need to find..." He didn't finish his sentence. At the end of the driveway to the factory he saw someone yelling and waving as he stood in front of a blue jeep. "Is that...Kevin?"

He started walking faster and then jogged towards Kevin as his friends tried to keep up.

When they reached Kevin, they hugged awkwardly.

"That's quite the chin bristle you're sporting," said Kevin

Joe rubbed his dark beard. "I'm trying something different," Joe said and introduced his friends. "This is Tank and Ben... this is Kevin."

They all shook hands. "What's going on, Kevin?" Joe asked, "What are you doing here?"

Kevin was looking past Joe. "Are those friends of yours?"

Joe turned around. A group of three men were walking towards them, led by Rafael Javier. The same Latino that had pummeled Joe at the jail.

"Hola, hermanos, I see you found me some transportation."

Tank spoke to his friends. "You guys better get in the jeep."

"What about you?" asked Joe.

"I'll be right there." He stood with his legs apart, and his hands clasped behind his back in front of the jeep. Ben jumped in the back, Joe sat in the front, and Kevin got behind the wheel.

Tank stood unwavering as the four men approached and stood in front of him.

"You need to tell your friends to get out of that vehicle, and then nobody will get hurt," said Rafael.

"I'm sure there are many other vehicles. You need to go find your own," Tank responded.

Before Rafael could react, Tank punched him in the throat. He gasped for air clutching his throat as he fell to the ground. The three men behind him paused in disbelief. This gave Tank the second he needed to punch the first man in the stomach. The second man took a swing, and Tank ducked and came up with an uppercut to the man's nose. The last man managed to hit Tank on the side of the head, knocking him over. The man swung back to kick Tank while he was down, but Tank deftly kicked at the side of the man's knee. There was a cracking sound as his leg bent sideways, and he fell sideways in pain. Tank jumped up and ran around to the side of the jeep and got in beside Ben.

Rafael was on his knees clutching his throat. His three friends weren't in any better shape. One of the men was trying to catch his breath. One was trying to stop the bleeding from his nose, while the other was screaming in agony while grasping his dislocated knee.

Kevin started the jeep and drove down the road away from their ephemeral prison.

"That was crazy!" said Ben. You're like Jackie Chan except your what, Russian?"

"I'm Canadian, but I was born in Ukraine."

"Well that was incredible, where did you learn to fight like that."

"Army and MMA."

"What? You're a mixed martial artist? I went to an MMA show once. One of my clients gave me tickets. I think his name was Kevin, just like our fearless rescuer here – wait a minute, how and why are you here, Kevin?"

"That is something I too would like to know," said Joe.

Kevin gave them a brief synopsis of how he had met Garret and had convinced him to drop the charges. He told them how he had tried and failed to get information from the police and how he had met Zach, Ayesha and Blender and Laurel. How they had all moved into a big mansion near Commerce City. He gave him the news of his friend Laurel's passing and how he had handed his letter to one of the guards.

"I went to the jail to try to visit you again, yesterday. I arrived just as those blue buses pulled in. I was told that you were all being moved to a larger facility, but they wouldn't say where. I raced back to tell Monique. She agreed that I should follow you to find out where they were taking you."

They drove on as Kevin relayed the story. "It was difficult to get through the new military checkpoints they are setting up. I assume they are quarantining every town in hopes of stopping the spread of the Scourge. I followed the buses all the way here. I almost lost sight of them at the last checkpoint. They were just starting to set up that checkpoint when I drove through. I don't think it's going to be so easy to get back."

Joe turned to him. "Why? Why did you go through all of that just for me? We've only met once. You hardly know me?"

A light armoured vehicle drove through the intersection in front of them.

"Because that's what Jesus would do – he would go after the lost sheep," he responded. They drove down the almost empty streets.

From the back, Ben spoke up. "Are you one of those Bible thumpin' Jesus freaks?"

"I try to be a good Christian, yes." He maneuvered the jeep around a pickup truck that had grey smoke streaming from the hood.

Three armoured vehicles passed by them going the opposite direction.

"I knew a Christian once," said Ben. "Actually, he was a Mormon. He tried talking to me about some Joseph Smith guy who had a vision. He believed in modern-day prophets, but he never warned me of an impending virus that was going to kill everyone. He died at the very start of the Scourge on his birthday of all days. Do you believe that? I thought…"

"Okay Ben, stop already," Joe called to the back. "Kevin, where are we going?"

"We are going shopping. You guys are going to need something a little warmer. We could be getting a cold snap soon, and I would hate to come all this way to save you, only to have you die of pneumonia."

CHAPTER 22

Monique looked out the window as Blender pushed the snow off the driveway with the ATV. Monique made Ayesha and Zach help keep the house clean and tidy, while Blender looked after the meals. She hadn't heard from Kevin since he left to follow the prison buses. She hoped he was okay.

Once the first snow fell, she told Blender to find something in the garage to plow it. He grumbled and complained until he found an ATV with a plow attachment. He was having a lot of fun driving fast down the laneway. When he came in, he had a big grin on his face.

"Was that fun?" asked Monique.

"Yes, it was. When you have the right toys, anything can be fun." He took his boots, coat and gloves off. "I saw something outside the gate."

"What?"

"Tracks. I've rarely seen anyone on this road, but today when I plowed outside the gate, I saw tracks. They were tire tracks from a vehicle that pulled to the side of the road near the entrance. I also found several boot prints leading up to the gate."

Monique rocked Olivia gently. "Okay, thanks for telling me."

"No, problem. I'll be in the kitchen if you need me."

An hour later, Monique put the baby down for her nap and

joined the others for dinner.

"We need to have better home security," said Monique as she scooped some cream corn on her plate. "There may be other people that want this house to themselves, so we need to be ready. Blender, have you found any guns in this house?"

"No, and I've looked everywhere. All I've seen for weapons are some golf clubs and a fire poker."

"Zach, are there any security cameras outside that we can tap into?" she asked.

"There are some security cameras, but I can't hack into them. I think they have an encrypted password," he answered.

"Tomorrow, I need two of you to go into Commerce City and get some security cameras and a gun."

Zach stared at her with his mouth agape. "Really? Can we find some chocolate too?"

"You," Monique pointed at Zach, "are in charge of getting the cameras. We need to have at least one for the backyard, one for the front yard and one at the front gate. We'll need a lot of cables to run from the house to the front gate..."

"No, we can use a wireless camera, but we might need an extender to reach that far," said Zach.

"Blender is going to have to find a gun."

"How am I supposed to do that?" he asked.

"Things are falling apart out there and you might have to get creative," she said.

The next morning Blender and Zach took the white pickup truck from the garage into Commerce City. Every time they drove into the city, which was usually once every two weeks, things seemed to be getting worse. More stores were either boarded up or closed. Fewer people were walking or driving. Credit and debit cards were useless, and cash was becoming less valuable. The government and the police services seemed to have dissolved. The only sign of order in the chaos was the military. There was some looting, but because the population had been decimated, some businesses remained untouched. Fresh food was in short supply, and many other necessities were dwindling as nothing new was being produced.

Occasionally, outside some businesses and homes, there were black flags. They were made of different materials, including ribbons, shirts, towels, socks and rags. They were on mailboxes, handrails, doorknobs and sometimes eavestroughs. There wasn't a lot of them, but they were all black. On previous visits to the city, they had been told that the black ribbons and flags were to signify that there was a dead body inside.

"Have you noticed how many military vehicles there are?" asked Zach.

"Yeah, I guess, why?"

"Every time we come to the city, there is less traffic, fewer people, but more military. Why do you think that is?"

"I guess the government is using the military to help keep society together."

"Maybe."

They drove into the city. The roads were not plowed, but fortunately not much snow had fallen.

"Where are we going to get a gun?" Zach asked.

"Let's get your camera's first, and worry about the gun later. Where do you suggest we find these cameras?"

"I remember a Best Buy near the stadium," said Zach.

"Weren't the front doors all smashed in? I'm sure the place has been looted."

"Maybe, but we just need a couple of WiFi cameras. They couldn't have taken everything."

"Look at that," said Blender pointing at the side of the road. A large transport truck was overturned on the side of the road. The back end was open, and it was empty inside, but there were lumps under the snow. "What do you think was in that truck?"

"Maybe pigs or cows," said Zach.

"How do you know that?"

"It's a livestock trailer, and those lumps are the animals that died when the truck crashed. I assume the vultures picked them clean."

"You're smart for an 11-year-old."

"I'm 12 and a half."

Blender drove the pickup to the Best Buy and parked near the door. The windows were smashed in, and the interior was a mess. The snow had blown in through the window, and there was a light blanket of white on the store's tiled floor.

"Are those hoof prints?" asked Zach, pointing to the prints in the snow.

"Maybe it's a deer," said Blender, "Let's just find these cameras. This place gives me the creeps."

Many of the shelves were overturned, and electronic devices were strewn across the floor. It was slow going, as they had to push items aside to get through. The lights were all off, but the light from outside was enough to see where they were going. They made it to the back of the store with the large screen televisions.

"We've gone too far," said Zach.

"What's that noise?" Said Blender.

Zach stopped and listened. There was a noise from the laptop section. It was grunting, and it was getting louder.

"Is that a pig?" asked Blender. "Maybe we can take it home so I can make some braised pork in sweet soy sauce."

Zach started to back up. "That pig has been out here for at least two months, and it may be feral."

"What are you talking about? It's a little pig." Blender started walking towards the grunting. "Here piggy, piggy, piggy…"

Out of the shadows, the pig emerged. It was big, black, hairy, and had two long tusks. It stared at Blender with its beady black eyes and then charged, making loud squealing and grunting noises. Blender screamed, turned, and ran towards Zach, who had already climbed on top of an empty shelving unit. The pig ran straight at the shelving unit, almost knocking the two of them off. As they watched, the pig rammed the rack a few more times and then paced around the rack.

"What now?" asked Blender with a look of terror on his face.

"Are you scared of a wittle piggy?" asked Zach in a mocking voice.

"That is not a little piggy. That is a wild boar!"

"It's a feral pig," Zach said, smiling. "You need to distract the pig by running *that* way." He pointed to the left.

"Why, what are you going to do?"

"I need to go *this* way," he pointed to the right, "and find the cameras."

"So, you want the pig to chase me so you can go shopping?" asked Blender.

"Well, we can't sit here all day. Besides, are you going to be the one to tell Monique that we couldn't get the cameras because of a little pig?"

"Fine, but if I get killed by this raging boar, I'm blaming you."

Blender waited till the pig wasn't looking in their direction. He jumped off the rack and ran. The pig turned and charged after him.

Zach climbed down and quietly made his way to the security camera section. He could hear crashing and loud banging from the other side of the store as the pig chased Blender around the store.

"Hurry up, Zach, I can't do this all day!" Blender yelled.

Finally, Zach found what he was looking for and made his way to the front of the store.

"Let's go, Blender!" he yelled and ran towards the car. Behind him Blender ran out of the store, but slipped on the snow-covered tile at the front of the store, landing on his butt. He made it back to his feet just as the pig came charging at him from behind. He ran towards Zach, yelling, "Start the car! Start the car!"

He made it safely to the car and shut the door. The pig snorted, shook its head and ran off.

"I hope you found what you were looking for," said Blender

Zach held up three boxes. "Yes, I did!"

As they were driving out of Commerce City, the pickup truck sputtered and died.

"We're out of gas, aren't we?" Asked Zach.

"Well, there aren't many gas stations open anymore, and I wasn't paying attention. Let's get out and walk. Maybe we can find another vehicle."

They started walking down the slushy street towards a small subdivision. "One of these houses must have a car," said Blender.

"Is that a cop car?" asked Zach. Past the next intersection, a police car was pulled over to the side of the road, beside a small church. There wasn't much snow on the car, so they knew it couldn't have been there very long.

They walked up to the side of the car and knocked on the fogged up window. They could see a figure on the inside. Blender slowly opened the door. The man inside was dead. Ribbons of dried blood snaked down his shirt from his mouth and nose.

"That's so gross!" said Zach.

"Maybe we should let someone know about this," suggested Blender.

"What are you going to do, call the cops?" asked Zach.

"That's exactly what I'm going to do," said Blender as reached across the dead policeman and grabbed the radio. "Hello, come in, anybody there?"

After a few seconds, a voice came on. "This is dispatch. Who is this? Over."

"Um...this is Blender...I mean Sherman Waters. I found one of your guys, and he's dead."

"Say 'over'," said Zach.

"Right. We have a dead policeman here, over."

"Are you in need of immediate assistance, over?"

"No, we're fine, over."

"Please put a black flag or cloth in a visible location and someone will pick up the body, over and out.

"That's it?" said Blender.

"They said over and out, so I guess that's it."

"Do you think we can move him into that church?" asked Blender.

"Maybe, why?"

"Because, then we can use his car."

Zach pointed at the policeman's sidearm. "I found your gun."

Blender removed the belt containing the pistol and put it behind the seat in the pickup.

They each grabbed an arm and dragged the body out of the car, down the sidewalk and up the steps of St. Edmund Catholic Church. The body was heavy, but slid easily over the fresh snow. By the time they got to the entrance of the church, they were both out of breath. The doors were not locked, and they pulled the body inside. As soon as the doors opened, a wave of putrid air hit them.

"Whoa! What is that smell?" asked Zach. They both covered their noses and walked into the sanctuary. The pastor lay crumpled on the steps of the podium with a bible clutched in his grasp. There were a dozen bodies strewn across the pews.

Blender looked at Zach. "Let's get out of here."

On the way out, Blender ripped down one of the black curtains and hung it on the church sign.

They looked at each other. "What do you think," asked Blender, "should we trade our vehicle in for one with a siren?"

"Oh yeah!"

As they drove back to the mansion, Zach tried the sirens and the lights as Blender drove and laughed. Zach went to touch the shotgun between the seats, but Blender stopped him. "That's only for the adults, Zach," said Blender.

When they got back to the mansion, they parked the car in the garage and brought their finds into the house. Monique shook Blender's hand. "I'm glad you made it back safely."

"Thanks," he said.

Ayesha gave Zach a quick hug, which he returned. Then the

four of them talked excitedly in the living room as the dog sniffed Zach and Blender.

Blender inspected the pistol.

"I see you found a gun," she said.

"The gun was the easy part," said Zach, "ask him about the little piggy he had to run away from."

"You were chased by a pig?" asked Ayesha.

"It was a wild boar and twice the size of Roxie," said Blender, "with razor-sharp tusks and it was as mean as a junkyard dog."

Zach laughed. "It was a feral pig."

"Shush!" said Blender, "I'm telling the story."

Monique smiled as Ayesha listened intently.

"As Zach here was leisurely shopping for cameras, I was risking my life," he continued. "It was grunting and growling…"

"Squealing," corrected Zach.

"Yes, it was squealing too. It sounded like the death screams of an angry demon. Its eyes were red with rage as it charged towards me. I raced out of the store with the speed of a man being chased by the devil. I dashed back to the truck with the boar's teeth gnashing at my heels. If it weren't for my brave sacrifice, we would never have made it out of there alive."

"That's quite the story," said Monique, "What about the gun?"

"We got it off a dead policeman," said Zach.

"Really?" said Monique.

"We also have a shotgun it's in the police car we drove home," said Blender proudly.

"Wow, did you do the siren?" asked Ayesha

"Oh, yeah," said Zach, "and the lights."

"Sounds like quite the adventure," said Monique.

"You know if we had found the gun first," said Zach, "we could have had braised pork for dinner."

CHAPTER 23

Rutger's Mall was not the largest mall in Chateaugay, Quebec. It was an older mall with two levels and over 100 stores. It had a movie theatre at one end, a large department store at the other and a food court in the middle. Kevin, Joe, Tank and Ben drove into the parking lot and parked near the doors. There were a few other cars in the large lot. Snow was starting to fall.

"Where is everybody?" asked Ben from the back. "Is it even open?"

"What day is it, Kevin?" asked Joe.

"I think its Sunday."

"Are malls open on Sundays?" asked Ben.

"I see lights on." said Tank.

"Let's find out," said Joe.

They walked up to a set of glass doors for the department store.

"I don't have a lot of money," said Joe, "and I'm assuming none of you have any money, so let's try to go easy on my credit card."

"It looks like it's open." Joe could see lights on inside. There was a large sign on the door that read: Protocoles de Virus and what he assumed were instructions below. "Does anybody know French?"

Nobody answered. Then Ben spoke up. "I knew a French guy. His name was Bob Riteaux. Bob isn't much of a French name, but he was French. I haven't seen him for years, not since…"

Joe pushed open the door and realized that the lock had been broken. Once inside, they stamped their feet to get the snow off their shoes and went through the second set of doors. The store looked like a tornado had swept through it. Racks and shelves were knocked over, clothes were strewn everywhere, and a cash register lay open and empty on the floor. The overhead fluorescent lights flickered but were still on.

"I guess we don't need your credit card," said Ben, "because it's Anarchy Day at the mall!"

"Look at all these footprints." Tank pointed at the floor. It was wet with many footprints. Tank knelt to get a better look. "These look like army boot prints."

"Hello!" called Kevin. "Anybody here?"

Nobody answered.

"I'm going to find some weapons," said Tank.

"Well, I'm going to find some food," said Ben.

"This doesn't seem right," said Kevin. "Maybe we should leave."

"It'll be fine," said Joe, "We need supplies, and the snow is starting to get worse out there."

"Okay, but let's keep track of what we take, so we can pay them back later."

"Let's meet right here in a half-hour," said Joe. They all left in separate directions.

Joe wandered down to the men's section where he changed into some jeans, a long-sleeved shirt, sweater and some insulated hiking boots. He found a backpack and walked around the store filling it with what he thought he might need. He found thick socks, a hat, mitts, a jackknife and some chocolate bars. Although much of the store looked like it had been ransacked, many items still had not been taken. Joe made his way out of the store and into the mall. The wide walkway between the stores was mostly empty except for a knocked over recycling receptacle.

None of the signs were in English, but he could translate 'cafétéria'. He started walking in the direction the arrow pointed. Most of the stores were caged shut with metal curtains, but a couple looked like they had been pried open. There were no other people. As he passed by a clothing store, he heard the clacking sound of someone rifling through clothes racks. It came from Couture Noir, which had its metal curtain pried open at one end. In the display window, female mannequins sported dark clothing and leather boots. This did not seem like the type of store any of his friends would patronize.

Maybe Ben is a cross-dresser.

"Hello?" he called into the store, but no one answered.

I'm sure I heard something in there.

He had to remove his backpack to fit through the gap in the metal curtain. One of the lights in the back was on. The rest of the store was only lit from the light coming through the curtain from the hallway. He had taken two steps when he felt something cold and metal pressed against the back of his head.

"Ne bougez pas!" It was a stern female voice. He froze.

"Hey, don't shoot, I'm not armed." He threw his hands in the air.

"Que fais-tu ici?" the cold metal still pressed against his skull.

"I don't speak French."

The woman switched to English. "What are you doing here?"

"I'm just looking for some warm clothing."

"What are you a cross-dresser? There are no men's clothing in this store."

"I know, I thought I heard something and..."

"Where did you come from? The army just cleared this place."

"We just got here." He was still facing forward with his hands in the air and couldn't see his ambusher.

"We? Who's we? Where did you come from?"

"Just a few friends and I. We just got out of jail." As soon he said it, he realized it might be the wrong thing to say.

"You don't look like a criminal."

"Look, we just needed a couple of things before we drive back to Ontario. We don't want any trouble."

"You're driving west?"

"Yes. Just let me leave the way I came in and you won't see me again. May I please put my hands down? My arms are getting tired."

The pressure from the metal on the back of his head eased.

"Okay, but no sudden moves. Do you have a car?"

"A jeep, yes." He slowly put his arms down.

"Can I ride with you? I would like to find my brother, Pascal. He's in Commerce City."

Joe slowly turned around to face her. She was not a woman. She was a teenage girl with long inky black hair. The girl had bulky army boots with silver buckles, baggy dark camouflage pants and an oversized black coat with MCR on it. She had a lot of dark make-up on her face, and held a large blue crowbar in her hand.

Joe held out his hand. "I'm Joe."

"I'm Camille." She moved the crowbar to her left, so she could shake his hand. The shake was firm and her rings pressed painfully into his hand.

"Are you into goth or something?"

"It's emo. No one does goth anymore."

"Sorry, what did you say about the army?" Joe asked as he climbed back through the gap in the curtain.

She followed him out. "You really have been in jail, haven't you?"

"Yes, I'm a little out of the loop. Where is everybody?

"The army is enforcing the state of emergency by kicking the looters from the stores and malls. They're sending everybody home."

"Why?"

"They say they're trying to maintain law and order, but I

think there might be something else going on."

Joe grabbed his backpack, and they started walking down the mall walkway towards the food court.

Camille continued talking. "I watched the army come in, send everyone home and then leave. As soon as they left, I came in to do some shopping."

"You mean to do some stealing."

"I suppose you plan on paying for everything you took. Besides, my bank card stopped working a long time ago."

Just as they were about to pass the hallway for the washroom, Ben appeared in front of them. Reflexively, Camille punched him in the nose. Ben keeled over, holding his nose.

"Whoa, hey easy there, Xena, he's with me," said Joe.

She stood watching Ben try to stop the bleeding. "Who's Xena?"

"The Warrior Princess," he said.

She looked blankly at him.

"From a 90s television show."

"Whatever. Before my time."

Ben straightened up as the flow of blood slowed.

"You okay there, big guy?" Ben asked.

"I'll live. Who's the punk rocker who just assaulted me?"

"It's not punk, its Emo."

"Camille, this is Ben. Ben, this Camille the warrior princess. She would like to drive west with us."

"Can't she drive herself?"

"I'm only fifteen."

Ben touched his nose and then looked at his hand to check for blood. "Where are your parents?"

"Dead."

"Oh, sorry. I had a niece about your age. She was into skateboarding. I think she went to Europe to find herself. She found that she liked drugs. I think the Dutch police sent her back home. You don't do drugs, do you? By the way you punch, I assume steroids. You know steroids do crazy stuff to your body."

As they entered the empty food court, the sound of clinking

dishes was heard from inside the Wendy's.

"Wait," said Camille, putting her hand out to stop them, "There's somebody here."

Joe tried to interject, "It could just be…"

Before he could finish, she had jumped on the Wendy's counter, slid across it, and then landed on the other side. She held the crowbar over her head as she crept towards the cooking area in the back.

Tank appeared around the corner, and Camille swung the crowbar towards him. Just before the weapon was about to collide with the side of his head, Tank's hand caught her by the wrist. He twisted her arm slightly, and she cried out, the crowbar clanging to the floor.

"Tank, it's okay, she's with us!" Joe called out.

He inspected her wrist and pushed the sleeve of her coat higher up her arm exposing scars on her wrist and forearm.

"You a cutter?"

She was still wincing. "What's it to you, Thor."

He shrugged and let go of her wrist. "I'm Tank."

"I'm Camille," she mumbled.

"Are you supposed to be goth or punk?"

"It's Emo, espèce de con!"

She bent over and grabbed her crowbar.

"Like Emo Williams the comedian?" he asked, disappearing into the kitchen. She followed him in.

"What's that smell?" Kevin came walking towards them from across the food court.

Joe realized that there was a smell in the air, and it was coming from Wendy's. "I think Tank's cooking lunch."

"Oh good, because I'm hungry," said Kevin. "Ben, what happened to you, did you walk into a wall? You got blood all over you, face."

"He was attacked by a little girl," said Joe, smiling.

Tank had cooked up some hamburgers on the Wendy's grill, and they all sat down at one of the tables eating.

"So, Camille," said Kevin, "Are you like one of those emo

kids?"

"Finally, someone living in the 21st century," she shook her head. "And you are what, a hipster?"

Tank leaned over to Ben. "What's a hipster?"

"I don't know," he replied, "I think it's like a hippie?"

"No, Camille, I'm not a hipster," said Kevin.

She looked up at him and swallowed another bite of her burger. "Oh really? What's with the neatly trimmed beard, skinny jeans and checked shirt? I bet you smoke a pipe and go to Starbucks too."

"No, I don't smoke…"

He was suddenly interrupted by a voice over the intercom. "Attention shoppers, would Joe, Ben, and the big idiota who broke my nose, please report to security immediately." It was Rafael.

"What is he doing here?" asked Ben.

"He must have followed us," said Kevin.

"I should have hit him harder," said Tank.

"Friend of yours?" asked Camille.

"We need to go," said Joe. They all stood up.

A deafening shot echoed across the food court, and Camille's arm flew backwards. Blood spurted out of her upper arm as she cried out. "Tabarnak!"

Tank grabbed her and pulled her down to the floor. "Everyone, into Wendy's, now!" More shots rang out as Tank hauled Camille behind the counter with everyone else.

"Great," said Ben, "Now they're armed."

Tank ignored him. "Everyone okay?"

"No!" Camille was holding her left arm as blood leaked out between her fingers.

"You'll be fine, just hold that as tight as you can. I'll carry you."

He flung her over his shoulder and carried her fireman style. He did a crouching run to the back of the kitchen. "Follow me, guys."

They obeyed, running along behind him. He opened the

door at the back of the kitchen and took a quick peek around the hallway, looking both ways. Tank then ran full tilt down the hallway with the others close behind. They could hear yelling and more gunshots back in the food court.

The narrow hallway had many doors, all with French labels. "Camille, find the janitor's room," yelled Tank.

"You just passed it!"

Behind him, Joe tried to open the door, but it was locked.

With Camille, still draped over his shoulders, Tank kicked the door in. The knob assembly clattered to the floor.

Inside, Tank put Camille on the floor, turned on the light and barked out orders. "Everyone inside. Joe, fix that knob so they can't tell that we're in here and find a long clean rag. Kevin, find some alcohol, peroxide, or a bottle of water. Ben, find some super glue, a screwdriver, or a pen. Camille, keep holding your arm up, and try not to drip blood on the floor."

They all did as they were told as Tank stood on the desk in the corner and lifted one of the ceiling panels.

Moments later, they were all assembled at the desk that Tank was standing on.

"All I could find was water and a pencil," said Ben.

"That's fine, just put it in your pocket for now. Kevin, do you have a phone?"

"Yes, but the cell networks don't work much anymore."

"That's fine. We just need the flashlight app on it. Joe, go turn off the light."

They could hear voices in the hallway, and they all stood silently.

Tank gestured for Joe to get up into the ceiling first. Tank helped him up, then lifted Camille to Joe, who helped her up as well. It was difficult to walk on the top of the walls without stepping or falling on to the fragile ceiling tiles.

Tank helped Kevin and, with some effort, Ben. Tank hoisted himself up and slid the panel back into place. Kevin turned off his phone light just as one of Raphael's men opened the door to the room. The light below turned on, and slices of light pierced through the joints of the ceiling panels as they perched silently above and held their breath. The man mumbled something, tromped around the room, then turned out the light and left.

They let out a collective sigh of relief but stayed silent.

From somewhere in the mall, they could here Raphael yelling. "I know you pendejos are here somewhere. When you come out, we will be waiting."

When they could no longer hear anyone below, Tank got Kevin to turn his light back on. Camille was sobbing quietly.

"Okay, Camille, this is going to hurt." Tank tied the rag Joe had found tightly around her arm just above the wound. He fed the pencil through the rag and used it to twist the tourniquet tight. Ben handed him the water bottle, which he used to clean her wound, trying not to spill too much water onto the tiles below.

Tank used the super glue to seal wound. The bleeding stopped, and he removed the tourniquet. He looked her in the eye. "Camille, you're going to be fine, okay? The bullet just grazed your arm."

"Thanks," she said quietly. She had stopped crying. Her dark eye makeup was now black tears streaked down her cheeks.

"What now?" asked Ben, "And is Tank our fearless leader?"

"I'm fine with Joe making the big decisions," said Tank.

"I'm fine with Tank keeping us alive when we are being shot at." Joe looked over at Tank, who nodded.

Ben coughed. "You okay?" asked Joe.

"I'm fine, I'm a little out of shape, and the dust up here is affecting my allergies."

"Well, let's move. Maybe we can make our way to the department store where we came in and sneak out without being seen." He looked over at Tank.

"Sounds like a plan Joe," he said.

They balanced on the walls and climbed over wires and duct work. It was awkward and slow, but they eventually hit a wall.

"Where do you think we are?" said Kevin.

"I don't know, I guess we're about to find out," said Tank as he gently moved one of the ceiling panels below. "I've haven't heard Rafael's men for a while now. Maybe they left."

He looked down through hole but all he could see was a carpeted floor and a bench. "Okay, I'm going down to check it out."

"Be careful," said Camille.

Tank lowered himself down. A few moments later, he announced that it was all clear. He helped Camille down and sat her down on the bench. Ben was coughing again and almost broke his leg when he jumped down. Joe and Kevin joined the others in what appeared to be the changeroom for the department store. The light wasn't on, but light streamed in from an open doorway to the store.

Ben held a fist up to his mouth and coughed again.

"Are you sure you're okay?" asked Joe.

"I'm fine, what's the plan?"

Joe thought he could see blood on Ben's hand, but before he could say anything, the lights went out, plunging the store into darkness. Multiple emergency lights came on immediately, casting ominous spotlights into the store.

In the distance, they heard shouting.

"It sounds like Raphael, and his guys are on the other side of the mall right now," said Tank. "We should grab supplies before those emergency lights run out of juice. Kevin, you should go warm up your jeep and bring it closer to the doors. Ben, Joe, go find some food, water, and blankets that we can take with us. We'll meet back at the exit doors in 10 minutes. Camille, you're with me."

Kevin left to get his jeep, while Tank and Camille went to the hunting section. Joe and Ben walked through the shadows towards the cashier area to find some snack foods.

"Ben, are you coughing up blood?" Joe asked.

"Yeah, I'm fine. I'm sure it's nothing. I had a cousin once who always coughed. Every time he..." he stopped mid-sentence and erupted in a fit of coughing. Joe looked down to see black splatter on the tile floor.

"Maybe you should sit down."

Ben stopped coughing. "Okay, maybe I just need to rest for a minute." He sat on the floor.

"I'll go grab some snacks and I'll be right back." Joe ran to the racks by the cashier. He realized he had left his backpack of supplies in the food court, so he grabbed a bag from behind the cash counter and filled it with chips, bottles of pop and filled his pockets with chocolate bars and beef jerky. Then he went back to find his friend. They walked slowly towards the exit doors where they met up with the others.

Camille was standing beside Tank, who was holding a large black compound bow and had a quiver of arrows on his back. "I can't believe they don't have any guns," he said.

Kevin was standing in the doorway covered in snow. "Bad news, guys. The jeep tires have been slashed."

"Can we find another vehicle?"

"Not tonight. There's a snowstorm brewing and it's as dark as sin out there. Looks like the power is out in the whole area."

"Okay, let's go upstairs," said Tank. They have beds up there and there's only one way up, making it easier to guard.

CHAPTER 24

Blender and Monique found tracks again outside the mansion gate the next morning. They got to work, making their home more secure.

Blender helped Zach set up the cameras. They placed one in the backyard overlooking the pool, one at the front door and one at the gate entrance. Ayesha checked all the windows to ensure they were all locked. Monique went through the police car in the garage. She grabbed a black duffel bag and threw in the pistol, shotgun, ammunition for both, two portable radios and pepper spray. Monique lugged the bag and a bullet-proof vest into the house and put it behind the desk in the study.

As per Monique's instructions, they all packed to-go backpacks with essentials. If there was any trouble, they planned to meet in the guesthouse at the back.

That night after supper, they heard a vehicle honking at the front gate. Zach checked his laptop and saw a brown pickup truck outside the gate. A large man wearing a brown winter jacket stood outside the truck, waving his arms at the camera.

"What do we do?" asked Blender.

"Let's just wait a bit and see if he leaves."

Five minutes later, he was still there, standing in the snow, illuminated by the truck headlights. Every thirty seconds he would walk back to his truck and honk the horn a couple of times. Then he would get back out and lean against the side of his truck, looking up at the camera.

"I don't think he's leaving," said Zach.

"I'm going out there," said Monique.

"Don't leave," said Ayesha.

"Ayesha, you watch Olivia – she's upstairs sleeping. Zach, you watch the camera feeds, and take one of the radios. I'll take the other. You let me know if you see anything I need to know about. Blender, let's grab some of the guns and ammo from the study.

Moment later they stood by the front door. Blender held the shotgun and Monique carried the pistol in her pocket.

"Blender, I need you to follow me, but stay out of sight. Roxie stays here."

"Do you think this is a good idea?" asked Blender.

"It's my only idea."

Minutes later, she was walking down the laneway, the snow crunching under her feet. Her flashlight announced her arrival to the man at the gate, who stood on the other side.

"Good evening," he yelled, his gloved hands holding on to the steel bars of the gate.

She stopped several metres back from the gate with one hand in her pocket. "What do you want?"

He held his hands back, "I'm not here to hurt anyone, I just need to talk." As he spoke, his words turned to steam in the glow of the headlight beams.

Monique pointed the flashlight at his face. He squinted and put his hand up to block the light. His face did not look like he bore ill intent. She stepped closer. "So, talk," she said in a stern voice and clicked off the flashlight.

"I know this isn't your house," he said.

She clenched on to the gun in her pocket but didn't pull it out. "It was given to us."

"I know that's not true," he said. "My wife used to work here as a housekeeper. She was with the owners when they died. They told her to lock the doors and leave after they died. After all the hours she spent slaving away cleaning this place for so many years, that's the thanks she gets? They paid her peanuts.

Even when they died, they couldn't do the right thing and tell her that she could live here. We *should* be living here."

"Well, you aren't and we are. I'm sure there are a lot of other houses you could live in," she said. She took a step back.

"No, no, I'm sorry, I don't mean to scare you. Let me start over - my name is Milosz." He offered his hand through the bars.

She did not move towards him. "My name is Monique. Like I said – what do you want?"

"I thought about coming here and forcing you guys out, but my wife, bless her soul..." He made the sign of the cross. "She said it wasn't right to kick you guys out, because you must have needed a place to live too. Anyway, we did find another house. One that was not as big as this one and didn't take so long to clean. When she got sick and died, I left and wandered into a C3."

"What's a C3?" asked Monique.

"It's a Community Command Centre. You haven't heard of them? They're run by the Army and provide food and shelter for those that need it. I moved into one of the local C3's and got talking with some people there. I found out that the Masterson's kid came back from the States. He and a few of his buddies had come out here. They discovered that someone was living in his house. I overheard them plotting to storm this place and take back his family's house. I knew from scouting out this place, that there were women and children living here, and I didn't want anyone to get hurt. I drove out here as fast as I could to warn you. His name is Warren, and he has at least four of his college buddies with him, and they are armed. I don't want to get caught in the middle of all this, so I'm leaving, but I thought I should warn you. If you want my advice, I'd say you should pack up and leave as soon as possible." He turned to leave.

Monique loosened the grip on the pistol in her pocket, stepped towards the gate and offered her hand through the bars. "Thank you, Milosz."

He shook her hand and nodded. "Good luck." He climbed back in his truck and drove away, leaving Monique in the dark.

She clicked her flashlight back on and started running back to the house. Blender materialized out of the shadows and ran to catch up.

"Did you hear all that?" asked Monique.

"Yeah, what are we going to do?" asked Blender

"We're leaving."

"We have guns now - can't we try to defend ourselves?"

"The two of us and two kids against five angry twenty-year-old's? Besides, it sounds like we unknowingly stole this house."

They ran down the laneway. "I thought that old guy told Kevin he could have it."

"Maybe it wasn't his to give."

"Monique, are you there?" said a voice in Monique's pocket.

She jumped, but then realized it was her radio.

"Yes, Zach," she said panting.

"We got company."

They ran into the house and over to Zach and the laptop without taking off her coat or boots. On the screen, she saw a purple pickup truck and a black SUV at the gate, which was now opening. The man who had just punched in the code looked up at the camera and gave them the finger.

Monique started yelling out orders calmly - which was not how she felt. "Ayesha go get Olivia."

Ayesha ran up the stairs.

"Blender, go to the study and grab the black duffel bag with the ammo and pepper spray."

He was on his way before she finished. "Zach, take this laptop to the basement and-"

"They're here!" he was pointing at the screen.

The front door opened, and a small canister was thrown in, before the door closed again.

"Go!" she yelled at Zach, who ran down the hallway. The room was filling with smoke. She ran to the stairs, her eyes burning, and flew up the stairs towards her baby. When she opened the door to the baby's room, it was empty.

From downstairs, she could hear the front door open and voices talking excitedly. Roxie was growling and barking.

"Ayesha," she called out, "where are you?" She was about to call out again when she heard a voice from the main floor.

"I hear someone upstairs. You check the basement…"

Monique didn't hear the rest as she ran down the hall, checking the other rooms. From behind her she heard one of the men at the top the stairs. Monique opened the closest door and went inside the bathroom as the man entered the hallway. She quietly locked the door and kept the light off.

"Monique…" her radio squawked before she turned it off.

The hallway light was still on, and she could see a shadow creep by the door. The hallway light went out, and everything went black. Even the night light plugged in below the mirror went out. She could hear yelling downstairs and the loud booming of a shotgun blast. There was more yelling and footsteps racing back towards the stairs.

She splashed her eyes with water, but her eyes still burned. As she left the washroom, she pulled the gun out of her pocket and clicked off the safety. She crept slowly down the hallway to the stairs. Just as she was about to take the first step down the stairs, she felt the cold steel of a gun barrel pressed against her temple.

"Don't move," a man's voice said.

"Look, we don't want any trouble. We were just leaving," she said as composed as she could. Her eyes were still stinging and she blinked rapidly.

"I'm sure you were," he said and turned his flashlight on. "I'm thinking we may want to keep you around for entertainment. You're pretty and -" he paused when he heard Olivia crying out from one of the rooms down the hall. "What was that?"

The moment she heard Olivia, Monique went from calm and composed to aggressive. She swiftly pushed the gun away from her head, and at the same time, shoved her own gun into his gut and fired. The man fell backwards down the stairs, his flashlight bouncing down ahead of him. He started to get up and reach for his gun when Roxie appeared at the bottom of the stairs.

"Kill!" yelled Monique, and the dog attacked the man before he could raise the gun.

Monique turned on her flashlight and ran to the room where Ayesha and Olivia had been hiding. They were both crying.

Monique knelt beside them and stroked Olivia's cheek. "Is the diaper bag here?" she asked.

Ayesha pointed beside her. Monique used the flashlight to find a soother and stuck it in Olivia's mouth, who stopped crying. She looked Ayesha in the eyes.

"Ayesha, listen to me. We are leaving, but I need you to stop crying for five minutes. You've had a tough life with people that didn't care for you, but you kept going. Tonight, I need you to trust me. I love you, and I will do everything possible to keep you safe, but I need you to be tough. I need you to be strong. Be strong for me. Be strong for little Olivia here. Be strong for your friend Zach. And even be strong for Blender." She cracked a small smile.

Ayesha stopped crying and let out a little giggle. She wiped her eyes and pursed her lips with determination. "Okay, what do you need me to do?"

"I need you to carry Olivia, and follow me downstairs. Do you have a scarf in your bag?"

"Yes."

"Cover your mouth with your scarf and keep Olivia's face covered. There's still smoke downstairs. Once we get to the back door, I need you to run to the guest house."

"What are you going to do?"

"I'm going to lead the way."

"What if those guys try to hurt us?" she asked.

"Then, I'm going to shoot them."

They left the room and walked down the hall. It was dark

upstairs, but one of the vehicles outside had its headlights pointed into the living room window downstairs. The beams of light illuminated the dissipating smoke. Roxie was still shaking the man on the stairs by the throat.

"Off!" yelled Monique, and the dog's jaws opened, and the dead body sank onto the stairs. "Heel!"

Roxie complied and walked with them down the stairs.

They could hear voices and movement from the other side of the house, but it didn't sound like anyone was nearby.

"Watch your step, but don't look down," Monique said as they stepped over the mutilated body on the stairs. They made it to the bottom of the stairs. As they walked through the living room, they heard a noise and stopped mid-stride.

"Monique is that you?" said a voice from behind them.

She turned to find Blender standing with the shotgun in his hands and a stunned look on his face.

"Blender, are you okay? Where's Zach?" she said.

Blender stepped forward into one of the beams of light coming through the window. "I killed a man," he said, staring at nothing.

"Come on we have to go," said Monique.

There was a loud gunshot from behind Blender. His face froze. With a stunned look, he fell forward. Blender was dead before he hit the carpet.

Ayesha screamed, and Monique fired her pistol towards the sound of the gunshot.

"Kill!" she yelled at Roxie.

The dog took three steps and then leapt through the air towards the man, snarling and growling.

"Run, Ayesha," she said harshly. Ayesha ran out of the living room towards the back of the house. Monique crouched behind a chair and pointed her gun towards where Blender had been standing. She could see the dog fighting with the man but couldn't find an opening for a shot.

As soon as she saw the gun fall from his bleeding hand, she yelled at Roxie, "Off!"

The dog let go of the man, and she took the opportunity to shoot him. He fell backwards, falling to the ground.

Monique ran out of the living room to catch up to Ayesha. She found her in the laundry room. "I told you to go to the guest house," she said.

Ayesha pointed. "There's a man by the back door. We can go through the window here, but I can't do it with Olivia."

Monique helped her out the window and handed Olivia down to her. "Can you find your way?" she asked.

"Yes, I think so."

Monique then managed to hoist the dog through the window. "Roxie," she yelled, "protect!" She pointed at Ayesha.

"Here, take my flashlight," she said to Ayesha, "but only use it if you really need to."

"Aren't you coming?"

"I will be, soon. I have to find Zach first. Now, go."

She waited till Ayesha, Olivia and Roxie disappeared into the back yard before slinking out of the laundry room. She couldn't hear anything except her heartbeat as she walked silently into the kitchen. Her eyes were starting to adjust to the dark. There was small flame from the stove pilot light casting an eerie blue glow. She heard someone bump the dining room table. She ducked behind the island counter and listened.

She felt a tapping on her back, and her heart leapt out of her chest. She turned, fearing the worst. A flashlight turned on for a moment, and she saw Zach staring back at her from behind his thick glasses. He had the look of total despair on his face.

"I saw Blender," he whispered, "he's dead."

"I know, Zach, but you have to do as I say or we will be too. When I stand up, I need you to run out the back to the guest house where Ayesha and Olivia are, okay?"

She hoped he was nodding in the dark.

There was the sound of movement on the other side of the counter. Monique stood and fired, but her shots ricocheted off the pots and pans hanging from the rack above the counter.

The man dove for cover as Monique continued firing in his

direction. She fired three more times. The gun flashes lit up the kitchen. She pulled the trigger again, but the gun clicked empty.

Suddenly it was silent and dark. Monique looked behind her. Zach was gone. She slowly backed out of the kitchen. A light flashed in her eyes, blinding her. She tripped backwards as shots were fired over her.

She looked up and saw the dark form of a man pointing a gun at her. She heard the shot and assumed she was dead, but the man clasped his side. He turned and fired two shots across the kitchen, then collapsed to the floor. Monique got to her feet and turned the flashlight on. Her attacker was leaning against the cupboard, holding his side, which was hemorrhaging blood. The gun lay on the floor beside him. She grabbed the gun and then shone the light across the kitchen.

It was Milosz, and he was bleeding badly from two bullet wounds.

She knelt beside him. "Let's see if we can stop this bleeding," she said, grabbing a tea towel from the counter.

"Are the kids safe?" he asked.

Within seconds the towel was soaked through, but she still held it tight against his wound.

"Yes, they're safe," she said. "You came back, and you saved me."

He smiled for a moment, then stopped breathing.

Monique wiped a tear from her cheek and stood up. She walked quietly to the back door, knowing there was one more attacker left. Slowly, carefully, she moved the sliding door aside. The cold night air blew in, and she stepped out into the snow. She heard footsteps behind her and swung her pistol up as she turned. Before she could pull the trigger, there was a bright muzzle flash and a gunshot. She felt the impact of the bullet in the centre of her chest as she fell backwards into the snow, and for a moment, everything went black.

Monique sat up in the snow. There was a throbbing pain where the bullet hit her. She touched her chest, expecting to feel the moist sensation of blood. Her fingers went through the hole in her coat and felt the large indentation in the bulletproof vest underneath. She got to her knees and looked towards the guest house which had lights flickering inside. The man that had shot her was running towards it.

Her chest was on fire, but she managed to raise the pistol and point it at the man's back and pull the trigger. The man fell to his knees and dropped into the snow. Monique ran by the dead man on her way to the guesthouse.

Ayesha and Zach were shaken but not hurt, and Olivia was fast asleep on the couch.

"Are we safe?" asked Zach.

"I think so."

"Blender is really dead, isn't he?"

Zach was trying to hold back his tears, but when Monique held him in his arms, the dam broke, and he sobbed uncontrollably. Ayesha hugged them both and they all cried together. Roxie lay down on the floor next to them.

Once they had regained some of their composure, Monique led them to the garage. "We're leaving," she said firmly.

Zach looked at all the vehicles. "Can we take the police car?"

"Yes, we can," Monique answered.

She double-checked the garage to make sure they were alone. Roxie followed Ayesha and Olivia into the back of the police car.

"I have to go back into the house for a second to grab the bag with the extra ammo, but I'll be right back," Monique said. "Stay, Roxie, protect."

Despite their protests, she left them and ran back to the silent house. She had to walk over several bodies as she made her way to the study. As she grabbed the duffel bag from under the desk, she noticed the box. It was the box that she had seen Kevin filling with the family photos. She pulled the box out from under the desk and looked at the framed pictures. One was of a couple – he was bald and she was pretty. She also found a framed acceptance letter to a fancy university in the States. Her flashlight pointed up to the wall where the replacement pictures that Zach had printed were now taped to the wall. One had Laurel holding Olivia, another had Blender and Zach eating together. Beside it was a picture of Ayesha playing with the dog in the backyard. Another photo showed her, Kevin and Olivia posing together in front of the house like a happy family in front of their new house. She ripped the pictures off the wall and tore them into pieces, angry tears streaming down her face.

She grabbed the duffel bag with the ammo and pepper spray and left the study. She said a quick prayer for Blender and picked up his shotgun. That's when she noticed that Blender's attacker was not there. The man that Roxie had bitten and that she had shot, was gone. She took off, running back to the garage. As she reached the side door to the garage, there was a gunshot, and a bullet shattered the wood siding beside her. She ducked and went through the door, closing it behind her. More gunshots rang out, and she could hear yelling.

She re-opened the door, but stood beside it. She popped her head out briefly and saw Warren bleeding from his shoulder. He was walking towards the garage. She held the shotgun up, stood in the doorway and pulled the trigger. The gun stock smacked against her shoulder, and she stumbled backwards. There was a bright light, and a massive *whoomph* as the propane tank beside the house exploded.

Monique ran to the car, but realized Zach was not in it. She looked to the other side of the garage and found Zach rifling through a box under a workbench.

"What are you doing, Zach?" Monique asked. "You need to get in the car."

"I need to find something – got it!" he pulled a black rag out of the box and ran to the car.

Monique turned the key and the car roared to life. She put it in gear and pushed the pedal to the floor. The push bar at the front of the car took the brunt of the impact as they crashed through the wooden garage door. Monique raced down the laneway, as the mansion burned behind them.

"Wait!" yelled Zach as they passed through the open gate.

Monique slammed on the brakes and the car slid a metre through the snow before stopping. "What?" she asked.

Zach opened the door and ran to the mailbox. He carefully tied the black cloth to the little plastic flag on the mailbox. He stood by the mailbox for a moment watching Blender's funeral pyre. The flicker of flames lit the tears streaming down his face.

He ran back to the car and sat in his seat. "I can't believe he's gone."

They all sat in silence as they travelled down the dark, snow-covered road. Thoughts and emotions swirled around in Monique's mind, as the snow swirled in front of the windshield.

Blender is dead. We have no home or food. Laurel is gone. I don't even know where I'm going or what I'm going to do. I'm looking after three kids and a dog by myself. Kevin, where are you? Are you coming back? Why didn't you tell me this wasn't our house? You fool. You knew. My shoulder hurts.

They drove into the dark, cold night in the direction of Commerce City.

CHAPTER 25

Joe, Ben, Tank, Camille and Kevin slept through the night without event. They blocked the doorway to the stairwell and Tank slept at the top of the escalator. The rest of them slept in the bedding section. Sometime during the night, the emergency lights had died, and the power had not come back on. Early in the morning, Tank woke them up. "Rise and shine people. We need to get going before Raphael's men find us."

Joe sat on the side of the bed and stretched. Ben was still sleeping in the bed next to him.

Joe walked over and shook him. "Wake up, Ben. It's time to go."

He didn't wake up.

Is he dead?

Joe shook him harder, "Wake up!"

Please don't be dead, please don't be dead.

Finally, Ben stirred and opened his eyes. "Water," he croaked.

Tank came over and handed him a water bottle. "You don't look so good."

Ben's skin was pale, and his eyes were red. Tank checked his pulse.

"I don't feel so good." Ben was struggling to sit up.

"We need to get him to a hospital," said Joe. "Everybody, get your winter gear on, we need to find a vehicle."

They donned their winter hats, gloves, and boots, grabbed their gear and walked down the escalators. Ben put his arm over Joe's shoulders to help him walk.

They didn't hear or see Raphael or his men as they passed through the department store. The snowstorm had abated, and the sun was rising. The morning rays of sunshine glistened on the fresh snow that was left behind by the storm. It wasn't windy, but it was cold.

"Okay, someone has to find another vehicle," said Joe. "Ben is in no shape to walk, and Camille shouldn't either."

Tank spoke up. "I'll stay here with Ben and Camille in case those men show up. You and Kevin can go find something."

Kevin and Joe trudged off making fresh boot prints in the snow.

"I think I saw a couple of car dealerships up a few blocks when we came in," said Joe.

"Are you suggesting we steal a car?"

"Unless you have a better idea. There are no buses or taxis, and I don't think we can get an Uber."

"I suppose. Where is everybody anyway?"

"Dead?"

"Do you think Ben is going to die?"

"I don't know."

"I hope Monique and the baby are okay."

"I'm sure they're fine. Just like Blender, Laurel, Ayesha and Zach."

Down the road, they found two car dealerships. The closest one was a new vehicle dealer selling shiny Hummers and Buicks. The front glass windows were broken, and the indoor showroom appeared empty. Half the building was blackened from a recent fire, and a thin trail of smoke rose to the sky.

"I'm thinking we might have better luck finding something at the used car dealership, further down."

Beside the new car dealer was Chateaugay Used Cars which remained untouched.

Joe found a rock to break the lock on the front door, but

when he tried it, he discovered the door was already unlocked.

"Maybe they're open for business," said Kevin.

Joe opened the door. "Did you bring your credit card?"

As soon as he opened the door they were hit by a wall of stench. Kevin almost puked but managed to swallow the acid bile that accumulated in the back of his throat. Joe covered his face with his scarf. "What is that smell?"

"I don't know," said Kevin as he covered his nose with his mitt. "It can't be good."

Joe looked behind the front counter and found the source of the smell. The rotting corpse of an older man was sprawled on his back on the floor. A frozen river of blood ran from his nose, mouth and ears to a frosted pool of red on the floor. His frozen eyes glistened as they stared up, sightless. A large silver cross on a chain sat on his chest, and a small red bible was clutched in his frozen white fingers.

Joe tapped the body lightly with his foot. The body was rigid and frozen. "If it's frozen, why does it smell?"

The reason became apparent when they saw the other side of the body. The man's sweater was pushed up, and blood, gore and entrails had leaked out.

They heard a low growl, and a shaggy brown dog emerged from behind a filing cabinet. Its teeth were bared and red with blood.

"Easy, boy," said Joe and held out his hand.

"Was he eating that guy?" said Kevin. "That's disgusting!"

"He's been stuck in here with no food." Ben reached into his pocket and pulled out some of his beef jerky. He unwrapped it and held it out. The dog stopped growling and moved closer.

Joe beckoned the dog to come closer and eventually the dog snatched it from his hands almost taking one of his fingers with it. Joe reached down slowly to let the dog sniff his hands. With a barking growl, the dog snapped at his hand. Joe pulled it away just in time.

"I'm going to find some water for this dog," said Joe.

"You do that. I'm not going anywhere near that beast. I'm going to see if I can find some keys."

Joe found the dog's water dish, which was bone dry. When he tried to fill it with water from the tap, he realized the pipes were frozen. Instead, he let the dog outside where it lapped up some of the fresh snow.

Kevin found the keys to an older model brown van with two rows of seats in the back. Kevin climbed into the driver's seat, and Joe sat beside him. The dog sat outside the van, looking at them.

"We're not taking that eater of human flesh, are we?" asked Kevin.

Joe got out of the van and opened the sliding door. The dog sat looking at him. Joe stepped back out of the way, and the dog hopped in. He slid the door closed and got back in the passenger seat.

The dog sat upright, and alert in the seat behind them. When Joe reached behind him to pet the dog, it growled and snapped at him.

"I guess he doesn't like to be touched," said Joe, pulling his hand back.

"And you want this killer dog as a pet?"

They drove back to the mall and pulled up to the door. Tank opened the door and the dog moved to the back of the van. Tank helped Ben in, who wasn't looking any better. Camille got in beside Ben in the middle row, and Tank got in the back with the dog.

"Good dog," said Tank tentatively.

"Careful," yelled Kevin from the front, "That dog eats people."

There was a bark and a snap. "Son of a..." Tank yelled.

"Told you!"

Ben coughed and blood splattered on his hand.

"Does he have the Scourge?" asked Camille. "Is he going to die?"

"I don't know," said Joe.

Kevin pulled out of the mall parking lot. "Do you know if there's a hospital near here, Camille?"

"Yes, Chateaugay General Hospital. You need to take a left at the next lights."

They didn't see any other vehicles on the road, and the van made fresh tracks in the snow.

As they pulled up to an intersection with traffic lights no longer lit, they heard the sound of a vehicle behind them.

"We got company," yelled Tank from the back. "Looks like a TAPV."

"A what?" asked Kevin.

"A tactical armoured patrol vehicle."

"The army?"

"Yes."

"Well, I'm pulling over," said Kevin.

"We don't have time for this," said Joe. "We need to get Ben to a hospital."

The choice was made for them when an army jeep pulled out from a side street and blocked the road in front of them.

Kevin slammed on the brakes, and the van slid to a stop just before colliding with the side of the jeep.

A uniformed man got out of the passenger side of the jeep. He had a holster holding a sidearm but didn't have it out. The driver stood outside his door with a large machine gun, but it wasn't pointed there way at the moment.

"I'll handle this," said Joe and got out of the vehicle with his hands in the air.

"Vous ne pouvez pas être ici, vous devez rentrer chez vous," the soldier barked, the steam puffing out into the cold morning air.

Joe called back to the van. "Camille, you need to get out here."

She climbed out of the vehicle and said something to the soldier who responded in French.

"What are they saying?" he asked.

"They say we shouldn't be out driving, and we need to go

back home."

"Tell him we have a sick man, and we need to get to a hospital."

She spoke in French to the man who responded and got back in his vehicle.

"What happened?" Joe asked. "Can we go now?"

"They want us to follow them to the hospital."

They got back in the van and followed the jeep across town.

"What happened?" asked Kevin. "What did they say?"

"They said it's not safe in the streets right now, so they will take us to the hospital."

Joe watched the houses go by as they drove. Garbage was piled up on the streets and many of the homes were boarded up. Some had black pieces of cloth or flags hanging in front of their house.

"What's with the black flags?" asked Joe.

Camille answered from the back as Ben coughed intermittently. "That's for the dead. If someone dies from the Scourge, you're supposed to put a black flag out front, and they'll pick up the body."

They drove up to Chateaugay General Hospital. There was a large noisy generator beside the parking lot. They pulled up to the emergency doors, and Joe helped Ben out. "I'm going to find a place to park, then we'll come and find you," yelled Kevin.

The sliding doors opened, and Joe helped Ben through. The lights flickered.

A male nurse with bright blue eyes ran up to them. "Puis-je vous aider?" he asked.

Joe regretted not bringing Camille, but she spoke up behind him.

Camille and the nurse spoke rapidly back and forth. The nurse looked briefly at Ben, then at Camille's bandaged arm. He left for a moment before returning with a wheelchair. They followed him through a pair of large automatic doors, around ripped plastic sheeting.

They walked down a hallway lined with patients on beds. It reminded Joe of St. Jude's except not near as busy.

"It's not very busy," said Joe.

Camille and the nurse talked as they walked.

"He says most Scourge patients have already died."

They entered a former cafeteria. It was now a makeshift hospital ward and was crowded from one end to the other with beds. Half of them were filled. There were no curtains or separators between the beds. Doctors and nurses walked the room tending to patients.

"Does Ben have the Scourge?" Joe asked as they helped Ben, who was uncharacteristically quiet into the bed.

Camille translated the question to the nurse who responded.

"He's not a doctor or a nurse. He doesn't know."

"He's not a nurse? Is he a volunteer? Why would anyone volunteer at a hospital during a pandemic?"

The nurse seemed to understand some of his questions. He stood in front of Joe, and his piercing blue eyes seemed to look into Joe's soul. "Qui donne aux pauvres prête à Dieu," he said and walked away.

"What did he say?"

"He who gives to the poor, loans to God."

A few minutes later, a nurse showed up and took some of Ben's blood.

Ben lay on his back, staring at the ceiling. Joe sat at his side. "Ben, are you okay? Should I be calling someone?"

"No. There's no one. My ex hates me, and my kids never even came to visit me in jail."

"Okay. If there's anything I can do for you, let me know."

"I'm glad you're here." He coughed again, and his breathing was wheezy. "You're the only friend I have left."

Beside them, Camille stood awkwardly. "In case you die, Ben, I just want to say that I'm sorry I hit you in the face yesterday."

Joe creased his brow and looked up at Camille. "He's not

going to die."

"No, it's okay, Joe. She's right, I'm not going to make it. Camille, it's okay that you hit me. It means you're tough. Tougher than me. You are going to survive in this crazy new world. I'm a nerdy overweight accountant. I was never going to make it."

Tears started to build in Joe's eyes.

A doctor came by with a clipboard. "Quel est ton nom?" he asked Ben.

Camille translated. "He wants to know your name."

With Camille's translation, Ben gave his name, age, birthplace and current address of residence.

Then his tone turned somber as he relayed the news, they all knew was coming.

"He says you have the virus," she told Ben. "He wants to give you something to help ease your suffering, but says you won't make it through the night."

Ben nodded, and the Doctor made an injection into his arm. "Je suis désolé," he said and left.

"Camille, why don't you go find the others and tell them where we are."

He sat beside Ben; their hands clasped. Ben looked up at him, "Take care of our little gang, okay?"

Tears leaked out of his eyes and a large lump formed in the back of his throat. He couldn't talk and didn't know what to say. Joe squeezed Ben's hand tighter.

"I'm just going to take a little nap," said Ben and closed his eyes.

"Good night Benaiah." Joe sat on the floor with his back up against the bed. The tears flowed down his cheeks and his grief exploded into hitching sobs.

The others came by, and Kevin said a little prayer. Nurses and doctors checked on Ben once in a while, but he never woke up. He died in his sleep later that afternoon.

A doctor checked on Camille's arm, re-wrapped it and gave her some antibiotics.

Joe walked out of the hospital in a numbed daze. They all

got back into the old brown van and drove away. Without Ben, most of the drive was silent.

CHAPTER 26

Monique, Olivia, Ayesha, Zach and Roxie drove towards Commerce City in the police car, but this time Zach didn't blare the siren or turn on the lights. The attack at the mansion and their hasty escape had taken a toll on all of them. It was late, and their adrenaline levels had subsided. The wind was picking up, and the blowing snow was making it hard to see. This was made worse by the fact that the road wasn't plowed.

"Where are we going?" asked Ayesha.

"We need a warm place to sleep for the night," answered Monique.

Zach looked out the window. "It looks like the electricity is out everywhere, I don't see any lights."

The capital city of Commerce was spread over a large area. It had a river on one side but was surrounded on all other sides by forest and farmland.

They drove through the blowing snow with frozen fields and trees on both sides. The whiteout conditions forced Monique off the road. They could barely see a few metres in front of them when they pulled off to the side.

"Is that a mailbox?" said Ayesha, pointing in front of them.

Monique flicked the high beams on and could just make out the outline of a mailbox through the snow. "If there's a mailbox, there must be a house here somewhere, but I can't see a driveway."

"I think there's a spotlight outside your window," said Zach from the back, "and I think the baby's hungry or something."

Olivia was crying. Monique found the handle for the spotlight at the bottom of her window. She was able to point it by turning the handle. They were able to navigate the long straight driveway which led them to a farmhouse on the left. There was a barn further down on the right. She stopped in front of the house and turned off the car. They were left in complete darkness.

"Whoa!" said Zach, "that's dark!"

Monique turned the car back on. "Okay, everybody get your flashlights."

She opened the car door, and an icy blast hit her. Monique closed it quickly. "Change of plans," she said as she started the car back up. "You all stay here, and I will go in a see if they have a fireplace I can get started. Once I know it's safe, and I have a fire going, I'll come back to get you."

Olivia's crying got louder.

"Maybe you should feed the baby," said Zach. "I can go start a fire."

"And what are you going to do if there's somebody in there?" asked Monique.

"It doesn't look like anybody's home," he answered.

"It's not safe, Zach," said Ayesha.

"Give me a gun, then," said Zach.

"I'll go inside to see if anybody's home and then come back. Then you can go start a fire while I feed Olivia."

Monique walked up to the front door and knocked. There was no sound from inside. She tried the door handle and was surprised when it opened.

Inside was just as cold as outside, but there was less wind and snow.

"Hello?" she called out softly into the darkness. Then louder, "Anybody home?"

Nobody answered. She turned her flashlight on and shone it around the small boot room. She opened a second door that led into a large eat-in kitchen and called out again, but nobody answered.

She ran back to the car to feed Olivia, who was now crying full throttle. Zach, Ayesha and Roxie left the car and went into the house. There was a wood stove in the kitchen with a small pile of kindling and wood. The two of them were able to start a fire, but had to figure out the damper before the house filled with smoke. By the time Monique came back, the stove was warm. They closed the doors to the kitchen to keep the heat in. Monique found some blankets in a hall closet, and they all cuddled by the stove. Monique snuggled close to Olivia, and the dog lay between them and Ayesha and Zach.

"You know what I could really go for right now?" asked Zach.

"What?" said Ayesha.

"Chocolate. A chocolate bar, a box of chocolates, smarties, chocolate ice cream, a chocolate macaroon or even a chocolate bunny."

"It's not Easter," said Ayesha.

"I know, and I won't get chocolate for Christmas either, but I can still dream."

"Sometimes it's good to think of things we love," said Monique, "when life is sad."

They managed to sleep a little before the sun rose and the wood stove ran out of wood.

"I'm freezing," complained Ayesha a few hours later.

"Me too," said Zach.

"Okay, let's get moving then," said Monique. I'm going to try to find some food in this kitchen and then make sure there is no one else in this house. You two can go out to the barn and see if you can find some firewood."

"Can't we stay inside?" complained Ayesha, "and look for food?"

Zach was nodding.

"If you find a dead body upstairs, are you going to drag the decomposing corpse outside and bury it?" asked Monique.

Zach nudged Ayesha, "I'm going to the barn."

"Wait for me!"

The weather had warmed up considerably, and some of the snow was melting under the morning sun. Ayesha and Zach walked through the slush to the barn. Roxie ran off to investigate all the new farm smells.

A snowdrift held the barn door shut, and they were unable to open it. Ayesha found a shovel nearby and started hacking at the snow.

"Here," said Zach, "let me try." For most of Zach's 12 years, he had always been a chubby, nerdy kid who wasn't into sports or any other strenuous activity. Over the last few months, that had changed. The rationed food forced him to diet, and he was getting a lot more exercise. Whether it was helping to clean the big mansion or running around the yard with Ayesha and the dog, his level of physical activity was raised significantly. However, the shoveling still left him breathless and sore. When enough of the snow had been removed, they opened the barn door and stepped inside. The barn was old and dusty but was intact enough to keep the snow out.

To the right was a tractor and other large farming machinery. To the left were stalls and some wooden doors. They found a tack room filled with saddles, riding helmets and to the right a row of empty stalls. Many of them opened up to the fenced-in field behind the barn. When they walked to the back of the barn, they looked across a snowy fenced-in field.

Ayesha pointed to a large gap in the fence. "Looks like the animals escaped."

"Or the farmer let them free before they left," said Zach.

There was a noise behind them in the barn.

"What was that?" asked Ayesha.

They slowly walked back into the barn towards the noise.

"I don't think we checked the far stall," said Zach. They heard the shuffling sound of hay moving. Just before they got to the stall, a black cat dashed across their path and into a hole in the wall.

Zach jumped and screamed, "Ahhh!"

"Are you afraid of a cat?" said Ayesha, laughing. She opened the stall door.

Zach shook his head. "It just surprised me, that's all."

He looked where the cat disappeared and then backed into the stall. When he turned around, he was hit in the face with a wet spray. He fell backwards, his glasses were covered in wet slime. When he looked up, he saw a furry white llama looking back at him.

Ayesha was laughing harder now.

"You could have warned me!"

"That wouldn't be much fun."

Zach wiped most of the llama spit off his glasses. He looked up and saw that there were two llamas. One was white and the other black. The back door in the stall was open to the field.

Ayesha was petting the black one. "Why do you think they're still here?"

"I don't know," said Zach, "maybe they didn't want to leave."

Ayesha closed the stall door, and they finished searching the barn. They didn't see the cat again and couldn't find any firewood, so they headed back to the house.

Back in the kitchen, Monique was loading the stove with wood. "I found firewood in the room off the back," she said. She closed the door to the stove. "And I found some food." She pointed to the table at some canned food including brown beans, pears, corn and sardines. "We can all pick one can to open, and we'll pack the rest."

They sat down at the table and started to open their cans.

"We have a problem," said Monique, "That is all the food I could find in this house, and there's not much wood left. We can't stay here, and the police car is almost out of gas. Did you see any gas cans in the barn?"

"I think there were a few cans of diesel, but I didn't see any gas," said Zach.

"We need transportation to get to Commerce City," said

Monique as she scooped some brown beans on the floor for Roxie. "I don't know how to drive a tractor, and I don't know if we'd all fit. I suppose we could start walking, but I need a way to carry Olivia and some of this food, in case it takes more than a day to reach the city."

Zach offered his corn to Ayesha, "Trade?"

She shrugged and gave him her can of pears.

"Are you two listening to me?" asked Monique sternly. "We are a team. If you want to survive, you need to learn, you need to adapt, and you need to be smart." She pointed to her head. "Otherwise, you will die."

Ayesha stopped eating the corn and looked down.

Zach kept eating. "I know how we can do it."

"Would you care to enlighten us?" asked Monique.

He swallowed his pears and searched the sugary juice for the last wedge. "There are two llamas in the barn. I think they can be used as pack animals. We could hook up a sled and put Olivia and the food in it. If we took both of them, we could take the guns and some blankets." He put the can up to his mouth and drank the peach juice.

"You're a genius," said Monique.

"I know."

Ayesha named the llamas Dora and Boots. There was only one sled which they tied to Dora. Olivia sat in an old baby carrier that they put in the sled. They tied their packs and some bags with their supplies to the back of Boots. The sun had melted more of the snow and it was a couple degrees above freezing. They sloshed through the snow up the driveway and onto the road. Roxie bounced around chasing rabbits, and sniffing trees.

"What will we do when we get to Commerce?" asked Ayesha.

"Our main concern is food and shelter. There should be some of both once we get into the city."

"I say we find a chocolate factory," said Zach.

"Yeah," Ayesha agreed.

"I could go for some chocolate," said Monique.

Later, as they continued walking down the empty road, Ayesha spoke up. "Do you think Laurel and Blender are in Heaven?"

"I hope so," said Monique.

"Do you believe in God?" asked Ayesha.

"Yes, I do."

"Why would God let so many people die?"

"Some people believe God has a plan. Some think this is a result of sin."

"What do you believe?" asked Ayesha.

"I believe that God has given us the gift of living another day and that He would want us to keep going."

CHAPTER 27

Joe, Kevin, Tank and Camille left the hospital and made it to the highway on-ramp before they had to stop.

A large military roadblock stood between them and the highway. Two large military transport vehicles were parked sideways on the road, and there were sandbags in the ditches on the side. Three soldiers with machine guns faced them. Their guns were all pointed in their direction. One of the soldiers walked towards them. Joe got out of the vehicle.

"Don't shoot!" he yelled with his hands in the air.

"Everybody out of the vehicle!" one of the soldiers shouted.

Kevin, Tank and Camille slowly got out of the vehicle.

"Everybody put your hands on the vehicle," the soldier yelled as he got closer. The other soldiers surrounded them. After being thoroughly searched, they all stood as ordered, in a line in front of the vehicle.

"Do you have any weapons in the vehicle?" one of the soldiers asked.

Tank spoke up. "We have a compound bow and some knives."

The soldier looked past Tank to the van. "Who else is in the vehicle?"

"Just my dog," replied Joe.

"Your welcome to pet it," Camille added.

"Are we under arrest?" asked Kevin.

"Not yet. You do know there is a state of martial law, right?"

"I didn't know that, sir."

"Why not? Where have you been?"

"I haven't listened to the news in a while."

"All non-essential travel is prohibited. You need to get back in your vehicle and go back home."

"We are *trying* to get back home. We live in Ingerwood, Ontario."

"Never heard of it."

"It's west of Commerce on the highway."

"The highway has been closed. If you don't live here, then you will need to go to the nearest C3."

"What's a C3?"

"It's a community command centre. They have running water, food, shelter and heat."

"What? No!" said Kevin, "My wife is looking after our baby girl, and I need to get back to her."

"I'm sorry, sir, that won't be possible. You need to go to the nearest C3."

"I don't want to go to a C3. I need to get back to my wife and daughter!" Kevin was yelling now.

"Sir, you need to calm down."

"Calm down? How am I supposed to calm down when you're telling me I can't be with my family?"

"Look, you want my advice?" He stepped closer to Kevin and leaned in. "Go to the C3 and send her a message. Most of the cell and internet networks are down, but there is a dedicated emergency network. Officially, it's operated by what's left of the military and government officials. Unofficially it's used to send messages between cities. If your wife is at a C3, you might be able to communicate with her. Then you'll at least know if she's okay."

"Thank you, sir," said Joe.

"Okay, get back in your vehicle and turn around. Do you know where the closest C3 is?"

"I do," said Camille.

They all climbed back in the van. Joe did a U-turn and drove back the way they came. Camille gave directions to the C3.

"Have *you* been to one of these C3's?" asked Kevin as he drove through the light snow.

"I've seen them - they look like homeless shelters."

"Where have you been living?" Joe asked her.

"With a friend from school. Our families died, so we moved into the nicest empty house on the block."

"Where's your friend now?"

"She died."

"Why were you at the mall?"

"I was bored and sad, so I decided to do some shopping." Camille changed the subject. "Does this mean you guys aren't going to drive me to Commerce?"

"Was it your brother that was in Commerce?" asked Joe.

"Yes, Pascal was going to University there. He's all I have left."

"Well, we're still going," said Kevin. "I'm not abandoning my family, and Commerce is sort of on the way. However, I would like to at least send Monique a message, so she knows I'm coming back."

They drove up to a small community centre, which was in a small suburb near the edge of the city. The parking lot was almost full. There was a large contingent of military vehicles parked near the entrance.

Joe, Kevin, Camille, and Tank got out of the vehicle. The dog jumped out too but didn't follow them. They walked up to the entrance, while the dog sat at a safe distance from the entrance and watched them. There was a soldier with a clipboard who met them at the doors and asked for their names.

"We don't want to stay here," said Joe. "We just want to send a message."

"Sorry, but no one goes in without registering," the soldier replied.

They all gave him their names, which he studiously wrote down on his clipboard.

"No weapons, no fighting, and no pets." The soldier pointed

to the dog outside.

"Fine," said Joe and looked back at the dog. "Sit, dog! Stay! We'll be right back."

"You really should name your dog, Joe," said Camille.

The dog looked at them for a moment and trotted off.

"Looks like you won't have to, he just ran away," said Kevin.

The soldier led them through a door. Inside, the air was warm and stuffy. He handed the top paper on his clipboard to a pretty brunette with short-cropped hair and brown eyes. "This is Corporal Callaghan."

Callaghan motioned them forward, pointing to a large table filled with neat little piles, each individually wrapped in clear plastic. "Grab your supplies, people. In your package, you will find your bedroll, pillow, soap, toothbrush, toothpaste and other essentials for your stay."

She led them down through double doors into a lobby area. Another soldier walked by and Callaghan asked him, "Private, did we resolve the heater situation yet?"

"No, Ma'am, but we're working on it."

"Well, get to it Private. I will not have all these people freezing to death under my command."

"Yes, Ma'am." He hurried away.

A few men and women were sitting around, but the lobby was mostly quiet. "To your right is the nurse's station, which is manned 24/7. If you have any type of medical issue, that is where you go. To your left is administration, which is where I sit. If you need any other supplies or information, you can make your requests there. Showers are in the next building."

They walked through a set of doors and then onto the iceless skating rink. The rink had been converted into a small city, resembling a methodically arranged tree. The trunk was a walkway that ran along the middle of the rink. Smaller pathways branched off to the right and left. These gave access to rooms of various sizes neatly separated with dividers.

"Reminds me of my last place," said Joe.

Men, women, boys, girls and babies all walked, talked and

played. At the base of the tree was the cafeteria. "Meals are at 7:00, 12:00 and 17:00," Callaghan continued.

"Okay, hold on," said Kevin, "We don't even need to stay here. All we need is to send a message to my wife back home."

"That won't be possible," she said curtly.

Kevin put his hand on her arm, "Why not? She's alone with our baby and…"

"Please remove your hand, sir."

"Oh, sorry…Ma'am. It's just that we were told that you had an emergency network system thing that we could send a message to another C3."

"I'm sorry, but that's for official use only."

"But this is really important," he pleaded.

"It's not to be used for personal use, sir. Those are my orders."

"Can't you make an exception?"

She continued staring forward and ignored the question. "Please find an empty room and make yourself comfortable. If you have any other questions, feel free to let me know. I'll be in the administration office."

She turned abruptly and marched away. Joe watched her leave.

Tank leaned over to him. "She's pretty, isn't she, Joe?"

He caught himself staring and immediately looked away. "What…no…I mean yes…I mean I didn't notice."

Camille was smiling. "Oh, I think you noticed. You may also have noticed that she seems colder than the snow we drove through to get here."

Joe was saved by an older man with wild grey hair that hung past his shoulders and a scruffy white beard. "Hello, there fellow travelers." He had a wide grin and bright blue eyes and walked over to them with a slight limp. "The name's Earl."

Kevin, Joe, and Tank introduced themselves and shook his hand.

"I see you met Cool Callaghan."

Camille looked over at Joe. "I told you."

"Yeah, she's not exactly the friendliest person here," Earl continued, "but she does get the job done. Speaking of cool, is it just me or is it getting colder in here?" He rubbed his arms, trying to warm them up.

"Do you think that someone else might let us send a message?" asked Kevin.

"Maybe. Walk with me and I'll see if I find you guys a decent room." They walked to the far end. "These cell walls aren't soundproof, but this room may give you a bit of privacy."

The room had five cots, a small table, and some empty boxes that Joe assumed were for storage. There was a privacy curtain boxing in one of the corners that had a small bench. In the centre was a dining table with six chairs. On one side were three comfortable chairs, a side table and some books.

"Wow, we're supposed to live here?" asked Camille.

"I know," said Earl, "you'd be better off finding an empty house. This place is more for those who can't take care of themselves."

Joe set his backpack down and sat on one of the chairs. "So why are you here?"

Earl stood in the doorway. "I hurt my ankle. It seemed like a better place than the hospital, and I prefer the cuisine. My ankle is much better now, so I will be hitting the proverbial road soon to find a more hospitable establishment." He said the last two words with a mock English accent. "Anyway, too-da-loo, boys and girls, good luck sleeping." He laughed again and left.

Kevin sat on the chair opposite Joe, while Camille and Tank sat on both ends of the couch.

"This place sucks," said Camille.

"I know," said Joe, "We'll be leaving tomorrow."

"*After* we send a message to Monique," added Kevin.

"Is it 17:00 yet?" asked Camille, cause I'm hungry.

"Where's your watch?" asked Tank.

"I left it behind in the last millennium, old man. There's a little thing called a cell phone. It tells the time, *and* it lets you communicate with the world."

"And where's yours?"

"It's dead along with all the cell networks."

"Bet you wish you had a watch now."

"Oh yeah, and where's yours, Captain America?"

"It interferes with my grapple."

Kevin broke up the exchange. "It's 16:50."

"That's ten to five," Tank said to Camille.

"I knew that," she retorted.

"Close enough, for me," said Joe. "Let's go find some food."

Earl was right, the food was good. They enjoyed roast chicken with potatoes and green beans. Earl joined them at the table in the noisy cafeteria.

"How are the lights and heat still on?" Kevin asked Earl. "I thought the power was out."

"They have generators for electricity, and they use propane for cooking. Their boiler system is supposed to be keeping us warm, but I heard it's not working right." Earl blew into his fist. "That's why it's getting colder in here."

That night, Joe fell in and out of sleep. He blamed his uneasy sleep on the noises and voices of the other refugees that echoed through the building.

Early the next morning, he woke up cold. The blanket that he had been given, wasn't enough to keep him warm. The temperature in the building had dropped significantly. He pulled off his covers, sat up and grabbed his coat. Kevin was tossing in his sleep while Tank snored. Camille was half asleep, shivering under her blankets. Joe took his blanket and put it over her before leaving. He walked out of the rink and into the lobby. He found Callaghan in the administration room sitting at her desk, bright-eyed and alert.

She looked up from the desk. "You look like you didn't sleep much."

He tried to rub some of the sleep out of his eyes. "I take it you haven't had much luck fixing the boiler."

"That's not your concern. It's being handled."

"I may be able to help."

She looked at him and paused for a moment. He used the moment to admire her facial features. Her skin was smooth and flawless, her piercing brown eyes...

She interrupted his thoughts. "What kind of qualifications do you have? Are you an engineer?"

"No, not exactly. I've done maintenance on three buildings for the last ten years."

"So, you're a maintenance man?"

"Two of the buildings I work in have a boiler heating system. One of them is about 100 years old, and I fix it all the time."

"So, you can't be very good if you have to keep fixing it."

"Look, do you want my help or not?"

"I guess it wouldn't hurt for you to take a look."

The two of them walked out of the lobby, through a doorway in the far end and down a dimly lit hallway.

Joe attempted small talk. "My name's Joe."

"Callaghan," she replied.

"So, do you have a family?"

"No, not anymore."

"How long have you been stationed here?"

"Two weeks."

They walked through a narrow doorway and into the boiler room. She pressed a button on a temporary LED light stand. It lit up the room and the boiler.

"Here it is," she said. "It's working, but it's not putting out much heat. I'm not an engineer, so that's all I know. Tools are over there, and there's a shelf with spare parts in the back. Don't break anything. Let me know if you need anything else. I'll be in my office." She turned and left.

The boiler was not the same model he was used to working on, but it had a similar design. He soon discovered the problem. The boiler had dirty burners and a faulty ignition switch. He was able to clean the burners, but was unable to find a replacement for the ignition switch on the shelves of spare parts. He went back to Callaghan to inform her.

From outside the administration office, he could hear Kevin talking with Callaghan.

"Can you please send a *little* message?" Kevin asked.

"I'm sorry, but it's against official policy," she answered.

"Aren't you in charge here? Can't you change the policy?

"I don't think so." She looked over at Joe as he walked into the room. "Joe, did you fix it?"

"Not yet, but I know what's wrong with it."

"What?"

"I'll make you a deal. I will fix it if you let my friend Kevin send a message to his wife."

"Are you blackmailing me?"

"No, I'm just making you an offer. I will fix your boiler, so all these people don't freeze to death, and you will help a new father who risked his life to save me, talk to his wife."

She looked at them with no expression for several moments.

"Fine. Just so you know, the emergency network is not very reliable, and it is by no means a phone system where you just have a conversation. We can send a message, but there is no guarantee that she will get it."

"That's fine," said Kevin, "Thank you, thank you very much, I appreciate it. Now how do I do this?"

"Hold on there, Mr. Hasty. First things, first. I need Joe to fix the boiler."

"I will need a new ignition switch."

"Okay, let me know what one looks like and where to get it. I'll send my men to retrieve one."

"I don't know the model number, but I suppose I could remove the broken one, and they could see if they can find a similar one."

"My men are good at what they do, but mechanical engineering is not what they do. You need to go with them."

"Wait. What?"

"Private Monty, get in here!" she yelled, and a well-built

dark-haired soldier stepped into the room.

"Ma'am." He stood at attention.

"You will take Lewis, Paquette, and Wortley and escort Joe here to the nearest mechanical supply store. He will assist you in locating an ignition switch, which you will bring back here as quick as is humanly possible."

"Yes, Ma'am!"

"Whoa, hold on a second here," Joe protested. "What about Kevin's message?"

"Please," Kevin pleaded. "I really would like to talk to her as soon as possible, so she knows I'm alright".

"Fine," she acquiesced. "You need to go now with my men, and I will see about this message." She motioned for Kevin to sit down.

"You're not coming then?" Joe asked.

"No," she said, "I will not. Now get out of here before I change my mind, and Monty, get him a vest."

CHAPTER 28

Neither Monique, Zach or Ayesha had a working watch, but since the sun appeared to be at its highest point, Monique assumed it was near noon. Zach and Ayesha were hungry and they were all tired. They had been walking with the llamas from the farmhouse, for a couple of hours.

Monique looked at the boarded-up gas station they were passing and announced, "Let's stop here for some lunch and a break."

Roxie's ears perked up, and she let out a single bark, her nose pointing down the road. "Get off the road, now!" yelled Monique.

As they shuffled into the gas station parking lot, they heard the sound of diesel engines. As they watched, jeeps, armoured personnel carriers and military trucks with canvas-covered backs rumbled by. Five minutes later, the procession ended.

"Are we at war now?" asked Zach.

"I hope not," said Monique. "You two need to find the bag with the hay and feed the llamas."

"Dora and Boots," Ayesha corrected her.

"I'm going to see if there is any food in the store," said Monique.

She managed to bend back one of the plywood boards using the squeegee from the gas pumps and smash the window. After climbing into the store, she stood in complete darkness. She turned on her flashlight and her mouth dropped and then closed into a wide smile. She went to the back of the store and unlocked the door.

"Did you tie the llamas up?" she asked when she reached the front of the station.

"Yes, they're all fed and secure," said Zach. "Did you find anything in the store?"

Monique picked up Olivia from the sled. "Oh yeah, I sure did." She started walking around to the back of the station. "Come with me."

They all followed her, including Roxie, who ran ahead sniffing.

When they reached the back door, Monique said, "After you." She opened the door for them.

Ayesha and Zach walked tentatively through the back door and turned on their flashlights.

"Whoa!" they both said at the same time. The store shelves were full. There were chips, candy, chocolate bars, pop, gum, pepperettes, beef jerky and a wide assortment of other junk food.

They attacked the store with wild abandon.

"Don't open the freezers, and don't eat anything that could go bad," Monique called after them. She grabbed a three musketeers bar, and a bottle of vanilla coke and sat behind the counter. She breast-fed Olivia while satisfying her sugar cravings.

The kids were ecstatic. The store was dark, and they used their flashlights to illuminate the sweet, sour and salty wonders. Monique watched with satisfaction as their beams of light bounced around the store. The sound of their young voices sharing in each other's discoveries. The crinkle of wrappers was punctuated with exclamations of delight as they uncovered new delicious treasures. Roxie got in on the excitement when Ayesha found some dog treats.

They had had a long eventful night when they left the mansion, had a short sleep at the farmhouse and then a long morning trek through the snow. They were all exhausted and were now well-fed.

The afternoon sun had warmed the air, and they all fell asleep. Monique napped slouched against the counter with Olivia resting peacefully on her chest. Monique snuggled on the bottom shelf with the toilet paper, while Zach used a jumbo-sized bag of Lay's ketchup chips as a pillow.

They slept for a long time till Roxie barked and woke Monique.

"Roxie, quiet," she yelled. Muffled voices could be heard outside.

"Get up, guys," Monique whispered. "There someone outside."

Zach and Ayesha got up quickly. They all walked quietly out the back door. Monique tried to shake the sleepy haze from her head.

"Stay here," she said before they rounded the corner to the front of the station.

There were four snowmobiles parked in front of the pumps, and four men stood outside the store. One of them was pulling at the plywood that Monique had partially pried off. Two others were going through their bags on the sled and the packs on the back of the Llama. The fourth man stood back watching. They all carried guns.

Roxie was baring her teeth and growling.

"Easy," said Monique then yelled out, "Hey, what do you think you're doing?"

They all immediately stopped and looked at her. The man standing watch pointed his shotgun in her direction.

It was at this point Monique realized that all her guns and her pepper spray were packed in the bags. She held Olivia close to her. "Don't shoot."

The man pointing the gun noticed the baby and lowered his gun slightly. "Are you armed?"

"No. I'm not. Please, don't shoot, I have a baby."

"Fine, but you need to stay where you are. If that dog attacks, I will shoot it. Stay where you are while we unburden you of your llamas."

"No!" said Ayesha as she walked into view, "Dora and Boots are ours." She crossed her little arms in defiance.

"Well, well, well," said the man, "What do we have here. I take it by the colour of this little one's skin that she is not yours. I suspect that this gas station isn't yours, and neither are these llamas. My friends and I are having a real craving for fresh meat. I'm sure that we could get a few decent steaks out of these two." He pointed at Dora and Boots with his gun.

"Shoot the llamas," he ordered his men.

Just as one of them raised his rifle at Dora's head, he was interrupted by the sound of a vehicle driving towards them.

A military vehicle pulled into the gas station.

Three heavily armed soldiers climbed out of the vehicle, pointing their rifles at the four men in front of Monique. A fourth soldier, who looked like he was the guy in charge, climbed out of the passenger seat and stepped forward.

"What's going on here Ma'am?" he asked, his hands on his hips.

"Nothing to worry about," said the man as he lowered his shotgun and held his hand up.

"I was talking to the lady," the soldier said.

"These men were trying to rob us," said Monique putting on her most vulnerable face.

The soldier looked at the man with the shotgun. "Are those your snowmobiles?"

"Yes, they are, but we were just..."

"I suggest you get on them and leave," his voice was authoritative and calm. "There is currently a state of emergency, which means I am within my rights to order my men to open fire."

The three soldiers pointing their guns all took a step forward. The shotgun man paused for a moment then boarded his snowmobile. The others followed his lead, and they sped off down the road.

"Stand down, men," he said and walked to Monique and

offered his hand. "I'm Captain Patricks."

"I'm Monique," she said and shook his hand. "Thank you so much for this."

"Are you okay, Monique?"

"I'm fine, we're just on our way to Commerce. Is it far?"

"No, Ma'am. It's about a half day's walk, but it's not safe, so you should stay out of sight." He was about to turn to leave and changed his mind. "May I make a suggestion?"

Monique was rocking Olivia, who was starting to fuss. "Of course."

"You need to arm yourself."

"We have guns," she said, "but they were in our packs when they surprised us."

"Then you should post a lookout or stay out of sight. There isn't much of a crime deterrent anymore except for what you provide yourself."

"Isn't the army going to provide law and order?" she asked.

"We have our own problems to deal with," said Captain Patricks.

"Like what?"

"Nothing you need to worry about just yet, ma'am. Have you heard of the C3's? When you get into Commerce, look for the C3 signs. They have food, water, shelter and security. They may not let you keep your llamas and dog, but it *will* be safe."

"Thank you," said Monique. "We just might check it out."

"Do you have a radio?" she said as he turned to leave.

"I do, but it's for official use only."

"I don't know where my husband is or if he's still alive, but if he is, he has no idea where I am. Is there any way you could, I don't know, find him somehow?"

"If he's alive, he may be at one of the C3's," said Captain Patricks, "They have a sort of unofficial messaging system."

"It would mean a lot to me if you could send a message out to Kevin Broderick that Monique, Ayesha and Zach are in Commerce City."

The Captain took out a notepad and wrote it down. "I'll see

what I can do. I would suggest you find yourself someplace safe soon. Things are going to get worse before they get better."

"Are people still dying of the Scourge?" she asked.

"Some, but that's not what I'm talking about. I'm not at liberty to say anything else." He signaled his men, and they all got in the vehicle and drove away.

Zach walked over to Monique. "What did he mean, things are going to get worse?"

"I don't know."

Monique decided that they would stay the night at the gas station. They tied the llamas up out of sight behind the store. Before it got dark, Monique got both of the kids to shoot the pistol a few times and try the pepper spray. Monique test fired the shotgun while she held it snug against her shoulder. This time it didn't hurt her shoulder.

They found a backup generator in the storeroom as well as a small electric heater behind the counter. With Zach's help, Monique managed to hook the heater up to the generator, so they wouldn't freeze to death in their sleep. The gas in the generator almost lasted until sunrise. When it did die, they got up and had a breakfast of orange soda, Snickers, Doritos and Little Debbie's. They packed as much food as Dora and Boots could carry and started walking towards Commerce City.

It was snowing lightly and was just below zero. Military vehicles passed by once in a while. Most of them slowed as they passed, but none of them stopped. As they walked, Monique noticed the high fences on one side of the road that were topped with razor wire. A few minutes later, they came across a big sign that read "Commerce Army Base." Beyond the sign was a short road with a big gate and a guardhouse. Guards with machine guns stood outside the gate. Roxie growled till Monique calmed her down. Ayesha waved, but nobody waved back.

"Do you think that's where Captain Patricks is?" asked Zach.

"He and a lot of other soldiers."

Beyond the gate, there was a lot of activity. It was busy with soldiers and vehicles.

"Is that a tank?" asked Zach.

Before Monique could answer, a fighter jet flew loudly overhead and appeared to land somewhere beyond the gate.

"Do they have a landing strip in there too?"

"We better keep moving," said Monique.

They continued trudging down the road through the snow, away from the army base. As they walked, their surroundings gradually changed. The country homes and farmer's fields became suburbs and stores. The gravel shoulders turned into sidewalks. The lonely fence lines disappeared and hydro poles and telephone lines appeared.

"We made it!" shouted Ayesha as they passed the *Welcome to Commerce City* sign.

A few military and other vehicles drove by, and there were a couple of other people walking the streets. The last time Monique had been here was during her honeymoon with Kevin. It was late summer, and the city was humming with excitement. It was alive with a myriad of families, children, business people, tourists, hot dog stands, and a host of people and activities. She had hoped to make it back here with the new baby to show her all the sights and sounds of the big city.

Today the city sounded like a Sunday afternoon at the library. There weren't any stores open – they were either boarded up or had been looted. There was also a lot of graffiti on the sides of buildings, bridges and windows.

Clouds had moved in, and without the sunshine, the temperature dropped.

On the right side of the road was a sign with a large brick foundation that read *Commerce City Museum*. Behind it were four interconnected buildings. The building at the front boasted an enormous glass-windowed atrium.

As they passed by the road leading to the museum, they heard a vehicle approaching behind them.

"Uh-oh," said Zach turning around, "That looks like the purple pickup truck that came through the mansion gates the

other night."
 "Warren is still alive?"

CHAPTER 29

Joe walked out of the C3 with Privates Monty, Lewis, Paquette, and Wortley. He noticed the dog sitting at a safe distance watching. He called to it, but the dog didn't move. When Joe tossed his last piece of beef jerky to the dog, it caught it in mid-air. Joe walked closer to the dog to pet it, but the dog growled, and Joe retreated.

"You coming?" yelled Monty.

"On my way."

Joe got into the armoured army Jeep, and they drove left to find the ignition switch. Private Monty drove, and Lewis fumbled with a map beside him. Joe sat in the back, wedged between Paquette and Wortley.

Paquette was a short fierce-looking woman who rarely spoke, and Wortley was a large man who seemed to always have an intense look on his face. It was a cool, grey, sunless morning. There was no snow falling, and the temperature was hovering just below freezing. A caravan of 10 army personnel carriers passed in front of them at one of the intersections. The green tarps covered the backs of the vehicles so Joe couldn't see if they were carrying people, supplies or if they were empty.

"What are they carrying?" asked Joe.

"Don't worry about it," said Monty from the front. "Nothing you need or want to know."

A short time later, they had to stop as a train flew by, leaving a trail of swirling snow in its wake.

"The trains are still running?" asked Joe.

"They are almost all that's left," said Monty. Airlines have all been shut down, and most highway traffic has been stopped. The army is trying to keep the trains running. They are fast and easier to manage."

"What do you mean easier to manage?"

"They can control the flow of people and goods. It's also safer from gangs or other security threats."

"What other security threats?"

"Nothing you need to know."

When they reached the empty parking lot of Grainger Mechanical, Monty called back to the C3 to let them know they had arrived safely. Joe was relieved to get out of the cramped quarters of the vehicle. Grainger was the largest store in a small strip mall. The mall was made up of a boarded-up spa and nail salon, a small pet store, and a looted and trashed convenience store. Joe started walking towards Grainger's, when Monty yelled, "Wait! We need to clear the place first."

"Why, there's nobody here."

Monty walked over to him. "There are a few looters and organized gangs roaming this city. If I don't bring you back safe, the Corporal will have my head."

Monty stayed back with Joe, while Paquette and Wortley cleared the store. When they came out, Wortley stayed with the vehicle while Monty, Joe and Paquette went inside.

Other than the door Paquette had kicked in, Grainger's was untouched and tidy. The store had eight aisles, all with full shelves. He found what he was looking for in an aisle at the back and grabbed three ignition switches. As he announced his find and was walking with the others back to the door, multiple shots rang out.

"Get down!" yelled Monty. Paquette may have been short, but she looked menacing as she crouched in front of him gun pointed out.

More shots were fired outside, and Wortley's voice came over Monty's radio. "Monty, come in, I've got multiple armed hostiles out here, and a big grey Hummer, over." His voice was calm but urgent.

"Roger, that Wortley. What direction, how many and what armaments? Over."

"We've got at least five behind a truck to the south."

More gunshots.

"They are armed with rifles, pistols and at least one semi-automatic, over." He was panting but still composed.

"Roger, that. I'm sending Paquette out." Monty was serious and methodical. "Joe you stick with me. Stay behind me, keep one hand on my shoulder, so I know your there. Paquette, clear the way." The three of them crouch walked to the front of the store to the last aisle by the door.

She popped her head around the corner so she could see the front door and pulled it back. When she neither heard nor felt any gunshots, she made a crouching run for the door. She kicked the door open and stepped outside.

Monty looked behind him at Joe. "Let's go. Stay low. Stay close."

Joe followed him to the door, gunshots still being exchanged outside. Suddenly he felt an intense pain in his back, and he fell forward onto Monty in front of him. He saw Monty's gun come up at the same time he heard the deafening shot above him. Joe was on all fours catching his breath when he was dragged by what he hoped was Monty. Rapid gunfire erupted all around him. When he caught his breath, he looked up to see Paquette rushing back in, her rifle spitting fire. There was a cry from the back of the store, more gunshots, and then Paquette was on the floor, not moving. Her gun lay on the floor beside her, and blood flowed out of a hole in her neck.

Joe sat on the floor staring, as Monty held the gun over his head and fired over the shelving unit. Monty looked at Joe's back. "Looks like the bullet never made it through your vest."

A shot fired from the back of the store found its way

through the shelves and pierced Monty's leg. He cried out and fell over, knocking Joe down in the process. Blood spurted out of his leg and on to the front of Joe's vest. Monty got up and pulled a grenade out of one of his many pockets. There was a ting and a click as he pulled the pin and let go of the trigger. He kept it in his hand for a full two seconds before lobbing it over the shelves.

There was a tremendous explosion, and pieces of the ceiling and glass rained down on them. Monty ignored it as he pulled out gauze and did a rapid wrap on his leg.

"Stay down," he ordered and peeked over the shelves. "I think we're clear." He crept towards the end of the shelving unit and then froze.

"Don't move!" The voice was coming from in front of Monty. Joe couldn't see the man, but he recognized the voice.

Monty stood up fully with his hands in the air, still holding his gun.

Raphael stepped out. "Drop the gun, pendejo!"

Monty dropped the gun, and it clattered to the floor.

Raphael looked around Monty at Joe, who was frozen in place. "Hola, mi amigo. I haven't seen you since our last date at the food court."

As Raphael was looking at Joe, Monty took the opportunity to grab Raphael's gun with one hand and pull out a knife with the other. The Latino reached to regain possession of the gun, which allowed Monty the opportunity to stab at him. The glancing blow sliced across his arm, and he yelped in pain. Raphael grabbed at Monty's hand which held the knife, but Monty charged at him with full force. The two of them fell backwards. As they fought, Joe ran over and picked up Paquette's gun.

"Stop!" yelled Joe. Monty and Raphael stopped fighting and looked up at Joe. Raphael stood up, holding his bleeding arm. Joe pointed the gun at Raphael's head.

"Don't move."

Raphael looked at him "You don't have the..."

Joe squeezed the trigger, and the gun recoiled in his hands.

Raphael flew backwards across the hardwood floor, blood spraying out of his shoulder. Monty immediately turned, grabbed his gun with one hand, and Joe with the other and hauled him out the front door. Joe stumbled back to his feet outside. When he looked up, he saw two men fall backwards at the same time he heard Monty's gun go off behind him.

"Go," Monty yelled. "Get in the truck and drive!"

He ran past the two dead bodies and paused for a moment when he saw Wortley lying dead in an awkward position. Monty shoved him from behind, and he continued to run to the driver's side and got in. Monty sat beside him, blood seeping through his bandage. He had a fierce look on his face. "Go," he simply said. Joe put the pedal to the floor and flew past the grey Hummer.

When they got back to the C3, Monty was treated for the gunshot wound to his leg. Joe had some minor glass and shrapnel lacerations on his neck and arms. He had large black and purple bruising on his back, and the medic said he had a bruised rib.

Joe installed the ignition switch that evening, and the temperature in the C3 rose to a comfortable temperature.

Kevin had sent a message on the C3 network and was still waiting to hear back. Joe and his friends stayed at the Chateaugay C3 for a week while they waited for a response. Joe's bruising had gone down, and so had his friend's moods. Kevin paced the room like a caged tiger. He kept praying and complaining. Every morning, and every evening he went to the administration office to ask if they'd received a message yet. He wanted to leave as soon as possible to get back to Monique, and at the same time, he needed to wait for her to respond. Tank tried to convince the army to give him a gun, but Callaghan adamantly refused. He spent his mornings practicing with his bow at a tree behind the community centre. He also taught Camille knife throwing, archery and some self-defence techniques. When she wasn't spending time learning violent skills with Tank, she was pouting about how there were no boys her age at the C3. Every day one or two more people would die, and their bodies were loaded onto a truck and taken away. The man Earl was bunking with died, and he moved into the extra bed in their room. He was often the lone upbeat voice in their room. He was quick with a joke and loved to play his harmonica.

What little news they had from the outside world was mostly bad. There were rumours of wars in Asia and Europe. Many major cities had the streets rife with viscous battles between roving gangs and the military. Nobody seemed to know the status of the current government either here or in the States. The only good news was that the Chinese had developed a vaccine that was supposed to start production soon. Meanwhile, the population of most countries was decimated and social order was almost totally broken down. The military seemed to be the only strand left holding together any sort of organization and structure.

Every morning, Joe went outside and fed the dog. It came back every morning, but still wouldn't let Joe touch him. One morning Joe went outside to throw some food for the dog when a line of troop carriers pulled into the parking lot. The weather had turned warm again, and much of the snow had either melted or had turned to slush. Corporal Callaghan came out of the building behind him. "Time to go, Joe," she said.

"What? Where?"

"Just got new orders from HQ. We're moving out. Most of the C3 populations have dwindled too much, so they are consolidating. We're moving to a larger facility downtown. You're welcome to join us."

She turned to leave but then stopped. "Oh yeah, have you seen Kevin?"

"I think he's having breakfast. Why?"

"He's got a message."

When Joe told Kevin he had a message, Kevin immediately ran to Callaghan's office.

He stood panting in front of her desk.

"What did she say?" he asked.

"The message says that Monique, Ayesha and Zach are on their way to Commerce City," she told him.

"That's it?"

"Yes, that's all it says."

"Are they at the C3 in Commerce?"

"I don't think so. It was sent by a Captain Patricks on her behalf."

"Can I send a message back?"

"You can try," she said.

"Tell her we're on our way."

Kevin was overcome with a wide range of emotions, including relief, joy, fear and confusion.

Why are they on their way to Commerce? Why aren't they at the mansion anymore? How will we find them?

What he was clear on, was that they needed to make their way to Commerce as soon as possible.

That morning felt like the end of a long weekend at a busy campground. People and army personnel milled back and forth throughout the facility. Everyone packed their belongings and piled them into the back of the army personnel carriers.

Joe gathered the group together in their little room to discuss their next move.

"Alright, people, we have to leave today, but we need to decide exactly how we do this."

"Let's just get in the van and start driving to Commerce," said Kevin.

"What about the roadblocks, how are we supposed to get around them?" asked Tank.

"Can't we just plow through them, Kamikaze style?" Camille piped in.

Earl stood at the back, "Kamikazes generally die when they crash. I'm not going with you guys if you have a death wish."

"Who invited you anyways?" Camille retorted.

"Are you saying this is an exclusive club?" asked Earl.

Kevin got back in the conversation. "There must be some back roads that can get us around."

"The back roads will be covered in snow drifts," said Tank.

The four of them argued amongst themselves till Joe yelled, "Enough!"

They all stopped talking and looked at him.

"We agree that our primary objective, as these army people would say, is to get to Commerce, right?" He didn't wait for an answer. "There are roadblocks on the highways, and the back roads may not be cleared of snow. I think we should take the train."

He was expecting the arguing to resume, but they just looked at him expectantly. "The trains are still running, and they're fast, so I think they are our best option. You are all free to make your own decision on what you want to do, including you, Earl, but I am going to find a way on to the train and go west to Commerce."

"I'm with you, Boss," said Tank.

"Me too," said Camille.

"I'm with you too," added Kevin.

Earl straightened up and raised a fist in the air. "I would be honoured to join you on your quest for freedom!" The last words were said louder for effect.

"For freedom?" asked Camille.

"Why are we going to Commerce, again?" asked Earl.

"To find my wife and child," said Kevin shaking his head.

Earl raised his fist in the air again. "...on your quest for Kevin to be reunited with his long-lost family!"

"And Joe's friends too," added Tank.

"I'm meeting up with my brother, Pascal," said Camille.

He raised his fist in the air again. "I would be honoured to join you on your epic quest to find Kevin's wife and child, Joe's friends and Camille's brother, Pascal!"

They all laughed.

"Why *are* you coming?" Camille asked.

"I always wanted to visit our grand capital and travel the country by train. Besides, I have nothing else to do." He turned to Tank. "Why are you joining this epic quest?"

"I just want to fight somebody," he answered.

"So, you're like the group's security detail?"

"Something like that."

They finished packing up their belongings, and Joe left to find Corporal Callaghan. He found her in the administration office. She was standing behind her desk. On the desk was a large empty box.

She looked up at him. "Feels like jour du déménagement," she said.

"What's that?" he asked.

"Moving day. It's a local tradition. Everyone moves on July 1st. My husband and son and I were going to buy a house out of the city. We would have moved from our little apartment to a nice little house in Charlesbourg."

Joe stood in the doorway and listened.

"On jour du déménagement, we would pack all our belongings on a big truck. Do you have any idea how hard it is to rent a truck on moving day? Maybe we would have to borrow my father-in-law's pickup truck and trailer..." she trailed off. "Now, instead of packing up to leave the city, I'm packing to go downtown." She looked down at the box. "And I have nothing to pack." Her brown eyes started to well up.

"Are you okay?"

She wiped her eyes. "Sorry. Why are you here?"

"I wanted to ask you about the trains."

"What about them?"

"How hard would it be to hitch a ride on one of them to the capital?"

"Not easy. They are for official use and are mostly used to transport essential goods or military personnel and hardware between cities."

"What about civilians?"

"No, they don't take passengers, yet."

"What do you mean, yet?"

"Once the Chinese vaccine is distributed, things will start getting back to normal."

"So, they have a vaccine?"

"From what I've heard, they not only have a vaccine but a cure."

"That's great, when will it be handed out here?"

"I don't know, for most people, it's a little late. Anyways, I'll believe it when I see it."

"So, how are we supposed to get to Commerce if the roads are blocked, and the train isn't taking passengers?"

"You seem like a resourceful group, I'm sure you'll figure it out."

"Did you want to come with us?" he asked hopefully.

She looked like she was thinking about it. "No, I can't. I have my duties here, and I have to take care of these people."

"Right, I see." He hung his head.

"I didn't tell you this…" She looked around to make sure no one was listening. "But there is a train that stops here in Chateaugay at Charny station. It continues west to Montreaux across the border into Ontario and then to the capital, Commerce City. It will be arriving at the Charny station this Saturday at midnight."

"Are they taking passengers?"

"Not exactly."

"Well, how are we supposed to…"

"As I said, you seem like a resourceful group."

"Okay, thanks. I guess I'll see you later then."

"Can you do me a favour?" she asked.

"Yes, anything," he said more enthusiastically then he intended.

She grabbed a pen and wrote an address on a piece of paper and handed it to him. "On your way to Commerce, can you check on my parents? I'm not sure they're alive, but I would like to get them a message to let them know I'm okay."

"Absolutely, I can do that. You must be worried about

them."

"A little. My Dad's a survivalist, and my Mom has a heart of gold. If anyone can survive this, it would be them. They're setup to live off the grid on a farm outside of Commerce City."

"No problem," he said, staring at her a little too long.

"I appreciate it." She leaned in and kissed him on his bearded cheek.

His eyes widened, and his face flushed. He turned in embarrassment and walked out of the room.

"Bon chance!" she called out.

CHAPTER 30

Monique realized that Zach was right. The purple truck coming up behind them was from the men that attacked them at the mansion. She had assumed Warren had died in the fire.

"Go! Now! Get inside the museum," she said. "Leave the llamas outside and take Olivia with you. Find a place to hide. I'm going to slow him down."

"Do I get a gun?" asked Zach.

Monique pulled the pistol out of her pocket and handed it to him. "This is a last resort only." She reached into one of the bags and pulled out the pepper spray. "Ayesha put this in your pocket. You need to be close if you are going to use this. Aim for the eyes." She looked at Roxie and pointed to Ayesha and Olivia. "Protect!"

The truck slowed down as it drove closer. Monique crouched behind the Museum sign as Ayesha, Zach, Olivia, Roxie and the llamas scurried towards the Museum.

The purple truck weaved back and forth on the road and then stopped. The door opened, and a man staggered out. At first glance, Monique wondered why the man was wearing short sleeves in winter. But as she got a better look, she could see why. He had a large bandage wrapped around his left shoulder with blood seeping through. His arms had angry, bulbous red blisters. The side of his head was covered in festering purple and black burns and his face wore a sneering grimace.

"Don't come any closer!" yelled Monique, standing behind the sign. She held the shotgun firmly against her shoulder, aimed above his head and fired.

The man flinched, then reached into the truck and pulled out a hunting rifle with a scope. Monique aimed her shotgun at him and pulled the trigger. There was a click but nothing else.

I'm out of ammo already?

She ran towards the museum and veered to the side towards the llamas. She put the shotgun down and started going through the packs looking for the shells. Before she found them, a bullet hit the side of the building beside her. She felt pieces of brick raining down on her. Monique took off into the museum. The atrium was lit up from the front windows. It was a large open space with a large reception counter. She stopped for a moment and listened for the others, but heard nothing. She ran down a hallway past some totem poles and into a large room lit only by one small window. The room contained artifacts, including a birch bark canoe, moccasins, a tepee, pottery and glass case with arrowheads. She frantically looked around for anything she could use as a weapon. The drunken assailant could be heard stumbling into the building.

Inside one of the display cases she spotted a wooden mohawk war club. It had a long handle the size of a crowbar, and the club end featured a large rounded ball. She had to break the display case with her foot to get it. The sound of the glass shattering echoed throughout the museum. She grabbed the club and hid inside the tepee. She stood poised beside the entrance with the club held over her head with both hands.

"I know you're out therrrre," the man slurred. "You took all that I had left in this world, you stupeeed blatch." He stumbled into the indigenous exhibit room.

"I don't know if you killed my Mom and Daaad, but I know you took their house. Then you killed my furrrends. We deeedn't want to hurt no one, and if you had just left, nooobody would have gottened hurt. But ooooh nooo! You guys start shooting at us in myyyyyy house! Now my friends are aaaall dead. My parents are deeeead. My house is all burned up. My arm is kiiilling me, and my face is tooootally messed up. My friend Jack Daniels helps a little biiit. Do you have aaaany idea how hard it is to shoot this gun with one arm when your druuunk? Did you know I was gooooing to be Warren Masterson, Esquire? I was a crack shot with this thing tooooo. I was going places. I was someone. But you? Who are you? You are a thief, a vandal and a murderer. Before I die, I will serrrrve justice this one last tiiiime."

His voice started fading as he left the room and walked down the corridor.

Monique quietly walked out of the tepee and followed him. In the distance, there was the unmistakable sound of a baby crying.

"It's the end of the wooorld people! This is nooo time to bring a child into this dyyying world. You took my family and myyyyy home. Now I will put youuu and your fammily out of their misssery."

She raced down the corridor, but couldn't see him. At the end of the corridor there was a sign with three arrows. One read, Pioneer Exhibit and pointed to a door that led outside, one read, Fur Trade Exhibit and pointed to a doorway to the right. The third arrow pointed straight ahead and indicated several other exhibits deeper into the building.

She could no longer hear Olivia crying, but Monique thought she heard Warren in the fur trade room and stepped inside. The room was dark, and there was a little light coming in from the entrance. She crept forward with her club at the ready, listening intently.

God, if your there, give me strength.

The further she walked into the room, the darker it got. She reached into her pocket and fished out her flashlight. She turned it on and saw Warren standing just a few metres in front of her.

Monique dove to the side as a shot echoed loudly. There was a sudden searing pain in her thigh, and she knew she had been shot. Her hands instinctively grabbed at the wound, and the club bounced on the floor. Monique looked up to see the dark shape of Warren standing over her. The gun was hanging by its strap on his shoulder, and he held the flashlight with his good hand.

Monique realized the club was out of reach, and the pain in her leg was intense.

"There you arrrre! Time to meet you maker you murderrring thief." Warren put the flashlight in his mouth and removed the rifle from his shoulder.

There was a gunshot from behind him, scaring both Warren and Monique. Warren swung around to find Zach pointing the pistol at him.

"Youuu missed!" said Warren. He still hadn't managed to get his gun in a one-handed firing position and instead flung his rifle at the boy with surprising strength. It wheeled end over end across the dark room before the butt-end of the gun struck Zach in the forehead. He fell over backwards as his glasses were knocked off his face.

Olivia, who was with Ayesha behind the snowshoe display, started crying. Warren removed the flashlight from his mouth and took a step in their direction. He stopped in his tracks when he heard a low growl from Roxie. Warren pointed the flashlight down and saw the dog baring its gleaming white canines. Just as he made a slight movement towards the knife sheathed at his side, Roxie was airborne. Warren fell backwards as the dog's jaws locked onto his arm, and he cried out in pain. With all his strength, rage, and adrenaline, he grabbed the knife with his other arm and slashed at the dog. He managed to hit Roxie with the hilt of the knife, briefly stunning her. The next strike sliced across Roxie's back, and she yelped and let go of his arm. Warren kicked at the dog hard, sliding it across the floor. He reached out to grab his rifle while Monique struggled to reach for her club. He was on his knees when he reached his gun and was having trouble manoeuvring the gun into a firing position with two injured arms.

There was the sound of spraying, and he screeched in agony, reaching for his burning eyes and face. Ayesha stood beside him with the pepper spray in her hands.

There was a gunshot. His screeches were cut short as his head exploded. Monique shone her flashlight and saw a thin trail of smoke rising from the barrel of the pistol in Zach's hand.

"That's gross!" said Ayesha looking at Warren on the ground.

"Is Olivia, okay?" asked Monique.

"Yes," answered Ayesha, "I wrapped her up in one of the fur blankets behind that counter."

Zach walked to the corner of the room and vomited.

Roxie shuffled over whining and lay down beside Olivia.

"You need to get that wound taken care of," said Zach looking at Monique.

Ayesha yelled at Zach, "make sure Olivia's okay and give me your belt."

Zach was about to protest but realized the seriousness in her voice. He pulled his belt off, threw it to her and ran to Olivia.

He wiped the puke off his chin and picked up Olivia awkwardly in a bundle of fur pelts. Roxie sat beside him.

Ayesha went to Monique with the belt.

"What are you doing?" Monique asked.

"We have to stop the bleeding, lift your leg," said Ayesha.

"Do you know what you're doing?"

"My mother was a nurse; I know first aid. Point the flashlight here."

She looped the belt under her leg and put it through the buckle. "Pull on the end as hard you can," she instructed Monique. When the belt was tight, she tried to put the prong in the hole. She realized there were no holes that far down the belt. "Maybe we can use the bad man's knife to cut a new hole."

They cut a new hole in the belt and secured it firmly around her leg and then placed a wool blanket from the exhibit on the wound. Monique cuddled Olivia with one arm and held the blanket against her leg with the other.

Ayesha went to the dog to assess its condition. Roxie had a slice across her back that was still bleeding a little.

"We need to get everyone out into the light, so I can tend to these wounds," said Ayesha.

Zach found his glasses and put them on. There was a crack in one of the lenses, and the nose piece was barely holding on. He turned his flashlight on and walked to the other side of the room. Moments later, he returned, dragging a contraption consisting of two long wooden poles attached to leather netting at one end.

"What is that?" asked Ayesha.

"It's a travois, drag sled, or wilderness wheelbarrow. It's a traditional Native American transportation device used for carrying loads overland. It was attached to a person, dog or horse," he answered.

"You knew all that?" she asked.

"No, that's what the plaque said." He set the travois down. "If Monique can climb aboard, I will get Dora and some rope."

They managed to drag Monique into the Atrium, where the warm afternoon sun shone through the windows.

Roxie's cut had stopped bleeding and wasn't as deep as they had feared. Zach had big red bump on his head. Monique, on the other hand, had a hole in the lower part of her thigh. The bullet had passed through, but they didn't think it had gone through any of the bones. The bleeding had slowed, but Ayesha needed a way to clean and sew the wound closed.

Monique started feeding the baby. "Zach, I need you to go through this place and find a first aid kit, and if possible, a needle and thread. Ayesha, you need to bring our packs in here and tie the llamas up out of sight."

Twenty minutes later, Ayesha and Zach returned. The llamas were safely tied up in the side parking lot. Zach had found a first aid kit, some alcohol, fishing line and a hook in the History of Fishing exhibit. They broke the barb off the hook, and Monique helped Ayesha clean and suture both the entry and exit wounds.

They gathered some fur pelts together, sat on them and had a late lunch.

"I'll be honest with you guys," said Monique, "We are in a bit of a jam here. I don't know what to do."

"Didn't that soldier say that there was a C3 with food and heat and stuff?" asked Ayesha.

"That's true, but I don't know where it is, and I don't know if the llamas could carry me anyway. We have shelter and some food, but without a heat source, we're going to freeze to death."

"I have an idea," said Zach. "I took a look out the door that had the Pioneer Exhibit sign. There's a little log cabin with a chimney. It may have a wood stove in it."

"That is an excellent idea!" said Monique. "After you're done eating, why don't you check it out?"

The pioneer exhibit was an old one-story relocated log cabin. It was constructed of massive logs and had three rooms. Half the cabin contained a sitting area, kitchen, and fireplace. The other half was divided into two rooms. There was a large firewood pile stacked outside the door.

That evening they sat in the cozy cabin listening to the sound of the hot crackling fire. Olivia slept soundly, cuddled in rabbit pelts gently rocking in the old wooden rocking chair on Monique's lap. Roxie curled up in front of the fire at her feet. Ayesha and Zach sat at the old oak table, eating smarties and ketchup chips.

"You know," said Monique, "we are going to need to find some real food eventually."

Ayesha was stuffing ketchup chips in her mouth. "What? This is real food."

"I agree," said Zach, separating his smarties on the table by colour.

Monique shook her head. "I suppose we had a bit of a rough day, so maybe we deserve some junk food."

"I'll need therapy," said Zach, "but chocolate will have to do for now."

Monique held her hand out. "Can I get some Smarties, please?"

Zach looked down at his little piles. "What colour?"

CHAPTER 31

The C3 parking lot was a flurry of activity as soldiers and civilians loaded the trucks and prepared to leave. Joe, Kevin, Tank, Camille and Earl made their way to the van. Joe took a quick look for the dog, but didn't see it.

As he walked to the van, a grey Hummer pulled in and stopped. The glare on the windshield prevented Joe from seeing who was inside.

He joined the others in the van and drove through the slush out of the parking lot.

They drove almost a block before Kevin slammed on the brakes. They slid to a stop a few metres from a dog sitting in the middle of the road.

"Who's this?" asked Earl.

"That would be Joe's crazy dog," said Camille.

Joe got out and opened the van's sliding door. "Come on, boy, let's go." He tapped his leg.

Tank moved into the back seat with Camille, leaving Earl in the middle row alone. Earl slid over and tapped the seat. "Come on, then, I don't bite," he beckoned.

Camille spoke up from the back. "Well, the dog does."

Eventually, the dog hopped up on the seat. Joe closed the door and got back in the front of the van. From the back, he heard a growl.

"I'm serious," Camille warned, "he does bite."

Kevin put the van in gear and continued driving.

"Okay, two questions," said Earl. "What is this dog's name, and why do you keep a dog that bites?"

Joe answered from the front. "The dog doesn't have a name, and he doesn't like being touched."

"Well, I think we should give him a name. How about Sir Bites-a-lot or MC hammer." No one said anything. "You know, 'don't touch this'," he rapped.

"We are not naming the dog!" Joe yelled.

The van drove on for a few moments of awkward silence.

"He's afraid to name it," said Kevin. "He's afraid that when it dies, it will be too sad."

"I think the dog's a girl dog," said Camille.

"Kevin, didn't you say this dog eats people?" asked Tank.

"Just his previous owner," answered Kevin.

"So why keep this man-eating canine?" asked Earl.

"Proverbs says that a wise man has regard for the life of his animal," said Kevin.

"Are you a preacher or something?" asked Earl.

"Nope, I'm just the driver. Speaking of which, what is the plan here, Joe?"

"We should scope out the train station, so we know where we're going. Then we should find a place to wait until Saturday night."

It was late afternoon by the time they got to the Charny train station, which was just outside of downtown Chateaugay. There was more traffic here, although much of it was military. They parked a block away from the station and walked the rest. The dog walked behind them.

As they approached the station, they could see that this was not an ordinary train station anymore. The parking lot was surrounded by a high chain-link fence. Inside the fencing, the train station building was barely visible. The parking lot was filled with military vehicles including jeeps, armoured personnel carriers, tanks and other instruments of war that Joe was not familiar with.

"What's the plan, Joe?" Kevin asked.

"We are going to try the direct approach. Everyone keep your eyes open and try to remember what you see," said Joe.

Tank was already scanning the area intently. They walked up to a security checkpoint consisting of a small building with large windows with sandbags in front of it. There was a large hinged gate that was closed. Five soldiers with machine guns stood in front of the gate. As they approached, two of the soldiers pointed their guns at Joe and his group. One of them yelled at them to stop. The group all stopped and put their hands in the air.

Another soldier came out of the small building. "Can I help you?"

Joe stepped forward, "Hi, we were wondering if we could buy a train ticket?"

"Sorry, the station is closed."

"Looks like it's open to me."

"Military personnel only. You need to go home. This is a restricted area."

"Isn't this a public area?"

"Martial law has been declared, and the military is in charge here. So no, this is no longer a public area."

"Are you sure you can't just find an empty car for us to ride in? We won't be any trouble."

"No. Now please turn around and go home."

"But…" he took a step forward.

"Don't take another step, or you will be placed under arrest!"

Joe stopped, his hands still in the air. "Okay, okay, we're leaving. Sorry to bother you." He turned and walked away. The others followed. Once they were out of hearing range, he asked, "Okay, tell me what you saw."

"I saw you taking unnecessary risk to achieve nothing other than to learn the fact that we can't buy train tickets, which we already knew," said Kevin.

"I saw a really cute soldier who I'm pretty sure was checking me out," said Camille.

Joe shook his head. "Earl, what did you see?"

"Oh, my eyesight isn't what it used to be. Everything past the fence was a little blurry."

"Well you guys are useful." Joe rolled his eyes. "Tank, your former army, you must be trained to be a little more observant than these fools."

"I did notice a few things," said Tank. "The fencing was four metres tall with razor wire on the top. The security checkpoint was manned by five soldiers with C7A2 automatic rifles. Inside the security building, there were two soldiers. On the roof of the train station, there were snipers as well as a Browning 50 calibre machine gun. Inside the fencing, there were multiple light support vehicles, Bison armoured vehicles, a BV206 tracked carrier, a couple of light armoured vehicles, at least one Leopard 2A4 tank and an Oerlikon GDF."

"Well," said Earl, "at least someone was paying attention."

"Doesn't that seem like overkill to you, Tank?" Joe asked.

"Yes, it looks like they are preparing for an attack and not just from local gangs."

"What do you mean?" asked Kevin.

"The Oerlikon is bad news."

"Sounds like a polish delicacy," said Earl. "What is it?"

"It's a Swiss designed, twin cannon anti-aircraft gun."

"Oh."

They all got back in the van and drove away. "Anyone have any ideas where we should go camp out for a couple of days till Saturday?" asked Joe.

"I say, we go to a fancy hotel," said Earl.

Kevin's suggestion of a church earned some groans from the back of the van.

"We should find a huge empty mansion," Camille proposed.

"I think we should go to an army surplus store, so we can load up on supplies," said Tank

"Your call, boss," said Kevin. "What's it going to be?"

Joe thought for a moment. "I think I like Earl's idea. Maybe we can find a decent hotel that hasn't been trashed and has a restaurant with a kitchen."

"What about heat?" asked Kevin. "It doesn't look like the power is coming on anytime soon, so it could get really cold at night."

"We'll stop and pick up some generators and heaters."

They managed to find a hardware store that hadn't been looted. They strapped the generators on the roof of the van and searched for a hotel.

They settled on a high-end hotel that was boarded up and didn't appear to have been looted or trashed. Tank pried a plywood board off and broke the window behind it. They brought the heaters and generators inside and set them up. Tank set up one of the heaters in the restaurant while Camille and Joe put the others in some of the rooms on the first floor. Earl wanted to move into the penthouse suites on the top floor, but no one was willing to carry a generator and heater up ten flights of stairs.

There was a lot of work to do at the hotel just to stay warm, fed and clean. Tank and Kevin made a run for gas for the generators, which they had to move outside because of the fumes. They also had to buy more heaters. Although the hotel may have been well-insulated, it was a large space to heat, and each of them wanted their own room. Each room needed its own heater.

The water was barely running since the pipes were starting to freeze. It was too much work to heat water for baths, so they all had quick cold showers.

They didn't bother opening the walk-in fridge or freezer as the power had been off too long. The gas in the kitchen still worked, so they were able to have hot meals with what they could find in the large pantry. Surprisingly, Kevin was a decent cook, and they were able to eat well. His only condition for doing all the cooking was that they let him pray before they ate.

Over the next few days, they all spent their time differently as they waited for the Saturday rendezvous with the train.

Kevin spent his time reading the Gideon bible he found in his room and preparing the meals.

Camille found black make-up somewhere and painted her face again. When asked about it, she said, "Just because it's the apocalypse doesn't mean I can't look good." She also continued her self-defence lessons with Tank.

Tank jogged a lot. He would jog up and down the hallways as well as the stairs. He also spent a lot of time in the fitness room in the basement. Camille practiced archery with him in the parking lot.

Joe joined Tank in the fitness room a few times, but refused to run up and down the stairs with him. He tried to get the gas furnace working, but it was nothing like the old boiler systems he was used to. He and Tank also came up with a plan to get on the train. Every night the dog slept on a small carpet in a corner of the lobby. The dog still growled at Joe when he tried to pet it.

Earl joked around a lot and read many of the books in the hotel library. He would often go up the roof of the hotel and watch the military trucks go by.

Saturday evening they all sat at the large dining table in the restaurant. They had just finished eating, and Earl had found some wine which he started pouring into glasses.

"Okay, I want to go over the plan for tonight." Joe nodded to Earl, who was holding the wine bottle near his glass. "We can't get on the train when it is at the station because it is too well guarded. The track just after the station is too open, and we could easily be seen. Tank, who is the only one able to keep his eyes open, saw a copse of trees on either side of the tracks just before the station. We are hoping that we can board one of the train cars at the end of the train from there. The plan is to hide in the trees till the train stops, then find a car that looks somewhat accessible and hop on."

"Won't they be locked?" asked Kevin.

"Probably," said Joe, "Which is why Tank will be carrying bolt cutters. We should all have backpacks with our supplies so we can run and jump on the cars quickly. Earl, can you run?"

"Hey, that's ageism, and I resent the implication," he said smiling, and poured wine into Tank's glass.

"Is that a yes?"

"Yes, my ankle is much better now." He brought the wine bottle over to Camille's glass. "I may be old, but I *will* keep up."

Just as Earl was about to pour the wine into her glass, Tank looked over at Earl with his brow creased and shook his head.

Earl pulled the bottle back.

Joe sat back and sipped his wine. "Earl, have you seen anything new from the roof?" asked Joe.

"Not much. A lot of military vehicles. Some of them are taking bodies away, but it looks like something else is going on too. There are a few roving gangs out there too. I think one of them spotted me."

"What? Who?" Joe sat up.

"I don't know. He looked Latino. He had a lot of tattoos and earrings and his arm was bandaged up. He was looking at the van."

"Was he alone?"

"No, there were a few mean looking dudes with him."

"We need to go, now!" Joe yelled. "Kevin, go turn off the generators. Tank, go grab your bow and arrows. Everyone, grab a weapon, your packs and a flashlight. We'll meet at the back door that goes to the parking lot in five minutes."

"What's going on?" asked Earl.

"Raphael is here to kill me."

"Who is…" Earl started to say.

"Shut up and do what you're told," yelled Tank.

As they all got up from the table, Camille held her hand up. "What's that?"

They all paused for a moment and listened. The dog growled in the lobby.

"They're here," said Joe. "Change of plans. Forget the generator. Grab your packs and meet at the stairwell in 60 seconds."

"What about the back door?" asked Kevin.

"They'll be there too," said Joe.

"Everybody, move!" yelled Tank, and they all sprang into action.

Joe ran to his room, grabbed his pack, and met the group at the stairwell. There was loud banging on the front door, but the intruders hadn't made it through yet.

They gathered in the stairwell with their packs and weapons. Tank had his bow and quiver full of arrows, Camille carried a large knife, Joe had a heavy cast iron pan, Kevin had a wooden rolling pin used for baking, and Earl had a steak knife.

"Tank, I need you to go down the stairs to make sure the basement is clear." By the time he had finished his sentence, Tank was flying down the stairs. The rest of them waited at the top.

Earl looked over at Kevin. "A rolling pin? Really? What are you going to do with that? Bake them to death?"

"Hey, your tiny little knife is smaller than the girl's," Earl pointed at Camille.

"Everybody, quiet!" commanded Joe. He opened the doorway into the hall and looked to the right past the lobby where the banging was coming from.

Suddenly he heard the back door behind him open. "Gotcha!"

He whirled around and was face-to-face with Raphael. He had a pistol pointed at Joe's head. His shoulder was bandaged, and he had a look of pure rage on his face. "I'm going to enjoy this."

The pan dropped from his hands as he put them in the air. "Hey, wait a second," he pleaded.

Before he knew what was happening, there was a blur of fur, and Raphael's wrist flew sideways as the dog clamped down on it in mid-dive. He fell backwards, and the gun fell out of his hands. Raphael then grabbed the dog by the scruff of the neck. He pulled the dog off his wrist and threw the dog. The dog made a yelping bark as it was slammed against the wall and went silent.

While Raphael was fighting with the dog, Joe retrieved his pan. He swung the pan with all his strength at the side of man's head. The pan vibrated in his hand as it collided with Raphael's skull. The man went instantly limp.

Joe dropped the pan and scooped up the lifeless dog. He carried it back into the stairwell, just as Tank came running up the stairs.

"There are men in the basement," Tank yelled. "We need to go up." The others followed him up the stairs. The generators only powered a few lights on the main floor, so the stairwell was dark. They shone their flashlights up the stairs as they climbed.

"After five flights, Earl was panting heavily. "Where...are...we...going?"

They could hear men below coming up the stairs after them. Tank didn't seem tired at all. "I have a plan. You guys go up two more flights then hide in one of the rooms on level seven."

They all started up the stairs. "What are you going to do?" Joe called back as he climbed the stairs, still holding the lifeless dog.

Tank held his bow in his left hand and pulled an arrow from the quiver behind him. "I'm going to slow them down."

Joe followed the others up to the seventh floor. He wished now that he had trained with Tank on the stairs. He heard a scream from below as he opened the door to the seventh level. When he walked into hallway, he could see the wild movements of flashlight beams. Kevin and Earl were trying to open the first door in the hallway.

A moment later, Tank came up the stairwell and into the hall.

"Not that one," he said and ran past them and down the hall. When he reached the middle of the hallway, he reared back and kicked the door in with his heel. They all followed him into the room and closed the door. As they caught their breath, Joe asked Tank, "Why this room?"

"They can't see the broken door from the stairwell."

"What now?" Joe asked, still catching his breath.

Tank had his ear to the door, listening. "When they go up a few levels, we run to the other stairwell and get out of here."

Joe turned to Kevin. "What time is it?"

"Almost eleven," he answered.

Joe looked at Tank. "We've got one hour to get to the train station, and they've likely slashed our tires."

Camille looked at the dog in Joe's arms. "Why is she not biting you?"

"I think she's dead."

"Then why are you carrying her?"

"She might not be."

Tank was still listening at the door. "Okay, time to move. Earl, you okay?"

He was still catching his breath. "I'm better than the dog, let's go."

They exited the room and crept down the hall. Tank gently opened the doors and listened. "Sounds like their above us now. Let's move."

Going down the stairs was much easier than going up, and moments later they made it to the main floor.

They ran down the hall to the window that they had originally broken into and climbed out. Once outside, Tank made them all turn their flashlights off. The night was cold and clear. There was a partial moon that cast an eerie glow on the snowy city. Joe could just make out the grey Hummer sitting in the corner of the parking lot at a weird angle.

"Over there." Joe pointed at the Hummer. "That's their vehicle. We should take it."

They all looked at the vehicle, but Tank was the first to notice the faint silhouette of a man standing in front of it. Tank put his finger to his lips to make sure everyone was quiet. Then he silently retrieved an arrow which he knocked and pulled back bow string. When he released it, there was a swoosh, and the man fell over, clutching at his chest. Tank ran toward the man. He pulled out a knife while he was running and slit the man's throat as he reached him.

"Whoa!" said Earl, "That was awesome."

Tank motioned them over to the Hummer. Joe ran with the dog.

He climbed in the back beside Earl. The Hummer was a big vehicle, but it wasn't meant to hold five adults and a dog. Kevin jumped into the driver's seat and turned the ignition. They drove away from the hotel, leaving their pursuers behind.

Tank gave Kevin directions as they found their way through the snow to the train station. In the back, Earl looked at the dog in Joe's arms.

"She's still alive." said Earl. He held his fingers to the dog's chest. "Pulse feels strong. She must only be unconscious."

"Pull over to the side of the road and turn out the lights," said Tank. "We're going to have to walk it from here."

Kevin looked at his watch. "It's after midnight now, so we're going to have to run."

They jogged down the road. Joe was relieved when Tank offered to carry the dog. Even with the extra weight, Tank was faster than the rest of them. They turned into a wooded area and ran through the snow. Fortunately, the temperature had cooled a bit that night, and most of the ground was frozen. Once they got further into the woods, they had to use their flashlights to see where they were going. They held their hands over the ends of the flashlights to try to dim the light so it wouldn't be spotted as easy. As they trotted through the snow, the slow chug of the train could be heard as it began to move.

"We better start running faster!" yelled Joe. They all picked up speed and flew out of the woods. The train was starting to gain speed, and they had to jog beside it to jump on. Kevin went first, stepping onto the bottom rung of the ladder that led to the top of the car. Once on, he held his hand out for Camille, who grabbed it and climbed up past him. He then grabbed the dog from Tank and climbed up to the top of the car with Camille. Tank, and then Joe followed. Joe looked back from where they came.

"Where's Earl?" he yelled.

The train was gaining speed, but there was no sign of the old man. Finally, Camille yelled, "There he is!"

Behind them, they could see a dark sharp emerge from the trees and run to the back of train and disappear.

"Did he make it?" asked Kevin.

"I think he got on the last car," replied Joe. The train was speeding up, and they struggled to hold on.

"The station's coming up soon", yelled Tank. "We need to lie down, so no one sees us as we go by." He motioned with his hands, and they all lay down flat. Joe was relieved that as they passed the station, there was no yelling or shooting.

As the train approached full speed it became difficult to hold on. The car that they were on was an oil tanker, so Joe knew they would have to find another car. They crouch-walked on the car towards the next train car. The thin layer of snow made their crawl slippery.

Tank, who was in the lead, held his hand up for them to stop. Then he pointed down, indicating they needed to go down to the coupling between the cars. They followed him down, with Kevin passing down the dog to Joe. The dog started to wake up.

The car in front of them was a storage car that could be loaded on to a ship or carried by a transport truck. Tank pulled the bolt cutters out of his pack, cut the locks and pulled open the door. The rest of them followed him in. Kevin pulled the door shut behind him. Once the door closed, the clatter from the train and howl of the cold wind suddenly stopped. Except for the thin rays of light peeking through the cracks in the door, it was dark. Camille was the first to find her flashlight and turn it on. The back of the car was full except for one metre where they stood. The rest was filled with crates. There was a narrow passageway down the centre.

The dog was starting to fuss. Joe sat on the floor, cradling the dog. Tank was moving through the passage, trying to get a look at the crates. "Tank," Joe called out, "you know first aid, right?"

Tank was still looking at the crates with his flashlight. "Yes, but not for dogs."

"Come, on," he pleaded, "Can you please just take a look?"

Tank came back, knelt and inspected the dog. He reached into his pack and pulled out a first aid kit. Tank opened it and pulled out a length of gauze. He looked down at the dog, who opened his eyes and growled softly. Tank handed the gauze to Joe.

"What do you want me to do with that?" Joe asked.

"She's got a sprained leg, I think. You should wrap it."

"What? Why can't you?"

"No way, your dog bites."

Joe talked softly to the dog and gently wrapped the leg. She growled at him but didn't bite.

"What about Earl?" asked Kevin.

"Yeah," said Camille, "shouldn't we be going out there to find him?"

"We can't do that," said Tank.

"Why not?" asked Joe.

"Because he's in the last car, and between us and that caboose he's riding are soldiers. I also saw a car with fully manned anti-aircraft guns."

Joe looked up at him. "Why are there manned anti-aircraft guns on this train?"

"Is it for protection against the gangs?" asked Camille.

"I think it's a little overkill for gangs," said Kevin. Camille shrugged.

"Those guns," said Tank, "are there for the same reason that the train station was so heavily guarded. It's the same reason the highways are blocked. It's the same reason that the crates in this car are full of ammunition and firearms."

They all looked at him wide-eyed, waiting.

"This country is under attack."

"What?" From who?" asked Joe.

"I don't know."

They sat huddled in the back of the car as the train clanked down the tracks. It was cold in the car, but at least they couldn't feel the wind. The dog slept peacefully in Joe's arms.

An hour later, as Tank got up to stretch, they heard the sound of boots walking on top of the car. Tank turned out his flashlight, and they listened in silence. One of the men on their car was yelling instructions that Joe couldn't make out. Someone jumped down in front of their door and opened it. The soldier had a light on the end of his rifle, which lit up the inside of the car, revealing the group inside. Tank went to grab his bow from the ground, but the soldier yelled, "Don't you dare!" The soldier went to grab his radio when Joe saw Camille make a quick movement. A small knife flew through the air and lodged itself in the man's arm. He gasped in surprise and then fell backwards through the open door behind him. A distinct squashing sound could be heard as the man disappeared under the train.

"Camille, you can't be killing Canadian soldiers," said Tank.

"Technically, the train killed him, besides what were you going to do with your bow?"

Before he could respond, the distinct sound of jets could be heard whistling overhead. At the same time, the booming *rat-a-tats* of the anti-aircraft guns were felt as much as heard. Suddenly, there was the sound of explosions. Tank threw open the door at the back of the car all the way. He stood between the cars and yelled one word. "Jump!"

When no one moved, he yelled, "Tuck and roll!" and grabbed Camille by her backpack and threw her off the train. Kevin stepped out slowly, and Tank threw him off too. Joe was sure he heard the man reciting the Lord's Prayer as he disappeared into the night.

Tank yelled at Joe, "Throw the dog." He threw the dog and then jumped after it before Tank had a chance to throw him too.

He cringed more than he tucked, and tumbled more than he rolled. Joe closed his eyes as he bounced across ground. When he finally stopped rolling and lay flat on his back, he opened his eyes. Flashes of light pierced through the cold night sky, and gunfire seemed to be coming from everywhere. There was a massive explosion and the night sky lit up like it was daytime. He was lifted off the ground and thrown through the air. Everything went black.

CHAPTER 32

The next morning at the cozy cabin next to the museum, Monique woke up to the sounds of fighter jets screeching overhead.
For the past few days, they had gotten settled in the little cabin. Monique's leg was still sore, and she suspected it might be getting infected.
She couldn't do much but sit in the cabin, feed and change Olivia and keep the fire going. Zach and Ayesha, however, were getting things done. They fed Dora and Boots the oats they had brought from the farm. Zach carried in more firewood from outside. They both went into the museum and explored it thoroughly for anything useful. Zach found some tape to fix his glasses so they would stay on his face by themselves. He also retrieved Warren's rifle and found three boxes of bullets in the purple pickup. Ayesha found some food in the museum store and the worker's break room and brought back more fur pelts, rabbit fur hats, mitts and snowshoes.

They brought all their loot back to the cabin.

"Those are some awesome finds, guys," Monique said, watching them smile proudly. "You didn't happen to find any disposable diapers, did you?"

"No, and there wasn't chocolate either," said Zach.

Ayesha shook her head, "I found some real food. I found a bag of oatmeal for Dora and Boots and some canned stew."

"With chunks of real llama!" joked Zach.

Later that evening, after eating their chunky beef stew, Monique and Ayesha changed her bandages. It wasn't bleeding, but was covered in yellow pus.

"I think its infected," said Monique. She was starting to feel a little sick and hoped it was just the junk food.

Ayesha started crying. "I'm sorry, I didn't do it right. I should have boiled the hook and fishing line and…"

"It's not your fault. You did the best you could. We'll put some more alcohol on it for now. Tomorrow you two are going on a field trip to get some supplies."

Zach looked up. "Normally, we would go to the museum for a field trip, not leave the museum for a field trip."

The joke lightened the mood, and Ayesha giggled and shook her head as she wiped the tears from her eyes.

"I'll make a list," she said, lifting Olivia and smelling her butt, "and the first thing on that list is diapers!"

The next morning, Zach and Ayesha put on their backpacks and headed out.

"Avoid all people. Do not talk or go near anybody and use the gun as a last resort to scare people away," Monique warned them before they left. She was starting to feel hot and woozy and laid back to take a nap.

Zach and Ayesha trekked into the light snow with Dora, the sled, the pistol, flashlights, Roxie and Monique's list.

The museum was near the suburbs, and they stopped at the first house they saw. Zach went up to the door and knocked. He heard a "who's there?" from inside and left before they came to the door. The next house was empty. But the moment Zach opened the door, the stench made him gag.

He backed out, covering this nose and mouth. "We have to remember to put a black flag on their mailbox, when we find one."

The next house was small and empty, and it didn't smell like anyone had died in it. They searched the house and found a sewing box with thread in every colour of the rainbow and few cans of beans in the cupboard.

"I think we can do better than canned green beans," said Zach putting the beans back in the cupboard.

The next house was a large two-story house with an empty driveway, and the windows boarded up.

"They wouldn't board it up if they were living in it, would they?" asked Ayesha.

"Note likely, but we might have a hard time getting in," said Zach. "Let's try around back." They left Dora in the front and walked around the side of the house. As they rounded the corner to the back yard, Roxie started growling.

"What is it, girl?" asked Ayesha, adjusting her backpack.

Neither of them could see or hear anybody, so they kept walking.

"It looks like they didn't put boards on the back doors and windows," said Zach as he walked to the back-sliding door.

"Uh-oh!" said Ayesha.

From around the hedges, five dogs appeared. They were all different breeds, including a Rottweiler, a Pomeranian, a Terrier and a Poodle. Their fur was matted and dirty, and they were baring their teeth and growling.

"It looks like the dog show from hell, said Zach as he tried opening the door.

A massive Rottweiler stood one step in front of the others. Roxie held her ground as the pack began to pace in front of them.

"Hurry up with that door," said Ayesha, her voice rising in fear.

"It won't...open." He pulled as hard as he could, but there was no movement.

"Can we break the glass?"

"Even if I could, they would just follow us in."

"We have to do something!" She was yelling now.

"Let me think," he said frantically searching for a solution.

"I'm going to try that window." He pointed to the small window above a garbage can.

"You can't leave me," she pleaded.

"Roxie will protect you, and when I'm in, I'll open the door."

He slowly made his way to the window, hugging the brick wall. One of the dogs snapped at him but pulled back as Roxie barked loudly and feigned a lunge. Zach climbed onto the metal garbage can and reached up to the window. He pushed and pulled, but it wouldn't budge. He pulled as hard as he could, but his gloved hand slipped. He lost his balance and the garbage can tipped over, spilling him onto the ground. He crab-walked backwards away from the Poodle, but it bit down on his boot. Zach used his other foot to kick the dog hard in the face, and it released its grip.

The dogs started to get more aggressive, making quick dashes towards them and snapping. Roxie fended them off, but Zach knew this wasn't going to last.

"Don't you have a gun?" asked Ayesha.

"You want me to shoot the dogs?"

Ayesha looked at the little snarling Pomeranian. "No, I guess not, but what if you shoot over their heads to scare them away?"

"I could try..." He aimed the gun over the dog's heads and pulled the trigger. Instantly the dogs went quiet. Some of the dogs scurried away, others shrunk back, but the big Rottweiler stood its ground. It barked a couple of times, and the other dogs returned.

"Plan C," said Zach and pointed the gun at the window he was trying to open, covered his eyes and fired. The glass shattered and the dogs paused again. Zach took their pause to put the garbage can back up and climb on top. He used his glove to break the larger shards that remained. He took his coat off and laid it across the bottom of the window and crawled through. His backpack got caught momentarily but then released, and he fell headfirst into a laundry basket. Zach got to his feet, ran out of the laundry room to the back door. Although he unlocked the sliding door, he was still unable to get it open. Ayesha was now banging on the window as the dogs were closing in on her and Roxie.

Zach took a step back to look at the door and saw the broomstick handle holding the door closed. He removed it and opened the door. Ayesha came in, but Roxie was unable to turn around without being attacked. Zach stepped outside the door with Roxie, yelled loudly and swung the broomstick at the Rottweiler. It connected with the side of the dog's head, stunning him for a moment. Zach then tackled Roxie, pushing her into the house, and Ayesha slid the door closed. There was a *thunk* as the Rottweiler charged headfirst into the glass door. Ayesha closed the curtain and threw her arms around Zach.

"We did it! We're safe!"

Zach awkwardly removed himself from her embrace. "Yes, that was quite intense."

"Ahhhh!" yelled Ayesha. "We forgot about Dora!"

"You open the curtains and keep their attention while I try to find a way to bring the llama in the house," said Zach.

The dogs were pacing around the back yard, and Ayesha had to open the door slightly to get their attention. Zach was unable to open the front door because it had plywood nailed to it. He went to the garage and found a small vehicle with a black cover. He walked around it and unlocked the garage door. Snow had drifted against the door, making it difficult to open. He heaved as hard as he could and managed to push the door open. Zach looked into the driveway, but the llama was gone.

Are you supposed to call llamas?

"Dora!" he yelled, "Dora, here boy...or girl." The llama did not come running, but he did hear some of the feral dogs from the back yard coming his way. He closed the door and went back inside.

"Where's Dora?" asked Ayesha.

"She must have got spooked and ran away. We'll have to find her later. Let's check this house out first."

Other than the fact that they were trapped, the house was like a gift from God. There were no dead or living bodies, and they were able to get most of the items on their list. Ayesha found a baby's room with diapers and cloths and other weird baby stuff. She found a cute pink bunny rattle that she added to her stash in her backpack. Zach went to the large bathroom and found a sewing kit in the vanity alongside an assortment of pill bottles. "What kind of pills are we looking for?" he yelled.

"Anything ending in 'cillin', aspirin, or...just take them all," she answered.

Zach's glasses had gotten worse. One of the lenses was cracked, and he couldn't see much out of it. The tape was not doing a good job of holding it together. When he found a pair of glasses in one of the bedrooms with a prescription close to his, he was ecstatic.

They met back up in the kitchen and searched the cupboards. There were a few cans of beans, beef stock and spices.

"Great," said Zach, "more beans."

Ayesha found a walk-in pantry and used her flashlight to illuminate the shelving inside. "Check this out," she said.

Zach came over to look. "Jackpot!"

The shelves were filled with cans of fruits, vegetables, stews and soups. There were also boxes of cereal, a large bag of oatmeal, crackers and cookies.

They kept checking the window to see if the feral dogs had left. Once, when they didn't see or hear them, they took a step out the back door. However, the dogs instantly appeared, and Zach and Ayesha retreated back inside. They decided to stay the night.

Zach found a small camping propane stove and a couple of small propane tanks. They brought them into the laundry room so they would have some heat that night. They piled as many blankets as they could find and made themselves a nest on the floor. With Roxie lying between them, they enjoyed a warm sleep.

The next morning, they got up and ate. There was no running water, so they had to pee in the corner of the garage.

The sun came up, and the temperature rose, and much of the snow was reverting to water. Zach stepped outside and looked into the backyard. From between two shrubs, the Rottweiler stepped forward and glared at him. Zach went back inside and closed the door.

"Are they still out there?" asked Ayesha.

"Yes, they are."

"What are we going to do?"

"There's a car in the garage," he suggested with a smirk on his face.

"What!? You can't drive!"

"How hard can it be?"

When they took the cover off the vehicle in the garage, they discovered a bright pink Volkswagen Beetle. They found keys on a hook in the kitchen. After piling their loot in the back seat beside Roxie, Zach opened the garage door, and started the car.

"It's not much different from my uncle's riding lawn mower," said Zach. "Besides, it's not that far." He put the car in drive and plowed through the small drifts in the driveway. Much of the snow had melted, but the slush made the roads slippery.

The car charged out of the garage. Zach turned the wheel hard to the left when they reached the road. The front end of the car veered to the left, but the back end of the car kept going straight. They hit the curb sideways.

"Ahhh!" yelled Ayesha. "Be careful!"

He drove forward towards the parked car in front of them.

"Car!" she yelled, "Don't hit the car!"

He squinted through his glasses. "I see it."

"Those aren't your glasses, are they?"

"No, mine are broken."

"Those look like girl's glasses."

"Yes, and this is a girl's car, but at least they work...sort of," he said as he fishtailed down the road.

They drove the few blocks to the museum narrowly missing a few more parked cars and the ditch.

"I feel like I'm on the Tilt-a-Whirl at the Ingerwood Fall Fair!" said Ayesha.

When they pulled into the museum, he was having fun in the little bug, and she was laughing hysterically.

They drove through the parking lot and up to the front of the log cabin.

"There's Boots!" said Ayesha. "And remember, we still have to find Dora."

They got out of the car and walked to the cabin. Roxie ran around the cabin sniffing.

Ayesha opened the door to the cabin, and they both stepped inside. The cabin was quiet and empty.

"Where's Monique?" asked Ayesha.

"I don't know," replied Zach.

They looked in the bedrooms, behind the cabin, and walked through the museum. They didn't see Monique or Olivia. They were gone.

CHAPTER 33

Joe woke up to a wet tongue on his face and the sound of a harmonica playing. He was laying on his side, and when he opened his eyes, he saw a fire. For a moment, he panicked.

I'm on the train and it's on fire! Where are my friends? What about the dog? Am I dead? Why do I hear a harmonica?

Then the fire disappeared as a black iron door closed over it with a creak.

Slowly, he started to gain his bearings. Joe realized that the fire was in a wood-stove, and he was lying on a couch. When he tried to sit up, the room began to spin.

He heard Kevin's voice, "Whoa there, boss. You need to take it easy."

He squeezed his eyes shut, trying to control the vertigo. "Kevin, is that you?"

"Yes, it's me. Don't sit up too fast. Here, have something to drink."

A water bottle was held up to his lips, and he took a couple of swallows. Some of the water dribbled down his beard. His vision cleared, and he looked around. He was in a tiny one-room cabin with a counter without a faucet, a cot, a couple of chairs, some boxes and the couch he was lying on. The dog was laying on the floor in front of the couch.

"Where am I? How long have I been sleeping?"

Earl stopped playing his harmonica. "You're in Kansas, and

it's been five years."

Joe shook his head, trying to clear the fog from his brain. "What? Five years?!"

"Earl, stop it, that's not funny," said Kevin. "We're in a hunting cabin on the Ontario side of the border. You've been out for a few hours."

"I thought it was funny," Earl wiped his harmonica.

Joe looked around again. "Where are Tank and Camille? And Earl, you made it?"

"Of course, I made it. You can't get rid of me that easily," said Earl.

The cabin door opened, and Tank and Camille walked in. Tank was carrying a small animal carcass that no longer had skin by the hind legs.

"What is that?" asked Kevin.

"Dinner!" answered Tank proudly.

"Hey, your awake, Joe," said Camille. Her dark make-up was smeared across her face.

The fog in his head cleared, but he had a pain in the back of his head. He sat up and stretched. "Okay, I'm awake. Now tell me what happened."

Kevin sat down beside him. "After we jumped off the train..."

"Thrown." Camille corrected him, and Tank rolled his eyes.

"Well, I jumped," added Earl.

"Me too," said Tank.

"As I was saying...after we exited the train - some of us with Tank's assistance - a missile or bomb or something hit the train, and exploded. The train had moved far enough away by that point, and we were spared from most of the blast."

"Not all of us," said Joe as he felt the large bump on the back of his head.

"Tank picked you up and dragged you into the woods to this hunting cabin.

"Nobody got hurt when they were thrown – make that *exited* the train?"

"The drifting snow is deep out here, and it cushioned our fall."

"What about the soldiers on the train, won't they be hurt?"

Tank answered. "I'm not sure if many of them made it, but in case the attackers had ground troops, we didn't stick around."

Joe looked up at Tank. "Do we know who they are?"

"I was army, not air force, so I'm not an expert on jets. What I do know is that I didn't recognize them, so I'm pretty sure they weren't American or Canadian."

Joe bent down to pet the dog, but it snapped at him. "I see the dog's back to her old self."

"She followed us back here and then lay down beside you," said Camille.

"Tank, I thought you said she had a sprained leg?" said Joe.

"No, I said I *thought* she had a sprain. I also said I wasn't a vet."

"Maybe you healed her when you threw her off the train," suggested Camille.

"What time is it?" Joe asked.

"I don't know," said Kevin, "My watch broke when I exited the train."

"The sun looks like it will set in another couple hours," said Tank.

"Maybe we should see if we can find another place to sleep. Something a little bigger than this little cabin," said Joe. "Are there any cities near here?"

"We found a road," said Camille, "and there was a sign for a place called Maveth that was six kilometres from here."

"Can we cook my rabbit first?" asked Tank, still holding the carcass by the legs.

They found some pots, plates and cutlery in the little cabin. They went through the supplies in their backpacks to find some suitable side dishes. Kevin said a little prayer and they had a late afternoon dinner of rabbit, Cheetos, canned peas and chocolate bars. The dog ate the rabbit bones.

"Tank," said Joe as they ate. "You still have your bow and arrows."

"Yea," he grumbled. "A train full of military hardware, and what do I get? Nothing. All I have is my little bow and arrow."

"Awww," mocked Earl, "The big warrior can't find his wittle guns?"

They all laughed.

After they ate, they put out the fire in the woodstove and left. The snow was knee-deep in the woods. The road hadn't been plowed or driven on and wasn't any better. It took them almost two hours to trudge the six kilometres to Maveth. Tank took the lead. The rest were able to walk in his footprints, with the dog walking behind them. Finally, they reached a sign that read *Maveth*. The slogan under it read, *The cozy little town you won't want to leave.*

The town looked deserted. They made the first footprints on the fresh blanket of snow down the centre of the main street. There were no cars, people or dogs. There were no lights on or smoke. There were a few cars parked on the side of the road, and several businesses had been looted, but most were boarded up. It was dead silent. The sun had just set, and the town was getting darker.

"This is uber-creepy," whispered Camille.

"I agree," said Earl just as quietly, "This is really weird."

"Where is everyone?" asked Kevin in a hushed voice.

Tank had an arrow knocked in his bow, and his head pivoted side to side scanning.

"Why are we whispering?" whispered Joe. He smiled as he was reminded of Blender. "If we whisper loudly, it defeats the point."

"Smoke!" Tank yelled, pointing down a side street.

Earl, who was walking next to Tank jumped. "Good gravy man, you nearly gave me a heart attack! I thought we were whispering."

They looked to where he was pointing and saw a thin trail of smoke coming out of a small red brick chimney. The chimney was on top of a long bungalow with a curved driveway in front of it. There was a car in the driveway, that was covered in snow.

"There are no tracks in or out of the house," Tank observed.

They walked down the side street towards the house and up the driveway.

Joe stepped up to the front door. "I guess we should knock?"

He knocked three times. No answer. He knocked again. Then heard movement inside. Tank held his bow and arrow aimed at the door.

Joe looked back at him. "Put the bow down, Tank, we aren't here to rob the place."

He lowered the bow but still held it at his side.

The door opened, and an old man with barely any hair left, and a face full of wrinkles opened the door.

"Good evening folks, how may I help you?"

"We were wondering where everyone has gone and…"

"Are you here to rob me? Because that would be stupid, seeing that I'm the only person left in this town, and you can have whatever you want."

"No, we just saw the smoke and…"

"Well, you might as well come in then, but can the oversized Robin Hood here please put his arrow away?"

Tank complied, and they followed the old man inside. He made them take off their boots and coats. "Is that dog with you?" he pointed to the dog sitting outside.

"Come, girl," Joe called, and the dog trotted in.

"She can come in," said the old man, "but she has to stay off the furniture. The wife hates dog fur on the couch."

They sat down in the large living room. The house had a slight odour that Joe couldn't quite place.

The old man grabbed some matches and lit a candle. "Are you hungry? I can get the wife to whip something up."

"No, thank you," said Joe, "We already ate."

Joe introduced everyone. The man shook all of their hands. "I'm John, and my wife is Gale."

"Where is Gale?" asked Kevin.

"She's in her bedroom. She's been very tired these past few days."

"Did you want Tank here to take a look at her? He's not a doctor, but he knows first aid."

"Oh, that's not necessary, I'm sure she's fine. Do any of you want some coffee? I have a French press and some hot water."

"I would love some coffee," said Tank.

"Yes, please," said Kevin.

"None for me," said Camille.

"No, thanks," said Joe.

John grabbed one of the candles and slowly hobbled around the corner into the kitchen.

Joe was still trying to place the smell. He looked up at the rest of them and whispered, "Wait here, I'll be right back."

"Where are you going?" asked Kevin.

Joe didn't answer. He got up and silently walked towards the hallway. John might be able to see him when he walked in front of the doorway to the kitchen, so he peered around the corner. John was facing the opposite direction, putting a kettle on the stove. Joe took the opportunity and dashed through the doorway into the hallway. With his flashlight he could see that the hallway was long and had doorways on either side. The first doorway on the left led to a bathroom. The next was an office on the right. A large bedroom on the left was empty, so he kept walking. Another smaller room on the right had nobody in it either. There were two final rooms at the end of the hallway. The odour was getting stronger. He put his ear up to the last door on the left, but heard nothing. He turned the handle and slowly pushed the door open. Suddenly he heard voices from the living room.

"Where's Joe?"

"He went to find a washroom."

Joe stepped out of sight and into the room. Inside the smell was stronger and he instantly recognized it. It was the same stench as the office of the used car place. It was the smell of death.

His flashlight revealed a woman's body on the bed. It was not moving, and the lacy white blankets were pulled neatly up to the old woman's chin. There was a pink silk sleep mask covering her eyes. He slowly crept closer to the body. "Hello, ma'am, are you okay?" He didn't expect an answer. He gently lifted the sleep mask and found dead eyes staring back at him. The stench was intense, and he replaced the mask, left the room, closed the door and walked back down the hall. When he got back to the living room, John said to him, "hope you didn't try to flush. The water's not running, so you have to use the bucket. Gale hates using the bucket."

"So where is everybody in this town?" asked Tank.

"They left. Most of the town died of the Scourge, but not me and my Gale." He sipped his hot coffee. "Last week, the army came by with a bunch of buses and took anyone that was still alive to Commerce to some sort of shelter."

"Why didn't you go with them?"

"Me and Gale have lived here all of our lives. We've raised six kids in this house. We aren't leaving now. We aren't leaving, not now, not ever."

It was quiet for a moment. "Where are you folks headed?"

Joe answered. "We are on our way to Commerce, but we need to get to a place to the east of the city first. He pulled out the paper that Callaghan had given him and handed it to John. "We were hoping to get to *this* address."

"That's actually not that far from here. It's about an hour and a half drive. I can draw you a map."

"We don't have a vehicle," said Joe, "and it would take a snow plow to get through the snow on the road."

John took another sip from his coffee. "I may be able to help you with that. My kids are grown up now and have moved away, but they loved to snowmobile on the trails out here. There's a big shed in the back with some snowmobiles. You're welcome to them. Gale and I are too old to use them anymore, and I don't think my kids are coming back to visit anytime soon." He finished his coffee and stared out the window with a faraway look. The light from the flickering candle illuminated his weathered face.

"Anyway, it's getting late," he said, finishing his coffee. "Your welcome to find a bed. We have lots of rooms, just not the bedrooms on the left. Those are mine and Gale's."

John had a big propane tank, which not only let him cook over his stove but also heated his house. That night they all slept well in the warm house, except for Joe. He tossed restlessly all night, knowing that there was a dead woman just down the hall.

The next morning was sunny, windless and cold. The snow sparkled on the ground. John had fed them a decent breakfast of oatmeal and canned fruit. They were able to start three out of the four snowmobiles in the shed. John insisted on filling all of them with gas and did so with shaky determined hands. John also gave Tank one of his hunting rifles with a box of ammunition. It was the first time Joe saw Tank smile.

Tank took the lead towing a small trailer. In it were the supplies from John and the dog. Kevin drove the second snowmobile with Camille behind him. Joe drove the last snowmobile with Earl. John stood watching them as they were leaving. Joe drove his snowmobile up to him. "You know, you're welcome to join us John."

"No, I couldn't leave my Gale."

"Uh, John, Gale isn't...you know...I'm not sure how to say this but...you do know that..."

John put his hand on Joe's shoulder. "It's okay, Joe, I know. But I'm staying. You gave me one more chance to do some good in this world. I still have one of my guns. You go and take care of these people." He handed Joe a map he had drawn for him. "Godspeed."

John turned back to his home and walked inside.

As the winter caravan of snowmobiles plowed down the street through the glistening snow, Joe heard the sound of a muted gunshot behind him. He blinked away his cold tears and drove into the sunshine.

The roads were clear of traffic, but they had to go around a few abandoned cars. As they got closer to Commerce, they crossed paths with a few trucks with winter tires and a couple of other snowmobiles. They were still 10 kilometres outside of Commerce when they turned off the main highway onto a small country road. There were some 4-wheeler, and other tracks on the roads. A few of the farmhouses had smoke coming out of their chimneys.

CHAPTER 34

The same afternoon that Ayesha and Zach left the museum, Pascal Donadieu sat in the dean's comfy leather sofa. He was alone in a warm professor's lounge with a stomach full of food, surrounded by books and games, but he was bored.

When the pandemic started, the final semester was just finishing. Pascal shared a tiny room with a basketball player studying engineering. Many of the other students, including his roommate, and most professors had died during the first wave. He was terrified that he would be next, but he didn't die. He was one of the 15%. One of the *lucky* ones that was immune. Most of the remaining students and professors that had survived had left to find their families. A small group of students and one professor stayed behind. They had formed a small commune that Pascal had joined. They ate food they had collected in the university cafeteria and lived in the residence dorms. The leader of the group, Professor Valnov, was an egotistical, power-hungry, cult-like leader.

When the cool fall weather came, Valnov told the students to build a fire in the gym. Pascal had insisted that this was a bad idea, but no one would listen. Valnov told everyone what to do, but never helped in any of the chores. Pascal left the group. A pretty blond girl named Desiree left with him. The next day a group of looters had seen the smoke and raided the place. They stole most of the food the group had collected.

They beat, chased away or killed the students. The raiders burned down an entire wing of the university then left. Professor Valnov disappeared.

Pascal and Desiree moved into the professor's lounge. They stole a truck and made a trip to Home Depot, where among other things, they picked up twenty-five propane tanks and a small propane heater. Desiree knew about a food distribution terminal where they stopped to pick up copious amounts of food. They brought back all of their finds to the University where Pascal could live his fantasy. It was like being stranded on a desert island with a beautiful girl. His fantasy turned dark, however, when Desiree got sick. The next day Desiree died, leaving Pascal alone.

One week later, he sat on a comfortable leather sofa and pondered his situation. He decided to take a trip to the museum. Before the pandemic, he had worked weekends at the Commerce City Museum. He was hoping it would look good on his resume when he graduated. He was in his third year of the Bachelor of Science program, and was planning to follow this up with a one-year honours degree in Archaeology. This was supposed to be the beginning of his epic career as an archaeologist. He should have been studying past civilizations, not witnessing the extinction of one.

He got up from his chair, turned off the propane heater, and went outside to his truck. It was late, but time didn't have the same importance anymore. He drove through the quiet dark city for 20 minutes to the museum. There were a lot of strange-looking tracks in the snow by the front atrium. A purple pick-up truck was parked outside, but he couldn't hear or see anyone. He went inside and used his flashlight to guide his way. Most of the exhibits appeared to be intact. He nearly tripped over a badly burned dead body in the Fur Trader's exhibit. Some of the glass shelving and enclosures were broken. As he left the room, he detected the smell of wood smoke. Pascal went outside and followed the smell to the Pioneer Cabin. He quietly walked in the dark through the slushy parking lot to the cabin. As he pointed his flashlight at the wood pile, he heard a strange spitting sound. He felt the warm wet spray from a llama's open mouth, who was standing in front of him.

"What on earth?" he exclaimed, wiping the spittle from this face. He walked over to the front door of the cabin and knocked. There was no light inside, but he heard the sound of a baby crying.

"Hello?" he said as he knocked on the door. He knocked harder. "Hellooo!" he yelled.

The door wasn't locked, and he opened it and stepped inside. He turned the flashlight on and found a woman lying on the couch with a baby crying beside her.

"Ma'am, are you okay?"

He felt her pulse. It was fast and she was burning up. The baby appeared to be healthy, but upset. The woman was mumbling incoherently as he carried her to his truck. He went back into the cabin and looked for baby formula without success. He brought the baby to the truck and drove back into the cold night.

A short time later, he reached the Commerce City Regional Hospital. It was one of the few places that still had electricity.

They took her into surgery, while he waited in the waiting room. A cute nurse with short blonde hair named Effy took the baby, fed, and changed her before giving her back to Pascal. An hour later, the doctor came out.

"Hello, my name is Doctor Guerroro," he said, "Your wife was suffering from sepsis."

"She's not my wife."

"We cleaned up, what I assume was a gunshot wound, and re-stitched it. We gave her antibiotics and something to help her sleep. As long as her fever goes down and the infection dies off, she should be able to get out of here in a couple of days."

"Thank you, Doctor. Now who can I give this baby to."

"You can take the baby home."

"But this isn't my baby! I don't even know that woman's name, and I have no idea how to take care of a baby?"

"You can talk to, Effy, here. She can give you some formula and directions to the C3. They may be able to help you there."

"But this isn't my baby," he protested.

"Maybe not," said Effy, "but you *are* the babysitter."

CHAPTER 35

Earlier that same day, Joe and his friends pulled up to the end of a long winding driveway. Large maples lined the driveway, and they couldn't see the house from the road. Joe stopped and pulled out his map.

"Is this the place?" asked Kevin.

"I hope so," said Camille, who was shivering behind him, "because I'm freezing here."

"I don't see any tracks," said Tank.

Earl jumped off the snowmobile. "Man, I'm cold." He walked over to the mailbox and brushed the snow off with his glove to expose the name on the side. "Yep, it says Callaghan!"

"Hop on," said Joe, "let's go check it out."

They followed Joe down the driveway lined with maples. It opened up to reveal a large old wooden barn and a yellow brick century home. The windows of the house were boarded up. They pulled the snowmobiles up to the front of the house. The dog jumped off the trailer and ran off sniffing.

Tank got his rifle out, but Joe stopped him. "We're not here to scare anybody, so just wait here with the gun."

"Hello!" he called out as he walked up to the front door. He knocked and called out again, but there was no response. He tried to open the door, but it was locked.

"What now?" asked Kevin.

"I assume they're dead," said Camille.

"Well, I have to know for sure." He found a small rock to

break the glass in the door and reached through to unlock the door. He stepped inside and called out again, but no one responded.

Camille, Earl, and Kevin followed him in, while Tank kept watch outside with his gun.

The house was covered with a layer of dust. Joe turned to look at the others. "Earl, you and Camille check out the main floor. Kevin, you go look in the basement, and I'll check out the rooms upstairs. They all nodded and followed his instructions.

At the top of the stairs was a small landing that led to a hallway. The landing had a wall with family photos. One showed Callaghan as a teen with her parents standing in front of the red barn. They all had big smiles on their faces. There was an old photo of what he assumed was her father in a soldier's uniform and a newer one of Callaghan in hers. There was another family photo of Callaghan with her husband and young son.

He walked down the hallway and looked into the washroom and bedrooms, but they were all empty and undisturbed. He went back down the stairs and met the others at the front door. None of them had found anybody either.

"The kitchen is clean and empty," said Earl. "All the food is gone, and it doesn't look like anyone has been here for a while."

"Has anyone found a note or anything?" None of them had found any indication of where Callaghan's parents had gone.

They left the house and walked back outside.

"Let's check the barn," said Joe and walked through the snow further down the laneway to the big red barn. There was a large set of wooden doors at the front. Beside them was a smaller door. As Joe approached the door, he heard it unlock. When he was a couple of metres from the door, it flew open, and a double-barreled shotgun appeared, pointed at his chest.

"Don't move."

Joe stopped and put his hands over his head. "Don't shoot!" He reached into his coat pocket to get the address that Callaghan had written down. "We're here because your daughter..."

There was an ear-piercing boom, and he saw the flash from the shotgun at the same time he felt a sudden pain in his chest and fell backwards.

He landed on his back in the snow and grabbed at his chest, but realized that it wasn't his chest. It was his shoulder and upper arm. He put his hands up in front of him. "Please," he pleaded, "we aren't here to hurt you."

"Then why is your big friend pointing a gun at me?" said the woman with the shotgun.

With one hand on his shoulder and the other in the air, Joe got to his knees and turned to look behind him. "Tank, put the gun down!"

The big man reluctantly obliged.

Joe started to stand up. "Your daughter sent us."

"Oh, yeah, then what's her name?"

"Callaghan." He stood up. His shoulder ached and was covered in blood.

"No, her first name, you nincompoop."

"Um...actually, she never told me..."

"Nice, try. You need to get back on your snowmobiles and leave, now!"

"No, wait." He spoke as fast as he could. "Your daughter is really beautiful, and has dark hair and piercing brown eyes. She had a husband and young son, and they were going to move to downtown Chateaugay this summer. She's a corporal in the Canadian Military. I think she said her father is a survivalist, and her mother has a heart of gold."

"Is she alive?"

"Yes, she's fine."

"What about her husband and my grandson?"

"I'm sorry..."

Her gun dropped a little. She looked up at the rest of the group, then back down to him. "She really said I had a heart of gold?"

"Yes, ma'am. I'm sorry for the intrusion. We can leave if you..."

"We better take a look at your shoulder." She lowered the shotgun and looked at Tank. "If you open these big doors, you can park your snow machines inside." She looked back at Joe. "You better come inside." She beckoned them to follow her through the door.

Kevin and Joe followed her. Earl went back to help Tank with the snowmobiles. The dog had run off exploring.

Camille walked beside the old woman. "Are you living in this barn?" she asked.

"Not quite, my dear. Follow me." They walked to the other side of the barn and into a small stall. The floor was covered in straw except for a large rectangular board in the centre. The board had a handle on it. She leaned over and pulled the board up. It swung open with a creak. Below it was a metal hatch with a wheel. She turned the wheel and opened the hatch, exposing a metal rung ladder leading down a square tunnel. They followed her down to a small room the size of John and Gale's living room. It was sparsely furnished with two cots, a table, four dining chairs and a shelving unit. They spread out the best they could in the cramped room.

"My name is Mildred, but everyone calls me Millie," said the old woman.

She got Joe to sit on one of the chairs and take off his coat, sweater and undershirt, so she could see his shoulder.

"Oh, it's not so bad, I only grazed you." She dabbed at the wound. "Camille is it?" she asked, "Could you be a dear and find some tweezers in the box over there on the bottom shelf?"

Mille plucked a few birdshot pellets from his shoulder and cleaned the wound with antiseptic.

"Do you shoot everyone who knocks on your door?" Joe asked, wincing as she poured the antiseptic.

"Your big friend Tank had a gun and I told you not to move...and my finger might have slipped."

Joe reached into his pocket and handed her the paper that

Callaghan had written the address on. "I was trying to give you this. Your daughter told me to find you, and…where's your husband?"

"Robert died a couple of weeks ago. I buried him out in the backfield under a pile of rocks. The ground is too frozen to dig. I'm not looking forward to burying him in the spring." She looked down at the note. "That *is* Erin's writing."

"I'm sorry about your son-in-law, grandson and your husband," said Kevin. "If you have some pickaxes and shovels, we will properly bury your husband for you."

"Really? I would appreciate that." Her eyes were glossy as she wrapped his shoulder in gauze.

Tank was looking claustrophobic. "We should do that right now, so we can get going."

"You should find what you need in the back of the barn, by the tractor. Robert is buried under some rocks by the big maple tree at the corner of the field, out back. That was his favourite tree, and I would like him to be buried there."

Tank, Kevin, and Earl went back up the ladder, leaving Millie, Camille and Joe down below. Camille took the bloodied dressings and put them in a garbage can in the corner.

"Can I ask you something," asked Camille.

Millie finished wrapping Joe's shoulder. "Yes, dear, what do you want to know?"

"Do you really live down here? It seems a little…small."

"I'm very resourceful," she answered, then changed the subject. "Tell me, how did such an odd collection of individuals end up wandering into my little abode?"

Joe spent the next hour summarizing his story as Camille napped on one of the cots.

As Millie was asking questions about his adventures, they heard barking and yelling from above. They woke Camille and climbed the ladder to the barn.

They exited the barn to find Tank with his gun pointed at a teenage boy standing beside a side-by-side utility vehicle with winter tires. His one hand was holding a rifle by the barrel, the other was in the air.

"I found this intruder," yelled Tank.

The dog stopped barking when she saw Joe.

"He's not an intruder, you big oaf, that's Tyler."

Tank lowered his rifle.

Tyler lowered his hand. "What's going on Millie, are you okay?"

"I'm fine, Tyler. Erin sent them to check up on me."

He handed her a large sack. "Here's your stuff Millie. I even found some dark roast."

"Thanks, Tyler. Everyone this is Tyler. Tyler here checks up on me and brings me my essentials."

"They all shook his hand and introduced themselves. Tyler, smiled timidly when Camille took his hand, and then moved on when Tank glared at him.

"We finished burying your husband, Mrs. Callaghan," said Kevin.

"Please, call me Millie."

"Would it be alright for me to officiate a small service for your husband, Millie?"

"That would be nice of you, Kevin. Can we do it right now?"

"Absolutely."

"Tyler, you're coming too," she told the boy.

Kevin offered his arm, and Millie took it. The two of them led the group behind the barn, with the dog walking with them. Earl walked beside Joe at the back of the line.

"Did you see all the animals in the barn?" asked Earl.

"No, what kind of animals?"

"She's got chickens, pigs, rabbits and even a donkey!"

"Really?"

"She can't really live down there, can she? I didn't even see a washroom or a kitchen, and the house didn't look lived in."

"I don't know."

They gathered around the grave under the big maple tree. Kevin stood behind the small wooden cross he had placed in the dirt and recited the Lord's Prayer. Millie spoke of some of her memories and said her goodbyes. Kevin led the group in a couple verses of Amazing Grace. Most of them knew some words, and the rest faked it.

Once it was finished, and they started walking back, Tyler asked Millie, "So, have you shown them?"

"No," she answered.

The rest of them listened to the conversation with confusion.

"Come on," he insisted. "It's getting late. You should at least let them stay the night. They're good people."

"Oh, we don't want to impose," said Tank, thinking of the tiny bunker.

"What do you say, Millie?" asked Tyler, "They even helped you bury Mr. Callaghan."

"Okay, fine," she said. "The Good Book says we should share in our blessings."

"What are you talking about?" asked Joe.

"I'll show you," she said, "but we'll have to carry your dog down that ladder."

She pulled some food out of her pocket and beckoned the dog over.

"My dog isn't exactly friendly," said Joe.

"He bites," added Tank.

The dog trotted over to get Millie's food, and she reached down to pet the dog.

"Careful!" yelled Joe.

The dog snapped at Millie, who pulled her hand away, and smacked the dog hard across the nose. The dog yelped and cowered. As they all looked on in disbelief, she bent over and pet the dog behind the ears. "What's her name?"

Joe was waiting for the inevitable moment when the dog would bite the poor woman's nose off, but it didn't happen. "She doesn't have a name."

Millie scratched the dog's neck. "Well, no wonder she bites. She needs some love, and you can't love a dog if you don't give it a name. I'm going to call her Shelby."

They walked up to the hatch in the barn, and she addressed Tank. "Would you be so kind sir to go down first and I can hand you Shelby?"

He shook his head with the look of a petulant schoolboy. "No way, he'll bite me."

She managed to convince Tank that if he left his winter gloves on, Shelby's bite wouldn't hurt.

Finally, they all made it down into the little bunker.

"What did you want to show us?" asked Joe.

"It's awesome, trust me," said Tyler, who was standing beside Camille.

Millie reached down behind the couch and pulled a lever. One of the walls slid sideways, revealing a wide passageway. Shelby took off running down the passageway and disappeared.

What they thought was a modest, sparsely furnished underground bunker turned out to be an immense subterranean survivalist shelter. It had a large community room, multiple bedrooms, washrooms, storage, a kitchen and a pantry.

Water was plumbed in from a drilled well. A bank of batteries was wired to solar panels on top of the barn. Heat and air conditioning were provided by ground source heat pumps. A monitor showed a live feed from a camera mounted on the side of the barn pointing at the laneway.

As they toured the facility, Millie explained that her husband, Robert, had bought the property from a rich cousin who was dying of cancer. The cousin had made a fortune investing in automotive stocks in the 1950s and spent millions on this massive underground shelter. Shortly before he died, he sold the property to Millie's husband. The shelter was in major disrepair, but Robert had spent years fixing it up.

"He was such an apocalypse junkie. He read all the books, watched all the movies and was always in here working. I think he was secretly excited when he heard about a pandemic sweeping the world. He stocked this place with food, weapons, and supplies. When he found out he was going to die of the Scourge, he was more disappointed in the fact that he couldn't use this place, than the fact that he was going to die."

"What about the animals in the barn?" asked Joe.

"Those were my idea. If this was a nuclear war, we would have to hunker down here for years, but since it's a virus that some people appear to be immune to...there is no reason to eat MRE's for the rest of my life. Besides, this was a working farm, so we already had the animals. I just moved them in the barn for the winter, so they're easier to take care of."

"What's an MRE?" Camille asked Tyler.

Tank answered, "Meals ready to eat."

"Well, this is incredible," said Kevin.

The rest of them agreed.

"You're welcome to stay the night. I have lots of room, and we can share a meal."

She showed them the showers as well as their rooms. They had to pull some cots and blankets out of storage, but she managed to find all of them a place to sleep.

Later that night they sat around the large dining table eating steaks, potatoes and vegetables.

"This is amazing, Millie. I haven't eaten like this in a very long time," said Tank.

"I have a question," asked Camille, "why such a big dining area and all the rooms?"

"The original owner was hoping to rent out rooms during the nuclear winter. Robert had planned to invite friends and family to ride out the apocalypse with us down here. It didn't quite work out that way. Many of our friends and family either died or lived too far away. So now it's just me down here. It does get kind of lonely, but Tyler does come by to visit - don't you, dear?" She playfully pinched his cheek.

Tyler told of his adventures. He was originally from Commerce and had just moved to the country. He didn't have anybody and said he would gladly help them navigate the capital city - especially if Camille was with them.

Millie brought out some Bailey's, Earl played his harmonica, and they sang, talked and laughed late into the night.

The next morning, they sat around the table again and ate a spread of eggs, toast, bacon and juice.

"You said last night, you were going to Commerce to find Kevin's wife and the kids," said Millie, "But what will you do when you find them?"

Joe finished his mouthful of eggs. "I haven't thought about it yet. I guess we should go back to Ingerwood to my apartment."

"You know you could come back here. You wouldn't have to travel so far, and I have lots of room."

Joe thought about it for a moment. "That's a really good idea. What do you guys think?"

"I think that would be great. I could use a safe place for my wife and baby," said Kevin.

Camille looked at Tyler. "I need to find my brother Pascal first, but I would like to stick around."

"I'm with you at least until the Chinese send that vaccine over," said Tank.

"What about you, Earl?" asked Joe.

"If it's okay, I would like to stay here. I'll slow you down anyway."

"I could use the help with the animals, and it's almost Christmas, and I don't think I could bear to be alone," admitted Millie.

After breakfast, they packed their things, filled the snowmobiles with fuel and packed more gas in the little trailer. They said their goodbyes and thanked Millie for her hospitality. She insisted on keeping Shelby, and Joe acquiesced. Millie gave them two radios.

"They only have a range of about 50 km, but it's a good way to stay in touch if you get separated," she said.

They climbed onto the snowmobiles. Tank towed the trailer again. Kevin and Joe had their snowmobiles to themselves and, despite Tank's reservations, Tyler and Camille road together on his side-by-side. Like its namesake, the side-by-side had two seats up front and a small bed in the back for storage.

They raced down the laneway, and out onto the road. It was sunny and cold, and there was another layer of fresh fluffy snow. They glided across the white terrain towards Commerce and an uncertain future, leaving a trail of wispy snow blowing in their wake.

CHAPTER 36

They had to stop once, just outside of the city limits to siphon gas from some parked cars outside a looted variety store. Tank went into the store and found a couple tourist maps of Commerce. He put one in his pack and gave the other to Joe.

It was late afternoon when they drove past the *Welcome to Commerce City* sign. Joe pulled over into the parking lot of G-Tech Engineering.

"We need to find a place for the night before we go into the city tomorrow morning," said Joe.

"Can we eat something, too?" asked Kevin.

"All right, let's find a safe place that might have food and heat," said Joe.

They drove on for a few minutes till Tank pointed out a small brick house with a big chimney. The house was empty, and there was a big wood stove in the living room. Tyler and Camille found some split wood in the shed in the backyard, and Kevin and Joe found a case of canned beans in the basement. Tank started a fire, and they all sat in the living room and ate.

"We need to discuss our next move," said Joe.

Kevin spoke up, "I'm going to the parliament buildings, I think I might know where Monique is."

"I'll come with you," said Joe. "With the train attacks and fighter jets everywhere, I'm not sure that the centre of the capital is the safest place to be right now. You may need help to stay safe," said Joe.

"I'm with you, Joe," said Tank.

"I need to go the University to find my brother," said Camille.

"And I'm going with her," added Tyler.

Tank looked over at Tyler with a noticeable glare.

"Are you sure you don't want to come with us?" asked Kevin. "We could go to the University afterwards."

"Like Joe said, the parliament buildings might not be the safest place right now," she said. "Besides, I survived on my own in Chateaugay. I have my knives, and Tyler has his gun."

Tank looked at Tyler. "If anything happens to her, I will tear your arms off and beat you with them."

Tyler looked back at him wide-eyed. "Yes, sir," he said, with a look of terror on his face.

Camille smirked. "We'll be fine."

"Do you have ammo for your rifle?" Tank asked Tyler.

"Yes, I have two boxes in the side-by-side."

"Do you know how to use the gun?"

"Yes, sir, it's my gun, and I used to go hunting with Dad."

Tank looked at both of them "I want you two to stay out of sight and only use the weapons if you get cornered. Call us on the radio if you run into trouble."

"Okay, Dad," Camille said mockingly, "We'll be careful."

The next morning Camille and Tyler headed south towards the University while Joe, Tank and Kevin went north to the Parliament Buildings.

The warm December sun was melting much of the snow, and Tyler and Camille were getting wet as they navigated the city streets towards the University.

There were a few army vehicles on the streets, as well as other trucks and SUVs. It felt strange to drive their side-by-side down the centre of the street but was also exhilarating. Tyler throttled up and sped across the wet snow. They approached the university. One of the buildings was burnt to the ground. Camille pointed to the residence building. Tyler stopped outside the front doors and shut off the side-by-side.

"I was only here once when we dropped him off on his first day," said Camille, "but I think I remember where his room is."

The doors weren't locked, and they walked into the small lobby. "It looks abandoned," said Tyler.

Camille pointed down one of the hallways. "I don't think he's here, but he may have left a note or something."

They walked down the hallway, which had garbage and papers strewn across the floor.

"I think this was this room," said Camille pointing at an open door.

They walked into the room. Both beds were empty, and the room was cold and dirty. They searched the room but found no notes or bodies.

"What size shoe does your brother wear?" asked Tyler as he looked in the closet.

"I don't know. Why?"

"Did he have really big feet?"

"I don't think so. He had regular feet, I guess."

"I see size 12 shoes and boots only."

"What does that mean?"

"It might mean that your brother took his shoes and boots with him, which means that he might still be alive. Do you have any idea where else he might go?"

"He worked part-time at the museum. He might have gone there, or he could be trying to get back home."

"Let's try the museum, just in case."

They got back on the side-by-side and drove west through downtown towards the museum. About 15 minutes into their trip, they heard a gunshot. Ahead of them, a group of people stood in front of a pick-up truck in the middle of the road. Tyler turned into the first available road. The road was a ramp that led into a parking garage. He followed the road up two levels and stopped. They heard the pickup truck following them and continued up the ramp.

"They're coming after us," yelled Camille over the noise of the side-by-side, "and this is going to be a dead end."

"I know," he replied. "When we stop, grab your bow and arrows, and we'll make a run for it."

When they reached the top level, he drove up to the stairwell doors and shut off the engine. Tyler grabbed his pack and rifle and joined Camille, who was already opening the door to the stairwell. They could hear the truck at the top stop, but they could also hear voices at the bottom of the stairwell.

"Any idea where we are?" asked Camille.

"Not exactly, I think we're in the theatre district. Come on, this way."

A few stair levels down, he opened a door that led into a long hallway. There were business offices on either side of the hall.

"Wait!" he yelled as she was about to walk through the door. "Take off your boots."

"What? Why?"

"Trust me," he said, taking off his boots. "We don't want them to track us. These boots will leave wet footprints for them to follow. We can carry them and put them back on later."

She took off her boots and held them. Tyler opened the door, they both walked inside the hallway. He let the door close slowly and quietly. They ran down the hallway in their socks, passing doorways, a coffee shop and a variety store. Light streamed in from the overhead windows. Everything was closed, and they didn't see anyone else.

Once they were sure they weren't being followed, they put their boots back on. "What made you think to take off our boots," Camille asked.

"I used to spend a lot of time tracking animals when I hunted with my father."

"Are you, like, indigenous?"

"Yes, I am Mohawk."

Their boots and voices echoed as they walked through the

hollow promenade.

"I thought you said you were from here?"

"That's right."

"But I thought...indigenous people lived on reserves."

Tyler laughed. "You know a lot of people might take offence to that."

"I'm sorry, I didn't mean to offend you or..."

"No, it's alright, I'm not that sensitive. I lived on a reserve half the time. My parents were separated. My father lived on a Mohawk First Nation reserve about two hours north of here, and I spent my weekends with him. During the week, I lived with my mother in Commerce, where I went to school."

"Why did you move to the country?"

"My mother got a job there."

"What about your Dad?"

"I was supposed to spend Christmas and vacations with... shhh."

They could hear footsteps coming towards them.

Tyler looked around frantically. "We need somewhere to hide!"

Camille looked around, but everything was closed.

She found a walkway that led to the Veldman Theatre. "Over here!"

They ran to the door and pushed it open as the voices and footsteps got closer.

They closed the door behind them and stood in the darkness. The footsteps in the hallway behind them got louder. Camille turned her flashlight on for a brief second. She tried to memorize the room before it was plunged back into darkness. They were at a side door for a large carpeted foyer. It was the reception area for the theatre. Further down and to the right were large wooden double doors.

She grabbed Tyler's hand and ran. "Let's go!"

Tyler tripped over something, and Camille reached out and pulled him up.

"Get up and follow me," she said.

"How do you know where you're going? Its pitch black in here."

She led them to the double doors and pushed them open.

"Okay," she said, "This time, pay attention. I'm going to turn my flashlight on for one second then turn it back off. Try to memorize what this room looks like."

She flicked her flashlight on and then back off. During the brief moment that it shone; they could see they were at the back of a small theatre with a large stage at the front. There was a long open row between the seats that went all the way to the stage.

They walked through the darkness until they got to the stage. They held their hands out to find it, then climbed onto the stage. They could hear someone walking around in the foyer and ran to the side of the stage. They groped in the darkness, afraid to turn the flashlight back on. Camille's hand touched a handle which, when she pushed it, opened a door. She dragged Tyler by the hand through the door. They stumbled through a corridor and found another doorway that led them into a small room. This door had a lock on the inside, which Camille used as soon as they were inside.

"Here," said Tyler. He grabbed a piece of fabric. "Put this under the door, so they can't see our light." They stood inside the door and waited till they couldn't hear footsteps or voices.

Tyler leaned his gun against the wall beside his pack. Camille put her pack and bow beside his and surveyed the room. It was a dressing room. Along one side of the wall were large vanity mirrors framed in lights with a chair in front of each one. On the other side of the room were racks and shelves full of costumes and props.

Tyler started looking through the props, and Camille went through the racks of clothes.

"Aha!" said Tyler from the other side of the room

Camille felt the lace on a fancy white wedding dress. "What did you find?"

She heard the snap of a lighter, and light flickered on the ceiling. Camille stepped back to look and saw that he had found a candle, which was now burning in front of one of the mirrors. He was sitting proudly on one of the chairs.

A moment later, Camille stepped out with the wedding dress over her clothes. She threw her arms out and put her head in the air. "What do you think?"

"I pictured you in more of a black wedding dress with spikes and chains."

"Oh, really," said Camille, "You pictured me in a wedding dress?"

"No... I didn't mean... I was just," he stammered.

"I'm just kidding," she laughed. She took the dress off and went back to the racks.

She came back out with a newsboy cap and fingerless gloves.

"Tada!" she said, but he wasn't there.

Suddenly a man jumped out with a black cavalier hat with a big red feather and an ornate sword pointed at her. She jumped back in fear. The man smiled, and Camille realized it was Tyler.

"You scared me!" she said, throwing her cap at him.

He deftly caught the hat with his sword and handed it back to her.

"M'lady seems to have dropped her hat," he joked.

She threw the hat into the racks of clothes.

They heard footsteps from somewhere in the building.

"He's still here," said Camille, "What are we going to do?"

Tyler put his sword down and laid his hand on the chair. "We could just stay here for the night. Maybe they'll be gone by morning."

"But it's cold in here, and I don't think your little candle is going to keep us warm."

There are plenty of clothes here we can use for blankets, and we can keep each other warm.

She looked up at him with a glare.

"No, I didn't mean that. I'm sorry, I just meant that we could use our body heat…I mean with our clothes on, and…"

"I'm just kidding, again," she laughed. "You're so easy."

"Yeah, well I can picture Tank ripping my arms off when he finds out I looked at you funny."

"That's possible," she said, "We'll make a bed – no an area to sleep – no, make that rest with our clothes on while we recite the Lord's Prayer."

He shook his head and gathered up some clothes.

Once they were settled and comfortable, (10 centimetres apart), and had blown out the candle, they lay in the dark talking quietly.

"Do you think things will ever go back to normal?" she asked.

"I don't know, I don't think so."

There was a brief moment of quiet before Camille spoke again.

"I'm still wearing these silly gloves," she said.

"You mean the apocalypse gloves?" he asked.

"What?"

"The apocalypse gloves. Haven't you seen any apocalypse movies? For some reason, they always wear fingerless gloves during the apocalypse."

"You're right, they do, don't they?"

"So now you are really ready for the apocalypse."

"Do you think this is the apocalypse? Is this the end of the world?"

"I don't know. I hope not. Most of the people we both knew are gone, but we're still here. It must be for a reason."

"You won't leave me, will you?" she asked.

"No, Camille, I'll stay with you."

"Good."

She moved her hands over and clasped his hand. She could feel his warm skin with the ends of her fingers.

"We're going to find my brother tomorrow, right?" she asked.

He squeezed her hand. "Yes, we will, but you can't tell Tank I touched your fingers."

CHAPTER 37

As Camille and Tyler slept in the theatre, Pascal was attempting to leave the hospital with the baby. It was dark and late, and he figured the streets might not be the safest place to be in the middle of the night. He turned around and went back inside.

"Effy!" he yelled.

She turned around. "I told you, you are going to have to care of that baby, till her mother is better."

"Yes, I know that, but I would rather go to the C3 in the safety of daylight. Is there somewhere here we can sleep?"

She looked around to make sure no one was looking. "Come with me."

Effy led him down the hall and up two sets of stairs. Pascal noticed that the second floor was much colder. The light from the green exit sign lit their way as they walked down the hallway. Partway down, she pulled out a set of keys and unlocked a door that said Dr. Ematha.

"Dr. Ematha is no longer with us, so I'm sure he wouldn't mind if you borrowed his office. There should be a heat vent in the ceiling. They are all closed up, but if you open in back up, it will be warm for you and your baby."

"She's not my baby."

"Okay, I got to go. Be sure you're out of here in the morning." She shut the door and left.

The room was nicely furnished with a leather couch, a large

desk, a large bookshelf, and a fridge and microwave. He flicked the light switch and jumped when it worked.

That rarely happens anymore.

The baby started crying. He rocked her, but it didn't seem to help. Pascal put her down on the couch and looked up at the ceiling for the vent. He had to stand on the desk, but managed to get the vent open and was relieved when warm air started blowing into the room. The baby was still crying. There was a small sink with slowly running water. He filled his water bottle and drank. The baby was still crying. He found the can of powdered formula and followed the mixing directions on the back. He held the baby in his arms and tried feeding her the formula. She took a sip, then spit it out and started crying again.

Now what?

He looked at the directions again and noticed the last instruction, which said to warm it up. He put the bottle in the microwave for 20 seconds, then took it out, shook it and tested the formula. It didn't taste to bad, and he hoped it was the right temperature. The baby was still crying.

He sat again on the couch with the baby in his arms and put the bottle to her lips. This time she took it. She contentedly drank while her blue eyes stared straight up into his. Her fingers grabbed on to his baby finger and squeezed. She released her grip and then squeezed again. She repeated this over and over as she drank. It felt like she was squeezing with every heartbeat.

"Your kind of cute for a baby," he said out loud, "but I'm still giving you back when your mother is better."

He looked up at the bookshelf. Most of the books were medical books. There was a book on Advances in Cancer Research, another was the Nord Compendium of Rare Diseases and Disorders. There were other books about bone diseases, bowel disorders and nerve diseases. He wondered what would happen with all this knowledge now that most of the population was dead.

I hope there are hard copies of all the medical research because I don't know if we'll ever get the internet back.

Suddenly the baby spat the nipple out and started crying.

Now what?

He rocked the baby and tried feeding it the bottle again, but she kept crying.

He hoisted the baby in the air. "What do you want?"

The baby burped and then spat up. The milk spittle landed in his face.

"That is the second time I have been spat it in the face today. You're worse than that llama!"

He fed her again, but the next time she stopped eating, he tapped her on the back till she burped.

Before the bottle was finished, the baby started to nod off.

Early the next morning, he woke with a start, wondering where he was and what the annoying sound was.

He realized where he was and the annoying sound was a baby who lying beside him, but no longer sleeping.

What's that horrible smell?

He lifted the baby up and smelled it. "That's nasty!"

He noticed that there was a package of diapers inside the door.

Thank you, Effy.

He had never changed a baby's diaper before, but after almost gagging, he managed to put a clean diaper on her.

Pascal went downstairs and asked about Effy, but was told that her shift had ended and she had gone home. He wondered if the doctors and nurses were getting paid.

He asked where the baby's mother's room was and was directed to Room 399. When he approached the bed with the baby in his arms, the mother started crying and tried to get up. One of the nurses came running over. "Ma'am, you can't get up, you're still sick."

"Let her hold her baby," said Pascal firmly. He gently laid the baby in her arms.

The tears streamed down the mother's face. "What happened? Who are you? How did I get here? Why do you have my baby?"

He told her how he had found her in the cabin and brought her to the hospital.

"I'm Monique, and this bundle of joy is Olivia, and we would like to thank you for all you have done."

"Your welcome. My name is Pascal, and she's a nice baby when she's not crying."

Monique smiled weakly. Sweat ran down her face. "I'm so tired…" she said as her head nodded forward.

"She needs more rest," said the nurse, "you need to take your baby."

"It's not my…" he stopped when he heard Monique mumbling something.

"What did you say?" he asked and leaned in to listen.

"My husband Kevin, he's…" she drifted into unconsciousness.

The nurse took Olivia and handed her back to Pascal. "She's going to need a couple of days to get over her fever. You can come back tomorrow to visit." The nurse shooed him out of the room. He carried Olivia to the stairwell to go upstairs to the office, when a voice yelled out from behind him, "Sir! Sir, you can't go that way, the exit is this way."

"But, I just…"

"Sorry, but that stairwell is off-limits," said the nurse.

As he reluctantly left the hospital, he saw two snowmobiles pull up to the emergency doors. A large man drove one of the snowmobiles that had a trailer with a body in the back. The other snowmobile carried a man and a little girl.

CHAPTER 38

Earlier that day, when Tyler and Camille had gone south to find her brother, Joe, Tank, and Kevin got on their snowmobiles and headed North. Kevin said that when he was on his honeymoon with Monique, they had gone to the parliament buildings. There was a monument in front of the parliament buildings that featured a flame in the centre. He had told Monique that his love for her was like the eternal flame that had been burning non-stop since it was lit over 50 years ago. She kissed him passionately. Kevin had a passerby take their picture with the parliament buildings in the background. He always carried the picture in his wallet. Kevin told Joe and Tank that if Monique was in Commerce City, there would be a good chance she might be at the flame monument.

On their way into the city, they passed an abandoned roadblock. As they got closer to downtown and the parliament buildings, they started seeing more military vehicles and jets fly by overhead.

They drove past some ostentatious mansions and saw a young girl with an unzipped coat and no hat or mitts. She was running into the road, waving her arms. The three snowmobiles stopped, and Joe was the first to get off and run to the girl. Kevin came up behind him while Tank stood by his snowmobile with his rifle out.

"Help, please," said the girl, who Kevin thought might have been a little younger than Ayesha. "We're being attacked!"

The girl was frantic, and tears streamed down her face.

"Okay, okay," said Joe. "Slow down and tell me what's going on. Who is being attacked?"

She was still catching her breath from running. "My brother, his friend, and our neighbour are still in the house, and there are a bunch of people with guns that are surrounding the house. I think they are going to kill everybody."

"What's your name?" asked Kevin.

"Ivette," she said, still sniffling.

"Well I'm Kevin, this is Joe and that big guy back there with the gun is Tank."

"Can you help us?"

Kevin looked at Joe, but answered before Joe gave him affirmation. "Yes, where do you live?"

They went back to tell Tank.

"What?" he protested, "We only have one hunting rifle. How are we supposed to take on a group of armed invaders with only one gun? If we stop to help everyone, we'll never find your wife."

Ivette looked up at him with her big tear-filled, brown eyes. "Please, Mister Tank, you have to help us."

"Come on," said Joe, "You can finally do some shooting with your new gun."

"Fine, but we do this my way."

They all nodded.

"How far is your house?" he asked.

"It's two blocks that way." Ivette pointed across the yard she had run from.

"We leave the snowmobiles parked here and walk."

The neighbourhood featured large houses that were homes to the rich and powerful elite of Commerce City. Large old maple and elm trees hung over expansive yards separated by what were once well-manicured hedges and ornate fences. As they cut across a yard with a frozen decorative fountain, Tank asked, "How did you get out of the house?"

"My brother shot at them when they attacked," Ivette answered, "and then told me to run away when they were distracted. I think they still saw me, but they didn't shoot."

"How many attackers and what did they have for firepower?" Tank asked.

"What?"

Kevin interjected. "Do you know how many people attacked your house and if they had guns?"

"I don't know, maybe four or five. I know some of them had guns, because they were shooting at us and the window in my room broke."

"How much further?" asked Tank.

"It's that house up there." She pointed to a large stone and brick house. It didn't have a fence or hedges around it but was surrounded by large oak trees.

"Joe, can you shoot?" Tank asked.

"Sure, I used to shoot a little when I was younger, but I'm not a crack shot or anything."

"Kevin, you stay here with the girl. Joe, you're with me."

They walked closer to the house and could see two men at the front of the house. Each man stood behind a tree with a rifle. They could hear gunshots from behind the house.

"Looks like we have two here at the front and at least three at the sides and back, they may all be armed."

"And we have one gun," said Joe, "those aren't very good odds for us."

"We have one gun with a scope in the hands of a trained professional," he replied, "and we have the element of surprise."

"So, what's the plan?"

"I need you to lay down under this tree and act injured. I will climb up this tree. When he comes over to check on you, I will jump down and kill him with my knife. We'll take his gun and even the odds a little."

"So, I'm the bait?"

"You make it sound bad."

"Won't he see you in the tree, and what's to stop him from just shooting me?"

"Unless he's trained, he won't look up, and he won't shoot someone who is injured."

"What if he's trained?"

"Then we're screwed."

Five minutes later, Joe reluctantly lay on the ground, groaning.

"Louder," whispered Tank from his tree branch. "He can't hear you."

Joe yelled out, "Help!"

A large man in a red and black checkered jacket lumbered over. He pointed his gun at Joe. "Who are you, and what are you doing here?"

"Please," Joe moaned, "I'm hurt, can you help me?"

The man stood there for a moment, then lowered his gun and walked over. When he was two steps from Joe, Tank dropped out of the tree. Joe looked up and saw the man standing with a shocked look on his face. Tank's hand covered his mouth as he fell forward, Joe saw a knife sticking out the top of his head.

He cringed at the sound of Tank removing the blade from the man's skull. Joe picked up the gun as Tank dragged the body behind the tree.

Joe looked at the gun in his hand. "How does this thing work?"

Tank came back with a box of bullets. "Here, put these in your pocket." Joe took the box. "This a lever-action rifle, like in the Wild West. After you fire, you have to pump the lever down and then back. That will load the next bullet in the chamber so you can shoot again. If you run out of bullets, load them one at a time in here."

"Got it. What now?"

"You stay behind this tree and count to 60, then fire your weapon in their general direction..."

"Wait, am I the bait again?"

"Well, yes, but at least this time you're armed. When they move towards your position, I will move in behind them and pick them off."

"But won't they be shooting at me?"

"Yes, but don't stick your head out. Just fire in the air once in a while."

Tank took off fast, adding to the collection of tracks in the wet snow. Joe waited behind the tree and counted. As he reached 30 Joe smelled smoke in the air and wondered what was burning. At 60 he took a deep breath and poked his head out. He saw a man in a blue winter coat facing away from him, looking at the house. He put the rifle snugly against his shoulder and used the sights at the top to aim at the man's head. He pulled the trigger and ducked back behind the tree. He could hear the man shout as he worked the lever to put the next round in the chamber. Joe could hear the man yelling, but there was no return fire. Joe peeked out from behind the tree and saw the man walking towards him, holding his gun with one hand. There was blood on his shoulder.

I hit him! The bait bites back!

There was another shot and then silence. He chanced another peek and saw the man in blue, face down in the slush. He waited, and suddenly a large man was standing beside him. Before he could take a shot, Tank grabbed his rifle, "Whoa there, John Wayne, don't shoot. I'm a friendly."

"Sorry, but did you see that? I hit him!"

"Were you aiming for his head?"

"Yes, and I just missed."

"Next time, aim for the centre of his body mass. There's more room for error. If you hit him anywhere, you're going to either kill him or wound him. If he's wounded, you can usually get closer for the kill shot."

"Where are the rest of them?"

"I think they're in the house, which is now on fire. You need to stay here in case they come out the front. I'm going in the back to flush them out. Go to the next tree and fire at any bad guys that come out."

"How will I know the difference between the bad guys and

the guys we are trying to save?"

"I have no idea. Maybe don't shoot the women and children and ask the others if they know Ivette?"

He ran off behind the house. Joe stood beside the tree with his gun pointed at the door. There was smoke coming out of some of the windows, and he could hear yelling and shouting and sporadic gunshots from inside.

Then the door opened, and a man came out.

Or is it a boy?

"Don't move or I'll shoot," Joe yelled as he aimed the gun at the centre of his chest.

The young man raised his gun in Joe's direction, and Joe pulled the trigger. The man stumbled, then fell into the snow. He tried to lift himself, but Joe worked the lever and shot him in the head. There was more shouting and gunshots inside. Joe stepped over the man whose blood was staining the snow red, and walked through the front door. He was met with a wall of smoke. The intense smoke caused him to start coughing, and he tried to cover his mouth. He thought he heard someone yelling, but couldn't see anything through the thick smoke. A dark shape came through the smoke and knocked him over. He looked up from the ground and saw the person who had knocked him over run out the front door.

Suddenly, he felt hands under his armpits and was dragged out the door.

"I thought I told you to guard the front door?!" yelled Tank.

"Sorry, I thought you might need help," he said, but Tank was already running after the man. Joe got up and took off after him. As he was running, he heard two gunshots. When he caught up, he saw Ivette crying and Tank standing with his gun in his hand and two men lying on the ground. One of them was Kevin.

"What happened?" he said as he knelt beside him.

"Someone abandoned their post," said Tank.

"I'm sorry, I was just trying to…"

"Never mind," said Tank. "Let's see what we got here." He

rolled Kevin over. There was blood oozing out of a bullet wound in his stomach.

"Am I going to die?" asked Kevin.

Tank took his hat off, and pressed it against the wound. "Yes, you are going to die, but not today. We need to get him to a hospital."

He lifted Kevin and started carrying him. "Go get my snowmobile, and we'll put him in the trailer."

"What happened to my brother?" asked Ivette.

"I'm sorry," said Tank, "but your brother and his friends are all dead."

She started balling.

"You can come with us if you want," suggested Joe and then ran to fetch the snowmobile.

A short time later, the four of them were speeding through the snow towards the hospital.

They pulled up to the front doors of Commerce City Regional Hospital, and Tank carried Kevin in. Joe and Ivette followed him in as a man carrying a baby walked out of the hospital.

CHAPTER 39

Pascal carried Olivia past the men and the girl from the snowmobiles. The weather was changing, and he felt a winter storm coming. As he drove his truck out of the hospital parking lot, Olivia started crying again. He pumped the heat up to full blast, and she stopped crying.

"Well, aren't we picky," he said, "let me know if it gets too warm. I'd hate for your highness to be uncomfortable."

He followed the directions that Effy gave him, and 20 minutes later he pulled into the C3. It was a former high school that had been turned into a C3 shelter by the army.

When Pascal checked in, they weren't sure whether to put him with the other mothers and babies or in the single men's section. They ended up finding him a small office on the 2nd floor near some of the other families. They gave him a box of baby items including diapers, formula, blankets and a baby carrier. The carrier was a pouch that fit over his shoulder and held the baby in front and kept his hands free. He tried it on and was impressed.

This could come in handy.

In the office he changed and fed the baby while jets screamed somewhere overhead. Pascal put Olivia down to sleep, then lay down and tried to follow her lead.

CHAPTER 40

Kevin was in surgery as Joe, Tank, and Ivette sat in the waiting room. Ivette cried for more than an hour, and Joe put his arm around her shoulder, unsure what to say or do to console her.

It was mid-afternoon by the time the Doctor came out and let them know that Kevin's surgery was over. The bullet had been removed, and the internal bleeding stopped. He was no longer in critical condition.

"Normally, we would keep him for a few days to make sure he's stable and doesn't have an infection. However, I'm going to give you his antibiotics now just in case."

"In case of what?" asked Joe.

The Doctor ignored him. "He's all sutured up and is in stable condition. He needs a lot of rest and can't be moving around for at least a few days, so you'll want to get him to a safe place where he can be comfortable."

"Why can't he stay here?"

"Things are happening fast in the city. I don't know how much longer this place will have electricity, and I've been hearing rumours about an imminent attack."

"What? By who?" asked Tank.

"Sorry," he said, "I don't know, but if you want my advice, it would be to take your friend out of here to someplace safe." He handed Joe a bottle of pills and walked away.

"What are we going to do now?" asked Tank.

"We should go to that flame monument to see if Monique left any kind note," said Joe. Ivette had stopped crying and was leaning into him, her eyes closing.

"Maybe you should stay here," said Tank. "I'll go and check it out."

"Alright, but be careful out there."

Tank nodded. "Here, take the radio. You should call Camille and Tyler if you don't hear from them by morning."

After he left, Joe slipped out from under the sleeping Ivette to take a walk. The hospital lights flickered.

A nurse came out of Room 399. "Sir, you shouldn't be here."

"Sorry, I was stretching my legs."

"You need to stay in the waiting room."

"I don't suppose you can recommend a decent hotel nearby?" he joked.

"Are you with the little girl sleeping in the waiting room."

"I guess, I just sort of found her today."

She held out her hand. "My name's Effy."

"I'm Joe."

"Come with me," she said and started walking away.

In the waiting room, she pointed at Ivette. "Pick her up and follow me."

She walked over to the stairwell doors. "I can't believe I'm doing this again," she mumbled.

Joe held Ivette in his arm as he followed her. "Pardon?"

"Nothing."

She showed him to Dr. Ematha's office.

"Make sure you're out of here in the morning," she said and left.

Joe laid Ivette on the couch and covered her with a blanket. He leaned back in the chair and fell asleep.

CHAPTER 41

Tank left his snowmobile, which was hooked up to the trailer and took Joe's snowmobile instead. According to his map, he needed to go straight north. There were more army transport vehicles in the city, but he couldn't tell if they were all going somewhere or just patrolling the city.

As he got closer to the parliament buildings, he came upon an army roadblock. It was heavily fortified with three manned C16 40 mm grenade launchers propped up behind a wall of sandbags. A Leopard 2A4 tank stood menacing with its main gun pointed down the centre of the road. Five fully equipped Canadian Special Forces stood at the ready.

Tank veered his snowmobile down a side road before he reached the roadblock. He drove down the side streets looking for a way around the roadblock, but found other similar ones at all point of access to the parliament buildings. The buildings backed onto Commerce River, so he drove toward the river hoping to find another way around. As he drove down streets lined with tall office towers, he saw something in his peripheral vision. It was a black form with an assault rifle disappearing into the side door of a building. He kept going for a minute, then parked his snowmobile between two vans. The building that the figure had gone into was one of the tallest buildings in the area, and he figured it might have a good vantage point. Also, the armed figure in black had piqued his curiosity. He loaded his rifle and walked to the building.

The footprints in the snow indicated that there were three men, and all of them wore identical boots.

He opened the door slowly, but stopped when he looked through the opening and saw a taut wire just above the floor.

Professionals.

He let the door close and walked around the back of the building. He found another door that led to a small restaurant-style patio. It was locked, and he used the butt of his gun to break the knob. This door did not appear to be booby-trapped. He stood inside the door and listened, but couldn't hear anything. Tank slowly crept through the cafeteria and into the hallway. He avoided the stairwell that the others had used and opted for the stairwell on the opposite side of the building. The elevator buttons he passed told him there were 20 floors.

He began his ascent.

On every floor, he stopped and opened the door to listen. Each time he neither heard nor saw anything. He stopped halfway up to catch his breath, and 15 minutes later, he made it to the top floor. Tank deftly opened the door and moved into the hallway. He could hear voices in one of the offices. Ahead he saw a man with a gun facing the opposite direction. Tank ducked into a doorway for a board room. The room was connected on the far end to a small office. He walked to the office, which had a doorway back into the hallway. He peered out the doorway and saw the man still facing the opposite way, but now he was closer. Tank slung the rifle over his shoulder and pulled out his knife. He was hoping to use the man as a temporary hostage until he found out if they were Canadian Forces. As he walked closer, the man turned and began raising his rifle towards Tank. The knife instinctively flew from Tank's hand and lodged itself into the man's jugular. The man grabbed at the knife as blood spurted out. Foreign voices came from the room the soldier had been guarding.

Tank unslung his rifle and shot the second man before he had a chance to get off a shot. The third man dropped the large binoculars in his hands, pulled out a pistol from his holster, and fired. Tank ducked as the bullet whizzed over his head. His gun jammed as he tried to fire back, so he threw the gun as hard as he could at the man. It hit him in the face. While he was still stunned, Tank charged at the man. There was an audible crunch of rib bones as Tank's shoulder collided with the man's chest and the pistol dropped out his hands. They both crashed to the floor. Tank grabbed the pistol on the floor and shot the man in the face before he had a chance to catch his breath.

Tank looked around to make sure there was nobody else. He also checked all the bodies for signs of life, but they were all dead. None of them had any papers, tags, ID or identifying marks. They were all of Asian descent.

Korean, Chinese, or Japanese? What are they doing here?

One of them had an encrypted combat radio. The large binoculars, the radio, and the view out the window led him to the conclusion that they were an advanced recon team.

From the window, he could see four of the roadblocks and the parliament buildings behind them. They were being guarded by a contingent of Canadian Army equipment and soldiers. There were tanks, anti-aircraft guns, and an M142 mobile rocket system. Voices from the combat radio broke him from his reverie.

These guys will be missing their check-in.

He upgraded his armaments with the dead soldiers' guns. Tank grabbed the QSZ-92 semi-automatic pistol, a CS/L26 50 round sub-machine gun and five grenades. He retrieved his knife from the first man's throat and the binoculars from his neck and ran down the stairs.

On his way down, on the 12th floor, he heard voices from below and exited the stairwell. He ran across the building, through several hallways and corridors, till he found the stairwell on the opposite side. He pulled the pin from one of his grenades and dropped it down the stairwell towards the booby trap at the bottom. Tank stepped back, and closed the door. He waited till he heard the satisfying explosion from below then searched for an office to hide in for the night.

CHAPTER 42

That night Tyler and Camille slept in the theatre dressing room.
    Pascal and Olivia slept at the C3.
Tank slept in the office tower.
Zach and Ayesha slept in the cabin.
Monique slept at the hospital.
Kevin slept in the same hospital down the hall, while Joe and Ivette slept on the 2nd floor.
None of them would get a full night's sleep.

CHAPTER 43

Whatever drugs they had given Monique to sleep were starting to wear off. She lay awake in her hospital bed, staring at the ceiling. The last couple of nights were a blur. She remembered being ill in the cabin when Zach and Ayesha left. The next thing she knew, she was in this hospital bed. Some Pascal guy had come to see her with Olivia.

Who is Pascal, and where is Olivia now?

Her leg was sore, but she could move it. She sat up in bed and let her feet touch the ground. When she put weight on her bad leg, it was a little painful, but bearable. She shared the room with another patient, and he was snoring loudly as she limped by.

She hobbled down the hall to the nurse's station which was manned by a lone nurse.

"Ma'am, what are you doing up?" asked the nurse.

"I'm just taking a little walk."

"You should go back to bed and rest."

"What's your name?" asked Monique.

"It's Effy."

"Effy, do you know where my baby Olivia is?"

"She's with Pascal, the man who brought you here. He seems like a nice guy."

"Are they here somewhere?"

"No, but I'm sure they'll be back in the morning."

Suddenly there was the sound of an explosion nearby. The building shuddered, and the lights flickered.

"What was that?" asked Monique.

"I don't know. You better get back to your room - and maybe put your clothes on. There's a major storm out there, and if we have to evacuate, you don't want to freeze to death."

Monique looked down at her thin hospital gown and hobbled back to her room. In a small cabinet, she found her clothes, boots and winter coat.

"What's going on?" said one of the other patients.

"I don't know, but you might want to get your clothes on."

He snorted, rolled over and went back to sleep.

Monique put her clothes on and was reaching for her boots when the lights went out. The emergency lights in the hallway came on, and she slipped her boots and coat on. She walked to the other patient's bed and shook him.

"Hey, buddy, wake up."

"Don't touch me!" he yelled, swatting at her hand.

She left him and went into the hallway. The fire alarm came on, and she could smell smoke.

"Get out of here!" yelled Effy.

She limped down the hallway as it began to fill with smoke. The sprinklers came on. The hospital, which was silent a few moments ago, turned into total pandemonium. Monique ran through the smokey chaos and into the snowy street.

I need to find Olivia. I hope Zach and Ayesha are okay. Will I ever see Kevin again?

She started limping in the direction of what she hoped was the museum. After a few blocks, she spotted a chain link fence surrounding a parking lot filled with transport and box trucks. The sign for the business was covered in snow. The gates were locked, with a loose chain. She was able to squeeze through the gap.

I'm glad I lost my baby weight.

Most of the trucks were parked in neat rows, except one box truck that was backed up to the loading dock. The driver's side and passenger doors were locked as was the rear door. The side of the truck had a #667 on it.

There was a smaller door next to the loading door that had a rectangular window in it. She found a tire chock to break the glass and then unlocked the door. Once inside, she used her flashlight to look around. There were racks, boxes, packaging and a small metal desk. In the middle of the desk were a set of keys with a small plastic fob. She picked it up and read the number on the fob: #667.

"Gotcha!" The word echoed across the plant. She wondered what kind of factory this was, but decided she didn't have time to investigate.

After unlocking the truck, she started it and turned on the heat. Monique took the smaller key off the fob and went to the back of the vehicle. She unlocked and raised the rolling door and took a look inside. There were stacks of boxes, and she could tell from the labelling what was inside them.

"Eureka!" she yelled in delight.

Jets flew by overhead. She closed the door and got back in the truck. The storm had subsided and the sun was beginning to peek over the horizon as the van smashed through the gate.

Olivia, where are you?

She drove through the snow towards the museum.

CHAPTER 44

Earlier, Kevin awoke to the sound of the explosion. He blinked awake and felt the hospital shudder.

Earthquake? Where am I? Oh, yeah, this is the hospital.

His stomach hurt, and there was an IV tube stuck into a vein in his arm.

At least I'm not dead yet.

Then the lights went out.

God, help me.

Then the fire alarm went off.

Seriously, God, I need your help.

He pulled out the IV and sat up. His head spun a little, and the pain in his stomach was intense.

There was a wheelchair near his bed, and he painfully struggled into it as the sprinklers came on. There was no one else in his room, but he could hear the chaos happening in the hallway as people yelled, screamed and ran.

Please, God, let me see my wife and child again.

He wheeled himself into the hallway as the sprinklers stopped, but the chaos continued.

CHAPTER 45

The sprinklers on the second floor did not turn on, but the explosion, hospital shudder and fire alarm woke Joe and Ivette.

"Get your jacket and boots on, now!" yelled Joe.

By the time they made it downstairs, the first floor was filled with smoke and mayhem.

He turned to Ivette.

"Put your scarf over your face, and go out those doors. Go across the street and wait for me there."

She looked at him silently, but didn't move.

"I have to find my friend," he told her, "but I'll meet you across the street. I promise. Now go!"

With a terrified look in her eyes, she scurried out the front doors amongst a throng of panicked patients.

The smoke was getting thicker, and he kept running into people trying to get out. Joe tried to remember how to get to Kevin's room, but it was getting increasingly difficult to navigate the hallway. The floors were wet from the sprinklers, the smoke was thick, and he was walking against the traffic. A woman in boots and a winter jacket limped by him.

Finally, he navigated his way to Kevin's hallway. Something hit him hard in his shin, and he cried out.

"Son of a..."

"Joe? Is that you?" asked Kevin from the wheelchair. "You're going the wrong way!"

"Kevin, thank God!"

"Yes, I will, but please drive me out of here first."

Joe pushed the wheelchair towards the exit. Now that he was going with the direction of traffic, it was much faster. They were both coughing, and their eyes were stinging. Joe was relieved to finally take a breath of clean air when he wheeled Kevin out the front doors. The relief was short-lived, when the cold snowy wind hit him.

Kevin was dressed only in his hospital gown, which was wet from the sprinklers, and the cold hit him like an ice block. Joe took off his winter jacket and put it over his shivering friend. The blowing snow made it hard to see. Joe pushed hard on the wheelchair to get it through the deep snow on the sidewalk. He kept going straight across the road. Patients, doctors and nurses were everywhere. There was another explosion behind them, and flames began to spew out of the windows.

When they made it across the street, Joe yelled loudly, "Ivette! Ivette, are you out here?"

Through the snowy darkness he panned the crowd till he saw a small child waving rapidly.

"Over here, Ivette. Come to my voice."

He saw a small figure trudging through the snow towards him. He reached out and hugged her. She was shivering when she hugged him back.

"Let's get out of here, okay?"

She looked at him and nodded.

He nudged Kevin, "I'm going to have to help you walk; this wheelchair is impossible to push in this snow. We need to find the snowmobile."

Kevin put his arm over Joe's shoulder, and Joe did the same. With Ivette holding on to Joe's belt, they shambled over to the snowmobile. Joe laid Kevin in the trailer, and with cold shaking hands, started the snowmobile. Ivette climbed on behind him and clung on to him tightly. As the hospital burned behind them, they plowed through the drifting snow into the frosty night.

After a few blocks, Joe pulled up to the side of a pizza restaurant where it was sheltered somewhat from the wind. He pulled out the radio in his coat pocket.

"Camille, Tyler, are you there? This is Joe."

There was a muffled crackle then: "This is Camille. We're here."

"Where are you? over."

"We're in the theatre district. What's happening with all the explosions and planes? Are we being attacked?"

"I don't know. We were in the hospital when it caught fire. Kevin is with me. We made it out, but now I'm not sure where to go. Are you guys safe?"

"Where is Tank?"

"He went to the Parliament Buildings."

"Shouldn't you wait for him."

"I can't. Kevin is hurt and I have a little girl with me. This storm is brutal and I need to find someplace safe and warm."

"We're on our way to the museum. It's where my brother worked. I don't think anyone would be there, and they may have supplies. It's on the edge of the city. It might be safer. It should at least get you out of the wind."

"Okay, I think I should have enough gas to get there.

"Do you know where it is?"

"Tank gave me a map. I can figure it out. We're on our way."

"We'll see you there."

CHAPTER 46

At the same time the explosion rocked the hospital, an alarm went off at the C3. Pascal woke up and grabbed Olivia.

A soldier in the hallway was making an announcement with a handheld loudspeaker:

"Attention, attention! All personnel must immediately go down the stairs and into the gymnasium and shelter in place. This is not a drill. Attention, all personnel must immediately go down the stairs and into the gymnasium and shelter in place..." The soldier repeated this as he walked down the hallway.

Pascal got his coat and boots on, bundled up Olivia, put on the baby pouch and put her in it. He put his backpack on and followed the crowd down the stairs to the gymnasium.

"What's going on?" he asked a woman walking down the stairs beside him.

"I don't know, and they're not telling us. They just say we're safer in here."

"I heard we're under attack!" said someone else. There was other murmuring and theories.

Once they reached the gym, Pascal sat against the wall in the corner and rocked Olivia.

The fluorescent lights in the gym went out and the emergency lights at the exits came on.

There was a brief din of excitement, but people settled

back down and waited.

Pascal and Olivia fell asleep.

He awoke sometime later to excited voices. When he opened his eyes, he saw the beams of flashlights dancing across the walls and ceiling. Pascal realized that the emergency lights had died and people were using their flashlights to see.

"They're gone!" someone shouted.

There were other cries and shouts.

"What?"

"Who's gone?"

"What's happening?

"The soldiers are all gone."

People began shuffling to the doors. There was pushing, yelling, kicking and swearing.

Pascal waited in his safe little corner with Olivia. When the crowd had left, he grabbed his flashlight from his bag and turned it on. It flickered and shut back off.

"Come on!" he yelled at the flashlight and hit it against his leg. It flickered back on dimly. He walked out of the gym into the hallway.

The C3 appeared to be abandoned by the army. There were people going through the supplies and walking around looking lost, but there were no army personnel. He heard shouting from upstairs and a gunshot echoed through the school.

"What do say, Olivia? Should we ditch this joint? Let's go back to the museum. Maybe it's a little quieter there."

He went out into the dark and snowy night and found his truck. He put Olivia and his pack in the truck and started it up. Olivia started crying.

"I know, you like the heat way up."

As he drove through the snow on his way out of the C3, he looked at the gas gauge. He was almost out of gas.

I hope we make it.

Within a few blocks of the museum, the truck sputtered and died.

"Looks like we're walking from here."

The storm was abating. There was a red glow in the Eastern sky, but the sun had not yet risen.

Pascal donned the baby pouch and put Olivia in it. He grabbed his pack and his flashlight and started walking.

After only a few steps he saw a large dark shape in front of him. He turned his flashlight on but nothing happened.

"Who's there?" he asked the dark figure, smacking his flashlight against his hand.

He heard strange grunting noise. It was getting closer.

He backed up against the truck and fumbled with the door handle, trying to get it open. There was another strange noise, and he felt something cold and wet against his neck.

He opened the truck door, put Olivia on the seat and closed it.

Pascal gripped his flashlight tightly, preparing to meet his attacker. When he turned around, Pascal was staring into strange rectangular pupils. The pupils belonged to a white llama.

Can this day get any weirder?

CHAPTER 47

Earlier in the theatre dressing room, the sound of fighter jets and explosions woke Camille.

"What was that?" she asked as she sat up.

Tyler rubbed his eyes. "It's probably Tank coming to kill me."

"Seriously, I hear something. It sounded like an explosion."

"Okay, let's check it out. Do you have any idea what time it is?"

"No clue."

Camille put her bow on her shoulder, and Tyler grabbed his gun. They both put their backpacks on and left the dressing room. They could hear the sound of jets overhead but nothing from inside the building.

"Let's go," she said as she walked out into the hallway.

They got to the stage, and Tyler shone his flashlight at the theatre seats. "It looks like no one has come to see our show."

"Show's over," said Camille and jumped off the stage.

They walked through the theatre and into the lobby.

Camille pointed to the front windows. "Looks like it's still night."

There was a loud explosion nearby, and the flash illuminated the blustery night.

"Whoa!" said Tyler, "what was that?"

"I don't know, but it doesn't sound good, we need to get out of here," said Camille.

"Let's find your side-by-side and drive to the museum."

They walked back through the hallway past the coffee shop and variety store towards the parking garage stairwell.

Camille stopped to peer through the security gate of the variety store. Tyler walked ahead. When he rounded the next corner, he stopped suddenly.

"Don't move!" yelled a voice. From where she was standing, Camille could see the back of Tyler, but not the person yelling at him.

Tyler's gun was in his hands, but it was pointed at the floor. He kept the gun in one hand and held up the other hand.

"Whoa…don't shoot," he said.

"Put your gun on the floor."

"Okay, I'm putting my gun on the floor."

"Weren't you with someone else?" the voice asked.

"I was, but not anymore. What about you? Are you alone too?"

Camille noticed that Tyler turned his head slightly towards her as he asked the question. She unslung her bow and nocked an arrow in it.

"My friends are around," the man replied.

"What do you want?"

"I like your side-by-side up there," the man said, "but I am having a hard time starting it without the keys. I need you to hand them over."

Tyler reached into his pocket, pulled out the key and paused.

"You mean this key?" He threw the keys to the side, and they slid across the hallway into Camille's view.

She pulled back her arrow and aimed it where she thought the man would make himself visible.

"Oops, they slipped," said Tyler.

"Don't move, idiot."

Camille could hear the man walking towards the key and pulled back the arrow further.

He stepped into view and reached down towards the key.

He stopped and looked up at Camille. Before he had a chance to raise his gun, there was a whoosh from the arrow and a wet thunk as it entered his throat. The tip of the arrow was sticking out the other side, and blood seeped out the entry and exit wounds. The man gurgled and slumped to the ground.

"Good shot, Camille," said Tyler.

"I was aiming for the head, but I guess that works too."

Tyler grabbed his gun and the key. "Time to go, in case he has friends nearby."

They ran to the parking garage stairwell and up the stairs to the roof. When Tyler opened the door, the snowstorm hit them with full force.

"I hope you know where you're going," said Camille, "because it's dark and stormy out here."

"So do I," said Tyler.

As they loaded their gear in the back of the side-by-side, a voice came over the radio in Camille's pocket.

"Camille, Tyler, are you there? This is Joe."

CHAPTER 48

Shortly before the explosion at the hospital, Tank woke up in the small office in the tall building. Jets screamed overhead and anti-aircraft guns shook the windows. From his vantage point at the top of the building he saw the army below scrambling to get to their battle stations. He watched as a JH-7 bomber was chased by a CF-18 hornet. Tank grabbed his gear and ran down the stairs. The door that had been booby-trapped was blown open from his grenade. A cold wind howled when he stepped outside. He couldn't see any soldiers, but he also couldn't see much of anything through the storm. Tank ran to his hidden snowmobile and started it up. Racing towards the hospital he heard the sounds of missiles, jets, gunfire, and explosions all around him. By the time he arrived, the hospital was fully engulfed in flames. When he pulled up in front of the hospital, he saw a lone woman standing in front, watching it burn.

"Excuse me miss?" said Tank.

She stood staring at the flames and didn't turn to look at him. "What?"

"Where are all the patients?"

"They took some of them away in buses, but most of them died in the fire."

"What about my friends? Kevin, the guy with the gunshot to the gut and Joe and that little girl?"

"I think I saw them leave on a snowmobile." She still stared expressionless at the flames.

"Are you going to be okay?" Tank asked.

"I could have saved more..."

"I'm sure you did what you could...can I take you somewhere? You're going to freeze to death out here."

"Yesterday, I had so much hope for mankind," she said. "A man brought an unconscious woman in. The man didn't even know the woman, but he gladly took care of her little baby. What was her name again? Anyway, that's when I knew that there are still good people in this world and maybe there is still hope. But now? Now I don't know. The hospital is burning, and there are still people inside, and they are all going to die."

"I'm real sorry ma'am," said Tank awkwardly trying to console her.

"Olivia was the name," she mumbled.

"Pardon me?" asked Tank, "Your name is Olivia?"

"No, my name is Effy. Olivia was the baby's name."

"Was the mother's name Monique?" Tank asked excitedly.

"Yes." She turned to him. "How did you know?"

"Where are they now? Are they still inside?"

"No, I saw Monique leave, but I don't know where she went."

"What about the baby? Where is Olivia?"

"She was with Pascal. He was such a nice guy."

"Who is Pascal? Do you know where they went?"

"They went to the C3."

"You're coming with me." Tank grabbed the woman by the hips and hoisted her onto the back of his snowmobile. She held on but said nothing as he drove the snowmobile into the storm.

When they arrived at the C3 they found it mostly abandoned. He asked a few people still wandering the facility but no one had seen Pascal or Olivia.

"Do you know where Pascal found Monique and the baby?" Tank asked her.

"He said he found them at the museum," said Effy.

CHAPTER 49

Just before the first missiles exploded in Commerce City, in the little cabin outside the museum, Roxie started barking.

"Zach, wake up!" Ayesha said and turned her flashlight on.

"Is the fire out again?"

"No, Roxie's barking."

Zach sat up and turned his flashlight on. "Do you hear that?"

"It sounds like planes," said Ayesha.

Zach got up and put his boots on. Ayesha slipped hers on too, and they stepped out into the stormy night with Roxie following closely.

"It sounds like fighter jets," said Zach, "but I can't see anything out here."

"It's freezing out here, can we go back in?" asked Ayesha.

Although Zach couldn't see the jets through the darkness and the blowing snow, he did see bright flashes over the city.

"Oh no," he said quietly.

"What was that?" asked Ayesha.

"They're bombing the city."

"What? Who?"

"Let's get back inside, before we freeze."

Roxie followed them in and they closed the door. Zach and Ayesha stamped the snow off their boots.

"My guess is, it's the Chinese." He opened the door to the stove and threw a log inside. "I wish the internet was still working."

Ayesha lit a single candle on the table and turned her flashlight off. "What are we going to do if Monique doesn't come back?"

"We'll figure something out. Maybe we should just go back to sleep."

"I'm awake now," complained Ayesha.

Zach sat beside the fire and looked at his pistol. "If someone comes here, we need to be ready."

"What do you mean?"

"I mean we need a plan, in case bad people come here."

CHAPTER 50

Tank drove the snowmobile up to the front of the museum. The buildings were dark but he could smell smoke. There was a purple pick-up truck parked in front of the entrance.

"Someone's here, follow me," he said to Effy as he got off the snowmobile.

Tank held his flashlight against the barrel of his gun and pointed it ahead of him. "Stay behind me."

"I thought we were looking for Monique? Who are you going to shoot?"

"Can't be too careful," he said as he walked around the side of the museum. He could see a dim flicker coming from the cabin beside the museum with a pink Volkswagen beetle out front. He turned his flashlight off and walked up to the cabin and knocked on the door. "Stay behind me," he ordered Effy.

The door opened and a little girl with dark skin stood in the doorway looking up at him. Beside her was a large German Shepherd sitting at attention with its teeth bared.

"Hello, little…"

Before he could finish, the girl spoke. "Don't take another step. With one word, this dog will go for your jugglear." Her voice was timid but firm.

"Look," said Tank, "I'm not here to hurt you, my name is Tank." He held out his hand.

"Don't touch me. There is a gun pointed at your head right

now. If you touch me, that gun will shoot you."

"I'm Effy," said the voice from behind Tank, "Don't let this big brute scare you."

She stepped between the little girl and Tank. "We're friends of Monique, is she here?"

"Really?!" said Ayesha, dropping the stern look on her face. "Is she okay?"

"She was at the hospital," said Effy, "and she was having her wound treated."

"Where is she?" asked Ayesha.

"Can we come in, please?" asked Effy, "It's really cold out here."

"I guess. You don't *seem* like bad guys." She patted Roxie on the head. "It's okay Roxie, they're fine."

The dog stood up and sniffed the visitors.

"Your dog looks well-trained, but I assume the 'gun pointed at your head' was a bluff," said Tank.

"Nope, that part was real too," said Zach as he stepped out from behind the wood pile, gun in hand.

"Impressive," said Tank.

"And Ayesha, its jugular, not jugglear."

They all went inside the cabin and exchanged names.

"Monique didn't just leave us?" asked Ayesha.

"No, Pascal found her unconscious here and brought her to the hospital."

"Who is Pascal?" asked Zach.

"He's a really nice guy who is looking after Olivia right now" said Effy.

"How do you guys know Monique?" asked Zach.

"I just met her at the hospital when she came in," said Effy. "When the fire alarm went off at the hospital, she was one of the first ones out. I haven't seen her since."

"I've never met her, but I know her husband Kevin," said Tank.

"Do you know Joe too?" asked Ayesha eagerly.

"Yes, we all travelled down here from Chateaugay."

"He's here?" yelled Ayesha. "Joe's here! Where is he? Is he coming?"

"I don't know, I lost contact with him when I left the hospital," said Tank.

"Someone's coming," said Zach as he pulled out his gun and walked to the door. He put his boots on and peered out the front window.

Tank got up and joined him. "Is that thing even loaded?"

"Yes."

"Would you really have shot me?"

"Yes. I also have a llama out back that I could have sicced on you," he replied with a smirk.

"Now you're bluffing."

"I don't know what bluffing is," said Ayesha, "but we do have a llama and his name is Boots."

Tank opened the door. "I'll handle this, wait here."

He took two steps forward and stood with his rifle at the ready. Zach stood beside him.

"I thought I told you to wait in the cabin."

"I thought you could use my help."

Tank recognized the side-by-side before it reached them. "Don't shoot, I know them."

Tyler and Camille drove right up to the cabin. "Tank is that you?" said Camille, and she jumped off the snowmobile and gave him a hug.

Tank looked at Tyler.

"I kept her safe…" said Tyler.

Tank nodded at him. "So, you did."

"Is it Joe and Monique?" asked Ayesha from the cabin.

They all went inside the cabin, which was getting a little crowded.

"Hello there," said Camille to Ayesha, "who are you?"

"I'm Ayesha."

"Well, Ayesha, I'm Camille and I had a little sister about your age."

"You're not Joe or Monique," Ayesha said pouting, "and I

don't know you. Is Joe your friend?"

"Yes. Do you know him?"

"Maybe. Does your friend Joe have black hair?"

"Yes," said Ayesha tentatively.

"Is your Joe a good guy who is nice to everybody?"

"Yes."

"Does he have a beard?"

"No."

"Well, he does now. Is your Joe a little quiet but a good leader?"

"Maybe."

"Did your Joe go to jail?"

"YES!"

"Well guess what?"

"What?" yelled Ayesha.

"He's on his way here, right now!"

"Really?" said Tank. "Is he with Kevin too?"

"Is he driving a snowmobile?" interrupted Zach, "because I think hear him coming right now."

Joe, Kevin and Ivette arrived to a great commotion. Ayesha ran to him, and they embraced, while she cried.

"You have a beard now!"

"Yes, but I'm still me."

Tank lifted Kevin out of the trailer and put him on the bed in one of the rooms. Joe told Tank how he had escaped the hospital and Tank said how he had found the parliament buildings heavily guarded. Camille regaled her story of how she bravely saved Tyler's life with her archery skills. Zach matched her story with his own story of fending off a wild pack of dogs to save Ayesha. They all laughed when Tank chimed in about how Zach and Ayesha heroically protected their cabin with nothing but a pistol, a dog and their wits.

Ivette stood awkwardly in the corner, till Ayesha talked to her. "I'm Ayesha, what's your name?"

She stood looking at Ayesha but didn't reply.

"Her name is Ivette," said Joe. "She doesn't talk much."

"Where were you living?" asked Ayesha.

Ivette remained silent.

"She lived in a big mansion," said Joe.

"Really? Me too," said Ayesha.

Ayesha talked to Ivette in the corner as the others swapped stories. Effy tended to Kevin's re-opened wound in one of the rooms.

"Someone else is coming," said Tank.

Zach ran to the window.

Tank nudged him on the shoulder. "Ha! I beat you this time."

The sun was starting to rise as a large box truck with #667 on the side drove up and parked beside Tyler's side-by-side.

When Monique limped out of the truck, she was mobbed with questions. She refused to answer any of them till she found and hugged Ayesha.

Joe yelled over the din, "Kevin's here!"

"What? Where?" asked Monique.

"He's in the bedroom in the cabin. Effy is looking after his wound. He was shot," said Joe.

"I have to go see my husband," Monique said to Ayesha.

The little girl reluctantly released her.

Monique ran through the small crowd and into the room with Effy and Kevin. Effy left the room and closed the door giving the couple some privacy.

As they traded stories in the main room, Kevin and Monique could be heard yelling, laughing and crying in the bedroom.

When Monique emerged from the room, her eyes were red and her cheeks were stained with tears.

Effy stood up and walked over to her. "I'm sure Pascal is taking care of your baby." She wrapped her arms around the older woman and let her sob on her shoulder.

There was a strange grunting sound outside.

"Someone's coming," said Tank and Zach at the same time.

Tank looked out the window. "What is that?"

"That's our other llama," said Zach.

"Dora?" said Ayesha.

"Are we expecting anyone else?" asked Tank, "because someone is walking with that llama."

Joe opened the door. "I don't know who that is."

"That's Pascal!" said Camille. She ran to her brother almost knocking him over with a hug.

"What is that llama carrying?" asked Tank from the cabin doorway.

Monique went on her toes to see over the throng of onlookers at the door.

Suddenly, she shoved her way through the throng and raced through the snow. "It's my baby!"

Moments later the cabin was alive with excitement as Kevin, Monique and Olivia were finally reunited with more tears and hugging.

Kevin was in a lot of pain. Effy found some sleeping pills in the collection that Zach and Ayesha had brought back and gave him two.

Pascal and Camille had their own little family reunion as Roxie bounced around the room from person to person.

Monique broke the sad news of Laurel and Blender's deaths to Joe. She hugged him, and they both cried for a long time.

Epic tales of harrowing adventure were told as they ate a breakfast of beans and canned stew.

When Olivia started crying, Ayesha ran into one of the rooms to get something and returned to Monique.

"I got you something for Olivia," she said and handed her the cute pink bunny rattle she had found in the house with Zach.

"Thank you, Ayesha. That was very thoughtful of you."

"We did get all the other stuff on the list too. Even diapers."

"You did great, Ayesha. I'm very proud of you. I'm sorry I wasn't here when you got back."

"I'm glad you're here now," said Ayesha.

Olivia was still fussing as Pascal handed Monique a bottle of formula. "This may be a little colder than she likes it…"

"Pascal, I don't how I could ever repay you for taking care of Olivia."

"No problem. I may appreciate the practice someday," said Pascal.

Monique looked at Effy and winked. "You're right he *is* a nice guy."

Pascal blushed.

Camille nudged her brother. "What's all that about?"

"What's with you and this Tyler guy?" he retorted.

"Touché."

As Olivia started to nod off, Monique went into the room where Kevin was sleeping. She lay Olivia down on the bed beside him.

She came back into the main room. "I have an announcement," she said. The excited conversations died down.

"I don't know when any of your birthdays are, but it's almost Christmas and I have just the thing for such an occasion. I know you have all just had an amazing breakfast of beans and canned stew, but I have something even more special to share with all of you." She looked directly at Zach. "Something that *you* in particular are going to enjoy."

Zach looked dumbfounded. "Me?"

"Yes, you. I need all of you to put your boots on and come outside to my truck."

She refused to answer any of their questions as they followed her outside to the big box truck. The snow and wind had died down somewhat as they all stood behind the truck waiting for the big reveal.

"Zach, you come up front here and help me open this door," Monique said.

She lifted the lever, and they both heaved on the door and rolled it up.

Zach stood in the back of the truck with a wide grin on his face as the others looked on behind him. There were gasps and laughter and clapping.

The back of the truck was filled with stacks of boxes of various shapes and sizes. The labels on the boxes made it easy to know what was inside them.

Zach rose his fists in the air in triumph. "Chocolate!" he shouted.

CHAPTER 51

The jets had stopped flying overhead and there were no more explosions that day. They all had had a long night and most of them slept a few hours in the cramped quarters of the cabin. Later that afternoon, Joe called a meeting and they all gathered around.

"This cabin is great," he began, "but it is not big enough for a group this size. I have a suggestion that I believe is the best option. As some of you know, there is a large underground bunker northeast of here. It is large, well-stocked and I'm sure Millie would be glad to take us."

"Is it safe?" asked Monique. "Who else knows about it and how do we know someone won't try to take it over? We found a big house that we thought was safe, but we were attacked."

"You can ask your husband, but I can assure you it's the safest place I know. The bunker is well hidden and I don't think there are many people that know about it. The only ones that know about it are in this room," said Joe.

"You can all do whatever you want, that's up to you. This city doesn't seem very safe lately and I don't know if those jets are coming back."

"I'm with you," said Tank.

"So are we," said Camille, pointing at herself and Tyler.

A little hand tugged on Joe's shirt. Ivette pointed at herself silently.

"Of, course you can come too Ivette," Joe said to her.

Ayesha looked at Monique. "We're going too, right?"

Monique looked at Zach who nodded.

"Yes, we're coming too," she said.

"What about Dora and Boots?" asked Ayesha.

"I don't know if a pair of llamas in a bunker is a good idea," said Monique.

"On top of the bunker is a big barn with chickens, pigs, rabbits and even a donkey," said Joe. "I bet Millie would be happy to add a couple llamas."

"If we eat more of the chocolate in my truck, we may have enough room to put them in there," said Monique.

"I can help you with that," said Zach.

They found a van with a full tank of gas in one of the houses nearby. Despite Zach's pleading, Monique would not let Zach drive the pink Beetle. He rode in the back of the van with Ayesha and Ivette. They tried to make Kevin as comfortable as possible laying in the middle seat beside Effy who tended to him. Pascal sat beside her.

As they were leaving, Monique stopped the van and got out. She walked to the museum sign and tied a black shirt to it.

"Who's that for?" asked Pascal.

"Warren."

"Who's Warren?"

"I killed him. He's in the Museum."

"Do you think anyone will come take the body anymore?" he asked.

"I don't know."

Pascal didn't ask any more questions and Monique didn't discuss it further.

She got back into the van and drove on.

Tyler had mapped out a route that bypassed most of the city. He led the caravan with Camille in his side-by-side.

Joe followed close behind them on his snowmobile with Monique's full van behind him. Tank took up the rear guard on his snowmobile.

No one stopped them on the way. They saw no roadblocks,

no army, and no gangs. It was as if everyone had gone into hiding. What they did see were black flags contrasting against the white snow. They were on mailboxes, front doors, on cars, in storefronts and in windows. Each one indicating another death. Another victim of the Scourge. Another body to be taken away.

Joe wondered if there was anyone that would take these bodies. The government was silent, the C3's abandoned, and the hospital gone. If the army survived, they would be preoccupied. Even if someone came to take the bodies, would anyone be left to bury them or mourn them? Most would never get a funeral or a plaque or a tombstone. The only monument to their life was the black flag hanging outside their home.

Millie and Earl welcomed them all into the bunker. Roxie and Shelby became acquainted and the llamas were put in the stall with the donkey. Millie fussed over the kids and Earl found rooms for everyone to put their belongings. They all had beds they could call their own. Joe asked about Corporal Erin Callaghan, but Millie hadn't heard from her yet.

That evening they all sat down to a hot meal, with boxed wine and canned juice. After a noisy meal of animated conversations, they settled into the rec room as Earl played his harmonica.

"Who do you think was in those planes?" asked Joe.

"I don't know," said Tank, "but they had some serious hardware."

"Why do you think someone would attack us, anyway?" asked Monique.

Zach joined in the conversation, "Did none of you guys ever listen to the news?"

"There hasn't been news for a long time, Zach," said Monique.

"I mean before all this. Did any of you keep up on world events or politics?"

"You read the newspaper?" asked Tank.

"Do those still exist?" asked Zach, "I did watch a lot of internet news and YouTube videos."

"So, smartie pants, who attacked us?" asked Camille.

"I saw Asian looking people who were doing some sort of recon by the parliament buildings," said Tank.

"Who are the ones that first said they had a vaccine?" asked Zach.

Pascal joined the conversation. "The Chinese."

"That's right and why did we never see a vaccine in North America?"

"This kid's smart," said Pascal, "and he's right."

"What are you guys talking about?" asked Monique.

"Zach is on to something here," said Pascal. "If the Chinese had a vaccine, they might have kept it to themselves. China is the most populous country in the world and have been running out of resources for years. They may not have created the virus, but they may be taking advantage of the situation. If they have found a cure or vaccine, they would just have to wait until most of us die off. When the time is right, they invade. Then they take our resources."

"So why has the bombing stopped?" asked Joe.

Tank answered. "That was just the first probing run of a much bigger invasion."

Thanks for reading. If you enjoyed this book, please consider leaving an review on Amazon, Goodreads or your favourite book site.

BOOKS IN THIS SERIES

Black Flag

Black Flag - Surviving The Scourge

A global apocalyptic pandemic called the Scourge is sweeping the globe, decimating the population. Society is disintegrating, leaving the remaining to endure the chaos. This is the action-packed adventure of a disparate group struggling to survive a societal meltdown.

Black Flag - Surviving The Invasion

The adventure continues as the intrepid group of survivors defend their homeland from Chinese invaders.

ACKNOWLEDGEMENT

Special thanks to my editor in chief, Carolyn Zorn for her ongoing support with this project.

ABOUT THE AUTHOR

Super Dave Klapwyk

Dave Klapwyk has diplomas in engineering and journalism. He has travelled and worked in a myriad of diverse places across Canada and around the world. His writing exemplifies his vivid imagination and wry wit. He lives with his beautiful wife and daughter in Ingersoll, Ontario.

Manufactured by Amazon.ca
Bolton, ON